Voncara Cove

Voncara Cove

George L Babec

MSTMicro Publishing
Knoxville, TN
http://www.mstmicro.com

This book is a work of fiction. All names, characters, locations, and events are products of the author's imagination. Any resemblance to actual persons, living or dead, business establishments, or locations are purely coincidental.

Copyright © 2015 George L. Babec

Pirate girl drawing by Nidhi Singh
Voncara Cove Treasure Map by Alex Klingenberg

Library of Congress Control Number: 2015918758

ISBN 978-0-9970222-0-9 (paperback)
ISBN 978-0-9970222-1-6 (hardcover)
ISBN 978-0-9970222-2-3 (e-book)
ISBN 978-0-9970222-3-0 (large print)

First Edition
November 2015

DEDICATION

Voncara Cove is dedicated to all those who are adventurous at heart. Explore through knowledge, for learning and imagination is the greatest journey of life.

Prologue

A vaporish twilight blanketed the cove as the cool misty morning drew near. Sultry whiskers of smoke arose from the many chimneys as the last smoldering embers of warmth melted away.

Patches of salty sea mist drifted upon the cool, crisp, breeze flowing from the ocean. A fox scratched at a decaying log in search of a juicy grub for breakfast.

Returning home from his evening hunt, a night owl, nestled into his hollowed tree trunk for a slumber as a tiny little mouse licked the dew from a buttercup growing in the field near the treeline to quench his thirst. The townsfolk lay, warm in their beds, enjoying a blissful sleep.

The morning's serenity was broken by a loud thunder-like snap in the sky that echoed within the cove, awaking Legauthaunti. He arose and walked to the cabin door. Cautiously, he peaked outside and peered through the morning mist. The sun was still tucked in beyond the horizon, softly illuminating the sky. A strange huge bird circled above the cove. Legauthaunti rubbed his eyes with his fists and tried to focus, but the bird was gone. He shrugged his shoulders and walked out onto the porch to get some wood for the fireplace.

SPLASH! Legauthaunti ducked and dropped his wood in the doorway. He caught something moving out of the corner of his eye within the cove. He curiously ran toward the beach to investigate. As he drew near, he stood and gazed upon a very strange looking ship, sailing beyond the cliffs. It quickly sailed out of his sight.

Being dumbfounded by his vision, he walked along the beach, staring out over the ocean. He paused and took a deep breath of the morning sea air but was stiffened by a cold shiver from the chilly breeze.

When he reached the mountains at the end of the cove he took a look around…seeing nothing, he decided to return home. After he walked a short distance, he heard splashing in the water. He spun around to see several strangely dressed figures walking up out of the sea. His eyes grew large and his cheeks tightened. Being concerned that the strange visitors were pirates, he ran back to town to sound the alert.

Chapter 1

Flames burst all around him as his ship soared through the outer atmosphere. Gnawing his teeth together and straining every muscle, he stretched out his legs pushing against the lower cockpit to pull back on the stick, but the angle of entry was way too steep. The fierce friction of the air stripped off pieces of the gunship as he plummeted downward. Never before had he encountered such a formidable enemy. Breaking through the outer atmosphere, the ship descending out of control, his thoughts shifted to his fiancé. She was so excited about the upcoming wedding and had not so patiently waited for so long...

~~ THREE YEARS EARLIER ~~

Jase Thunderbelt and Alrand Dawlsome were best friends. Their parents, being next-door neighbors since before they were born, were quite close. They lived just outside Summerset, a small, quaint, charming little town surrounded by rolling hills, trees, and farmland. Their home was part of several small neighborhoods bordering large fields of overgrown grass, wheat, and arrays of wild flowers scattered across the countryside.

Each neighborhood looked similar with many cookie-cutter homes featuring a large front porch, a pathway leading out to a synthetically colored electronic facade fence, and a driveway occupied by one or two Laviniun Cruisers.

Laviniun Cruisers were invented by a scientist named Sinbra Laviniun. He discovered the relation between gravitational force and the subatomic cercumvalance of electrons. Using this knowledge, he created the first anti-gravitational, omnidirectional craft capable of defying gravity and using gravitational forces to thrust the craft in specific directions, based on user input. The craft's batteries could propel it up to four hundred sects per charge, but the wireless power transmitters were normally placed close enough along the roadsides that the batteries simply acted as a buffer for proper power regulation. Laviniun cruisers were available in many different shapes and sizes, and varied dramatically in price based on brand and options. Jase's family owned a simple Hydro Turbo X model designed to carry up to five people comfortably.

In just a few days was the Summerset Pirate Festival, a well-known event held every year during school break. Patrons came from all over to attend the festival and the whole town was turned upside down with so many visitors. Much of the town's economy was based on a good turnout so everyone did their bit to both look and play their parts. The town was completely transformed into a virtual pirate paradise. Vendors transcended on the town from many sects away to set up booths to sell their pirate garb and souvenirs. That sat well with Jase; he would spend all of his allowance throughout the year to prepare and fine-tune his competition costume. After all, he had won first place in the youth and teen division for the past three years.

Jase and Alrand jumped on their bikes and headed towards town. Normally there would be little traffic as scarcely a cruiser would pass by, but traffic always picked up during Pirate Fest. As they passed by Mare Street, they stopped off at the house of Nattellie Candella. She enjoyed following Jase on his many adventures and found him very interesting.

Jase knocked on the door and called out, "Nattie, you coming?" The door slowly opened. "Yes, Mom. I won't be home too late." Nattie turned toward Jase as she stepped out the door with a big smile on her face.

"Hi, Jassie!"

"Hi, Nattie."

"Come on, guys," Alrand said. "Let's go." The three of them headed off towards town.

As they road, Jase asked, "Are you ready for the Pirate Festival yet?"

"I'm not sure what I'm going to wear yet," Alrand said.

"Wait, that's the most important part!"

"Jase, will you stop with the pirate stuff already!"

"What's wrong, Alrand? Can't find anything that fits?" Nattie giggled.

"Ha, ha. Funny, Nat. I'm not that fat."

"I'm just jokin' with ya."

"I know. I just don't see what Jase sees in all this pirate stuff anyway."

They reached the top of a large hill leading down into town when Alrand asked, "Guys, are we going to stop at the power transmitter to rest this time?"

"Sure," Jase said.

The transmitter provided all of the homes in the area with wireless power and made an electrical medium pitch hum. They liked to stop and rest there because of the great view of the town and the ships passing by on an intercoastal waterway that ran from north to south along the eastern edge of Summerset. Ships would stop to take on provisions and refuel at a dockyard midway through the town along the waterway. Folks could sit, eat, and watch the ships passing through at a very well kept concrete boardwalk with seating areas and tables.

Souvenir shops and places to eat ran all along the boardwalk leading down to the fairgrounds, the predominant feature of Summerset at the southeastern edge of town. Many piers extruded out into the water where small and medium-sized ships could be moored. The main food market, containing multiple stores, sat between Main Street and the harbor area and was accessible from both the front and back, by the waterway. Also accessible from the front and rear, below the food market was the Hardware and Farm Supplies Center. Alaxrandus Rare Books was located on Fairgreen Street, one street west of Main Street, just a couple of blocks down from Skaters restaurant.

"Jase, I suppose you're going to want to stop at Alaxrandus on the way, right?" Alrand asked as he let out a short sigh.

"Of course," Nattie said. "You know he can't pass up the chance to buy another pirate book."

"At least you get another chance to talk with Kimberly, Alrand."

"Jase, shut up!"

"You know you like her."

"You don't have to tell the whole world!"

"Like we're the whole world," Nattie giggled.

"Besides, she's not interested in me anyway."

"Nattie can ask her for you, to see if she likes you?"

"Sure, I can ask her."

"NO WAY! Stop it! You better not say anything, either one of you!"

"Chicken." Nattie said.

"Shush, Nat, before I swat you." Nattie poked Alrand with her foot. "Ouch, Brat!"

The three of them lay back on the grass looking up at the sky. Nattie lay in the middle of the two boys and tapped Jase on the chest.

"What?"

"Nothing…"

"I'm just thinking," Nattie said in her cute little tenacious way. Jase was a bit tall for his age but so was Nattie; she was about five inches shorter than Jase. She rolled over, put her chin on Jase's chest, and asked, "So what do you want for your birthday, Jassie?"

"I don't know; surprise me."

"Okay, I will."

"I will be fifteen also, in two months," Alrand said.

"Oh, yay! You both will be as old as me. I'll no longer be your elder." Jase laughed and pinched Nattie. She grabbed his hand before he could tickle her.

"You know, Jase, things were a lot quieter before she moved back into town." Nattie smacked Alrand on the side of his head. "Ouch!"

"Ha, ha! That's what you get, dumb head."

Nattie only moved back into town two years ago with her mom after her dad died. She had known Jase since she was only seven years old and they got along remarkably well. After her dad died, her mom felt it would be best if they moved back to the small town to be near friends and family.

"Let's go, guys. I got my allowance and I want to find the perfect pirate book. I need more ideas to help win the competition." Jase took Nattie's hand and helped her up.

"Come on, Alrand," Nattie said. She grabbed his hand pulling him to his feet. "Ugh."

"Okay, I'm not that heavy, Nat."

"You are to me!" She yelled as she took off running but Alrand only chased after her for a couple steps.

Most of the remaining ride into town from the tower was downhill. The three of them ducked their heads down and glided very fast along the road until they reached Alaxrandus Rare Book Store and parked their bikes. Jase was filled with excitement and anticipation as he expected to find another treasure, a rare pirate book to give him an extra special edge for the competition.

As they entered Alaxrandus, they could smell that unique, wonderful scent of old books, cedar wood, and scented candles. Being fourth generation owned, the bookstore had not changed much in two hundred years. Stepping into Alaxrandus was like stepping into a combination of an old pirate ship and an old church. The ceilings were very high with wooden rustic support columns every ten feet, holding up wooden panel boxes that made up the crossbeams.

The walls were made of ancient-looking coarse wood with lots of character, covered with antique tapestries intermingled with wooden bookcases. The main chamber opened up to the second floor with a catwalk around three of the outer walls protected via cast-iron railings. The back of the second floor extended into an extra-large seating area and a set of steps leading down to the first floor where a teller counter stood left of the staircase. Another staircase in the back of the second floor led up to the third floor apartment that the Alaxrandus family used for offices and storage. The whole store was dimly lit with old-fashioned oil lamps and candles keeping with the theme. The soft flickering lights created moving shadows against the walls that added to the ambience.

Alrand noticed that Kimberly was working at the teller counter. He smiled and walked in her direction. He didn't mind Jase spending hours looking for the perfect book because it gave him considerable time to talk.

"Hi, Kimberly." Kimberly looked up and smiled, brushing her blond hair from her face.

"Hi, Alrand. Is Jase back for another book hunt?"

"Of course, isn't he always?"

"Yeah, pretty much. He should just move in here. But that's okay because I enjoy the company. It's so boring sitting here waiting for someone to come in to shop."

Jase started his quest to find another pirate book with Nattie following close behind. He picked up one book after another, blowing off the dust, inspecting them, and placing them back onto the shelves. After two hours of searching, Jase said, "Nattie, I'm not finding anything so far."

"Jassie, let's go upstairs and look."

"Good idea." After continuing to search for another hour, Jase said, "Nattie, let's go," with a disappointed look on his face.

Nattie took Jase by the arm and pulled him over to the narrow row of bookshelves on the opposite side of the second floor. "Let's look over here."

"No, Mr. Alaxrandus said these books aren't the kind I'm looking for."

"So, let's just look, you never know."

"Okay, I'll give it a try."

"Besides, I don't think Alrand is ready to go yet. He is enjoying his time with Kimberly."

Chapter 2

Jase traversed the narrow path with Nattie still arm in arm to continue searching.

He scoured through the many rows of dusty books seated in the wooden shelves along the east wall. Still, with no success. Pausing for just a moment, Jase took a deep breath and let out a deep, "Ugh, I don't seem to be finding anything that will help me win the pirate contest."

"Jase, keep looking. There's only a few book cases left on this side."

"I need to check the books up there. We need a ladder."

Nattie walked down the narrow track between the railing and the bookcases. She carried back an old wooden ladder with hooks on the top used to hold onto a metal bar that ran along the upper half of the tall bookcases. Jase took the ladder and attached it at the very last bookshelf along the wall.

As he climbed up the ladder, he noticed the spine of a book that looked different from the others. In fact, the spine of the book was not like any other book he had ever seen before. It appeared to be made of dark brown leather with black around imprinted text and images. Each side of the spline had a small, narrow, ladder-like design stamped into the leather. A crest of some kind was stamped near the top centered between the two ladder designs. It was hard to read the imprinted title of the book with so many years of dust buildup. Jase pulled the book gently from the bookshelf and climbed down the ladder. The book seemed very heavy for its size.

"What did you find?"

"I don't know…this looks amazing. Let's get a lamp and take a good look at it," Jase said in a high-pitched whisper. His eyes were wide open and his eyebrows lifted high.

They briskly walked over to the second floor parlor and sat down at one of the small, round, wooden tables. Nattie lit an oil lamp and turned it up as high as it could go. Jase brushed off the spine and cover with anticipation to reveal, to his amazement, an intriguing title and imagery, *Thundering Cannons, by U.S. Wells.*

"Oh, Jassie," Nattie said as she put her hands on his left shoulder and leaned her chin on top of her hands looking down at the intriguing book. The handcrafted leather cover had an imprint of a large black cannon resting on a woodgrain carriage with four wheels. A background image, as if created from a hand sketch, was imprinted in the leather in the form of a tall wooden battleship. The book was about nine inches wide, ten inches high, and three inches thick.

Jase opened the book carefully. "Nattie, feel this." She rubbed her fingers across the leather cover.

"Oh my, it's so soft." The leather wrapped around to the inside where the rough-cut edges were fastened to wooden slats that made up the very thick cover. The slats were thin strips of wood bound together side by side. The leather covering itself acted as a hinge that attached the cover to the inner binding of the spine. Pieces of yellowed thread lay across the first page coming from the binding.

Jase's breathing increased and his palms started to sweat. He opened the book to the middle and started to read aloud, "The wind caught the sails filling them with the power of the sea air. 'Bring her about, hard to starboard.' The Pirates were caught off guard and began to panic…"

Jase's heart raced and his imagination ran wild. He closed the book. "Come on Nattie, I have to have this. Let's go see how much they want for it." Jase took Nattie by the arm, pulling her in the direction of the staircase leading down to the first floor of the shop. She almost stumbled as Jase tugged her along. They darted down the stairs, "Kimberly, how much is this book?"

"Jase! You startled us," Kimberly said.

"Sorry."

"Okay, let me see what you found."

The Alaxrandus bookstore still used old-fashioned card catalog price listings. Kimberly had urged her father to switch over to a new automated teller system but he refused. *'We must honor the old ways in the spirit and principles on which this bookstore was founded by my great-grandfather.'*

"Jase, what is the title of the book?" Kimberly asked.

"It's *Thundering Cannons, by U.S. Wells.*"

"Let me see here…It looks like its forty-five tutarian."

Alrand blurted out, "Wow, forty-five tutarian?"

"Why so much?" Jase asked. "I only have twenty five."

Creek — crack — squeak. Kimberly's grandfather made his way down the steps to the teller desk.

"Hi, Grandpa."

"How are you today, youngsters?"

"Hi, Mr. Alaxrandus," Jase said.

"Grandpa, why is this book so expensive? Jase wishes to purchase it but he only has twenty-five tutarian."

"Well, let me take a look at it…hmm." He lifted his eyebrows and bit on his lip. He looked at the kids and then back at the book with a puzzled expression.

"Grandpa, what is it?"

"Where did you find this book, Jase?"

"Up on the last bookshelf on the right side gangway."

"Amazing...I haven't seen this book in many years. I thought it was lost in the fire. This book is the reason this bookstore exists. My grandfather's book obsession started after he found this book so many years ago."

"What makes this book so special, Grandpa?"

"Well, Kimberly, legend has it that this book has hidden secrets. U.S. Wells supposedly published three different books. When used together, they lead to a hidden treasure. If you believe in such things."

"Do you think it's really true, Mr. Alaxrandus?" Jase asked.

"My grandfather thought so. Unlocking the secrets of this book consumed his life; he searched for many years but never found the other two books. He enjoyed traveling the world searching for clues and collecting rare books.

"I remember times when he would return home from his many adventures packing wooden crates of books and artifacts. He obtained so many books in his search to find clues that he finally decided to open the bookstore. It helped support his work by selling many of the rare books he discovered in lands all over the world. Many governors from faraway would come and visit the famous Alaxrandus Rare Book Store to purchase books and relics."

Chapter 3

"**T**here are no relics now, Grandpa?"

"True, they were sold off many years ago. But your father and I continue to collect rare books when we can, to keep the bookstore alive today."

"Isn't it hard to find rare books today, Mr. Alaxrandus?" Jase said.

"Ah, not if you know where to look, my boy. Many gentleman and nobleman possess large collections of ancient works. Many have been forgotten and are auctioned off to the highest bidder. We still keep a lookout for books authored by U.S. Wells.

"That's a very special book, Jase. The manuscript was handcrafted and self-published. The binding was sewn together using needle and thread; the cover is made of doe suede and wood held together with horsehide glue. The same glue that is used to make string instruments, which is very strong."

"So your grandfather never learned anything more about the book, Mr. Alaxrandus?" Nattie asked.

"Oh, no, he learned much about the book. Unfortunately, his journal was lost in the fire we had at the bookstore many years ago. After the fire, the journal was not to be found, nor was *Thundering Cannons*. I'm so happy to see it wasn't lost after all."

"Can you think of anything else your grandfather may have

learned about it?" Jase asked quickly with a raised voice.

"I remember when my grandfather returned home from one particular trip very excited. He said he found something incredible."

"What was it?" Alrand gasped.

"He wouldn't tell us. He went straight into the parlor to study his notes. I do know that his trip was to a place called Voncara Cove located in Fawneather. It's a land well known for its ruthless pirate attacks in ancient days. Jase?"

"Yes?"

"I want you to have it, no charge."

"Really?"

"Yes, I want someone to own the book that will appreciate it and continue to uncover its secrets. That is, if it's okay with you, Kimberly?"

"It's okay with me, Grandpa. I mean, I have heard you talk about these things before with Dad but I didn't really know all of this. I want Jase to figure out its secrets and tell me all about it. After all, he is a pirate himself." Everyone laughed.

"He does spend every waking minute in here looking for pirate books," Alrand said sharply.

Jase smiled and bounced up and down. "Thank you so much, Mr. Alaxrandus, and Kimberly."

"You're welcome, very welcome. I hope you enjoy it."

"It's getting late and I'm getting hungry. Let's go to Skaters," Nattie said.

"Would you like to come with us, Kimberly?"

"No, I can't. I wish I could but I have to go somewhere tonight. See you later, Alrand. It was nice talking to you."

"Bye, Kimberly. It was very nice talking with you also."

"Bye, Mr. Alaxrandus, Kimberly. Thanks for everything!"

Jase, Alrand, and Nattie went outside to get their bikes and rode a few blocks to Skaters, a favorite hangout of the youth of the town.

Skaters had a red and white checkered tile floor, white tile walls with the occasional red tile speckled in here and there, and a full line of red tiles about waist high all the way around the outer walls. It was always very bright and well-lit inside, even at night. There were places to stand and eat, booths for up to six people, and a food and ice cream bar with high stools on the right side as you walked in the door. The counter top along the half-moon-shaped bar was marble white with red, blue, and orange speckles all over. Along the wall behind the bar was a wealth of stainless steel containers full of every topping imaginable. Skaters was well known for its ice cream and real beef hamburgers. They were also known for their ice cream shakes in every possible flavor. On the weekend, they always played very loud and trendy modern music to draw the young students in for a good time. An old-fashioned music box that took coins to operate and a small dance floor was located at the back of the restaurant.

Jase opened the door and let Alrand and Nattie walk in. As Nattie passed by, she ran her fingers across Jase's face.

"Thank you, sir." They bustled up to the bar to order. Jaftney, a young college girl, was working that night. She always worked for Skaters during summer break and was very nice to everyone. She had a great personality and everyone was drawn to her pleasant demeanor.

"Hi, Jase. What will you have tonight?"

"Umm, I guess I will have the crako burger and a septberry shake."

"Nattie?"

"I'll have the same."

"How about you, Alrand?"

"I think I will have the chocolate licorice shake and the breeam cheese burger, large."

"Okay, guys. Coming right up."

Jase placed his new book up on the counter and opened it to page one to start reading. Nattie put her hand on Jase's shoulder and leaned her head up next to his to get close enough to look down at the book. The text was printed with a unique, old style type set that was very appealing to the eye. Jase read several pages before Jaftney came over with their ice cream shakes. "Awww, you two make such a cute couple."

"Oh, no, we're just friends," Jase declared. Nattie leaned back over her seat and started to drink her shake. She leaned forward shrugging her shoulders and arching her back. Her throat started to feel tight and her stomach began to knot up taking her smile away. She held back a tear as her pretty blue eyes started to water.

Jaftney brought their food and placed it on the bar. "You okay, Nattie?"

"Oh, I'm fine," Nattie stated in a whisper as she wiped her eyes. Jase continued to read and Alrand ate his burger. Nattie picked a little at her food but her appetite had diminished. The rest of the meal was fraught with silence.

"Nattie, are you going to finish eating?" Alrand asked.

"I'm not really hungry anymore and it's getting late. I have to get home soon or my mom will be mad at me."

"It is getting pretty dark out. Jase, are you ready to head home?"

"Okay, just let me finish reading this page." Jase took one last slurp of his drink, closed up his book, and they headed out to their bikes. They rode to the bottom of the big hill where they hopped off their bikes and pushed them up the large incline.

Alrand, sensing the silence, said, "So how's the book so far, Jase?"

"Well, I'm just getting started but they settled in this cove because they had a shipwreck. They were stranded but settlers there helped them. I don't understand something though."

"What's that?"

"It said that five people survived the shipwreck but then it seemed like there was only five people total because they all survived."

"So?"

"Don't you see? How can only five crewmembers crew a tall ship? It takes a lot more than five people."

"Maybe it was a small ship?"

"I don't think so. I can't wait to figure this out."

"What did you think about what Jaftney said?"

"Said about what?"

"The two of you being a couple?"

"I know. That's so gross."

"SO! You think I'm gross, Jase Devan Thunderbelt?"

"What? I didn't mean..."

"Shut up! I never want to talk to you again!"

"Nattie, wait! Nattie, where are you going? Nattie!"

Nattie ran up ahead as fast as she could, pushing her bike up the hill without looking back. Her chin quivered; she couldn't help it as tears ran down her face. Her heart raced and her face was all red. She couldn't get away fast enough.

"What's wrong with her?"

"You don't know, Jase?"

"I didn't mean to say she was gross. I just meant that we are just friends."

"Are you blind?"

"What do you mean?"

"Jase, she's crazy about you? I mean, she's always hanging all over you all the time. You haven't noticed?"

"I never gave it that much thought. I didn't mean to hurt her feelings I just never thought of her that way."

"You are so lucky. She is so pretty and you haven't even noticed her?"

"Now I feel bad. Let's try to catch up to her. Hurry." The boys pushed their bikes as fast as they could but Nattie had already reached the top of the hill and started riding again.

When the boys finally reached the top of the hill, they rode as fast as they could to catch up but she was already heading into the house. They could hear her mom saying, "Why are you so late?" Then the door closed and they couldn't hear anymore.

The boys felt it would be best not to knock on the door with Nattie being so upset. "Let's go home and we can talk to her tomorrow. Maybe she won't be so mad at you then."

"Okay, I hope you're right. I need her help to figure out this book." So the boys headed for home.

Nattie ran past her mom and right up into her room crying along the way. Her mom quickly ran after her. Nattie ran to her bed to hide her face in her pillows. "What's wrong, sweetie?" Nattie just continued to cry. Her mom sat on the side of the bed and stroked Nattie's long black silky hair. "Are you okay?"

"I don't want to talk about it."

"Sweetie, what is it? Are you hurt?"

"Mom, it hurts so bad."

"What, honey?"

"Jase thinks I'm gross. All he cares about is that stupid pirate book. He doesn't even know I exist."

"Why do you say he thinks you're gross?"

"He said so. Jaftney said that she thinks we make a cute couple and he said that's gross."

"Honey, let me tell you something, something my mom told me at about your age. Boys don't mature as quickly as girls do. It takes them more time before they look at girls in that way. Just give him some time; he will see how very beautiful you are."

"I don't think so, Mom. He doesn't care about me at all." Nattie's cheeks were soaked with tears.

"Sweetie, you don't really think that's true. The two of you have been inseparable for the past two years."

"Then why doesn't he care about me?"

"Jase is a very nice boy, and I know he cares about you."

"Well, he doesn't act like it." Nattie gasped a few quick jerking breaths and let it out all at once with a sigh.

"Awww sweetie, just wait until tomorrow. I know Jase will be here knocking on the door asking for you, like usual."

"Mom, I told him I never want to see him again."

"Sweetie, I'm sure he knows you didn't mean that."

"I just want to sleep, Mom."

"Nattie, don't worry. Everything will look better in the morning. I promise." She gave her a kiss on the forehead. "Good night, Nattie."

"Good night, Mom." Nattie lay still then her little chin quivered and she started crying again until she finally fell asleep.

The boys reached home and Jase said, "Alrand, do you want to spend the night."

"No, that's okay. I'm sure you will be reading your book driving me crazy all night with pirate stuff."

"Aren't you interested in the stories that Mr. Alaxrandus told us?"

"Ha, ha. I'm sure he just made all that stuff up. You know he is like five thousand years old."

"Yeah, right, I guess. See you tomorrow."

Jase went up to his room in the lower attic on the front end of the house. He had a room downstairs but he recently moved up to the attic where he was allowed to decorate to his heart's content. One of Jase's old books depicting a famous pirate battle, *Mayhem at Sea*, had a page that pictured a pirate captain's quarters, which served as his main inspiration.

The attic walls were lined with wooden planks and the ceiling opened up to the rafters supporting the roof. Jase and his dad purchased some old surplus wood from the local hardware supply store that was originally part of a very old barn. They used the rustic-looking wood to build his bed frame, computer table, and a window seat under the high circular window overlooking the street. Jase hung some cheap, thin, decorative throw rugs on some of the walls to look like the tapestries in Alaxrandus Bookstore. He hung some pirate flags and ship signal flags from the rafters in random places around the room. A pirate's round top chest sat at the foot of the bed that Jase used to hold his most precious treasures.

On the right side wall, Jase placed two pickle barrels that looked much like old-fashioned wine barrels and attached boards to make a rustic bookshelf to hold his many books. He was able to get a large, wooden spindle from a crew of men burying a communications cable near town. He cut the lower spindle circumference down enough to insert chairs underneath and placed the spindle near the entrance of the room as a makeshift captain's table.

The local thrift store had some very old chairs that Jase and Nattie stripped down and distressed to make them look more like chairs that would be found in a pirate captain's quarters. On the right side of the door, he hung a pegboard holding two pirate coats, three pirate hats, and a pirate belt with a large buckle. Jase had a few pirate swords mounted on the wall across from his bed.

He walked up the staircase and went into his room. He turned on his block and tackle pulley lamp on the rustic nightstand next to his bed for reading. He couldn't wait to dig in and really get into this new book. He opened the cover and noticed something he missed before.

Chapter 4

The same crest stamped into the spine of the leather cover was drawn on the lower left-hand side of the title page. The inside of the crest looked like a hawk with a shield over it and some kind of banner held in the hawk's beak with words but they were not readable. The hawk held something like arrows in its right foot and some kind of plant with the left. Just inside the crest's outer-circle on the left was a number 1. At the top, was printed the number 29 and on the left the number 16. At the bottom was the letter 'N'. Jase wondered what the crest meant. Why was it on both the spine and the title page? The crest on the spine didn't have any numbers or letters around the inner circle. He started reading, page after page until...

Captain Wells taught Legauthaunti how to create a great forge powered by coal harvested from the hillside. All of the settlers helped to gather raw ore from a cave on the far end of the peninsula. They used a forge to heat the raw ore to a molten glowing vat of metal. Legauthaunti pulled the peg allowing the liquid metal to flow into the clay-lined wooden form. After several days, they pulled the form away to reveal a beautiful ten-foot cannon! Ten men hoisted the cannon up onto a carriage with four strong wide wheels.

Lieutenant David Anderson reported in, "Sir, the last stone was finally laid. The cove wall is completed."

"Good work, Anderson, just in time. Gather a crew together and get the cannon in place. We will have a great surprise for the pirates when they show up this time."

"Sir, do you think we can stop them from trying to enslave these people?"

"We must."

"Sir, we could use the Resonate Frequency Injection Gun."

"No, we can't take that chance."

Jase immediately picked up on the strange, out of place text, printed in a different typeface. *What is a Resonate Frequency Injection Gun?* He had never before heard of anything like that, let alone, in a pirate book and why couldn't they take a chance and use it? It must be something powerful if this Lieutenant guy is suggesting using it on the pirates. Jase read on, his mind racing and eyes wide open. There was no way he could sleep now…

"The pirates should have invaded the village by now, captain. Do you think they saw the stone wall and moved on past the cove?"

"No, Anderson, look on the horizon. There's a storm headed this way. I believe they were caught in the storm."

"Sir, that would be great for us. At least it would be if all of their ships were lost." Lieutenant Ultaman climbed up to the lookout, "Sir, at two o'clock, a sail!"

"Man the cannon! Take aim!"

"Sir, wait! Look, they are heading into the rocks. The storm surge is too great and they can't turn in time." The ship caught a wave and crashed into the large

rocks at the southern end of the cove. The storm was quickly approaching and the ship listed on its side, Captain Wells had to make a quick decision. Let the pirates perish in the storm or try to rescue them. The screams of women could be heard echoing in the cove.

"Men, quickly. Get to the longboats. We must try to rescue as many as we can."

"But, sir?"

"There are woman on that ship! Get moving."

"Yes, sir!" The captain knew there was a chance that the pirates had already plundered other towns and enslaved folks on their vessel.

Jase continued to read about the daring rescue. Waves were crashing against the boats. Thundering lightning strikes grew ever closer as they pulled the men and women in the water to safety. Only fifteen were able to be rescued and brought ashore. Three women and twelve men...

"Anderson, keep them under guard at all times. Separate the woman from the men and get them some dry clothes. We need to question everyone. Bring me the women first. One at a time."

Lieutenant Anderson ordered the men to keep the pirates under guard. He provided the women with dry clothes. One of the ladies, well, not so much a lady, would not cooperate. Anderson brought her before the captain.

"Sir, I believe that this woman is a pirate!"

"What is your name ma'am?"

"I ain't no ma'am. Get your hands off me!"

"Miss, you're not going anywhere. If you cooperate, you will be treated well, No one is going to hurt you."

"My name is Tristy Brody and my father will be a-comin' for me!"

On the upper center of the page was a sketched color image of Tristy Brody. She was well dressed, as if a daughter of a rich man, but her clothes had seen better days. She had long flowing black hair and a slender build. Her dress was red with black and gold trim and a black corset covered her torso. The lower dress skirt slanted down to the right at an angle so one side was longer than the other, revealing part of her leg. Her top hung off the shoulders and had pleated and ruffled sleeves.

Her black boots had a two inch heal and black leather laces running up the sides. *She is a cute pirate. She kind of looks like…Nattie.*

Jase's thoughts drifted from the book and he started to think about Nattie. *She's cute also. I bet she would look good in that pirate dress.* He started to miss her and felt bad about what happened earlier. *I really didn't mean to hurt her feelings.* Just then, he wished he could give her a hug and tell her he was sorry. It was too late to call her. *Maybe I could sneak out, go over, and wake her up? No, she's mad at me.* He laid there thinking about her for a while, how she had such a cute smile with those little dimples on her cheeks and how she would always laugh at everything he said, even if it wasn't funny. She had been such a nice friend and always supportive no matter what. Jase started missing her even more as he drifted asleep.

Chapter 5

"**J**ase! Time to get up! Come on, sleepy head. Come and eat, and then you need to do your chores before you do anything else today."

"Ugh, it feels like I just fell asleep." Jase got up and went downstairs to eat.

"Breakfast is on the table. What time did you get in last night? I didn't hear you come in."

"Not too late, I went up to read my new pirate book."

"Did you find a good one?"

"This is a very special book. Mr. Alaxrandus told us all about it. It has hidden clues that his grandfather tried to uncover and then he started the bookstore."

"Ooh, that sounds like the perfect book for you. What are your plans for the day after your chores are done?"

"I need to go see Nattie. I said something yesterday that hurt her feelings."

"Awww, she is such a sweet girl. You better be nice to her. She has been through a lot. You know she really likes you, right?"

"That's what Alrand said."

"Make sure you empty all of the trash cans and get the trash bins to the street."

"Okay, Mom." Jase continued to eat his breakfast.

"Hello?"

"Hi there, Alrand. Jase is in the kitchen."

"Hi, Mrs. Thunderbelt. Hey, Jase."

"Hey, I have something to show you."

"What is it?"

"Here look." Jase opened his new pirate book to the sketch of Tristy Brody. "She looks a little like Nattie. Don't you think?"

"Yeah, a little. I like that pretty dress."

"Look at this." Jase showed Alrand the out of place typeface about the Resonate Frequency Injection Gun.

"Wow, that's so neat! What do you think it means?"

"I don't know. Have you ever heard of such a thing?"

"Never." Jase did his chores, and then the boys walked up to Jase's room. "I need to jump into the shower real quick. Then we can go get Nattie."

"Do you think she will want to see you? Maybe you should get her some flowers or something."

"Oh, maybe that will help."

Jase got into the shower and Alrand, now a bit intrigued with the pirate book, started to look through the pages for other out of place typeface. About halfway through the book, he found another section that looked out of place…

With the ship badly damaged and more enemy ships in the area, Captain Wells decided to find a place to take cover, out of sight of the enemy.

"Anderson, see that cave in the cliff over there?"

"That might work, sir."

"Bring us about and take her down." The ship descended and just kissed the water. Anderson pulled her nose up and skimmed along the sea until their velocity slowed and they came to rest sending a large wave before

them. The crew rigged sails to maneuver the ship into the cave. There was concern that the crashing waves and rocks could sink her. Fortunately, it was high tide and the ship just fit.

"Anderson, set a watch for enemy ships. Everyone is to keep a side arm close until we know it's safe. Hopefully we have evaded the enemy."

Jase finished his shower and dressed.

"Jase! Come look. Check this out." Alrand pointed to the page with the strange typeface.

"No way!"

"I know. Are you thinking what I'm thinking?"

"It sounds more like a sky craft than an ancient battleship."

"But this book is hundreds of years old?"

"That's not possible?"

Alrand turned on Jase's computer and opened the Global Information Network (GIN) to do a search on U.S. Wells. He didn't expect to find anything but to his surprise there was a library site that published an online list of forgotten authors. A small blurb read:

"U.S. Wells, a lesser-known author, is rumored to have published three books. Only one copy of each book was ever created. The first and last book titles are unknown but the second book, *Three Tall Ships*, was reproduced from the original, and published by Angelica Simate. It is believed that all originals have been lost for many years. If any of the original works existed today, they would be priceless, providing additional historic accounts of the amazing history of Voncara Cove, in Fawneather, during the infamous pirate era."

"Jase, check it out!"

"So, there are three books and only one copy of each?"

"Except for the reprint." Jase's heart now excitedly racing, he did a search on *Three Tall Ships*, by Angelica Simate.

"How much is it?"

"It says zero copies available."

"Try searching other GIN sites." Jase searched many sites but there were no copies available anywhere that he could find. "Jase, if we're going to Nattie's house, we better go soon. She will think that you don't want to see her. It's almost mid-day."

"Oh, no, time is flying. We seriously need to hurry."

Jase and Alrand ran downstairs. Jase grabbed a pair of scissors and went outside to cut a red rose from his mom's rose bushes. The two boys rode over to Nattie's house as fast as they could pedal.

Jase knocked on the front door. Nattie's mom answered, which was unusual when Nattie was home.

"Hi, Ms. Candella."

"Jase, I don't know if Nattie is up to going out today."

"I know I upset her yesterday but I didn't mean to hurt her feelings. Please tell her I am very sorry and I need her help. It's very important."

"Wait here and I'll see if she is up to it."

"Thank you."

Nattie's mom went up to her room and knocked on the door.

"Nattie, Jase is here to see you." Nattie was still lying in bed. Since Jase didn't show up earlier, she was hurt that maybe he didn't want to see her anymore. She sat up in bed, her hair a frizzy mess and her eyes were a bit red and droopy.

"Nattie?"

"Yes, Mom."

"Jase is here to see you." Nattie's heart raced. She jumped out of bed and ran to her bedroom door.

"Mom, I'm a mess."

"Do you want me to tell them you'll see them later?"

"NO! Wait. Let me get a robe. Did he say anything?"

"I will let you talk with him but he did say he needs your help with something."

Nattie ran downstairs. She opened the door and stood in the threshold. She was almost as tall as Jase standing there. Jase could see the rough shape she was in and thought she was so cute with her hair all frizzy. He never saw her before without her hair and everything else completely perfect.

Jase handed her the red rose in his hand and said, "I'm sorry, Nattie." She started to cry. Jase felt so bad, he reached out and gave her a hug. "I'm really sorry." She hugged him so tight, with tears running down her cheeks. "Are you okay?"

"Yes, I am now. I didn't think you wanted to see me anymore."

"Sorry, Nat." Alrand said. "We were doing some research on some amazing things about this book and we lost track of time."

"Yeah, we meant to come get you much sooner."

"I want to hear all about it. Can you wait here so I can get ready?"

"Sure, we'll wait."

"Don't go anywhere. I won't be long, okay?"

Nattie ran up to her room to get cleaned up. She looked in the mirror. *Oh, I look horrible! I can't believe that Jase saw me like this!*

The boys sat on the front porch and waited for what seemed like forever. Finally, Nattie hopped out of the front door, sat down next to Jase, and put her arm around his neck with a big smile on her face. Jase noticed that she looked perfect again, not a hair out of place.

"I figured you would be reading your book all night," Nattie said.

"I was, but then, I saw this picture of a pirate girl and she was so pretty. It got me thinking about you. I think she looks a lot like you. Don't you think?" Jase showed her the sketch. "Isn't that such a pretty pirate dress?" Nattie just looked at Jase and smiled.

"So you think I'm pretty like her?" Jase turned a bit red and looked away.

"Well, yes." Nattie gave him a big hug.

"So, Jassie, what did you find?" Jase couldn't help but notice her beautiful smile. He was so glad to see her smiling again. He stared at her for a few seconds and smiled back, not saying a word. "What, Jase? Why are you smiling like that?"

"I don't know. I just am." Jase turned bright red. "Let me show you what we found. You are going to love this."

Jase showed Nattie the different typeface for the Resonate Frequency Injection Gun.

"That's amazing! Actually, that's impossible. An ancient book talking about an RFI gun. How is this possible?"

"What is an RFI gun?" Jase asked.

"I don't know. I have never heard of an injection gun but resonate frequency is a scientific term. It's when something oscillates based on its physical characteristics. Like when you ride down the road at a certain speed and the cruiser vibrates. They use resonate frequency circuits in radio wave transmitters and receivers also."

"How do you know that, Nattie?" Alrand asked.

"We learned about it in electronic arts class."

"Maybe you did, us normal people play ball." Nattie stuck her tongue out at Alrand.

"I just don't get it. It's like they traveled back in time or something."

"Nattie, that's nothing. Jase, show her the water landing."

"What? There's more?"

"Here look." Jase showed her the text:

"The ship descended and just kissed the water. Anderson pulled her nose up and skimmed along the sea until their velocity slowed and they came to rest sending a large wave before them."

"Amazing, I can see why Mr. Alaxrandus' grandfather was so interested in the secrets of this book. I just don't understand how this is possible." Nattie's mind now intrigued about the possibilities, "Is there anymore?"

"We didn't see any more out of place text but I looked on the GIN for U.S. Wells and found this." Jase showed her a printout of the lesser-known author's information.

"Jase," Nattie gasped. "So this book could be worth millions of tutarian?" Nattie's heart pulsed like a zillion beats per second along with the boys. "We have to find the second book!"

"We tried, just before we came over. We found a lot of sites that show the book, *Three Tall Ships*, for sale but none of them had any in stock."

"Did you do a search for Angelica Simate?"

"No, we didn't even think about that."

"Good idea, Nat."

"Can we do it later? I want to go to Skaters. I'm starving. I didn't eat anything since last night."

"Sure, Nattie." Jase got up and helped Nattie to her feet. The three of them road into town and stopped at Skaters to get something to eat. Nattie thought about the pirate dress. She still needed to decide on a final costume to accompany Jase to the Pirate Festival.

After ordering their food, Jase showed Nattie the seal in the front of the book. "Jase?" Nattie whispered with her soft voice. "What do you think the numbers mean?"

"I was hoping you would know."

"Hmm, one, twenty-nine, and sixteen. I haven't a clue."

"What about the N at the bottom?"

"The key could be in the words in that banner."

"But I can't see what they say. I used a magnifying glass but they're not clear enough."

"The first letter by itself looks like a capital E. but I'm not sure."

"It's a very neat looking symbol."

"Yeah, it looks like a coat of arms or something."

Skaters' front door bell clanged as Tawlsur Garish and his two motley goons walked inside.

"Oh, great," Alrand garbled under his breath. Tawlsur failed a few years in school, which he took advantage of in a tormenting since. Students avoided him as best as they could.

"Looky what we have here. The three goofballs." Tawlsur reached over and tried to grab the right side of the pirate book from Jase. He quickly pulled the book away and hopped off the stool, standing face to face with Tawlsur. "Ooh, you gonna challenge me, Jase? You must have a death wish." Jase's heart pounded and his neck throbbed as he started to sweat. *Am I really going to fight this guy?*

Chapter 6

In a desperate blink of an eye, Nattie jumped off her stool and punched Tawlsur right in the middle of his face as hard as she could. He stumbled backward tripping over one of his goon's feet and fell hard on the floor, giving his head a good thump. Completely shocked, the other two boys stepped back away from Tawlsur and leaned down asking if he was okay.

"Nice shot, Nattie!" Alrand said.

"Tawlsur, you okay?" his friend asked.

"Ouch, my nose is bleeding. Why did you do that? I was just playing around." The town sheriff walked into the door as the two boys helped Tawlsur get up. Jaftney called him as soon as the commotion started.

"What's going on here, kids?"

"Nothing really," Jase answered.

"What happened to you, Tawlsur?"

"I tripped over a chair."

"I see. You should be more careful, son," the sheriff lightly snickered. Tawlsur and his goons quickly headed out the front door. "About time someone stood up to that bully," the Sharif said.

"Yeah, it was Nattie."

"Nattie?"

"I don't know. I just reacted."

Jase put his arm around Nattie's waist and gave her a kiss on the cheek. "Thank you, Nattie, but don't ever do that again. He could have tried to hurt you." Nattie just looked up at him with her big cute smile. *I would do anything for my Jassie.*

The three of them finished eating and headed over to the docks. With a slight gusty wind blowing, they could hear clanging and tinkling of the rigging snapping against the masts of the many sailboats moored at the piers. The fresh breeze felt good on that moderately warm evening. They walked down the boardwalk toward the fairgrounds with Jase holding Nattie's hand.

"Alrand, do you know what you're going to wear yet?"

"I think so. Can I borrow your blue pirate coat?"

"Sure, I have my new red, brown, and gold one. How about you Nattie?"

"I wasn't sure until this morning but now I know exactly what I'm going to wear."

"Really? So?"

"It's a surprise. You'll just have to wait until the festival, handsome."

"Hey, no fair."

"Jassie, I need to go home. Mom and I have some shopping to do and I have some things I need to do tomorrow."

"So I can't see you tomorrow?"

"Well yes, but I have a lot to do so you can stop by, but I won't be able to go anywhere."

"Okay, as long as I can see you." Nattie held Jase around the waist as they walked. Jase put his arm across her back and his hand on her shoulder and leaned his head over against hers. "When do you have to go?"

"I really need to go now so we will have enough time to get the shopping done."

The three of them rode their bikes to the big hill and started to push them up the large incline toward home. They talked about the amazing discoveries they found in the book until they reached the top. Then they stopped under the tower to rest, leaning up against the concrete base of the tower. Nattie rested her head against Jase's chest and put her hand on his shoulder, "I could stay here all day." Jase rubbed the center of her back.

"Guys, I don't think we should tell anyone about the secrets we found in the book or how much it's worth," Alrand said.

"Why not?" Nattie asked.

"I just think we should wait until we know more. I don't want anyone to think we're crazy or anything."

Nattie laughed, "Why would they think we're crazy?"

"I don't know. Whatever."

"I think he's right, Nattie. I don't want anyone to know just yet."

"Okay, I won't say anything."

They headed to Nattie's house. She gave Jase a hug, "See you tomorrow."

"Okay, smiley." Nattie winked at Jase and went into the house.

"Mom, quick!"

"What is it, Nattie?"

"Please help me. I need to get cloth, I need to sew together a pirate dress, and we only have two days."

"Let's go to the store and get what you need. Do you have a pattern?"

Nattie's smile vanished, "No," she stated in a sad voice. "But I do know what it should look like."

"That's okay, honey. We can get a pattern that's close and then modify it as needed."

"Oh, Mom, that's a great idea!" They headed off to the store to get the cloth and supplies needed to construct a quality pirate dress. Nattie almost skipped along as they walked. She couldn't wait to create a pirate dress that exactly matched the red and black dress that Jase was so fond of in the pirate book.

The boys reached home, "Alrand, want to spend the night?"

"Yeah, let me tell Dad and I'll be over." The two boys ate dinner and went up to Jase's room. They talked for a while but Jase was so tired, since he didn't sleep much the night before, he just fell asleep.

The next morning, Jase and Alrand got up early and headed downstairs. "Are you two hungry?" Jase's mom asked.

"Mom, we want to eat at the docks this morning."

"Right, today's the big day. I know you always love when the tall ships start coming in for the pirate festival."

"Yeah, I'm going to take lots of pictures."

Jase's mom gave him some money for breakfast, "Have fun!"

"Thanks, Mom."

The two boys headed over to Nattie's house. Jase knocked on the door and waited. Nattie answered and gave Jase a hug.

"Hi, handsome."

"Hi, smiley."

"We're going to watch the ships come in. You want to come?"

"Yes, but I can't. I have so much to do."

"We will miss you."

"We?"

"Okay, I will miss you."

"I will miss you too. I want to see you later though. Can you come by later tonight?"

"Sure, what are you doing anyway?"

"Just working on something with Mom."

"Okay, see you later then." Jase leaned in and gave Nattie a little hug.

"Bye, Jassie."

Jase and Alrand rode very quickly into town. They found a table under an outside canopy at their favorite restaurant on the boardwalk, with a great view of the harbor inlet. Jase could hardly wait to order breakfast as he gazed upon several of the smaller ships that had already arrived. The air was cool and the sun was rising above the horizon, illuminating rippling streams of orange shimmers across the water. Traces of sweet-smelling pipe tobacco lingered from a passing tourist.

"Jase, I'm surprised Nat isn't here with you."

"I know. She's up to something."

Alrand laughed, "I wonder what it is?"

"With her, who knows," Jase snickered. "I can't wait. I am so going to win this year. My costume is the best ever. My new frock coat is so remarkable."

"I just wish I could go with Kimberly," Alrand said.

"Just ask her. You know she likes you."

The boys were served breakfast and they scarfed down their food quickly. Jase was about to put a bite in his mouth when... BOOM!

He jumped, throwing his fork on the ground. Several birds took flight squawking loudly. A young lady standing nearby screamed then covered her mouth. She laughed and turned flush when she noticed everyone looking at her. A few seconds later, another BOOM! And again, BOOM! The famous Zondanaut had arrived. Puffs of smoke drifted toward the boardwalk. The air smelled of gunpowder.

"Excellent! That was great!" Alrand said.

"I know! I so jumped!"

The famous ship had been featured in many movies created about piracy on the high seas. It was of solid design and lacking no detail. The fascinating thing about the ship is that it was an exact replica of the ancient Zondanaut battleship, which was designed and launched as a pirate hunter and was commandeered by pirates on her maiden voyage. In the hands of the pirates, she was undefeated for many years until finally taken by the sea in a massive storm. The wreckage was never found but rumors of her plunder scattered all over the seafloor had lured many treasure seekers over the years.

Jase rushed over to the mooring area to take pictures of the great wooden battleship as she drifted into place alongside the boardwalk.

"I love this, Alrand."

"Yeah, it is pretty neat."

"Ahoy there!" Shouted Jase with his hands cupped like a loud speaker around his mouth.

"Ahoy! Garr, how are ye, matey?" spoke one of the crewmembers.

The boys laughed. "I love your ship!"

"Would you like to come aboard, matey?"

"Really? That would be so great!" Jase said as he turned to Alrand, "It would be so nice to get pictures of the deck and crew without all the tourists on board in the picture."

"Yeah, that's a good idea."

"Stand back as we lower the gangplank!"

The crewmembers tied up the ship and set the gangplank into place. "Come on board, mateys."

"Do you mind if we take some pictures of you and the crew?" Jase asked.

"We wouldn't have it any other way, laddie." Jase and Alrand took many pictures on the main deck. Some of the crew posed for a few shots. "What's your name, laddie?"

"Jase, sir."

"That would being picaroon to you scallywag!"

"Ha, Ha. You guys are so great! I love your uniforms and those are some really tremendous frock coats!"

"So ye know the ways of the sea, do ye?"

"I would love to crew a ship like this someday."

"Come boy, let's meet the captain."

"Really?"

The pirate led the boys up to the quarterdeck to meet Captain Abbott. "Sir, these two young lads would like to crew our ship someday," the crewmember said in a true pirate fashion.

The captain turned toward the two boys with an evil-looking grin on his bearded face. His big black tri-fold pirate hat seated upon a head of black matted dreadlock hair held firm in the quickening breeze flowing across the deck.

"So ye thinken you can crew on my ship?"

"Absolutely!" Jase said.

"Ye must pass the test first, but be ye warned; it's not for the faint-hearted!" *Oh no, what is Jase getting me into now?*

"I'm not afraid. Let's do it!" Jase said. The crew started laughing.

"Do we have to walk the plank?" Alrand asked.

"No, laddie. Ye have to climb the rigging to the crow's nest."

Some of the crew yelled out a long, "Ooh."

The captain leaned over to Jase, "Ye sure ye are up to the challenge now?"

"I'm ready!"

"Me too!" Alrand said.

"First Mate, take these scallywags up to the crow's nest."

The three of them walked to the main deck by the rigging. "Listen up. Always keep three pints of contact on the ropes at all times. Take your time and keep your footing. I will be coming up directly beneath you. Can you handle that?"

"Definitely."

"Yeah, definitely." Jase and Alrand climbed up the rigging very slowly. The ship rocked a little in the breeze and choppy water, which was amplified the higher they climbed. About halfway up, Jase looked down and paused for a few seconds.

"Jase, you okay?"

"Yeah, I forgot the first rule."

Alrand laughed, "Yeah, don't look down." They continued up and finally climbed into the crow's nest.

"Wow, we can see the whole town from up here!" Jase said as he held on tightly.

"I can't believe how high up we are. Hey Jase, look! Another ship is coming."

"Nice!"

The mysterious Killick had arrived. No one knew the origin of the Killick except that some merchant fisherman found it adrift without a crew and claimed it under maritime law. It was later sold to the maritime museum and routinely placed into service for special events like the pirate festival.

Jase snapped quite a few pictures of the Killick and of the town before they started the climb down to the main deck.

Captain Abbott met the boys, "Passing the test, ye are now honorary members of our crew for the weekend."

"Thank you so much! This was so excellent!"

"Would you boys mind showing us around the town a little and direct us to the best places to eat and get supplies?"

"We'd be happy to."

Jase and Alrand led the men all around the town. They told them about the famous Alaxrandus Rare Book Store and took them to Skaters to eat lunch. As they headed back to the ship, Jase could hear the sound of a snare drum. A young sailor from one of the seven tall ships, now moored along the boardwalk, walked along the waterside beating on a drum. Jase watched as people followed the sailor, forming a line behind him and dancing about. It reminded him of a fable he once read as a child. Eventually the line of individuals reached about a hundred people.

"Alrand, don't you think that's a bit odd?"

"Yeah, really odd. How did he know that they would all follow him?"

"I don't know."

"Thank you, young pirates, for showing us around. We need to get back to our ship to prepare," the captain said.

"Thank you!"

"You're welcome. Stop back by during the festival," the captain said.

"Okay, we will."

"Jase, let's go by Alaxrandus. I want to ask Kimberly if she will come to the festival with me."

"Nice, and let's see if she wants to come to my birthday party tomorrow."

"Oh! Good idea." Alrand smiled as they walked.

When they reached their bikes, they rode to Alaxrandus Bookstore. The bell on the door clinked as they walked through. They walked to the teller counter where Kimberly would normally be sitting but she wasn't there.

"Hey, guys!" Kimberly said. She smiled, looking down at the boys from the second floor catwalk.

"What are you doing up there?" Alrand asked.

"Watch this!" Kimberly let loose several pieces of folded, weighted, paper with the tops cut into two and folded down. They slowly spun toward the floor like little helicopters.

"Oh, Kimberly, that's so neat!" Jase said.

"Hey, I want to try."

Kimberly and the boys played with the paper spinners for about an hour until it was time to close the store.

"Kimberly, Alrand has something he wants to ask you."

"Jase!"

"So ask me. I'm sure I will say yes." Alrand turned all red and was stunned for a moment.

"Well, I was just wondering if you would like to come to the festival with me."

Kimberly patted Alrand on the shoulder, "I would love to come to the festival with you."

Alrand smiled and looked Kimberly in the eye, "Okay, great. Do you want us to come by here and get you?"

"No, I will meet you by the entrance to the fairgrounds."

"Okay," Alrand said. The boys started to walk toward the door.

"Oh, Kimberly, do you want to come to my birthday party tomorrow?" Kimberly laughed. "What's so funny?"

"Nattie already invited me."

"She did? She didn't tell me."

"She just invited me a couple hours ago."

"She was here?"

"Oops, you weren't supposed to know that. Please don't tell her I told you, okay?"

"What was she doing here?"

"I can't tell you. It's a surprise."

"Hey, that's not fair!"

"I have to lock up, guys. See you tomorrow, okay?"

"Okay, bye, Kimberly," Alrand said.

Chapter 7

The boys rode to Nattie's house very excited about their day. Jase walked up to knock on the door but Nattie opened it first and jumped from the doorway almost knocking him down.

"Nattie, don't kill Jase before his birthday."

"Ha, ha. Very funny, Alrand." Nattie kissed Jase on the cheek, "Boy, have I got a surprise for you!"

"What is it?"

"You have to wait until tomorrow, birthday boy."

"Arrrgh, I don't want to wait." They all laughed.

"Come sit on the swing with me, Jassie…I missed you today." Alrand sat up on the wood railing across from Jase and Nattie.

"I wish you were with us…we had a wild time."

"We so did. Jase, as usual, got us into trouble."

"What did you do Jase?" Nattie said in a stern but soft voice.

"I just accepted a challenge from the captain of the Zondanaut so he would let us become part of his crew."

"You did not."

"Yes, he did, but we had to pass a test first."

"What test?"

"Oh, we just had to climb the rigging up to the crow's nest on top of the ship."

"What? Really? Did you do it?"

"Yep, we both did."

"Awww, I wish I was there. I just knew you were going to have a lot of fun."

"You should have come with us."

"I couldn't but at least I'm almost finished…"

"Finished what?"

"What my mom and I are working on. So, what else did you do?"

"We showed the crew around the town and we ate at Skaters with them."

"The whole crew, costumes and all?"

"Yep."

"Jase, I think I'm going to head home now."

"Why?"

"I'm going to call Kimberly to talk for a while."

"Nattie, Alrand finally asked Kimberly out."

"What did she say?"

"She said she would go to the festival with him."

"I told ya so."

"Shush, Nat, see you at the party. Bye, Jase."

"See you tomorrow."

"Give Kimberly a kiss for us, Alrand."

"Nat, you are such a brat!"

"If that means cute, then I guess I am!"

Jase put his arm around Nattie and she leaned her head against the front of his shoulder. "I really did miss you, Jassie."

"I missed you too. It wasn't as fun without you there." They talked for about an hour then Nattie's mom told her to come in for the night. Nattie took Jase's hand and he walked her to the door. "Good night, Nattie."

She gave Jase one last hug, "Sweet dreams, my Jassie."

Nattie got up very early the next morning and went to Jase's house. She knocked on the door very gently. Jase's mom answered and they whispered rather quietly as to not wake anyone.

"Good morning, Nattie."

"Hi, Mrs. Thunderbelt. I have the special recipe for the cake."

"This will be so fun. I'm glad we decided to do this."

"I know. I'm so excited and Jase will be so happy when I give him his present."

"What did you get him?"

"I'm not telling."

"Oh, a big secret?"

"I can't wait to see his face when he opens it."

"Let's get the cake started so it will be done on time." They mixed up the vanilla cake mixture and poured it into several different sized baking pans. "How many layers total, Nattie?"

"Let me see here…it says up to seven thin layers or four thick layers."

"We will make enough for five thick layers and cut them down as needed."

"Look, here is the shape of the fold-up pattern."

"Ooh, that will be nice." Once the cake pans were placed into the preheated oven, they started to make breakfast. "Nattie, would you go wake up Jase and have him come down to eat breakfast?"

"Okay."

"Good morning, Nattie," Jase's dad said as he walked down the staircase.

"Good morning." Nattie pranced up the staircase into Jase's room and stood beside his bed.

He was so cute sleeping there, she thought. She picked up a large hawk feather on the side of one of Jase's nightstands and rubbed it against his nose. Jase let out a little snort in his sleep. Nattie flexed her shoulders and covered her mouth as she tried not to giggle. Again, she tickled his nose with the feather. He let out a sharp sigh and rolled over a little. Nattie couldn't help but to start giggling.

"Nattie? What are you doing here?"

"Get up, my little sleepyhead. It's time to eat." She pulled his hand to get him up and sat next to him. "I got you something and you're going to love it."

"Where is it?"

"You can't have it yet. You have to wait until you open your presents." Nattie kissed him on the cheek, "Come and eat breakfast while it's hot."

Jase and Nattie went downstairs and sat down at the table. The smell of baking cakes and bacon filled the air. Jase's mom brought them both pancakes in the shape of pirate hats along with some eggs and bacon.

"Mom, that's so neat."

"You're welcome." While they ate, Nattie reached over and pinched Jase on his side.

"Hey!" Jase tickled Nattie and she fell off the chair. They both laughed so loud.

"What are you two doing over there?"

"Nattie is so ticklish."

"You know I am." Jase took her hand and helped her back into her chair.

"Jase, when you get done eating, you need to go find something to do. Nattie and I have work to do and you can't be in here until we are done."

"Okay."

They finished eating and Nattie let out a little burp. After a second or two, Jase started laughing, and then Nattie followed.

"What's so funny?"

"Baby burp," Jase said.

"That's not funny."

"But that was such a cute little baby burp."

Jase's mom overheard and started laughing in the kitchen. Nattie smacked Jase, "You better not say that to anyone. Everyone will start calling me that." Jase laughed hysterically and almost fell off his chair.

Jase's mom came over giggling and gave Nattie a hug, "I love you, Nattie. You're such a sweet girl."

She pulled her long silky black hair back out of her face and patted her on the back. Jase finally caught his breath. Nattie punched him on the shoulder with her usual huge smile.

"You are so bad!"

Knock, knock, knock. "Hi, Alrand. Come on in," Mrs. Thunderbelt said.

"Hey, Jase, Nat."

"So, lover boy, did you talk with Kimberly last night?"

"Cut it out, Nat. And, yes, as a matter of fact. We need to ride over and get her. Her mom doesn't want her riding all that way by herself with so many people in town for the festival."

"You and Jase can go. I have to stay and help Mrs. Thunderbelt get everything ready for the party." Jase went upstairs to get cleaned up.

"Nat, what did you get Jase for his birthday?"

"Not telling, but he's going to love it!"

"Tell me. I won't tell anyone."

"Nope, you'll just have to wait." Alrand bumped into her on purpose. "Watch it, dumb head, or I'll whack you!"

"Sure, like I'm afraid of you, smarty."

"You better be. I know where you sleep."

Jase's mom laughed, "You're so cute, Nattie." Jase came downstairs and walked into the kitchen where everyone, except

Alrand, scurried around getting ready for the party.

"Let's go get Kimberly."

"Bye, Nattie." Alrand went outside to get on his bike.

Jase leaned over to whisper in Nattie's ear, "See ya later, baby burp."

"Hey!" Jase took off running toward the door with Nattie chasing close behind. He ran down the back steps and Nattie jumped on his back with her arms around his chest and neck. "Got ya! You brat!" She gave him a kiss on the side of his forehead. "Happy birthday, my Jassie."

"See you in a bit." Nattie went back into the house to help get the special cake ready for Jase.

"Nattie, Jase is going to love this."

"I just hope it turns out okay."

"I'm sure it will. Besides, Jase will love it because you made it for him."

"I really hope so."

The boys arrived at Kimberly's house and Alrand knocked on the door. Kimberly walked out and smiled at the boys.

"Hi, Alrand."

"Hi, Kimberly, you look very nice today."

"Thank you." The three of them rode to the bottom of the big hill and pushed their bikes. "Alrand, what are you going to do after you graduate?" Kimberly asked.

"I really don't know. I haven't thought about it that much."

"What about you, Jase?"

"I haven't really thought about it much either."

"You guys need to start thinking about it soon."

"So, Kimberly, do you know what you're going to do?"

"I sure do. I'm going to join the Proelium Concordia."

"Really?"

"So you're going to fly fighters in space?"

"No, silly, exploration detachment."

"That's so excellent!" Alrand said.

"I know. My mom was not so happy about it. She would love it if I stayed and worked in the bookstore my whole life. How boring is that?"

"So, do you go in right after graduation?"

"No, I signed up to start in six months. I can finish my schooling there and graduate as an officer."

Alrand frowned and said, "So you're leaving in six months?"

"It's okay, Alrand. I'm not leaving for good. Plus we can always video chat on the GIN." Kimberly put her arm around Alrand. "It will be okay, Alrand. Trust me."

Jase, Alrand, and Kimberly arrived back at Jase's house. The other guests had already arrived. Jase opened the door for Alrand and Kimberly.

"No, Jase. I'll get the door. You go ahead," Alrand said.

Jase walked in the back door and passed through the kitchen. "Surprise!" everyone shouted. Nattie and Mrs. Thunderbelt walked over, each holding one side of a huge pirate ship cake with lit candles and sparklers crackling embers of red, yellow, and silver into the air. The ship was brown like wood and used three dowel rods to hold up three sets of white paper sails in full array. The ship had black topped railings and black chocolate cannons. At the base of the ship were white chocolate waves covered mostly with blue fluffy icing.

Jase jumped when everyone shouted. He was caught off guard since it wasn't really a surprise party. He was truly amazed at the detail and the dazzle of the cake before him. "Wow, that's so crazy! I love it!"

"It was all Nattie's idea. She worked very hard to get it ready for you."

"Thank you, Nattie. It's so great."

"Blow out the candles, birthday boy!" Nattie said in a very sweet voice.

Jase blew out the candles and everyone started to sing a pirate, happy birthday song:

"I love to watch tall ships, sailing on the sea.

A pirate I am I tell you, I pirate I must be.

Today I'm a year older, than I really want to be.

Sailing amidst the ocean, I am truly free. Arrrgh "

Everyone laughed at the silly song that Jase's dad made up for his birthday. They sat the cake on the table and cut pieces for everyone. "Wait, I want to get a picture first!"

"Don't worry, Jase. Nattie used your camera and took a zillion pictures of it for you." Nattie gave Jase a hug, squeezing him tightly.

"Nattie, you're so great."

"You know, I try."

"I mean it, Nattie. This is beyond anything I would have imagined. Thank you."

"You're welcome, my Jassie." She gave him a little kiss on the cheek. Everyone sat down around the kitchen and dining room eating pirate cake and talking. Nattie sat next to Jase, tapping at his ankle with her foot as they ate.

"Time to open presents!" Jase's mom said. Jase opened his presents one by one. Of course, most of his gifts were pirate-related.

"Here open this one next, Jase," Jase's dad said. Jase tore off the paper while Nattie put it in the trash bag. He opened the box and took out a new pirate hat.

"Wow, this is phenomenal, Dad! This is the best one yet and it matches my frock coat for tomorrow."

"It sure does. That's why we picked that one. We knew you

would want to wear it tomorrow."

"Try it on, Jassie." Jase adorned the spectacular black leather pirate hat with feathers and braided leather strands with beads hanging from a golden circular clasp affixed to a red, felt-like base.

"Ooh, you look so good in that hat, Jassie."

"That's the last present, Jase," his mom said.

"Wait, there is one more," Nattie said. She got up and ran to Jase's room where she hid his present while he was out. She went back downstairs and handed the big box to Jase. "Open it, Jassie." Intriguingly, Jase tore off the wrapper and pulled out a smaller, thin, and stiff present. He tore off the wrapper to reveal, *Three Tall Ships, by Angelica Simate*. Jase tucked in his bottom lip. His eyes teared up a bit but he held them back. He gave Nattie a hug and whispered, "How did you do this?"

"Kimberly helped me to find it at the bookstore and we ordered it for overnight morning delivery."

The book was very old but in great shape. The black hardback cover had detailed inlaid golden imprints of three tall sailing ships on the ocean. The spine, inlaid with golden text, simply stated the title and author's name. The back of the book displayed the text, 'In fond memory of my great-grandmother, Angelica Brody, after whom I am named. You are so loved.'

"Nattie!"

"I know. I saw it when it arrived."

"The author must be related to that pretty pirate girl Tristy Brody!"

"It makes me wonder why Angelica published a reprint of the book since there was originally only one copy. Kimberly's grandfather was very fascinated by this and would like to borrow the book from you to read it sometime," Nattie said.

"Okay, sure. I mean, he did give me the first book which is priceless."

After the party wind down and the guests started to leave, Jase,

Nattie, Alrand, and Kimberly went up to Jase's room. They sat around Jase's makeshift pirate table and Jase looked at the new book while Nattie peered down at it with her head against his shoulder. Jase opened the book to the inner cover to reveal the same seal that was in the first book, *Thundering Cannons*. The outer ring of the seal had different markings. To the left side of the outer ring was the number 2 and the top of the seal had the number 94. To the left side of the seal was the number 45. The bottom of the outer ring had the letter 'W' written. "What do you think these numbers mean, Nattie?"

"Don't know but I think maybe the two means the second book?"

"Oh, maybe you're right. What about the other numbers?"

"Since the numbers are different from the first book, but everything else is the same, it must mean something important," Nattie said. "Jassie, I have to go."

"Wait, you can't. I want you to go through the book with me and it's not very late yet."

"Sweetie, I have to go get ready for tomorrow. You want me to look good in my pirate outfit, right?"

"Yes, but can't you stay for a little while? Please?"

Chapter 8

"**O**kay, but I do have to go soon because I have a lot to finish up. Don't read this without me, okay?"

"But...Okay, I promise."

Jase read the book out loud as Nattie followed along the text,

After the battle, the crew set into land to repair their damaged ship and take on water. Once the ship was ready for sail, they rigged up a tackle and pulled cannons from the sunken pirate ship. One of the crew found a chest wedged in a crushed section of the ship's hall. They brought the chest onboard and the captain gave the order to break the lock to inspect its contents.

They tried with all their might but couldn't break the lock. After some time had passed, Anderson ordered the crewmembers to take the chest into the captain's quarters and shut the door. A strange sound that they had never heard before echoed within the cabin. Anderson then exited, dragging out the open chest.

Inside the chest were the prized possessions of the dispatched pirate captain. Anderson pulled out coins, jewelry, guns, and a few pieces of clothing along with

some parchments that appeared to be treasure maps. One piece in particular stood out amongst the rest — a fine gold necklace with a locket of rubies, diamonds, and sapphires. Anderson reached down, suppressed the necklace from view, and slid it over to put into his pocket.

Jase read several more pages until they reached the text,

Anderson held Tristy in his arms. "I have something for you." He pulled out the beautiful necklaces he stole from the pirate chest and put it around her beautiful neck. "I love you so much."

"It's so beautiful, David! Where did you get it?" Anderson knew taking the necklace was wrong but he could not resist the temptation of trying to win the heart of the beautiful Tristy Brody.

"He was in love with her, Jassie. I wonder what happens to them."

"Let's read on and find out."

"I really have to go, Jassie. I wish I could stay but I have to get some stuff done."

"Okay." Jase shrugged his shoulders as they walked toward the door, "Don't be mad. I'll see you tomorrow."

"I'm not mad at you at all. I just…"

"What?"

"Nothing."

"Nattie! Your mom's here to pick you up!" Jase's mom called up from downstairs.

Nattie gave Jase a quick hug, "Bye, Jase."

"Bye, Nattie. See you tomorrow." Nattie ran downstairs and out to the cruiser.

"Nattie, do you know what time it is? You are going to miss your hair salon appointment!"

"Sorry, Mom. We were reading Jase's new book."

"How did he like it?"

"He loved it. When he opened it, he almost cried."

"He did?"

"Well, almost. He was so happy and he really loved my cake also."

Nattie and her mom reached the hair salon just in time and she was able to get her hair done before they closed for the day. It took over three hours for her long hair to be permed. Afterwards, Nattie and her mom headed home to finish up her pirate dress for the festival.

Jase went downstairs to get another piece of the delicious cake. Alrand and Kimberly followed him down. The three of them sat at the table talking and eating, "Jase, why did Nattie have to leave?"

"She said she had things that her and her mom needed to do for tomorrow."

"Alrand, you should see what I'm going to be wearing tomorrow," Kimberly said.

"What does it look like?"

"You will have to wait till tomorrow."

Jase laughed. "How does it feel, Alrand? Nattie does that to me all the time. She makes me wait for everything." They all laughed. Jase paged through his new book. He didn't want to read it without Nattie but he could skim through it without really reading. He turned to the back page that displayed a detailed drawing of Voncara Cove. It was more like a map really, but also contained sketched details of cliffs to the left of the cove, the defensive wall along the sea line, and some buildings within the town. There was a sketch of a tall sailing ship floating in the cove and a neat map compass depicting magnetic north.

"Hey, guys, look at this."

"That's neat," Alrand said.

"It's a map of Voncara Cove."

"Jase, does it show the location of the treasure?"

"No," Jase snickered. "I don't think they would make it that obvious."

"Jase, you two need to take Kimberly home now. Her mom just called," Jase's dad said.

"Okay."

The three of them rode their bikes to Kimberly's house. Alrand reached out and gave Kimberly a hug before she went inside. "Goodnight, Alrand. I had a great time."

"I can't wait to see you tomorrow. Where do you want to meet?"

"I will meet you at the old three-rail fence near the fairgrounds. My mom said she wants to get pictures of us before I run off with you guys."

"Okay. Good night, Kimberly."

"Good night. Bye, Jase. See you tomorrow." Jase waived goodnight while sitting on his bike.

Jase and Alrand rode toward home. They stopped at the tower at the top of the big hill. The sun was setting over the town and the sky was dappled with thin orange and yellow-tinted clouds. The power transmitter at the top of the tower hummed and the air was quite warm with a gentle breeze that picked up the scent of wild flowers growing in a nearby field.

The boys sat and talked while watching the sunset. Jase missed Nattie and wished she were there to watch the sunset with him.

"What do you think of Kimberly, Jase?"

"I think she is a lot of fun."

"I really like her. I wish she wasn't going away in six months."

"I couldn't imagine Nattie going away. I would go crazy."

"I don't think you have anything to worry about, Jase. Nat would never go anywhere without you."

"I remember when she was little before they moved away. She was always so shy and quiet." They both laughed.

"What happened to her now? You can't shut her up. It was so crazy how she punched Tawlsur Garish in the face."

"I know. That was classic...we better get home; it's getting dark."

The boys rode past Nattie's house. "Alrand, wait. I want to talk to Nattie for a second."

Jase went up and knocked on the door. "Hi, Ms. Candella. Could I talk to Nattie for a second?"

"Jase, she is very busy working on something right now."

"No I'm not!" Nattie scurried around in the other room for a minute. Then her mom stopped her from coming out.

"Nattie!" whispered her mom sharply. "You said you wanted to surprise him tomorrow with your new hair and costume!"

"Oh! I totally forgot! Awww, but I wanted to see him."

"He can wait one night to see you."

"Jase, I can't come out right now!" shouted Nattie from the dining room. Nattie's mom walked back to the door.

"Jase, she wants to see you but you two will just have to wait until tomorrow, okay? She has a lot to do so she will be ready for the contest."

"Okay, Ms. Candella. Sorry for stopping by so late. We were just on our way home from dropping off Kimberly."

"Well, she can hear you from here."

"See you tomorrow, Nattie!"

"Bye, my Jassie." Nattie's mom closed the door.

"Nattie, I told you he really liked you."

"You were right, Mom. Like usual." She tickled Nattie's tummy.

"Mom, stop it!" They both laughed.

"You are so silly, girl."

"I get it from you, ya know."

Jase and Alrand headed home. "Alrand, do you want to ride to the festival with us tomorrow?"

"I can't. We will have to meet up at the fence with Kimberly."

"Don't leave until my mom gets a picture of us though, okay?"

"Okay. Good night, Jase. See you early tomorrow."

Jase went up to his room and got ready for bed. He really wanted to read the pirate book but he promised Nattie that he would wait for her. He just laid there but couldn't fall asleep. He figured he would just read a little tiny bit and opened the book to somewhere in the middle.

Captain Wells walked into the Dirty Dog Tavern. The room was dimly lit with flickering candles and a warm crackling fire burning in the fireplace. His meeting was to be with a hooded man in dark clothing. He would be wearing a small red sash around his left arm. The captain feared to wait too long because he knew it would only be a matter of time before his ship was discovered, just off the pirate's coast. He sat down at a table near the back of the room where he could keep an eye on everyone. His pirate disguise had thus far concealed him from the shady sultry characters drinking and carousing.

After waiting for some time, he was just about to get up and leave when two hooded men entered through the door. One of them had a red sash around his left arm. He looked around the room and spotted the captain, and walked in his direction. The other man worked his way to the far side of the bar and sat down in a fashion that allowed him to watch the entire room. The hooded man sat at the table across from the captain.

"Do you have it?"

"It's right here in my pocket."

"Let's see it."

"Information first please."

"How do I know you haven't already claimed the treasure for yourself?"

"The treasure is of no interest to me."

"Listen carefully," he whispered. "You can easily capture the ship by taking it the day before it's released from dry dock. This is the most advanced ship ever created. Her main gun is built into the hull. The cannon was forged after the design of your long guns."

"What?"

"Keep your voice down. You want to be killed?"

"How did they get my designs?"

"You have a spy among you."

"Do you know who?"

"No, but I would keep an eye on Anderson."

"David would never betray me. He knows what's at stake."

"Just don't mention me to anyone. This cannot come back on me."

"When are they planning to release the ship from dry dock?"

"The day after tomorrow. So you must take the ship

tomorrow or we will all pay."

"Now give me the map." The captain handed over one of the treasure maps they found in the chest recovered from the sunken pirate ship.

"You are a man of your word. I must be going now. Remember what I said, you must take the ship tomorrow."

Jase's eyes were wide open and his imagination running wild. He wanted to read on but he didn't want to break his promise to Nattie.

He put down the book and thought about the pirate festival until he finally fell asleep.

Chapter 9

The air was cool and brisk for a summer morning. Birds outside the attic window enjoyed themselves chirping and singing. They woke Jase up a bit early but he didn't mind. He jumped out of bed, excited about the first day of the pirate festival. He decided to make some last minute changes to his sword frog, which he fashioned himself from a piece of leather hide. He opened up his leather working toolbox, selected a few leather stamps, and took out his wooden mallet. Tap, tap, tap. He went to work imprinting additional detail into the lather. Jase always loved working with real leather because of the unique smell. He opened up a bottle of red leather dye to touch up a few areas around the cross swords and skull imprints to make them stand out a little more during the costume judging. The dye had a sharp but not displeasing tang to it as it filled his nose.

"Jase, what's all that banging up there?"

"Sorry, Mom. The birds woke me up so I'm working on some of my leather stuff for my costume."

"Get ready. Breakfast is almost done."

"Okay." Jase finished up quickly and wiped off any extra dye on the leather. After he put his tools away, he headed downstairs to eat.

"Are you ready for the big day?" Jase's mom asked.

"Definitely. I just hope it doesn't fly by too fast. I wish the festival was longer."

"I bet you do." Jase quickly rushed through breakfast and headed upstairs to put on his costume. He put on his black baggy sailor's pants and fancy, white, swashbuckler shirt with ruffles around the wrists, neck, and chest. The upper fringe had white lacing stitched from the center of the chest up to the neck. He put on his black leather captain's boots that folded over at the top and stitched up the black lacings.

He slipped on his black leather vest and secured his waist with his custom-made black pirate belt and large buckle. He pulled over his sword frog and affixed his sword, knife, and replica flintlock pistol. The outfit was finished off with a beautiful decorative brown, black, and red, wool frock coat. The coat was a replica of one worn by a famous ship captain that sailed during the pirate era.

The lapel was black with white strips for the buttonholes and brown cloth-covered buttons. Jase placed his dreadlock pirate wig on his head then laid his new pirate hat upon it. He could smell the scent of wool cloth and leather. He took a deep breath and let it out. Lastly, he clipped on some beads, shells, and trinkets threaded onto leather strands that hung from his hair, hat, and sword handle.

He looked in the mirror and just smiled. *I got this. This is my best costume ever!* Jase proudly clopped down the stairs in his big boots.

"Well, what do you think?"

"Jase, is that you or did a pirate come and steal you away?" his dad laughed.

"Jase, you really do look like a pirate captain."

"Thanks, Mom." They took many pictures before heading outside. Alrand and his parents were waiting so they could take pictures of the two boys together. Once they were finished, Jase and his parents headed over to Nattie's house.

Jase waited outside near the porch steps to gauge Nattie's reaction when she saw his costume. His dad knocked on the door. "Good morning, Anna."

"Hi, Gavin."

"Nattie, are you ready? Jase and his family are here?"

"I'm coming, Mom." Nattie rushed to the door, stopped, took a deep breath, and stepped out onto the porch. Jase's eyes opened wide and his jaw dropped. He stood frozen in time staring at Nattie. He blinked a few times and shook his head as to break his trance.

"Oh my! You are the most beautiful thing I have ever seen." Nattie's mom placed her hand over her lips so they couldn't see them quivering as she held back tears. She knew how hard Nattie worked to try and impress Jase.

Did I just say that aloud? "Nattie, you look just like Tristy Brody. Your hair is so pretty and curly."

Nattie wore tall black pirate boots with black lacing and a two-inch heel. Her dress was red with black trim, hanging off her shoulders. Her ruffled sleeves were pleated and she wore a black corset tied up tight in the middle, and her dress hung down at an angle just like Tristy Brody's.

Her face was decorated with dark black eyeliner and some cute little wash-off facial tattoos. Her lips were covered with scarlet lipstick and her blush was rose-colored on a tan foundation. She wore a cute little red and black woman's pirate hat with red, brown, and pink feathers. Nattie's long, curly, and freshly permed silky black hair rested over her shoulders and back.

"Nattie, you are truly beautiful."

"Thank you, Mrs. Thunderbelt."

"Wherever did you get that lovely dress?"

"I made it."

"No! Really?"

"Well, with help from Mom."

"No, it was mostly Nattie. She worked very hard," her mom said.

"Your hair is so pretty," Jase's mom said. "You two come stand over here on the top of the porch so we can take some pictures."

Jase was afraid to touch her. His heart raced and he couldn't take his eyes off her. Nattie took Jase by the hand and they walked up the stairs to pose. Nattie put her arm around him. "Jassie, what's wrong?"

"Nothing, it's just…"

Nattie giggled, "It's okay, Jassie. You can put your arm around me. You look very handsome."

"Thank you, you smell wonderful. I love that perfume."

"Well, I had to try to cover up the smell of my perm. Did you smell my hair?" Jase leaned over and smelled Nattie's hair.

"It smells okay to me." Jase put his arm around her skinny waist and they posed for pictures.

"My, you two do make a very sweet couple." Jase's mom said. Nattie looked up at Jase to gauge his response. He looked down at her and smiled.

"Yes, Mom. We do make a *great* couple." Nattie smiled and squeezed Jase's waist tight. She didn't care about the rest of the day. She was already in heaven and anything else was just a bonus.

"Are we ready to go?" Jase's dad asked.

"Oh, I almost forgot about the pirate competition," Jase said.

Nattie hugged him and laughed, "That's a first." Everyone climbed into the cruiser and headed for town.

After paying for the tickets at the front entrance of the fairgrounds, Jase and Nattie set off to find Alrand and Kimberly. Jase tried to take Nattie's hand as they walked but she put her arm around his, holding on tightly while walking in her high heal boots.

An older couple stopped them as they walked, "Hi, sorry to bother you two but could we take your picture? Your costumes are so impressive!"

"What costumes?" Nattie said. They all laughed at the insinuation that this is their normal dress and that they are really pirates.

"Sure," Jase said. He put his arm around Nattie and they posed for the picture.

"Thank you. You two make a very cute couple."

"Awww, thank you," Nattie said with a big smile.

"Nattie, is that you?" Kimberly asked as she and Alrand walked over.

"Yes, it's me!"

"You are so beautiful!"

"Yeah, Nat. You really do look great. Love the hair."

"Thank you. Wow, a compliment from Alrand?" They all laughed. "Kimberly, I love your dress," Nattie said.

"Thank you." Kimberly wore a colonial looking yellow dress that hung off her shoulders. She was a little mature for her age and filled out the dress nicely.

"Yeah, I think she's cute." Alrand said.

"You're sweet." The two couples held hands and walked to the competition entry booth. They entered their information and waited for the next group orientation session. A pretty lady dressed in a pirate outfit began to give the orientation speech to the group of pirate competitors.

"Please listen carefully, as the rules have changed a little this year. Each individual must complete all five events in addition to the costume judging. The five events are worth fifty percent of your total score and the other fifty percent is from costume judging. The information packet shows the times of the individual events and a map to each event location.

"You will also find a list of items for a scavenger hunt. If you can find all of the items on the list before tomorrow's award presentation, you will receive an additional five points for a maximum of one hundred and five. The costume judging will be later today. Look at your packet for judging times and location. This year we have a special prize.

"The winner of each division will receive a gold-replica pirate coin worth five hundred tutarian inlaid into the base of a pirate ship designed trophy. Please be safe and have a great time."

"Wow, Jase, this seems like the hardest competition yet." Alrand said.

"Yes, but the prize is really nice also."

"Jassie, where should we go first?"

"Jase, there is a lot of stuff on this scavenger list. It looks like twelve items," Alrand said.

"Yeah, but some of these items are easy to get. Look at the first item — a complementary competitor's pirate compass from the Buccaneers and Souvenirs Agora. Let's go there first. That compass sounds neat," Jase said.

The two couples, guided by the map, walked toward the location of the ship. As they walked, Jase turned toward Nattie's ear, "Nattie, do you see all these people are looking at us?"

"Yes, I think they really like our costumes."

"Or they just think that you are a really cute pirate." Nattie pulled Jase toward her and kissed him on the cheek, leaving lipstick behind. Alrand quietly snickered because Jase didn't know. Nattie turned her head and placed her finger up to her lips beckoning Alrand to be quite.

"Hey look, guys. I think the shop is on a pirate ship. The Blackrock Interceptor."

"Oh, it is, Jase. Look over there," Kimberly said.

"Nice ship!" They went up the gangplank onto the main deck. They could smell the freshly coiled hemp rope laying near the main pylon. They went down into the hold to the gift shop.

"This is a neat shop. I could spend hours in here."

Nattie pulled Jase's arm, "We don't have time, Jassie. Oh, miss? Where do we get the competitor's compass?"

"Right here. I just need to see your entry forms." She handed each of them a rustic looking compass with calligraphy numerals and fancy decorative graphics. Each compass was laid in a small, hinged, wooden case. The case cover had a glass see-through center.

"Very nice! I love this compass. Do we get to keep these after the scavenger hunt is completed?" Jase asked.

"Absolutely, these are yours. Feel free to look around at our other items. By the way, I really love your costumes. Yours are the best I have seen yet."

"Really? Thanks."

The shop owner walked over to Jase and Nattie. "Would you two mind if I took your picture for a flyer we send out after the fair? I will give you forty tutarian in store credit if you wish to participate."

"Okay, sure," Jase said. "Okay with you, Nattie?"

"Uh-huh, sure."

The storeowner walked them up to the quarterdeck and had them pose. Jase drew his authentic replica sword and crossed swords with Nattie's. Afterwards, Jase and Nattie went back down to spend their store credit. Jase looked around a bit holding Nattie by the arm. He spotted something — a pretty, golden butterfly necklace with a setting of various high quality imitation stones. He thought about the necklace that David gave Tristy in *Thundering Cannons*.

"Nattie, would you mind if I used the money to buy something?"

"I don't mind."

"Can you wait outside for me?"

"Why?"

"Just because."

"What are you up to, Jase Devan?"

"Nothing; it will only take a second."

"Okay but hurry." Nattie reluctantly left the store, sliding her fingers across his hand as she left. She went up to the main deck to wait with Alrand and Kimberly.

Jase asked to see the necklace and inquired about the price. "It's fifty-five tutarian."

"Wow that's a lot...okay. I'll take it." He placed the necklace into his pocket wanting to wait until the right moment to present it to Nattie.

He walked out to meet up with the others and the two couples walked toward the first event, which was the rope swing.

"Hey, Jase, this one is aboard our ship, the Zondanaut!"

"Woohoo, that's our ship!" The couples walked up to the main deck.

"Ahoy, lads and lassies!"

"Hi, guys," Jase said.

"Jase, is that you?"

"It sure is."

"What a mighty fine costume."

"And who did you capture here?"

"He didn't capture me; I captured him." The crewmember laughed.

"Jase, where did you get this pretty lady?"

"This is Nattie; she's my girlfriend."

"Well, hi there, Nattie. You have a very beautiful outfit."

"Thank you, sir."

"I'm no sir, madam. Nope, I'm a scallywag for sure." Nattie laughed in her sweet little voice with a big smile on her face. "I guess that being the reason for the lipstick on your face, lad."

"Nattie, did you put lipstick on me?"

"Who me?"

"Trust me, lad. Keep it there; it's a nice look for a pirate captain," laughed the pirate crewman. He whispered quietly to Jase, "Don't let this one get away, lad; she's a real looker."

I'm Jase's girlfriend. Nattie was all smiles and hugged Jase.

"So what brings ye to our humble pirate ship?"

"We are here for the competition." The crew had rigged up netting above the main deck so that competitors could safely swing on a rope from the quarterdeck down to the main deck. To pass the competition, one simply had to swing down without falling in the net. Jase, Alrand, Nattie, and Kimberly safely completed the rope swing and Jase asked if they could do it again.

"This is so great. I love it," Alrand said.

"This one was fun," Kimberly said.

"Jassie, what's next?"

"It looks like knot-tying."

"Oh yay, my favorite." Kimberly said. She wasn't really into the competition but she wanted to fit in with the others so she participated, mostly to spend time with Alrand.

"See you later, guys!" Jase said to the ship's crew.

"Nattie, keep an eye on that one. Keep him out of trouble!" the ship's captain said.

"I will."

"Arrrgh, mateys. Have fun. Come back and see us again."

"We will, you scallywag!" yelled Nattie as they walked away laughing,

"Nattie, you are so cute," Kimberly said. Nattie smiled.

The four of them worked their way to the rope-tying competition area. There were so many things to see along the way. The fairground fields were filled with rows and rows of vendor tents set up to sell lots of different things including antiques, pirate trinkets, artwork, crafts, clothing, and food.

"Hey, guys, keep an eye out for any booths with swords," Jase said.

As they walked through the field between the tents, Jase found a pretty butterfly perched on top of a tall flower. He gently picked it up, pinching its wings together and turned toward Nattie, "Looky what I got."

"Jase! Please don't hurt it," Nattie said.

"I'm not going to hurt it. You want it?"

"No, let it go. Please!"

"Okay, okay, don't get upset. I didn't hurt it, see." Jase released the butterfly and it flew onto Nattie's shoulder. She walked to the closest flower and gently nudged it off.

"Let's go, guys." Alrand said.

They passed by one of the smaller amphitheaters and Kimberly noticed they were performing a dog show.

"Hey, Nattie, look."

"Awww, Jassie, let's watch the dogs for a minute. They are so cute." They started the show with four dogs of varying breeds side by side on the stage. All together, they sat up with their paws in the air. The trainer rewarded the dogs after returning to all fours. He then placed a yellow ball on the nose of each of the dogs and told them to wait. After some time, he said "Okay" and each dog caught the ball in its mouth.

"Nattie, they are so cute," Kimberly said. The dogs ran off the stage for a moment while the trainer set up an array of tall bars with little metal platforms at the top across a span between two tall metal towers. Each tower had a set of steps leading up to a carpeted platform. One of the dogs ran out wearing a doggie pirate outfit.

"Awww," the girls said.

The trainer motioned the dog to run up to the first platform. The dog obeyed and stood on the platform of the left tower. The trainer motioned the dog to cross the span on the little footrests on top of the array of bars but the dog shook its head NO. The whole audience laughed. Again, he motioned the dog to cross. The dog bowed down its head and placed it between his front paws.

"Awww," Nattie said.

The audience enjoyed the dog's defiance of its master. Again, the trainer motioned the dog to cross. Nattie unexpectedly shouted from the rear of the amphitheater, "Don't do it!" Everyone in the audience started laughing. The dog finally traversed the span, carefully placing its paws on the small little platforms. The audience stood up and clapped loudly.

"Okay, let's go get the knot-tying done because I want to do the shooting competition next," Jase said. "We only have half an hour before it starts."

Using the map, they located the booth for the knot-tying competition. Jase completed tying his knots in record time with a perfect score. He enjoyed studying knot tying in one of his mariner books that his dad purchased for him a few years before. He knew every knot by heart. Nattie also received a perfect score; she was a very quick learner and had a very analytic mind. Alrand only missed one knot and with Alrand's coaching, Kimberly just passed with the minimum score required.

They walked toward the shooting range for the next competition. "Alrand, wait," Kimberly said. "I think I see some items on the scavenger hunt list."

Chapter 10

They each purchased a set of imitation gold and silver pirate coins, and a leather coin purse, that would have been used by common folk during the pirate era. Nattie purchased Jase's set for him. "Nattie, you didn't have to do that?"

"I wanted to." Jase put his arm around Nattie and gave her a kiss on the cheek.

"So we have five of twelve items now," Alrand said.

"Nice job, Kimberly, spotting those."

"Thanks, Nattie."

Once they reached the shooting range, they received a safety briefing. An attendant loaded the mussel loader rifles for them. The air smelled like gunpowder from the previous shooters. Jase scored a perfect score five out of five hits. The target was a large circular black spot on a large white poster board set at about fifty feet away. The competitor only had to hit somewhere within the black area to count. Nattie was up next.

"Miss, this rifle has a kick to it. Would you like me to use less powder so it won't kick as much?"

"No, please set it up the same as you did for him."

"Are you sure?"

"Yes."

"Nattie, I think you should listen to him," Jase said.

"No, I got this."

Nattie pulled the rifle in close to her shoulder and fired her first shot. She stepped back and handed Jase the rifle.

"Nattie, you okay?"

"That did hurt a bit." Jase rubbed her shoulder. "I held it tight like he said but it still kinda hurt."

"You need to stand with one foot back some at an angle and allow your body to move with the gun. Try to keep your body loose and relaxed while holding the gun tight to your shoulder."

"Okay, I'll try again." Nattie fired the next four shots successfully for a perfect score. Alrand also scored a perfect five out of five.

"Guys, I don't know if I can do this," Kimberly said.

"It will be okay," Alrand said. "Sir, can you use the minimum amount of powder for her please."

"Yes, and it won't be as loud and will have a lot less kick."

"Alrand, am I holding this correctly?"

"Here, let me show you. With less powder, you need to aim for the top of the target." Alrand coached Kimberly and she fired her fist shot.

"Nice, bullseye!"

"Really? I had my eyes closed." They all laughed. She fired her next four shots missing twice.

"Three out of five is pretty good for your first time, Kimberly," Alrand said.

A subtle breeze blew the aroma of grilled steaks in their direction. "Jassie, I'm getting hungry. Let's find a place to eat."

"Okay."

The two couples walked around for a while until they reached an area with several food tents. Nattie and Jase shared a meal since they both generally liked the same foods. They found an open table where they sat down to eat in view of the harbor and the tall ships.

"I'm so starving and my feet are killing me, Jassie. It's so crowded. I can remember when the festival was a lot smaller but now the fairgrounds and the boardwalk are almost totally filled with people."

Alrand said, "I know; it's crazy."

"Jase, what's next for the competition?" Kimberly asked.

"I think we should do the rigging climbing." Nattie and Alrand laughed.

"Didn't you already do that yesterday?" Nattie said.

"Well, that didn't count, silly."

"I know," Nattie said as she pulled Jase closer to her.

"This should be easy though."

"Maybe easy for you guys," Kimberly said. "We have high heels and dresses."

"Actually, that may help us, to keep the ropes from slipping off from under our boots," Nattie said.

"Well we have heals on our boots also," Jase said.

"Jassie, I want funnel cake."

"Okay." Jase walked over to order and Alrand followed.

"Nattie, how's things going with Jase?"

She smiled widely, "Great!"

"He is very handsome in his costume."

"I know. I could eat him up." They both laughed.

"How are things with Alrand?"

"I think he really likes me but he's so timid."

"I know he likes you. I'm sure he wants to be your boyfriend."

"Why doesn't he just ask?" Nattie laughed.

"If he's anything like Jase, he'll never ask." They both giggled.

The boys walked back with funnel cake and drink refills. "What's so funny?" Alrand asked.

"Oh...we were just talking about stuff."

"Yeah, wasn't that dog show funny? How the dog shook his head?" Nattie said.

Kimberly laughed, "That was so funny. I wonder how they got the dog trained to do that."

They all pulled off pieces of the funnel cake and started to eat.

"Do you mind if we stop by that clothing tent on the way? It looks like they have some nice pirate stuff," Jase said.

"Sure, Jassie. Besides we already have three competitions done and we have two days."

"Jase, what time is our costume judging today?" Alrand asked.

"It looks like it's in two hours and it's close by."

They finished eating and ventured into a large tent to look at all of the pirate and colonial type clothing and accessories. They had several rows of fashionable frock coats, which Jase couldn't resist. Kimberly noticed many rows of corsets on sale. Before the festival, she tried to find one that looked good with her costume but was unsuccessful. The corsets were arranged by color so she found a section with both brown and yellow. She sorted through quite a few of them.

Nattie pulled Alrand aside and whispered in his ear, "You should ask Kimberly to be your girlfriend."

"Nat, stop it!" He whispered in reply.

"Alrand, she told me she wants you to ask her."

"Really, you're not playing with me?"

"I'm dead serious. Ask her."

Jase was not far from Kimberly who found a corset that she really liked. "Jase, can you tie this for me?"

"Sure."

"Alrand, go!" Alrand walked over to Jase and Kimberly.

"Here, I'll tie it for you." Alrand started tightening up the corset lacing. They stood in front of a mirror where Kimberly could see the results.

"What do you think, Alrand? How does it look?"

"Wow, it's perfect; it really makes your costume stand out now. I like it."

"How much are these?" Kimberly asked.

"It looks like twenty-five tutarian."

"Awww, that's too much."

"I'll help you get it."

"That's sweet but I don't know."

"We'll all help you get it, Kimberly," Nattie said. "Jase?"

"Yeah, sure. It does look very nice and the judging is coming up so I think you should get it." Nattie waved her hand beckoning Alrand to ask her the important question.

"Kimberly, I want to ask you something."

"Yes?"

"Here, Kimberly." Jase handed Kimberly seven tutarian from Nattie and himself to put toward the corset.

Nattie grabbed Jase by the arm and pulled him outside the tent. "Nattie, what are you doing?"

"Give them some room. Alrand has something he wants to ask her."

"What's he asking her?"

"Let's go over here, Jassie." They walked over to the other side of the tent to look around.

"What did you want to ask me, Alrand?"

"Well, it's not easy." He paused for a second and started to turn red. "Relax, Alrand, just say it. I won't bite you…well I might but not that hard." They both laughed.

Alrand smiled and said, "Will you be my girlfriend?"

Kimberly smiled, "Uh-ha. I thought you'd never ask."

"Really, why didn't you say something?"

"Why didn't you?"

Nattie walked over when she saw Kimberly smiling. She knew he must have asked. "So?"

"We are officially a couple," Alrand said.

"Yay." Nattie gave them both a hug together.

Jase walked over, "Nattie, what do you think about this coat?"

"Jase, Kimberly and Alrand are now boyfriend and girlfriend."

"Nice."

Kimberly and Alrand went to pay for the corset.

"Jase, that's a nice coat but I like yours better."

"What about this brown sash if I tie it around my head."

"Put your hat on and let me see."

"Ooh, I do like that. You should get it." Jase paid for the sash and they all walked toward the next competition.

The rigging climb was set up next to a wood barn. The rigging was anchored to the ground on the lower end and attached to the building at the upper end. There was a thick layer of hay at the base. To successfully complete the test, one simply had to climb high enough to press a buzzer near the top. Two competitors could climb at the same time so Jase and Nattie went first. They got about three-quarters of the way to the top when Nattie stopped.

"Nattie, look at me. It's just a little further. Don't look down; just look at me."

"Jase, it's too high."

"Look at me; watch me. Now take another step. You can do it."

"Go for it, Nattie," Alrand yelled. She finally reached the buzzer and stretched her arm up to press it. The buzzer sounded but the ropes jiggled, she grabbed hold of the rigging with both arms and held on tight.

"It's okay Nattie, take your time." She climbed back down very slowly.

"Jase, I didn't like that."

"It's okay; you're done now." She held Jase for a while to calm herself. Jase could feel her heart pounding. Alrand and Kimberly climbed up next. They also succeeded in pressing the buzzer.

"We need to hurry over to the costume judging. That took longer than I thought," Jase said.

They just reached the judging booth in time. There were bleachers of onlookers watching. Kimberly was first to walk down the catwalk. The boards cracked and squeaked a little with each step. She smiled as she received applause and a few whistles. Her new corset made a big difference in her costume authenticity.

Jase turned to Nattie and said, "I have something for you. I want you to look your best for the judging." Nattie looked up at Jase and smiled. He reached into his pocket and took out the butterfly necklace.

"Ooh, Jase, it's so beautiful!" She pulled her hair up and let Jase reach down to put the necklace around her neck. She couldn't resist and pulled him closer and their lips met for their first real kiss. Jase was caught off guard and almost lost his balance but then melted away into her arms. Nattie started to giggle a little and they both smiled as they separated. "Thank you Jassie for the beautiful necklace," Nattie said with a big cute dimple smile as she looked up at Jase with her beautiful blue eyes.

"You're welcome, Nattie."

"Jase, you're up!" Alrand shouted.

Jase was quite distracted thinking about that wonderful kiss as he walked out onto the catwalk. He received a standing ovation for his excellent costume but the cheering was nothing compared to Nattie's soft tender lips. He walked off the platform and waited while Nattie took her turn being judged.

She walked out on the catwalk and the crowed went crazy with clapping and whistling. She paused for a moment and curtsied. The crowd loved her and carried on with shouts, calls, and whistling. Nattie smiled from ear to ear. *This is the most wonderful day of my life!*

Jase clapped and loved to see her having such a good time after putting so much time and effort into her costume. She walked off the catwalk and Jase gave her a tight hug. She couldn't have imagined a better day. "Nattie, they loved you!"

After a few other contestants were judged, Alrand walked out onto the catwalk. Something must have got into him because he put on quite a show. He pulled his sword and struck multiple poses. The crowd loved it and he garnered quite a bit of applause.

"Jassie, why didn't you do that?"

"Because all I could think about was you."

"Awww." She put her head against his chest and hugged him. Jase rested his head against hers until Alrand was finished.

"Alrand! That was great!"

"Thank you, Kimberly."

"I figured I needed to do something after Nattie stole everyone's heart out there." They all laughed. "Nattie, you were great. Everyone loved your costume."

"Just call me Tristy the pirate."

"Nattie, that's so cute," Kimberly said. Nattie gave Jase a quick kiss and they walked toward the docks.

"Guys, I think we are done with competition stuff for the day. There's no more event times until tomorrow."

"Jase, what's left?" Alrand asked. "We only have the sword fighting lesson and finishing up the scavenger hunt."

"Jassie, can we go sit and rest for a little bit. My feet are killing me."

"Okay, Nattie."

The four of them walked to a table overlooking the harbor and sat down. Nattie was limping a little. "Nattie, are you okay?"

"My feet really hurt."

"Here, let's take off your boots." Jase held her boot up and loosened the lacing. With a bit of effort, he pulled off her first boot and loosened the lacings on the second.

"That's much better. My feet are throbbing." Jase propped her legs up on his lap and massaged her left foot. "Ooh, that feels so good."

"Kimberly, how are you doing?" Alrand asked.

"I'm okay, just a little tired. We did so much walking today."

"I know we did, but it was so much fun," Alrand said.

"Jassie, do the other foot now." Jase switched feet and massaged her right foot when she jerked her foot away some.

"Does that tickle?"

"Yes, some," Nattie giggled. "Don't stop."

"Jase, how long until the fireworks?"

"They don't start until after it gets dark, so like, three or four hours I guess." They sat and talked for a while until they were fully rested. Nattie leaned her head on Jase's shoulder and played with her new necklace.

"This is so pretty, Jase."

"Just like you." She pushed him a little with her head letting him know she liked his compliment.

"You guys want to go look in some of the shops?"

"Okay, maybe we can find some of the scavenger hunt items while we look."

"Good idea. What do we need?"

"Let me see, we need a flask of non-alcoholic sparkling apple wine, a block of cabin cheese." They all started laughing.

"What's cabin cheese?" Nattie started to giggle. That just struck her as so funny. She couldn't stop laughing and had everyone else laughing also.

"Nattie, stop it."

"I can't help it," she giggled. She tried to stop laughing but the harder she tried, the more everyone laughed.

"Nattie, stop it. I can't breathe," Kimberly said. She was laughing so hard she couldn't catch her breath. Alrand didn't help matters any,

"Cabin cheese, what's that?" he said sarcastically. That really got Nattie laughing hysterically to the point she couldn't catch her breath either.

Jase laughingly said, "Okay, breathe, in, out, in, out." Some folks walking by caught on and stared to grin and laugh a little. Finally, they calmed down but then a passerby made the mistake of asking them what was so funny.

Nattie giggled out, "Cabin cheese." Then they all started laughing again. Finally, after a few more minutes had passed, they settled down and continued to walk.

Kimberly said, "Dare I ask what the other items are?" That got Nattie giggling again but she bowed her head down and pinched her nose to try and stop. Jase put his arm around her waist as they walked. "You're so funny, Nattie."

"We need a small burlap bag of oats, a red pirate lanyard, a tin of pirate mints, and a mystery item."

Nattie barely giggled out the words, "What does it say about the mystery item, Jassie?"

"Hint — if it were real it could not contain a sword."

"That makes no sense." Alrand said.

"Jassie, what could it mean?"

"I think I know. There are two things that can contain a sword, a sword sheath and a sword frog. I think they are talking about a real frog because it couldn't actually hold a sword."

"Oh, that makes since, but that means we have to find real frogs?"

"I guess."

Chapter 11

"**I**'m not hunting frogs, Jassie."

"Maybe a fake frog statue or something like that would work," Kimberly said.

"Let's just keep an eye out for any frogs."

"Or cheese," Alrand said. Nattie smacked Alrand and started giggling again.

They looked through many interesting shops as they walked. "Hey, Jase, there's a wine shop over there."

"Yeah, maybe they have the apple wine." They went in and looked through the wine bottles but no apple wine. Then Kimberly stumbled across a pirate flask of apple wine.

"Here it is. Hey! Here are the bags of oats also."

"Wow, Kimberly. You really have a knack for this," Nattie said. "Guys, over here."

Each of them purchased a flask of apple, non-alcoholic, wine and a burlap bag of oats.

While they were checking out, Jase asked the cashier, "You wouldn't happen to know where we can find a red lanyard, would you?"

"Have you tried the gift shop at the Voncara Cove Exhibit?" Jase's eyebrows rose up and his eyes widened. He looked at Nattie and she at him.

"Where's the exhibit?" Alrand asked.

"It's at the south end of the fairgrounds in the permanent buildings." They hurried out of the shop.

"Did you guys hear that?" Jase said.

"Jassie, we have to see this."

"I know. I had no idea there even was an exhibit for Voncara Cove."

The four of them walked briskly toward the south end of the fairgrounds in search of the exhibit. Along the way, a young lady with a photographer stopped them. "You are so perfect! I love your costumes. How would you like to be on the cover of *About Teen Magazine*?"

"Really? That would be great!" Nattie said.

The young reporter had them pose in a lot of fun and clever positions. "This lady really knows what she's doing," Jase whispered to Nattie.

"Yeah, she's pretty good." She took a picture of the two boys holding their swords up as if they were fighting, and took a picture of the two girls bending over with their heads almost touching while looking over at the camera. The two girls looked like they were forming the shape of a heart. She also took several pictures of them all together and as individual couples. When she was done with the pictures, she did a quick interview with everyone for some background.

She asked Nattie, "What's your favorite part of the festival?"

"That's easy, my boyfriend." She put her arm around Jase.

"Let me get a few shots of you two hugging." When she finished she got their addresses. "I'll send you some copies of the magazine when it comes out."

"When will it be printed?" Kimberly asked.

"It will be ready in a few days. They normally are available a few days before the actual month of release."

"Will we really be on the cover?" Nattie asked.

"Trust me. I'm pretty sure you will. I have been looking for you all day."

"For me?"

"All of you. You have the look I was searching for."

"Thanks!" Jase said.

"You all have a great time and thank you very much!"

"What a day, Jassie."

"Could it get any better?"

"Well, we could find some cabin cheese," Alrand snickered.

"Oh no, don't start that again," Jase said.

Jase took Nattie's slender little arm in his and they all continued on their previous quest to find the Voncara Cove Exhibit.

"Nattie, you are so pretty in that outfit."

"Oh, Jase. Look!" From a distance, they could see two large ships' cannons on carriages just outside of a large entranceway.

As they approached the entrance, they could see a sign displaying, *Historical Voncara Cove Pirate Exhibit*. The sign was all lit up with multi-colored lights. They walked on the red-carpeted entranceway.

"Nattie, sit on the cannon. I want to take your picture." Nattie posed in a few different positions, and then Jase asked Kimberly to take a few of them together. He sat on the cannon next to Nattie and put his arm around her. A security guard came out and asked them to stop climbing on the cannons.

"Yes, sir," Jase said.

"Jase, there you go again, getting me in trouble!" Everyone laughed.

"Well, at least we got the shots before he said anything. These are great. I'm going to have them framed." They walked into the exhibit. It was decorated like the historic cove with fake trees and photos hanging on the walls. There were weapons display cases all around the outer walls. Jase took lots of pictures, half of them of Nattie. They held hands as they walked around the cases looking at the swords and nautical instruments.

"Jase, look at these swords. They're for sale."

"Nattie, look at this one. It's so neat. I want it!"

"Jase, it's five thousand tutarian."

"Oh, wow."

"JASE, look!"

"What?"

"I can't believe it. Look at this sword. It's Captain Wells' sword."

The sword was in excellent condition, yet very aged. The workmanship rivaled any sword ever made. The handle had inlaid gold, silver, and pearl. It lay open only a few inches out of its sheath revealing some engravings on the blade. The exposed area had two partially visible lines of text. The first line read, *U.S. Wells* and the second, - *TPN*.

"Nattie, we need to see the rest of the blade but I doubt they will ever let us into the case."

"What is it, Jase?" Alrand asked.

"It's the actual sword of Captain U.S. Wells from my book."

"No way? Excellent!"

"Jase, I wish my grandfather was here with us. He would love this."

"Here, step back everyone. I want to take some pictures." After taking a few pictures, Jase noticed that Nattie was gone.

"Guys, where did Nattie go?"

"I don't know. She was here a second ago."

Nattie walked back across the room with a young man following her. They walked over to the display case. The young man opened the case and using gloves, as not to touch the sword with his hands, picked it up and pulled the blade a few more inches from the sheath. The exposed area revealed an engraving of a compass further down from the text on the second line, *TTS – TPN*. Jase took some pictures of the blade.

"Thank you, Tupac," Nattie said. He closed the case and returned to the information booth.

"How did you get him to do that, Nattie?"

"I just told him we're working on a project and it would be helpful if we could see the rest of the writing on the top of the sword."

"What do you think the letters mean?"

"I think the letters on the sword are old mesirage numbers which were used for mapping coordinates hundreds of years ago. That's why I wanted to get the guy to show us the rest of the numerals. Without them, we wouldn't know where to look."

"Look for what?" Jase asked.

"The treasure, silly."

"You think the sword points to the treasure?"

"I don't know yet. We need to get a reference to convert the numerals. We should be able to get them off the GIN at home." They continued to look at the display cases until they made their way to the souvenir area.

"Guys, look, a red lanyard."

"Good job, Alrand."

"Thanks, Nat." Jase found a great miniature cannon replica that he purchased along with the red lanyard for the scavenger hunt. He also purchased one for Nattie.

"Thanks, Jassie."

"Only a few items left now."

"I'm hungry," Kimberly said to Alrand. "Guys, let's go get something to eat and find a place to sit for the fireworks. It's starting to get a little dark."

Jase took Nattie by the hand and they set off to find a booth to purchase something to eat.

After searching a bit, they found the tents where they wanted to get dinner. The girls went to find a table while the boys stood in line to order their food. After they made it through the lines, they took their food and drinks to find the girls.

All of the tables by the marina were taken so they found a place to sit right on the edge of the boardwalk where they could put their feet over the side and have a view of the fireworks barge in the harbor. Kimberly saved their places and Nattie waved the boys over.

While they were eating, the sun was setting and the sky came alive with brilliant harmoniously colored clouds and an orange glow reflecting off the rippling water. A smooth breeze gently rocked the boots moored in the arena, causing the rigging to cling and clatter. The familiar setting was peaceful and calming after such a wonderful exciting day.

When they finished eating, Nattie put her head against Jase's arm and put her arm around his waist.

"Jassie, this was the bestest day ever." Jase leaned his cheek against her head. "Jassie, you okay?"

"Yeah."

"You're kind of quiet."

Jase lifted up his head and looked at Nattie and she at him. He hesitated and his cheeks turned bright red. He put his arm around her. *She is so cute in that outfit.* He leaned a little closer but then stopped. Nattie looked away, took a deep breath, and let it out all at once in a little huff. Jase's heart raced and he felt so hot in his pirate coat so he took it off and sat it down next to him. He put his hand on the back of Nattie's neck and gently pulled her chin so she would face him with his other hand. He looked into her eyes and leaned toward her. She tilted her head up and leaned toward him and their lips met for a gentle kiss. They both smiled for a second, and then continued. Nattie put her hands on the sides of Jase's face to hold him close, and then put her arms around his neck. Nattie started to giggle a little.

The first firework shot in the air with a bang and burst overhead in the shape of a red heart.

"Oh, Jassie, look. That one was for us." Jase put his hand around her waist as the next firework shot in the air. The two couples enjoyed the half-hour display until the incredible grand finale.

"Jase, I'm going to take Kimberly to her parents. See you two tomorrow."

"Okay, see you later."

"Bye." Nattie said. Jase and Nattie were in no hurry to end their day so they sat there for a while and talked.

"Jassie, I want a cute doggie like that one in the show. He was just so cute. I want to kiss his face."

"It was funny when you told him not to cross."

Nattie giggled, "That was funny. Can we stay here forever? I don't want to go home. I will miss you too much."

"I wonder if we could get your mom to come over for a while. I have an idea that I need your help with, but first I need to look at the seals in the front of the two books and you need to figure out the letters from the sword."

"YES! Let's ask. Then I can come over for a while."

"Let's go find them."

They hurried to the parking lot and found their parents waiting for them. "There they are! Did you two love birds have a good day?"

"Mom!" Nattie said. "We had the bestest day ever! Can we go to Jase's house for a little while? We have something we need to check out in Jase's book?"

"Yeah, we found something very interesting at the Voncara Cove Exhibit and we need to look at the new book," Jase said.

"You are welcome to come over for a while if you would like, Anna," Jase's dad said.

"I don't know, Nattie. It's been a long day and I'm pretty exhausted."

"Please, Mom, just for a little while?" Nattie's mom knew that when it came to Jase, a little while would end up being hours but she gave in not wanting Nattie to be sad.

"Okay, I guess, but only for a little while."

"Okay, Mom. You're the greatest." Nattie gave her mom a big hug and a kiss.

They arrived home. Nattie and Jase ran up to his room. "Jase, can you help me take off my boots?" Nattie asked. She sat on the edge of his bed and he held up each leg, loosened the lacing, and pulled off the boots. "Oh, that feels so good to have those off my feet. They look nice but they don't feel so well after walking in them all day. So what's your idea, Jase?"

"Can you look up the numerals from the sword?"

"Okay." Nattie searched for the Mesirage Numbering Scheme on the GIN. "Write this down, Jase. T is equal to ten so TT is twenty and S is nine. P is equal to six and N is equal five." Nattie added up the sequence of numerals based on their values and mathematical rules. "TTS is twenty nine and TPN is sixteen and a five? Wait that doesn't make sense."

"Yes, it does, Nattie. Look at the seal in the first book. The top number is twenty nine, and the right number is sixteen."

"But, Jase, where would the five go?"

"It's not a five, it's actually an N. See the bottom of the seal in the little compass looking arrow?"

"Oh, the letter N. I got it. It's the latitude. Twenty-nine degrees, sixteen minutes north. The N stands for north. I should have seen that before. Jassie, get the second book."

"Nattie, it's ninety-four and forty-five with a W."

"Okay, so that's ninety-four degrees, forty-five minutes west."

"Now what?"

Chapter 12

Nattie looked up the coordinates on the GIN world map. "Jassie, look! Those coordinates are in Voncara Cove. But this makes no sense. That's in the water just off the coast."

"Nattie, Mr. Alaxrandus said we needed all three books to find the treasure. Couldn't there be more information in the third book that makes a difference somehow?"

"I don't know, but even if we had it, how would we get there? That's on another continent."

Jase took Nattie by the hand and they walked downstairs. "Dad, can we take a trip to Voncara Cove?" His dad almost spit up his coffee and started to laugh.

"What?"

"Voncara Cove in Fawneather."

"Son, do you know how much that would cost?"

"No."

"The flights alone could cost up to a thousand tutarian per person."

"What if Nattie and I saved up the money to go. Would you let us?" Jase's dad looked at Nattie's mom. She just shrugged her shoulders and smiled as to say you're on your own with this one.

"Jase, how do you think that you and Nattie could come up with that much money?"

"I'll get a job."

"Do you know how long that would take to save up that much? I'll tell you what, you come up with the money for the trip and then we will make a decision."

"Okay, deal."

"Now, you know it could take you well over a year to make enough money for just one ticket."

"I can get a job also, to help pay," Nattie said.

"Why is this so important to you two?"

Jase looked at Nattie and she was silent. After a few moments, Jase said, "After we visited the Voncara Cove Exhibit and saw all of the pirate history, it seems like a really neat place to go. We really want to see it in person." Jase was afraid that his dad would just totally dismiss his request if he thought it was for something foolish like a treasure hunt.

"Well, Nattie will have to discuss this with her mom but I don't think either of us would allow you to go to another country on your own at your age. Maybe in a year or two, after you have a chance to save up the money."

"Nattie, it's getting late and we all have a big day tomorrow so we need to get going."

"Awww!"

"Nattie, you promised me."

"Okay, Mom. I need to go upstairs and get my boots first."

"Well, hurry up." Jase and Nattie ran up the stairs as fast as they could.

"Jase, I was so afraid you were going to tell him. You know he would never let us go if you told him about the books."

"I know, that's why I didn't tell him."

Nattie picked up her boots and walked over to Jase and they kissed. Jase hugged her around her waist. "I can't wait until tomorrow, Jassie."

"I know. I will never sleep now."

"Nattie! Let's go," her mom yelled.

"I have to go, Jassie." She walked to the door, dropped her boots, and ran back to Jase for another hug and a quick kiss. She took Jase by the hand and he walked her downstairs and out to the cruiser.

"Good night, Nattie."

"Bye, my Jassie."

Jase went back upstairs and got ready for bed. As soon as his head hit the pillow, he was out cold. The same was true for Nattie. They were so exhausted from their very long, exciting, and revealing day. Nattie thought, *This was the best day of my entire life. What will tomorrow be like? Could it be as good as today? What could possibly be better? Maybe my wedding day when I marry Jase.* She smiled and drifted asleep.

The next morning, Jase was still sound asleep. His mom knocked at the door, "Jase, are you going to get up sometime today." He startled awake and looked at the time. "Jase you up?"

"Yes, Mom. I'm getting ready."

"You better hurry up." He got ready as fast as he could and rushed downstairs to eat. "Jase, Alrand has already left to go to the festival. He said they will meet you at the same place as yesterday," his mom said.

"Okay." They all loaded up into the cruiser and headed over to Nattie's house. Jase knocked on the door. "Hi, Jase. Why don't you all come in for a minute? Nattie is still getting ready."

"Mom, is Jase here?" Nattie called from the bathroom.

"Yes."

"Jassie, come here real quick."

"Hey, Nattie."

"Hey, can you lace up my corset?"

Jase smiled, "Sure." He helped her get the rest of her costume in order and brushed her hair, "I really love your hair, Nattie."

"Good. I'm going to keep it this way forever." She leaned back and gave Jase a little kiss. "Jase, I'll meet you downstairs in a sec."

"Hurry, we need to get going." Jase went downstairs with the others. A few moments later, Nattie pranced downstairs with her boots in her hand.

"Nattie, are you going to put those on?" her mom asked.

"Not till I have to." She giggled and went over to Jase and kissed him on the neck leaving a lipstick kiss behind. "Oops." She ran into the kitchen and got a rag to wipe off his neck.

"Nattie, you are so silly," Jase's mom said.

"I think we need to keep an eye on these two."

"I'm getting that impression."

They drove to the festival and Nattie asked Jase to help her put on her boots. Then Jase and Nattie set off on their adventure for the day. Nattie took Jase's hand and pulled him along as she skipped down the red brick pathway to the entrance of the fairgrounds.

"Hi, Kimberly!" Nattie shouted from a distance.

"Hey, Jase, Nat. What took you so long?" Alrand said.

"We were up late but we found the location of the treasure."

"You did!"

"Well maybe. You know that sword?"

"Yes, from the Exhibit."

"Well, the numerals match the numbers on the seal in the first book. When we put the two sets of numbers together from the first two books, it pointed to a spot in Voncara Cove on the GIN."

"So, the treasure is actually real?"

"We don't know. We need a way to get there and find out."

"You didn't tell anyone, did you?"

"No, I just asked Dad if I could go there when I saved up enough money."

"How are you going to get the money?" Alrand asked.

"Jase, you know the bookstore better than anyone. Ask my dad if you can work there since I will be leaving in a few months. They will need to hire someone."

"That's a great idea, Kimberly. Thanks."

"You're welcome."

"Come on, Jassie. I'm bored. Let's do something," Nattie said as she pushed up against Jase's shoulder.

"Okay, next we need to do the sword fighting lesson. That's over near the Voncara Cove Exhibit I think, as best as I can tell from this map."

Nattie led the way skipping and singing. "Come on, pokies."

"What's gotten into you, Nat?"

"I'm just happy."

"Evidently."

"Come on, Alrand." Kimberly started skipping along with Nattie and the two girls started giggling.

"Alrand, pirate captains don't skip," Jase laughed. Nattie grabbed Jase's hand and pulled him along hurriedly until they found the building where the competition sword-fighting lesson was given.

Jase stood up tall and eagerly walked into the main entrance. It was arranged like the inside of an old castle. The walls were lined with a faux stone finish and tapestries. A large square dark-colored mat on the center of the floor, with red tape, marked off the borders of the competition area. Along the left wall were seven suits of armor, each with an elegant sword sheathed at the waist.

The longsword-fencing instructor met them near the entrance and welcomed them. "You are my first students for the day. I need your contest entry forms please."

The instructor explained the rules of the competition and gave a safety briefing, "Safety above all else. I don't want anyone getting hurt today. You will be judged on style, form, and ability to follow instructions. You can earn a maximum of ten points from this competition. Who would like to go first?" Of course, the two boys couldn't resist and both eagerly raised their hands. "Okay, you first," the instructor said to Alrand.

"Each of you can select a suit of armor and when it's your turn, draw the sword from the sheath. Be careful, the swords are not very sharp but they are real and can inflict injury. So no playing around."

Alrand drew one of the swords, "This is so excellent!" The instructor went through a basic pre-programmed sword-fighting lesson and showed Alrand all the different techniques used in battle. He then helped him to put on the protective gear and taught him the different maneuvers that could be used to disarm his opponent.

"Okay, now try to use what I taught you and disarm me."

"Really, are you sure?"

"Give it all you got." Alrand swung his sword as best as he could. It started to feel heavy in his arms. "Remember to keep your form, hold your sword high, and swing with power." Alrand tried again.

"Very good. Anyone who can disarm me will automatically receive the maximum score."

"Who's next?"

Nattie had snuggled up to Jase as it was a bit cool in the hall and he was quite content with her in his arms. "Kimberly you can go ahead."

Kimberly was not really looking forward to a sword-fighting lesson but she thought the instructor was cute so she eagerly pulled a sword from a suit of armor and started her lesson. She listened to each instruction. It also helped that she learned from watching Alrand's lesson.

"You are quite good at this, Kimberly. Very good form. Try swinging from a higher position." Kimberly did okay, and then she smiled at the instructor and went back to her seat.

"You want to go next, Jassie?"

"Okay." Jase asked if he could use his own pirate sword.

The instructor inspected it, "This is a very nicely designed sword. Are you sure you want to nick up the edges?" Jase thought for a moment.

"Go for it, Jassie. It will make it look more like an authentic pirate sword." That was all the encouragement Jase needed.

"Sure, let's go for it."

They began the lesson. Jase took everything in like a sponge, absorbing every maneuver and so did Nattie as she intently watched Jase sitting strait up in her seat.

"Okay, try to disarm me," the instructor said. Jase swung his sword with all his might, trying each tactic he learned. He almost kept perfect form but was blocked each time. "You did very well, Jase."

"Nat, go get em," Alrand laughed. Nattie turned and stuck her tongue out at him and went over to Jase.

She gave him a kiss and took his sword. "I'm ready!" Nattie said. "I don't need any instruction. I could see the others' lessons."

"Are you sure?"

"Yes." They put on her protective gear. Jase thought she looked cute as she walked around the instructor with her sword high in the air. She took her time and maneuvered herself within the border of the mat. She took a few practice swings at the instructor who responded with blocking tactics. All of the sudden, Nattie lunged forward with her sword, catching the instructor off guard, and then quickly changed direction, knocking the sword from his hands.

"Whew, Nattie!"

"Yeah!"

"Very nice," the instructor said. He picked up his sword quickly, "Again." Nattie took her time and strategically swung the sword with tactical accuracy. Sparks flew off the blades as they crashed together. "You are quite the natural. Have you had lessons before?"

"Nope, I'm Tristy Brody. I'm a pirate." Jase, Alrand, and Kimberly laughed at Nattie's boasting. The instructor enjoyed the competition and played along with her. In a final maneuver, he disarmed Nattie sending the sword flying.

"Oops, guess I got a little carried away there, young pirate girl," the instructor laughed. "Very good job though."

"Thanks."

Nattie walked off the mat a little out of breath and picked up the sword. "Whew, that's hard work!" She handed the sword to Jase. He inspected the blade, now fraught with scars and nicks.

"Nattie, you were so great out there. How did you do that?"

"I don't know, Jassie. I was just having fun."

"Okay, Tristy. Let's go." They all laughed. Nattie punched Jase on the shoulder and put her arm around him.

"What's next, Jase?"

"I guess we just need to find the rest of the scavenger hunt items. We have about three hours before the deadline."

"Jassie, I hope we can find them in time." They visited shops and looked though quite a bit of merchandise to see if they could find the remaining items.

"Hey, look at those swords. Let's go in there," Jase said.

"Jassie, look at this one. It's kind of like U.S. Wells' sword."

"Oh, that is nice. But it's a little too expensive. I don't want to spend all my money."

"Jase! Nattie! I found the wooden box of pirate dice."

"Nice, Kimberly." Alrand gave her a hug. "Good job."

Jase picked up a set for Nattie and himself. "Nattie? Where did she go now?"

"Jase, you need a leash for her," Alrand said.

Kimberly smacked him, "Be nice!"

Nattie walked around the aisles with a sword and sheath tucked under her arm. "Here, Jassie," Nattie said with a big dimple smile. "I bought it for you."

"Nattie, that was so much! Why did you do that?"

"Because I wanted you to have it." Jase stood still for a second and said nothing. He wiped his eyes, gave her a hug, and put his head down against hers.

"You're my cute Tristy." She giggled. Alrand noticed some neat little key chains and thought one might make a cute little gift for Kimberly. He noticed some of them were little frogs holding swords in their hands and wearing pirate hats.

"Jase, look, do you think these will work for the scavenger hunt?"

"Yeah, those are perfect."

"I will get these," Alrand said. He walked to the teller counter and purchased four frog key chains. Kimberly gave him a little kiss on his cheek.

"Thank you, Alrand." He smiled and put his arm around her.

They continued to look for the two remaining scavenger hunt items. "Nattie, there's a sign for a ship tour."

"Do you want to do it, Jassie?"

"That would be neat."

"Jase, we don't have much time left," Alrand said.

"Look at that ship though. It's so big. I really want to do this."

"You two go ahead. I think Kimberly and I will keep looking."

"Alrand, come on. It could be fun."

"Yeah, let's do it," Kimberly said.

They paid to take the ship tour and walked up the steps to the main deck. The ship was a hundred-gun, multi-deck, wooden warship. "Guys, are you seeing this?"

Jase and Nattie posed for a picture next to a large cannon sitting in the center of the second deck by one of the framing posts. The ship smelled like old wood and it creaked and cracked with the movement of the water.

Chapter 13

"**Y**ou're really loving this, Jassie."

"Yeah I am." As the tour finished up, they entered the captain's quarters. The room was decorated very elegantly as if the captain was royalty. The tour guide talked about life of the sailors onboard the vessel and about the food they ate. On the way out, he gave away samples of cheese that was preserved in the same manner as was used back in the pirate era. He handed each of them a little burlap bag with the printing upon the side that displayed, *Cabin Cheese*.

"Oh no!" Alrand said.

Nattie started laughing. The further they walked the more she giggled. "I will never hear the end of this." Alrand said.

"And you didn't want to come," Nattie giggled.

"Shush, Nat."

"Kimberly, pinch him for me," Nattie said.

Kimberly chased Alrand off the ship and caught him by the arm. Alrand didn't really want to get away from her anyway. She pinched him and gave him a hug.

"Jassie, what's left?"

"Just a tin of pirate mints and then we're done."

"Jassie, we've been almost everywhere. Where are we going to find them?"

"I don't know." Nattie started to ask the workers at every tent if they knew where they could find the mints.

There were some ladies sitting around who just completed a show. They were all dressed up in their pirate costumes. Nattie walked over to them, "I love your costumes."

"Thank you, sweetie. I really like yours also. Are you in the pirate competition?"

"Yes."

"You should do great with that outfit. You have very beautiful hair."

"Thank you. We are actually done except for our scavenger hunt. We can't find the last item and we are almost out of time."

"What are you looking for?"

"It says a tin of pirate mints."

"You mean like these?" One of the women asked as she held up a metal container that said, *Pirate Mints.*

"Yes! Where did you get that?"

"I don't remember exactly but it was somewhere around the main amphitheater."

"Ooh, thank you so much!"

They all ran to the amphitheater and split up to try and find the mints. "Everyone meet back here in ten minutes."

"Okay, Jassie." They all went their separate ways to search. Jase, Kimberly, and Alrand all met back up but Nattie was nowhere to be found. They waited for about another ten minutes then decided to start looking for her. Jase hurried around the tent to search and almost fell over Nattie hurrying from the other direction.

"I found them, Jassie!"

"Alrand, Kimberly! I found her. Where were you?"

"I found the mints but forgot I spent all my money."

"So what did you do?"

"There was this little lady behind me in line. She said she would buy them for me. I told her not to but she insisted. She said I was the cutest little thing and she wanted to buy them for me." They all laughed. "Jase, we need to hurry and turn all this stuff in. We only have half an hour."

They hurried along and made it to the sign-in booth to receive credit for the scavenger hunt. Nattie was the first in line to display her items. "Hi, is this where we turn in the items for the scavenger hunt?"

"Yes, place your items here so I can see them and take a picture." Nattie placed all of her items up on the counter.

"Can I use this froggy key chain for the mystery item?"

"Yes, you can. You are the first to get all twelve items."

"Yay!"

"That's excellent," Alrand said. After they finished they started to walk toward the dock.

"Jassie, I'm so starving! Can we go to Skaters?"

"Do you two want to go to Skaters with us?" Jase asked.

"Yeah, I'm starving, Alrand. How about you?" Kimberly said.

"Me too." They walked past the amphitheater on their way and Nattie asked Jase, "Can I have five tutarian?" Jase gave her ten and she said, "Wait here one sec." She ran into the tent where she found the mints and purchased something she wanted to buy for Jase before she realized that she spent all her money on his sword. Moments later, she came out with a huge smile on her face and handed a bag to Jase.

"What's this?"

"Open it up, Jassie." Jase opened up the decorative box with pirate ships imprinted on the top to reveal a pirate ship, soap on a rope.

"Ooh, no way? That's so excellent!"

"Where did you get that, Nat? I want one!"

"I will get one for you," Kimberly said. Nattie took Kimberly by the hand and showed her the assortment of soaps.

"Kimberly, smell them. Don't they smell wonderful?"

"Oh yes, you're right. Do they have any scents for women?"

"I don't think so."

"Which one do you think Alrand would like?"

"I think he would like the black one because it has the strongest smell. He seems to like that." Nattie and Kimberly skipped out of the tent and over to the boys. Jase hugged Nattie. "Thank you, Tristy. This is great."

"You're welcome, Captain."

Kimberly handed Alrand his soap on a rope, "Smell it, Alrand. Do you like it?"

"Wow, that's nice." He gave Kimberly a hug. "Thank you."

She smiled, "You're welcome."

They walked a good distance to Skaters. "We have to head back in about an hour so we can get a seat for the announcement of the winners." Fortunately, Skaters was not as busy as the food tents at the fairground. "Nattie, I mean Tristy, you want to share something with me?"

"Sure, Jassie." They all ordered their food and took the time to relax a bit.

Nattie started to tear up a bit as she sat next to Jase.

"Nattie, what's wrong?"

"My arms and shoulders hurt."

Jase massaged her shoulders some. "Does that help?"

"A little. Do my arms."

"My arms kinda hurt also," Kimberly said.

"I bet it was the sword fighting," Alrand said.

"That must be it, Nattie. You must have overdone it. You were really swinging that sword hard." Jaftney brought their food over.

"You okay, Nattie?"

"No." She started crying a little.

"She hurt her muscles sword fighting."

"Sword fighting?"

"Yeah, it was a lesson for the pirate competition."

"Oh, you want something to take for the pain?"

"Yes, please." Jaftney brought her back some aspirin.

Jase kept massaging her shoulders and gave her a hug. "Are you feeling any better?"

"A little."

"Are we ready? We need to get a seat for the judging," Alrand said. They picked up all of their stuff and started the long walk back to the amphitheater. Nattie was walking a little slow.

"Nattie, you okay?"

"I think I'm falling apart, Jase. My feet hurt, my shoulders, and my arms."

"Here, jump on my back." Nattie held on to Jase's back and he quickly walked to catch up to Alrand and Kimberly. After he caught up, he passed them by rather quickly.

"Come on, pokies," Nattie said.

Jase put Nattie down as they approached the fairgrounds. They walked over to the amphitheater and stopped for a second to take it all in. The presentation area was decked out with incredible pirate decorations. There were tropical looking faux trees with coconuts and ships cannons. Both sides of the raised platform had ships railings with open gun ports on the sides. There was a centrally located mast with ropes and rigging affixed to the ships railings and tie downs. Gunpowder barrels and cannon balls were stacked in various locations next to coils of rope.

The seating area was already very full. "We could stand, up near the front," Alrand said.

"No, Nattie needs to sit down." There were a few scattered seats left way in the front. They walked all the way down and found a place for the girls to sit. The boys stood down by the platform a few feet away.

Jase looked around at the competitors and smiled because he didn't see any real competition. *I got this.*

"Alrand, can you take some pictures of me when they give me the trophy?" Jase asked.

"Hey! How do you know I won't win?"

Jase laughed. "If you win, then I will take the pictures." Alrand pushed Jase.

"Nattie's right. You are a brat."

"Okay, Mr. Cabin Cheese." They both started to laugh and looked back at the girls. Nattie came running up from behind.

"Boo!" She hugged Jase around his waist. "Are you guys laughing at me?"

"What gave you that idea, Nat?"

"Cuz I know you."

The announcers walked out on the stage. "Attention, all contestants, the moment you've been waiting for." They started by presenting the awards for the youth competition.

"Next up, the winners of the Teen division. The first runner up, with a total of one hundred and three points, Jase Thunderbelt!" Jase hung his head down for just a second but then he thought, *I guess second place isn't that bad.* He walked up to the platform and waited for the winner to be announced. His shoulders hung down a bit and he frowned as he looked out over the audience.

"Our first place winner and grand champion, Teen division, with a perfect score of one hundred and five points…Nattie Candella!"

Nattie gasped! "I WON!" She jumped up and down, "I won!" She danced her way to the platform to stand next to Jase, bouncing on her toes and smiling. She gave Jase a hug and the crowd seemed to love it as they clapped and cheered. Nattie took Jase's hand. "Jase, bow." Jase bowed down before the audience and Nattie crossed her legs and curtsied. The crowed clapped louder and continued their applause. Nattie put her hand over her lips and blew kisses to the audience. Her infectious smile and youthful enthusiasm was contagious and the crowed loved her. Jase smiled so big. He thought, *I am so glad Nattie won. She really deserves it.* He gave her a big hug and put his arm around her waist. Once all of the announcements were complete, they presented the expensive and elegant trophies to the first place winners and cash awards to the two second place winners.

They walked off the platform to meet up with the others. Nattie jumped up and down and ran over to Kimberly with Jase by the hand. Their parents had already met up with Alrand and Kimberly during the awards.

"Nattie, I'm so proud of you!"

"Thanks, Mom." She said with her cute dimple smile. Nattie started to hug everyone. Jase felt warm and content. "I never would have won if it wasn't for my Jassie." Nattie handed the trophy to Jase. "You can have this."

"No, Nattie, you worked very hard for that. It's yours."

"But I want you to have it. And besides, it's very heavy and I don't feel like carrying it." Jase's mom laughed at Nattie.

"Nattie, you are so amazing." She gave Nattie a hug.

"I will hold this for you but it's yours. You deserve it," Jase said. Nattie put her arm around him and they all headed toward the parking lot to go home. "The end of another grate day!" Nattie said.

On the way home, Jase took Nattie's hand. She put her head against his shoulder, took in a slow deep breath, and gradually let it out. With her heart finally calming after all the excitement, she fell asleep. "Awww, Jase, she must be so exhausted," his mother said. Jase gently lifted her out of the cruiser and carried her to the porch. She woke up and gave Jase a hug. They said their goodbyes for the night.

Jase slept in the next morning. The bright sun shined though the high stained-glass attic window, casting colorful panels upon the wall. He awoke to the smell of buttermilk pancakes and maple sausage. After eating breakfast, he hurried to pack his backpack for the day, making sure to include his new book. He met up with Alrand and rode to Nattie's house.

She was rocking on the porch swing with her feet dangling, swaying about as the boys rode up.

"Finally! I've only been waiting all morning," Nattie said with a big smile. She jumped off the porch and gave Jase a hug, and the three of them set off for Alaxrandus Rare Book Store. "Jassie, when are you going to talk to Mr. Alaxrandus?"

"Today I hope. I don't want anyone else to get the job when Kimberly leaves for military school. I hope he will hire me."

"I'm sure he will. You know the bookstore better than anyone. Alrand, you doing okay back there?" Nattie asked.

"Yeah, I'm just a little sore and tired from yesterday."

"You want to stop at the tower?" Jase said.

"No, I want to hurry and see Kimberly."

When they walked into the bookstore, Jase took a deep breath of the wonderful, familiar aroma, of the scented candles and seasoned wood. The metal clanging bell on the door announced their presence.

"Hi, everyone!" Kimberly said.

"Hi, Kimberly, is your dad in this morning?"

"Oh, I'm sorry, Jase. He won't be in until this afternoon."

"That's okay, we can wait."

"Nattie, how are your shoulders and feet feeling today?"

"Much better, thank you."

"Jassie, are you going to look at books while we wait?"

"No, I brought my new book. I wanted to read some with you."

"Oh yes, please. I love it when you read to me. You get so excited."

"Why don't we all go up to the parlor? I would like to hear some also," Kimberly said.

The four of them walked up the creaky old steps to the rather dark parlor and lit some lamps. The light flickered across the pages creating dancing shadows.

Jase started rereading about the captain's meeting with the hooded man in the Dirty Dog Tavern to catch everyone up to where he last left off. Nattie leaned on his shoulder and followed along as he read aloud.

Chapter 14

"Lieutenant Ultaman, maneuver into position up ahead and prepare to drop anchor. We need to keep a good distance or this mission will be over before it starts."

They anchored the ship just off the pirate coast near some cliffs hoping not to be discovered. The captain knew that they would never be able to capture the ship in dry dock if the pirates learned of their presence. They were outnumbered a hundred to one. Anderson suggested to the captain that he and his men go ashore to create a diversion by blowing up several barrels of gunpowder on the far side of town. The captain was hesitant to send Anderson on this mission. What if he really is a spy for the pirates? After considering his proposal, the captain felt it was the best option and decided to have faith in Anderson, giving him permission to proceed with his plan.

"You know what's at stake, Lieutenant. You must not be discovered and we have to make sail before daybreak or we could end up at the bottom of the sea."

"Sir, trust me, this will work." Anderson said. He gathered up his men and they covertly rowed a longboat up the shoreline until they found a place to sit and hide. Captain Wells kept a close lookout for enemy ships. His men were ready and anxiously awaited the word to go ashore and capture the Black Malice, still in dry dock. They planned on overpowering the guards so that they could release the ship to slide into the sea. Everything hinged on Anderson drawing away the town by the diversion so that the pirates wouldn't notice the ship sailing away until it was too late. They waited for two hours, yet no explosions.

Did Anderson betray me?

"Men, keep a close look out," ordered the captain.

"Sir! Look who we found hiding in the galley?" The crew dragged Tristy Brody up to the deck. The captain felt a shiver run up his spine.

"Why haven't you tried to escape? How did you get on board?"

"Please, Captain, I meant no harm. I am only here to help David take the ship."

"What do you mean, take the ship?"

"I know of a secret way to get to the dry dock so that the ship can be taken without anyone knowing."

"Why didn't you mention this before?"

"Would you have believed the word of a pirate?"

"Why should I trust you now?"

"Captain, these are not my people, they are my enemy. The day you pulled me from the water was the

same day they captured me and forced me onto their ship. We only wish to be free. My father and his crew are hunted by these cursed pirates and they wish to see us dead."

"Captain, we can't trust her. She's a pirate," Lieutenant Ultaman said.

"Prepare to make sail!"

"Sir, look! The Black Malice, she's in the water!" The captain had to make a decision fast. Trust that Anderson was truly in charge of the ship and wait, or make sail and run as fast as the wind would carry them.

"Prepare to make sail! All crew be ready for battle," the captain said. "Open the gun ports, no one fire without my consent. Ultaman, make way and maneuver us into battle position. Sharpshooters, to the top sails."

As they sailed toward the Black Malice, the captain could see Anderson at the helm and the ships gun ports were still closed. Could Tristy be telling the truth? Anderson lied about his reason to go ashore. Could he be trusted?

Cannon fire rained forth and echoed loudly off the sheer cliffs alongside the coast. The crew ducked down quickly.

"Hold your fire! Ultaman, get us out of range of those shore cannons." The pirates had discovered their ship had been taken but it was too late for them. The Black Malice was already too far from shore for them to do any real damage. The captain ordered the crew to head for home.

Once their two ships were anchored in the cove, Anderson was ordered before the captain.

"Sir, I can explain."

"Anderson, I trusted you."

"Sir, we captured the ship and no one was hurt."

"You should have come before me rather than acting on your own."

"If I came to you with a plan devised by Tristy, would you have allowed it?"

"Certainly not!"

"That's why I didn't tell you."

"Anderson, I am taking a big risk telling you this. We have a spy among us."

"And you thought it was me?"

"By your actions and willingness to trust Tristy, yes. If you ever disobey me or lie to me again, I will have you shot. Is that understood?"

"Yes, sir."

"And tell me why you trust this pirate enough to disobey me in the first place?"

"Because she loves me and I trust her with my life."

"With your life?"

"I would die for her, sir."

"Well you may get that chance. We can expect retaliation from the pirates and we will be outnumbered in both men and ships."

"Captain, why can't we just use the RFI and take those ships out once and for all?"

"Anderson, I have long believed that turning on the RFI will draw our enemy down from the sky. We just can't take that chance."

"Look, more out of place text! How did I miss that when I paged through the book?" Jase said.

"Jassie, this is crazy. There could not have been any weapon like this RFI gun back then. What kind of enemy could possibly come down from the sky? There were no flying ships back then," Nattie said.

"Yeah, and they have two enemies, the pirates and the other enemy that attacked their ship in the first book."

"I wonder why using the RFI gun causes the enemy to come attack them?"

"I don't know but this is so neat. I want to see how the battle goes." Jase gave Nattie a little kiss on the cheek because she looked so cute sitting there thinking so hard with the lights flickering across her face.

Nattie bit his shoulder, "Ouch! Brat!" Jase tickled Nattie. She screamed and hopped off her chair. Alrand and Kimberly laughed.

"Nattie, you are so ticklish," Jase said.

"Okay, stop it. Keep reading."

"Well, sir, in that case I have another proposal."

"Let's have it."

"If we release Tristy and provide her passage on one of our ships, she can get her father and his crew to join us. Then we will have three tall ships to fight."

"Anderson, even if I trusted Tristy, there is no way I can trust her father nor release one of our ships. The pirates can show up at any moment."

"Then what are my orders, sir?"

"Take our two ships and conceal them on the other

side of the peninsula until you hear the long guns firing. Then bring the ships to bear behind the enemy, trapping them in the cove between our ships and the shore cannons. Make use of the new ships long gun and try to take out one of their ships as fast as possible to even the odds."

"Sir! Sorry to interrupt."

"Yes Ultaman?"

"Tristy, she has fled! She has taken a fishing vessel and escaped."

"Anderson?"

"I didn't know, sir. Honest. We must go after her or she could be captured."

"Anderson, she is on her own now."

"Sir! I have to go after her."

"Anderson, I need you here, that's an order. Do not cross me. Now follow your orders." Anderson walked outside and looked to the sea. My Tristy is out there somewhere. His heart ached for her. Will I ever see her again?

Nattie took a deep breath and sighed. "He really loves her, Jase. That's so sad. I hope they get to see each other again. I think she is dumb to leave him like that."

"Nattie, it's just a story."

"I don't think so, Jassie. I think it's a true story, and what if she never comes back?"

"I think she will because she loves him also."

"I think it's so cute," Kimberly said. "He looked out at the sea and was missing her already."

"Read more Jassie."

The ships were maneuvered into place. The crews

stood by waiting for the emanate pirate attack.

"Sir, when can we expect them?" his first mate asked.

"It could be any time now; day or night," replied Anderson. Many hours had passed and the moon had risen over the water reflecting beautiful bright streaks across the fluent waves of the ocean. Anderson looked up at the moon wondering if Tristy was looking and thinking the same thing. His first mate noticed the sad look on David's face.

"Sir, I'm sure she's safe. She is smart and tough, and she knows the sea."

"I hope you're right. I should not have allowed her to escape. I should have put a guard on her. I would have never guessed she would leave me that way."

"Kimberly?"

"Up here, Dad."

"What are you doing?"

"We are just reading from Jase's new book," Kimberly said.

"Mr. Alaxrandus, could I talk to you for a minute?" Jase asked.

"Sure, come up to my office." The two of them walked up to the third floor and sat down in the office. "What can I do for you, Jase?"

"Kimberly said that she will be leaving to join the Proelium Concordia and I was just wondering if I might apply for a job since she won't be working in the store anymore."

"I think that's a splendid idea, Jase. You know most of the bookstore, and how we conduct business. We can start your training in a couple weeks."

"Thank you! That's great."

"What was that book you were reading from downstairs?"

"It's U.S. Wells' second book, *Three Tall Ships*."

"Interesting. Kimberly told me you found the second book. Any prospects on the third?"

"No, sir; no trace of it."

"Well, that's a shame but keep looking. I bet you'll be the one to find it. Please send Kimberly up for a second, would you?"

"Yes, sir; see you later."

"Bye, Jase."

Jase walked downstairs smiling.

"Jassie, did you get the job?"

"Yep. Voncara Cove, here we come!"

"Yay!"

"Kimberly, your father wants to see you."

"Okay, don't read any more until I get back."

Nattie jumped up and wrapped her arms around Jase. He picked her up by the waist and swung her around until they both felt dizzy.

"Jassie, I love this story. I can't wait to see what happens with Tristy and David Anderson. They are just like us, don't you think?"

Alrand started laughing loudly, "You are so funny, Nat." She stuck her tongue out at him.

"You're my silly Tristy," Jase said. He gave her a long kiss.

"Don't you two ever stop?" Alrand said.

"Why don't you kiss Kimberly?"

"I'm waiting for the right time."

"I dare you to kiss her when she walks down here."

"No way. I'm not doing that with you all watching."

"Chicken." They could hear Kimberly walking down the steps.

"Kiss her, Alrand," Nattie said under her breath.

"What are you all whispering about?" Kimberly asked.

"Nothing," Alrand said as he gave Nattie an evil eye.

"Jassie, I'm getting hungry. Can we all go to Skaters?"

"Sure."

"Let me ask my dad if I can come since we're not really busy today," Kimberly said. She ran upstairs for a few seconds then came running back down, "I can go."

"Yay," Nattie said. The two couples walked to Skaters.

They found a table and sat down. The aroma of grilling burgers filled the air and a trendy song played.

Nattie started to giggle.

"Nat, why are you so giggly?"

"Because I'm so happy. My mom said I have a bubbly personality."

"Alrand, she's so happy because she's with Jase," Kimberly said. Nattie scooted closer to Jase and put her arm around his neck. She inched up and gave him a kiss on the cheek.

Jase hugged her and smelled her hair, "You smell so good, Nattie."

"Thank you, Jassie. I can't wait until we can go to Voncara Cove. It will be so much fun."

"I just hope it doesn't take too long to get the money."

"Jase, what if someone has already found the treasure?" Alrand asked.

The waitress came and took their orders. Jase played with Nattie's soft hair behind her back. "From what my grandpa tells me, no one has ever had all three books at the same time. So how could anyone find the treasure?"

"That's a good point but I don't really care if there's treasure. I just want to go there," Jase said.

"Me too, Jassie. With you."

After they finished eating, Kimberly said, "I have to get back to the store, guys. Alrand, do you want to come with me?"

"Absolutely," Alrand said. "See you guys later."

Nattie and Jase walked to the docks and sat down on a bench.

Chapter 15

"Jassie, I want some funnel cake."

"You're still hungry?"

"No, but I want some." She gave Jase a really cute look.

"Okay, cutie. Wait here. I'll be right back." Jase handed her the book and walked to a nearby snack shack. When he returned, Nattie had her shoes off and her feet up on the long bench. He lifted up her legs and sat down resting her legs on top of his.

"Jassie, when we're done, do you want to go home and read some more?"

"Okay." They finished their funnel cake and walked to their bikes to ride home. When they reached the top of the big hill, they stopped in the field under the power transmitter to rest.

They lay back on the thick freshly mowed grass. "Read to me, Jassie, please." She looked at him with her cute blue eyes and big dimple smile.

Jase laughed, "What are you doing to me, girl? I can't ever say no to you."

"Why would you want to?" Nattie giggled. She laid her head on his chest looking up at him and he kissed her forehead. He read from the place where they left off.

The sun was barely peaking up over the water

when there sounded three loud cannon blasts that echoed off the cliffs of the cove. "They've arrived," Anderson said.

"Make sail, men. Quickly now." They maneuvered their ships upwind of the pirates, sailing just outside of the range of the shore cannons.

"Take aim with the long gun," ordered Anderson. They turned the elevation adjustment for the estimated range.

"Fire!" The huge cannon ball hurled forth, high in the air, with its trajectory dead on as it plummeted downward. The explosion on impact sent splinters flying in all directions with a loud bang and bright flash.

"Direct hit, sir!"

"Reload quickly," Anderson said.

Caught off guard, the targeted pirate vessel received a crippling blow and listed to one side. The three remaining pirate ships adjusted course and headed toward the two Voncara Cove vessels.

"Ready, sir!"

"Take aim...Fire!"

"Another direct hit, sir, just below the water line."

"Great work, men!" The pirate ship went down fast and started to break apart.

"Sir! The main long gun has cracked! We dare not risk another shot."

"Lieutenant Anderson! A sail on the horizon to the west."

"Men, concentrate all fire on the two remaining

pirate ships." The tactical battle ensued for over an hour as each ship tried to maneuver into position for each cannon barrage.

The defender, which was the first ship built by Captain Wells, had sustained major damage. The Black Malice had not fared much better.

"Sir! The fourth pirate ship is almost upon us. We can't take them on and survive. Our mast is severely damaged." Another ship snuck up behind the defender unnoticed.

"Sir! Look! They have her! That's it then; we've lost the Defender."

The Galveta, with her ports closed, sailed past the Defender, and met the fourth pirate ship head on. They boarded her and attacked the pirate crew. Anderson could see Tristy waving her arms on the deck.

"It's Tristy's father's ship, men. We have a chance." David's heart pounded heavily. The other two pirate ships tried to turn tail and run but the wind was against them. Anderson gave the order to chase them down and end their plunder of innocent towns. All but one pirate ship was sunk. The crippled ships anchored in the cove. Anderson made his way to the Galveta to find Tristy lying wounded on the deck.

The captain of the Galveta, Tristy's father, said, "It's a mortal wound, I'm afraid."

"Jassie, no! No way!" Nattie's eyes started tearing up. "Keep reading!"

Anderson ordered his men to quickly take Tristy to shore. He rushed her to Pamela Surenski, their crew *physician.*

"Is there anything you can do for her?" David asked.

"We need to take her into surgery right now. She has lost a lot of blood."

David stood with his hand on his forehead not knowing what to do with himself. He walked around outside of the makeshift hospital waiting for news for many hours.

The day led into the night, and still no word on Tristy. Her actions to risk her life to get help from her father saved the crews of Voncara Cove. David could hardly contain himself. He was so helpless to do anything. He chiseled a heart in one of the stones of the sea wall he had overseen being built with the inscription, "David and Tristy, now and forever."

Nattie let out a little whimper and a sigh. "Do you think she will live, Jase?"

"I don't know. If this story were made up, then I would say yes. If it really happened, then I don't know."

"I don't want her to die, Jassie. It's too sad."

"We better get heading home, Nattie; it's getting late." They rode to Nattie's house and went inside.

"Hi, Mom."

"What are you two up to tonight?"

"Mom, it's so sad. Tristy might die."

"Who?"

"Tristy, from the pirate book. We made her dress, remember?"

"Oh." She gave Nattie a hug and patted her back. "It will be okay, sweetie. Maybe you shouldn't read anymore."

"But I have to know what happens, Mom."

"Well, just take a break for tonight, okay?" Nattie took a deep breath and let it out.

"Okay. Come on, Jassie." She took Jase by the hand and they sat on the front porch swing to talk for a while. Jase put his arm around her and they started kissing as the sun disappeared behind the trees.

"Nattie, it's time to come in now. Say good night to Jase."

"You say it first, Jassie."

"No, you say it first." They kissed a little more.

"Nattie!"

"Okay, Mom! Ugh," Nattie said. She looked at Jase for a second then they both started to laugh. "Let's say goodbye together," Nattie said.

"Good night, my handsome."

"Good night, my beautiful Tristy." Nattie walked toward the door but wouldn't let go of Jase. They stood at the door and had one last kiss good night.

"I can't wait to see you tomorrow, Jassie." Nattie beamed and winked. Jase winked back and then headed home. Nattie watched him leave from the living room window.

Jase stretched and rolled over in bed. The sun was bright but an unusual group of colors glimmered against his bedroom wall. He arose out of bed and stood on the window seat to look outside. The sun was rising just under the clouds. The brilliant light illuminated the tops of the trees and reflected off the tree trunks like arrays of yellow and orange mirrors, yet the clouds in the sky were as black as night. *Oh, wow, that's so neat.* He ran outside and took a few pictures. He couldn't wait to see Nattie and tell her about the wonderful sight.

He went back inside. His mom had already started to cook breakfast.

"Hi, Mom."

"Hey, Jase, you're up early this morning?"

Jase looked at her with a smile, "Did you see that incredible sunrise?"

"I sure did."

"Nattie and I are going to watch the tall ships leave today."

"You two seem to be getting along very well." Jase just smiled back and his cheeks turned a bit red. "You hungry?" Jase could hear a faint knock at the front door.

"Mom, I think someone's at the door." He walked over and heard it again, a faint taping. He opened the door to find Nattie standing there with tears streaming down her face. He could see her lips and chin quivering. She ran into his arms and held him as tight as she could.

"Nattie, what's wrong…what's the matter?" Nattie just continued to cry with her face hidden in Jase's chest.

"Oh, Jassie," she whispered so faintly.

Jase rubbed her back gently and asked, "Nattie, what's wrong? You're scaring me."

"Jassie, I have to go away." Jase's heart sank and he feared to ask what she meant. He could feel a cold, lonely, despair welling up from inside and he felt like crying. He just held Nattie tight and could hear his mom talking to someone in the other room.

A few moments later, his mom walked over and held both of them together. "Nattie, it will be okay." She continued to cry, tears were running down her cheeks and soaking Jase's shirt.

"Oh, Nattie," Jase's mom said as she started tearing up with concern. "It's not forever."

"Mom, what's going on? Please someone tell me."

"Jase, Nattie has been given a great honor. She has been offered a seat at the Institute of Advanced Sciences for this coming school year. It's an accelerated youth program for gifted teenagers. It will be great for Nattie's future."

"Where is this? She has to go away for a whole year?"

"I'm not going!" Nattie said.

"Nattie, sweetie, it's only for one school year and the two of you can video chat over the GIN."

"I don't care. I'm not leaving Jase."

"Nattie, you should not have run away like that. Your mother called and is worried about you. You need to head home because you two need to talk." Nattie just held tightly to Jase and said nothing. "You two must be hungry. Why don't you both come into the kitchen and have some breakfast."

Jase sat Nattie down in a chair at the table and he slid a chair right next to hers. He took a tissue and wiped the tears from her eyes and cheeks. She just closed her eyes and let Jase gently wipe the moisture from her eyelids but she couldn't hold back the tears.

Jase gently kissed her. She put one arm around Jase's neck and her other hand on his face to hold him close and she kissed him as if it was for the last time. "I won't leave you, Jassie. I don't care about the stupid science thing. I'm not going."

"Breakfast is ready. Jase, why don't you come and make a plate for Nattie and yourself?" Jase prepared their plates and carried them back to the table. His mom gave Nattie a hug and kissed her on the cheek. "Jase, after you two are done eating, I'm going to take Nattie home."

"But, Mom, we were going to go to the harbor and watch the ships leave."

"Jase, no argument. Nattie has to go and talk with her mom."

They took a long time to eat breakfast. Nattie just picked at her food with a very sad frown on her face; she had no appetite. She whispered into Jase's ear, "Let's run away, Jassie." Jase placed his hand on her thigh; he could feel her shivering. It was a cool overcast morning and she ran out of the house with only a pair of shorts and an old tee shirt. Her legs were freezing. Jase went and got a jacket and put it on her. "Jassie, I mean it. Let's run away."

"Where would we go?"

"I don't care. Mom is going to make me leave and I'm not going. I don't care what she says."

"Maybe I can come with you."

"I don't see how. If I go, you won't be able to stay with me. I will have to stay in a girl's dorm and boys aren't allowed. The first two weeks they don't even let us use the GIN."

"When would you have to leave, if you go?"

"In two weeks."

"Two weeks? That's crazy...at least we can spend that time together though."

"Jase, I'm not going!"

"Okay, Nattie. I was just saying." Nattie held Jase and started crying again. Jase felt a lump swell up in his throat and an empty feeling in his stomach.

"Jase, it's time. Take Nattie out to the cruiser so we can take her home."

"Come on, Nattie." Nattie wouldn't let go.

"Come on, you two. Right now." Jase pulled Nattie to her feet and put his arm around her waist and they walked to the door.

"Jase, why won't you run away with me?"

"Nattie, I would go anywhere with you but we don't have anywhere to go and no money."

"We can sell the pirate trophy coin."

"Nattie..." They walked out to the cruiser and Jase opened the door. Nattie just took off running as fast as she could into the field across the street.

"Jase, go after her!" Jase ran after Nattie but she was sprinting like the wind. Finally, she slowed when she made it into the woods, way on the other side of the field by a trail leading to the Intracoastal Waterway.

"Nattie! Wait!" Nattie fell down to her knees crying. Jase ran to her, sat her up, and held her close. Nattie hugged him so tight. Tears ran down her face. Jase teared up and tried not to cry seeing her so upset.

"Jassie, please don't make me go back."

"I won't, sweetie." Jase's heart thumped so fast. They just sat there for a while and held each other.

Chapter 16

"Jassie, please run away with me, even if just for today."

"Okay, Nattie." He kissed her and then helped her to her feet. They put their arms around each other and walked down to the Intracoastal Waterway. The air was warming up and rays of sunlight shined through the dense clouds and bounced off the rippling water. They walked for several sects in the woods along the waterfront. Neither one desired to talk about that morning's events. Nattie took in a deep jerking breath and let out her sorrow all at once, pretending that nothing had happened and everything was just fine. She felt free again and looked up at Jase. "I really love it when you smile at me, Nattie."

"Then I will have to smile at you forever."

After a while, the waterway narrowed as they walked toward Halkers Pass. The small little town was abandoned a hundred years ago when the Summerset Sea Port was constructed. However, some of the buildings remained. The weather had grown warm so they decided to swim across the waterway and visit their favorite little hangout, the old Halkers Mill. The mill was used to process grain carried by ships from area farms. A little stream ran alongside the mill and flowed into a wooden trough used to feed the mill's water wheel. A few years back, Jase, Nattie, and Alrand repaired the water wheel and managed to get it working. Nattie rigged up a small, old-fashioned, power generator, with help from the boys, so they could have power at night. The power transmitter near town didn't reach out far enough so the generator idea worked out quite well.

The mill was constructed out of solid hardwoods and was very weathered, yet quite solid. The roof was made of gray slate tiles upon the third floor framing. Jase and Nattie walked into the milling room where large millstones attached to gears and pulleys. The water wheel drive belts had been removed many years ago so the grinding stones were disconnected. The building smelled very dusty and of old wood.

They walked up the solid, thick, hardwood steps to the third floor and over to the large deck overlooking the waterway. Jase laid his jacket down on the edge of the deck and Nattie sat down with her legs hanging over the side and her arms and chin resting on the second rung of the railing around the deck. Jase sat next to her and put his arm around her.

Nattie started to get upset and her insides turned, "Oh no! Jassie! If I leave, I won't be here with you for the pirate ship reenactment. I can't go, I just can't."

"I don't want you to go either. Maybe we can talk to your mom and ask her to let you stay?"

"Jassie, I tried. She got mad and yelled at me. She said if I didn't stop, I would be grounded and not be able to see you at all."

"What did you say?"

"I didn't. I just ran away and came to you."

Nattie held Jase's face in her hands and they kissed. A tall sailing ship from the festival floated by on the waterway and they watched it pass. The canvas of the sails ruffled in the quiet breeze. They were high enough to look down at the crew on the deck.

"Jassie, two days ago was the happiest day of my entire life. Today has been the worst day of my life. I would miss you too much. I can't do it."

"Nattie, I don't know what to do. I would go crazy without you. What if you left and I never saw you again?"

"Don't ever say that! Don't you ever say that!" Nattie's tummy made a loud growling sound.

"Nattie, you have hardly eaten anything all day."

"I don't care. I just want to be with you."

"Let's catch you something to eat."

Jase got up and helped Nattie to her feet. They walked downstairs where they kept a fishing rod hidden and sat down at the waterway wall. Nattie laid her head down on Jase's lap while he fished and fell asleep. Jase was careful not to wake her until he finally caught something. They went up to the top floor and made a fire in the old fireplace to cook. They had done this many times before when they didn't feel like going home to eat while working on the mill.

Nattie scarfed her fish down as if she hadn't eaten in a week. "You feeling better now, sweetie?"

"Yes. Thank you, Jassie." She said as she let out a little burp.

"For what?"

"Spending the day with me. My mom will never let me see you again after we go back."

"I don't think she would do that."

"That's what she said. Can't we just stay here forever?"

"I wish we could."

Jase sat against the wall across from the fire. Nattie rolled up Jase's jacket as a pillow and laid on his lap nice and warm. She was so tired. All of the emotion and events over the past few days had thoroughly taken its toll on her and she fell asleep. Jase ran his fingers through her hair and massaged her neck. After a while, the warm air started to make him sleepy. He laid his head back against the wall and fell asleep.

As the sun began to set and the night creatures started to stir, a young owl landed on the deck railing making quite a fuss. Jase woke up and noticed the sun was setting and the sky was riddled with orange-colored puffy clouds. He gently woke Nattie and they walked out to sit on the deck to watch the sun go down.

"It's so pretty, Jassie." She leaned her head back so Jase could give her a kiss as he sat behind her.

"Nattie, we have to head home soon. My parents are going to be so mad at me."

"But we will never be able to see each other again. We will both be grounded and then I will have to leave."

"We have to go home sometime."

"Please, Jassie, just a little longer."

"Okay, a little longer." They watched as the sun touched the trees.

"Hey, you guys!" yelled Alrand. Nattie gasped. Alrand walked out on the deck, "Hey, you two."

"Alrand, you scared me!"

"Sorry, Nat. Are you two okay?"

"Yes, we're fine," Jase said.

"I figured I would find you here."

"Did you tell anyone?"

"Of course not, but you need to come home now. The police and your parents are at Nat's house and they have half the town out looking for you."

"Oh, great!" Jase said. "Are my parents really mad?"

"I don't know. Your father looked mad. He had to leave work and all, but Nat, your mom is really upset."

"Jase, I don't want to go. She is going to ground me for life."

"Nat, you have to."

"Shut up, Alrand. I don't have to do anything!"

"Nattie, calm down," Jase said. She just started crying again. Alrand gave the two of them a hug.

"I'm sorry, Nat, but you really need to go home."

"Alrand, are they up there?" yelled Kimberly.

"Yes, they're coming down."

The three of them walked downstairs and outside to meet up with Kimberly, who walked over to Nattie and hugged her.

"I'm sorry you're so upset, Nattie. I know everything will be okay. All right?" Kimberly rubbed her skinny little arm.

"I guess so." Jase took one of Nattie's hands, Kimberly took the other, and they started walking. There was a waterway crossing two sects up so they headed in that direction. There was an air of silence during their very long walk home. Nobody wanted to say anything upsetting to Nattie. They reached the waterway crossing then continued north until they reached the path through the woods that led to the big field.

When they approached Nattie's house, they could see lots of people and some police cruisers parked in the driveway. As they drew close enough for Nattie's mom to see them, she ran in their direction. Nattie got scared and instinctively tried to bolt but Jase had hold of her and wouldn't let go for anything. When Nattie's mom reached them, she hugged both of them, crying.

"I'm so so sorry, Nattie." Nattie started to cry also.

"I'm sorry, Mom." They hugged for a few minutes and gained their composure.

"Nattie, you scared me so bad."

"I'm sorry, Mom. I really am, but I can't leave Jase."

"Nattie, you don't have to go if you don't want to."

"I don't?" Nattie took a deep breath and let it out.

"Can you two meet me inside after I finish up out here? Please?"

"Okay, Ms. Candella," Jase said.

Nattie and Jase went inside and sat on the couch next to each other. Jase's dad came in to talk with them.

"Are the two of you okay?"

"Yes, sir," Jase said.

"Good, now don't ever ever do that to us again! You understand me!"

"Yes, sir."

Nattie's mom walked in and sat down on the edge of the couch next to Jase. "Nattie, I am leaving the decision up to you, if you promise me that you will seriously consider going. Can you promise me that?"

"Yes."

"And Jase, you have to promise me that you will respect her decision."

"Okay, I will."

"Jase, you need to go now. We have some serious things we need to talk about. Nattie, you can say goodbye but don't you leave the house." Nattie walked Jase to the door and hugged him.

"Good night, Jassie. I hope I can see you tomorrow."

"Good night, sweetie. Sleep well. I will be thinking of you."

After everyone left, Nattie sat down next to her mom. "Nattie, I was so worried about you today. I was going to punish you but I think you are capable of making the correct decision and I know you will want to spend this time with Jase before leaving." Nattie sat attentively with her head cocked and her hair hanging down in front. Her mom began a well-prepared speech, "Before you say anything, hear me out. If you take this opportunity at the school, you are guaranteed to receive a scholarship if you get decent grades. I don't have the money to send you to college."

"Mom, I don't care about college."

"Well, let me ask you this…what if Jase gets into college and you want to go with him? Without the scholarship, you won't be able to go. That's four years. Can you handle that?" Nattie frowned and her eyes teared up. Her bottom lip protruded out and quivered, she couldn't help it. She started to cry again. The only thing worse than having to go away from Jase for a year would be to stay home while Jase went away, especially for four years.

Nattie managed to get out a few words while she was crying, "Okay, Mom. You win, I will go." Her mom hugged her while she sat on the edge of the couch crying. "Can I go to bed now?"

"Sure, honey. And think about this; you will not be gone for a full year and you will be able to come home to visit twice during the school year. So you will be able to see Jase."

Her words were of little comfort. Nattie went up to her room and climbed into bed, still wearing her shorts and old tee shirt. She cried for a while but couldn't fall asleep. She had slept so much during the day. *How am I going to tell Jase? He will hate me…*

Jase and his family returned home. His dad took him up to his room in the attic to talk. "Jase, what you did today was unacceptable. I know Nattie ran off and you were just protecting her, but you should have come home."

"Dad, Nattie was so upset. I have never seen her like that before. I couldn't leave her and there was no way she was coming back home."

"Jase, you are a young man now and you have certain responsibilities. Running off like that was wrong for both of you. Decisions should always be made with a sound mind without emotion clouding your judgment. Tomorrow you will accept Nattie's decision, whatever it is."

"Yes, sir."

"Why don't you get cleaned up for bed?"

Nattie still laid in bed wide-awake, her brilliant mind racing with so many thoughts. *What will school be like? What will Jase be doing while I am gone? Will he miss me after so long or will he forget me?* The thoughts never stopped. She went over a hundred different ways in her mind to tell Jase but none of them seemed good enough. She glanced over at the window and could see daylight seeping through the curtains. Morning had come and her mind still raced. She felt as if she had no tears left to cry but was all choked up inside. She dreaded having to tell Jase the news, yet she could hardly wait to see him.

She jumped out of bed and got cleaned up and prepared to leave. "Nattie, you up?"

"Yes, Mom." She rushed downstairs where her mom stood.

"Nattie, do you want me to take you over to the Thunderbelts'?"

"Yes, please."

"You must be starving. Aren't you hungry?"

"No, I don't want to eat. I need to see Jase."

"I think you should eat something first."

"Mom! Please, I can eat at Jase's house."

"Okay, okay. Let's go."

When they arrived at Jase's house, his mom was already working on breakfast. "Nattie, Jase is up in his room if you two want to talk." Nattie's mom had already talked to Mrs. Thunderbelt and informed her of Nattie's decision.

Nattie slowly walked up the steps. *What am I going to say to Jase?* She knocked on his door, which she never did before. She was so nervous and so tired. Jase opened the door.

"Nattie." Jase held her tight but sensed something was wrong. She was not her joyful self. "Nattie?" She took Jase by the hand and they sat down on the edge of the bed.

"Jase, please don't be mad at me."

"You're scaring me. What's going on?"

"I am accepting the position at the Science Academy." Jase's heart almost stopped. A cold shiver ran up his spine.

"Nattie, no. You said there was no way you would go." Jase said in a sorrowful voice.

"Jase, I have to go. I don't want to leave you but I have no choice." Nattie bowed her head and shrugged her shoulders.

"Nattie, you can't go. I won't let you." Jase put his arm around her.

"Jase, please don't make this harder than it is."

"I don't understand."

Nattie couldn't bear the thought of being without Jase, she hugged him tightly, "Jase, I don't want to go but I have to. My mom said I can come home to visit two times during the school year so we can be together."

"Jase!" yelled his mom.

"Yes?"

"Come down here please."

"I'll be back in a second, Nattie." Jase left the room and went downstairs. Nattie was so tired and upset, she crawled up to the top of the bed and laid on the pillows and fell asleep.

Jase went over to his mom to see what she wanted. "Jase, don't you dare give Nattie a hard time about her decision. She is doing what she has to do for her future."

"Mom, I was just trying to understand."

"Jase, trust me. Nattie wants nothing more than to be here with you but she understands how important this is and has made the right decision." Jase bowed down his head in despair. He missed Nattie already just thinking about it.

"Can I go back upstairs now?"

"Yes, but you be kind to Nattie. She has had a rough few days."

Jase went upstairs to find Nattie sleeping peacefully. He just sat there and looked at her. He touched her hair and gently rubbed her back. He let her sleep and finished getting ready, and then he went downstairs to eat.

"Jase, where's Nattie?" his mom asked.

"She's sleeping."

"I don't think she slept at all last night worrying about everything," Nattie's mom said.

"My heart really goes out to her, Jase," his mom said. "I think we should just let her sleep until she wakes up."

Nattie's mom left and Jase just stayed at home, quietly keeping busy in his room until early evening when Nattie finally woke up.

"Jassie, what time is it?"

"It's evening."

"Why didn't you wake me?"

"You were so tired. I just watched you sleep. You were so pretty laying there."

Jase brought her something to eat. She sat up in bed and ate dinner. She and Jase started making plans and marked his calendar with the dates she would be able to come home and visit. She printed out a long calendar and hung it on Jase's wall so he could mark off each day until she came home. She put little hearts on the days that they would be together and a huge heart and smiley face on day she would complete the year.

"Jassie, I miss you already. This is so hard."

"I was missing you while you were sleeping."

"You should have awoken me."

"I care about you Nattie and I wanted you to rest and feel better. I don't want you to get sick or anything."

Nattie kissed him, "Jassie, can we go get some funnel cake?"

Jase laughed, "Okay, Tristy."

"Oh wait. I'll be right back." Nattie went downstairs to her side purse and pulled out the pirate trophy. She took it up to Jase's room and sat it on the nightstand next to his bed.

"I want you to keep this, Jase. I want you to think of me every time you see it, when you go to bed, and when you wake up." Jase frowned and looked at Nattie, and then he bowed his head down in despair. She hugged him, "Jassie, please don't be upset, it will be okay. You will see, okay?"

"If you say so." Nattie gave him a tender kiss then put her forehead against his.

Chapter 17

They went into town and ate their funnel cake. Afterwards they walked around the shops and boardwalk by the waterfront.

The next two weeks Jase and Nattie spent every possible second together. Their relationship took a very serious turn as they both prepared their hearts, knowing they would be so far away from each other.

The night before Nattie's departure, they fell asleep together on the couch downstairs. Jase's parents just left them there, not wanting to wake them for another sleepless night.

Jase woke up early in the morning with Nattie still in his arms. They smiled at each other, and then Nattie's lips drew downward and her bottom lip pouched, "Jassie…"

"What, sweetie?" She wiped tears from her eyes.

"Jase, you and Nattie get cleaned up. We need to take her home to get ready to leave for school," Jase's mom said.

The past two weeks were the best they had ever spent together, knowing that they would be apart for so long. No amount of preparation could ease the pain in Jase's heart. They were so quiet all morning and there was complete silence on the ride to Nattie's house. Jase held her tight with his cheek resting on her head.

Nattie got her things together and Jase packed them into the cruiser. Jase rode along so he could see her off from the skyport. As they drew near to the Skytrans terminal, they could see skyships taking off into the air heading to their various destinations.

Skyships utilized the latest in Laviniun hover technology that allowed them to perform vertical takeoffs and landings. The laviniun generators limited the effects of gravity felt by passengers, when maneuvering through the atmosphere. For intercontinental flights, skyships would execute extreme assent into the upper atmosphere allowing them to settle into a very low orbit around the planet. This allowed very long flights of nine or more hours to be shortened to less than two hours. Intracontinental flights, being much shorter in duration, would normally stay within the atmosphere but would rapidly climb to cruising altitude.

Skyships were generally white in color with distinctive markings related to the individual company logos. The fuselage was wide with a low profile and adjustable wings slanted down and back from both sides of the craft. They were extended during takeoffs and landings but would be retracted for faster flight at altitude. The wings ran the full length of the ship with a long, half-moon-shaped, trailing edge at the wing tips.

Two omnidirectional induction pulse engines capable of operating in both the inner and outer atmospheres centered in the middle of each wing and were able to turn in all directions. Nattie had always been amazed by the ingenious design of skyships and had always longed to fly on one.

They arrived at the Skytrans terminal a bit early so Jase and Nattie walked out onto the flight observation terrace alone, to watch the skyships taking off and landing. Standing there together for the last time before she had to leave, Nattie tried not to cry but she couldn't help it. Jase teared up, seeing Nattie so upset and thinking about how lonely it will be once she's gone.

"I am going to miss you so much, Jassie."

"I am going to miss you to, Nattie. I already do."

"I love you, Jassie, with all my heart." Jase stood still, his heart racing and his palms growing clammy.

He looked into Nattie's pretty blue watering eyes, "I love you too, Nattie, with all my heart."

"Oh, Jassie." They held each other tight until Nattie's mom stepped out.

"Nattie, it's time." Jase wiped her cheeks with his sleeve and Nattie held his arm and leaned against him.

They walked to the departure gate and Jase helped Nattie to get everything situated so she could board the skyship. Once they started boarding the passengers at the gate, Jase and Nattie hugged each other tight and kissed for a few seconds, then Nattie took her suitcase by the handle while still holding Jase's hand. She slowly walked toward the gate until only their fingertips touched. She walked up to the gate, a deep feeling of cold sprung up inside her...her throat got tight and the flow of emotion and utter fear completely overwhelmed her. She let go of her bag with a whimper and a shout of desperation and ran back to Jase holding him as tight as she could.

"Mom, I can't do it. I can't go." Jase put his hands on either side of her face to calm her and kissed her.

"Nattie, it will be okay. I promise."

After a few moments, Nattie said, "Jassie, turn on your GIN video when you get home in case they let me talk to you, okay?"

"I will, my beautiful Tristy." Nattie gave Jase one last hug and kiss and ran for the gate before it was too late to board. As she disappeared out of sight, Jase's heart sunk as if he would never see her again. He just stood there, looking at the gate with a vacant expression on his face. Then, for a brief moment, Nattie peeked around the corner, blew Jase a kiss, and then disappeared again. Jase just smiled and thought, *That's my Nattie.*

Nattie reluctantly walked into the skyship to find her seat. The flight was only about half full and she was able to get a row of seats to herself. She wanted time alone to think. She took out the beautiful butterfly necklace that Jase gave her and held it in her hand. She imagined how wonderful it would be if Jase could be there with her.

The ship started to move and Nattie held on tight. It only took a few minutes for the ship to depart and fly up into the atmosphere but she was afraid to look out the window or loosen her grip from the seat handles.

Nattie's mom drove Jase home from the skyport. He sat with his head held low and a frown on his face. "Awww, Jase. Before you know it, she will be back home. I miss Nattie also but the time will go fast. You will see."

Once home, Jase went straight up to his room. He kicked off his shoes hard against the wall and paced about. He didn't know what to do with himself. He hurt inside and he couldn't do a thing to take away the pain. It was as if part of him was missing and he felt incomplete. He sat on the edge of his bed and imagined Nattie sitting there next to him, talking away about everything, leaning on his shoulder, with her little arms wrapped around his arm. He imagined her smiling at him with her beautiful dimples. He climbed into his bed, laid his head back, and closed his eyes for a while, thinking about all the good times they shared together.

Nattie's flight arrived at her destination and she found her way to the luggage pick up area. She rushed as fast as she could because she wanted to call Jase before leaving the terminal but an announcement over the intercom warned all Science Academy students to catch the last high capacity cruiser for the day, heading to the school within the next twenty minutes. She rushed quickly but ran out of time and just barely caught the cruiser before departure. The ride from the skyport to school was about half an hour. Nattie sat looking at the floor with a deep frown on her face and her eyebrows were low on her forehead. She wasn't even interested in the exciting, big city views, outside the window.

The City of Nightera had a population of about six hundred

thousand and the heart of the city centered around an industrial seaport supporting large cargo ships and their marketable goods. The downtown harbor area was quite beautiful, especially at night when all the lights of the tall buildings reflected off the water. A public park and boardwalk surrounded the inner harbor area where individuals could walk and sit on park benches to enjoy the city views.

The northeastern corner of the harbor gave way to several city blocks of science museums, library buildings, public research facilities and the science academy buildings. The student dorms were spread out around the surrounding areas, many sitting just outside the harbor boardwalk and seawall to the north. They were the coveted dorms of the students because of the surrounding scenic beauty of the harbor and easy access to shops and local hangouts.

The transport dropped off the students at the main registration building. Nattie made her way up the numerous steps, struggling with her luggage, to get to the main entrance. The face of the registration building was as if it were constructed of unpolished rough white marble with four huge decorative white columns, climbing several stories high, that supported a student patio. The patio had large stone railings around three sides and the far end led into the student cafeteria, just inside.

Nattie nestled herself into one of the long registration lines along with the other students. The school supported up to fifteen hundred students every semester and was never lacking a single seat.

Two boisterous young ladies joined Nattie at the rear of the line. She could hear them talking as if they knew the school very well. One of them accidently bumped into her,

"Oh, I'm sorry."

"That's okay."

"Hi, my name is Endnova Tripoli."

"I'm Nattellie Candella, but you can call me Nattie." They shook hands and Nattie almost smiled for the first time of the day.

"This your first year, Nattie?"

"Yes."

"I could tell by the terrified look on your face." Nattie kinda laughed and smiled at Endnova.

"Do I look that pathetic?"

"No, girl. You're okay. We've all been there. We know how it is."

"So you've attended more than one year?"

"Oh yeah, this is my third and Daisha's second."

"Hi, Nattie," Daisha said.

"Hi, Daisha."

"Pleased to meet you."

"Thanks, you too."

Endnova was a tall slender seventeen year old with a dark tan complexion, long black hair, brown eyes, and a big heart. She liked to push the school rules and really loved the city.

"So, Nattie, do you like to live life on the edge?"

"At times, I guess."

"Have you registered for a room yet?"

"No, I didn't know I could."

"Yeah, you should have gotten a form with your submission packet."

"Oh, I never submitted anything to the school."

"Then how did you end up here?"

"The school selected me for some reason. I didn't even know about the school until two weeks ago."

"Ah, you're one of those."

"One of what?"

"The gifted ones."

"Is that bad?"

"Not for you."

"I've been trying for three years to get a scholarship but only the smart ones get them."

"Wait! I thought everyone who came here could get one?"

"No, girl. Only like the top fifteen percent can get them. This is my last chance; if I don't get one this year, I can't come back. All current students get priority though, over new submissions. If you don't get one this year, you can come back next year and try again."

Nattie's smile disappeared and her lips tightened. Her heart rate went wild and she started to feel hot. Her eyes started to water but she managed to hold back any tears. "Girl, it's okay. Nothing to be upset about," Endnova said as she could see Nattie was about to cry. Nattie felt hurt, like she was lied to, and vowed deep in her heart that she would ace every test and get a perfect score on every project so she would never have to come back or leave Jase ever again.

"I thought every student here was supposed to be gifted?" Nattie said.

"Well, some students are more gifted than others. This is not like high school; you have to basically kill yourself just to get a passing grade."

They finally reached the registration desk. Nattie received her introduction packet, class schedule, and was able to select an available dorm room. "Nattie, pick our dorm. There is an opening in our room," Endnova said.

"Okay."

The three girls gathered up their luggage and waited outside for a school shuttle to take them to their dorm.

Jase moped around the house most of the day and didn't really feel like doing anything. He wondered how Nattie was doing and was worried about her. "Jase, you want something special for dinner tonight?" his mom said.

"No, thanks. I'm not really hungry anyway." He turned on his video chat over the GIN, hoping to hear from Nattie. He sat on his bed and waited for hours just hoping for at least a few seconds with her. He decided to read a little more from *Three Tall Ships*. He opened the book to the point where Anderson carved a heart into the stone wall.

Finally, there was some news. Anderson was called to the makeshift hospital. When he arrived, Pamula walked out of Tristy's room, gave David a hug, and softly whispered. "David, I'm afraid she's gone. There was nothing I could do to save her."

Anderson could hardly believe what he had heard. He went in next to Tristy's body and wept. He stroked her hair and kissed her forehead.

"This is not goodbye, my love, I will see you again on resurrection day, and we will be soulmates for all eternity."

Jase felt like ripping the book in half, as if, somehow, Tristy's fate was tied to Nattie's. He threw the book up against the wall and wished he could talk to Nattie more than ever.

Nattie and the girls made it to their dorm room, which was surprisingly nice. Nattie selected a bed near a window overlooking the harbor. The furniture was spaciously arranged in each room to support three girls. Nattie had her own wardrobe, large desk, bed with nightstands, and a bookshelf that was about four feet high. The bottom of the wardrobe had four drawers for folded clothing. She had lamps on the nightstands and a little adjustable reading lamp above her bed. Nattie just put her suitcases on the floor next to her bed and sat down with her legs crossed. She looked out the window at the harbor and wiped her watering eyes with her sleeve. She really missed Jase and wished she could talk to him.

Endnova walked over, sat on the bed next to her, and gave her a hug. "It will be okay, Nattie. Everyone gets homesick at first but you will get used to it."

"I'm not homesick. I miss my boyfriend."

"Oh, someone's in love."

"What's his name?"

"Jase Thunderbelt."

"What's he like?"

"He's my best friend." They talked for a little while and Nattie told her all about the pirate competition. She kept wiping her eyes and her nose started to run and turned red from her rubbing it.

"Hey, Daisha, why don't we blow off orientation and take Nattie over to Rashnaies Restaurant so she can call her boyfriend?"

"Yeah, for sure," Daisha said.

"Won't we get in trouble?"

"Only if we get caught, girl. Besides, everyone will be going outside to walk to the orientation anyway. You want to talk to your boyfriend or what?"

"Yes!"

"You got to live your life on the edge, girl. Enjoy life a little."

"Yeah, it's like our literature teacher always says. A happy ending is gauged by the controversy that precedes it."

"Without a little controversy, you can't have a happy ending."

"Okay, um, so like, the more problems you create for yourself, the happier you will be? That really doesn't make sense." They all laughed.

"Trust me, girl. After a year with us, it will make perfect sense."

The three of them went outside with the other students to walk to orientation. They ducked in between two dorms and ran toward the seawall.

Chapter 18

Nattie followed them to Rashnaies Restaurant. They walked inside and Nattie could smell pizza making her feel a little hungry. The interior of the restaurant was very pleasant with plants around the outer walls and booths on the left and right of a long path through the center of the dining room. The booths were divided into many smaller sections to give a homey warm feeling with many little lights decorating the ceiling. In the very back was a large game room with a bar and monitors to watch sporting events. The three girls proceeded to the back so Nattie could place her call.

Jase decided to write a letter to Nattie but he dare not tell her about Tristy. He wrote a few lines when he could hear someone calling.

"Hello?"

"Jassie!"

"Nattie! Are you okay?"

"Yes, I miss you so much."

"Hi, Jase!" Endnova and Daisha yelled.

"Who was that?"

"That's my new roommates."

"How's the school?"

"I don't like it. Everything is so industrial and the city is so big and noisy. I do like the harbor though. It makes me think of you every time I look out my window and see the boats."

"I just started to write you a letter."

"What does it say?"

"Well, I just started to write but it says I miss you and I love you."

"I love you too, Jassie."

"I can't talk long because we don't want to get caught. It will be two weeks before we can use the GIN but I can call you on the weekend."

"I wish I was there with you."

"I do too." Nattie told Jase all about her flight and about her two roommates.

"Nattie, we better get back to school." Endnova said.

"You two go ahead. I will catch up."

"Nattie, they will do a head check soon. We all need to get back."

"Jassie, I have to go. I love you."

"I love you, Nattie."

"Bye," Nattie said as Endnova pulled her arm.

"Come on, we need to run!" The three of them ran back to their rooms and slipped inside without being noticed. "You feeling better, Nattie?" Endnova asked.

"Loads better, thank you."

"You just stick with us. We'll watch out for you."

The dorm supervisor stopped by each room to make sure all students were accounted for and to verify their room selections. She handed each student his or her dorm responsibilities and cafeteria passes. The girls went to the cafeteria to eat dinner. Nattie expected gross food as she can be very picky but to her surprise, they had many desirable selections available. She was starving, having eaten very little all day. She loaded up her tray and they went out to the patio, overlooking the harbor, to eat dinner.

"So, what do you think, Nattie? It's not so bad here, right?"

Endnova said.

"Well, if my boyfriend was here, it would be perfect."

"Nattie, you are lucky to have someone like that," Daisha said.

"I'm going to miss the pirate ship reenactment and I will be stuck here for my birthday in a couple of months," Nattie said.

"Oh really, don't worry, girl. We're gonna throw you a huge party."

"That's okay. I really want to concentrate on my grades. I don't want to have to come back here next year."

"Nattie, the teachers here are way different than high school. They teach college-level material and each teacher has their own way of grading, especially when it comes to papers. You will need to learn what each teacher wants to get high scores. Some of the teachers are a bit prideful so sucking up tends to go a long way. Whatever you do, don't argue with a teacher. Remember that they are right about everything whether that's true or not. Some of the teachers compete to make their classes the hardest and they act as if their class is the only one you have. You end up with so much homework, it's impossible to get it all done. You have to prioritize and pick which classes need your attention the most and just get done what you can," Endnova said.

"Yeah, they are like, so why didn't you get the work done? You try to tell them that you had twelve hours' worth of homework and only four hours to get it done but do they listen? Nope, they just act like you're goofing off and blowing off their class," Daisha said.

"That sounds horrible, like a nightmare."

"Now you're catching on. Some of the teachers are nice and care about us; they grade fairly and understand how hard it is to get all of the work done."

"How about math and science classes?"

"They are my favorite because you can actually get good scores by learning the material," Endnova said.

"I like science and math," Nattie said.

Jase got up the next morning and got the mail for his mom. He found a new issue of *About Teen Magazine*. He and Nattie were on the front cover and there was a full multipage article inside with several pictures of Jase, Nattie, Alrand, and Kimberly in their pirate costumes. Jase smiled at how nice Nattie looked in her costume. He really missed her cute smile and her warm touch. He met up with Alrand and they went to get Kimberly.

"Alrand, sorry you and Kimberly are not on the front cover. They should have had all four of us on there."

"I know; she told us that we would all be on the cover."

"How do you think Kimberly will feel about it?"

"I don't think she will care; things don't seem to bother her much. She is always so calm about everything. I really am not looking forward to her leaving but I think it will be harder on me than for her."

"I know. I feel like everything is changing so fast and I have no control over anything. I wish things could stay the same."

"Jase, do you think Nat will be different when she comes back?"

"I hope not. I don't think I could take it. I miss her so much and I don't want anything to be different between us."

"I know she won't feel any different about you. She has been in love with you since she was like what, seven years old?"

"I hope you're right. It didn't bother me when she went away with her family back then, but now...it's so sad the way her dad died. I felt so bad for her when they came back but I was also happy that she returned."

"Yeah, I know. I used to be your best friend."

"Alrand, you still are my best friend. Girlfriends don't count, you know."

"Yes, they do."

"Do not."

"Do too."

"Do not."

"Okay, let's ask Kimberly."

Nattie got up to get ready for her first day of school. She put on the best outfit she brought with her and fixed herself up nice.

"Nattie, wow! Look at you, girl."

"What?"

"You're all fixed up and all. You look really pretty." Nattie smiled.

"Thanks, Endnova. I really needed that."

"Well, we're off and running now. Full speed ahead. Let the games begin."

"You're funny."

"Stay tuned, you ain't seen nothing yet."

"Make sure you have your map. Most of the classes are in different buildings."

"Have it right here." The three girls started their first day of school.

Jase and Alrand arrived at Kimberly's house. Kimberly waited for them and walked outside.

"Hi, Alrand." Alrand gave Kimberly a hug and a kiss.

"Hi, Jase, how are you?"

"I don't know. Okay, I guess." Kimberly gave Jase a hug.

"That's from Nattie. She said to give you a hug for her after she left." Jase felt numb. "You sure you're okay, Jase?"

"Yes, I'm just missing Nattie."

"Kimberly, question? When it comes to best friends, do

girlfriends count?"

Kimberly laughed. "Of course, they count. Why wouldn't your girlfriend count?"

"Told ya, Jase." The three of them stood there for a second thinking the same thing. If Nattie were there, she would have said something witty and silly.

"I know, Jase. I miss her too. Other than Alrand, she was my best friend."

"Did you see the magazine?"

"I did. You two look so good on the cover. I was surprised that they didn't use this other image on the cover with all four of us. I think we all looked very good together. Did you read what the article said?"

"Not yet."

"You should read it. She talks about you and Nattie being in love."

After classes were done for the day, Nattie returned to the dorm room.

"There she is!" Endnova said.

"Our own celebrity! Woohoo!!"

"What are you talking about?"

"YOU Girl! On the cover of *About Teen Magazine*!"

"Oh, I completely forgot about that!"

"You look good, girl. Is this your Jase?"

"Yep!"

"He's cute, Nattie. You better keep him away from me." They all laughed.

"I need to go get a copy."

"No, you don't. I bought you two copies."

"Listen to this. Nattie Candella and Jase Thunderbelt were the first and second place winners of Summerset's thirty-eighth annual pirate competition, teen division. The two love-stricken teens stole the hearts of the audience when presented with their awards. Everyone was completely taken in by their youthful exuberance and playful manner. At one point during the ceremony, Nattie blew kisses at the audience and received a standing ovation. The young couple is an inspiration of the hope of true love as they gave their hearts to one another."

"She said all that? I wonder why she didn't put Alrand and Kimberly on the cover."

"I guess you and Jase just stole the show, after all you did win the competition."

"I guess she must have watched the awards ceremony because she took the pictures the day before."

"Will you sign my copy, Nattie?" Endnova said.

"Sure, why not."

"So, Nattie, how was your first day?"

"I liked it. The classes sound very interesting. I am looking forward to physics class."

"You're crazy, girl. That's the hardest class in this school."

"Maybe, but the final project sounds really fun. I have a really neat idea for something I want to build."

Endnova laughed. "Fun? You and I have a totally different idea of the definition of the word fun."

"I don't know; it just sounds like a challenging and rewarding assignment."

"Okay, if you say so."

"So what's your idea?"

"I don't want to say yet. I need to do a little research first."

. . .

Jase, Alrand, and Kimberly walked around a while at the docks and then had a snack at Skaters. Jase was a little moody and didn't say much. They all went home early to get ready for their first day of school.

Jase's first day back at school without Nattie was hard. He rested his head on his arm and tapped his pencil while watching the clock. Every minute seemed like forever. Everyone kept asking about Nattie, where she was, and how she was doing. Jase finally smiled when he learned about a work program where he could take his core classes in the morning and work in the afternoon, provided he could get approval. Keeping busy, working towards saving for their trip to Voncara Cove sounded much better than sitting in school all day missing Nattie. He would much rather work in the bookstore with Kimberly trying to achieve their goals.

When Jase returned home from school, he talked to his mother and found her receptive to the work program idea. She figured it would help him to keep his mind occupied rather than sulk over Nattie all year.

He changed and headed off to his first night of work at the bookstore. He met up with Kimberly who would be teaching him about operating the shop for a few months until her training commenced with the Proelium Concordia.

"Hi, Kimberly."

"Hey, Jase, how are you holding up?"

"It was really hard. I thought the day would never end."

"I've had days like that. I'm sure you really missed Nattie."

"I'm missing her right now. I wish I could at least talk to her."

"I'm sure she's doing fine, Jase."

"Hey, Kimberly, do you think your dad might allow me to work here during the day if I can get on the work program at school?"

"I don't know. Maybe; it couldn't hurt to ask."

Later that evening, Jase had a chance to talk with Mr. Alaxrandus, "Jase, I think that's a great idea. I was concerned that I may need to hire more help, so this works out well for both of us."

"Thank you, Mr. Alaxrandus." Since Jase saved his winnings from the pirate competition, and his recent allowance, he already had over four hundred tutarian. He figured it should be easy to get the rest of the money by the time Nattie returned home. They could try to take their trip in the coming summer.

Nattie really missed Jase and wished she could talk to him but she immersed herself into her schoolwork. Her classes had been easy thus far and she enjoyed learning and discovering new things. Her teachers were impressed with her enthusiasm and desire to excel. The other students seemed to be drawn to her cute and passionate demeanor, along with her friendship with Endnova and Daisha. Appearing on the cover of *About Teen Magazine* also made quite a popular impact amongst her classmates.

Every day, Nattie wrote letters to Jase telling him how much she missed him and about everything that transpired since the last letter. Endnova would douse her letters with perfume. "Trust me. Guys love it when they get sweet-smelling letters from their girlfriend."

Jase smiled and felt warm every time he went to the mailbox, hoping to find a letter or two from Nattie. He was never disappointed. He really loved Nattie's neat and creative handwriting. She had a cute style all of her own. He would answer every letter during the slow time between customers at the bookstore but he longed to hear her soft voice again.

Chapter 19

Nattie finally reached the end of her first week at school, and was allowed to talk on the phone over the weekend. She hardly slept. She lay with her mind racing, thinking about all the things she wanted to say to Jase after he got off work.

Endnova and Daisha got all fixed up to go out and have fun with their classmates.

"Nattie, you sure you don't want to come?"

"No, I'm going to wait here until I can talk to Jase."

"Girl, you've worked hard. You need to live it up a little. Take a little break."

"Are you kidding? I finally get a chance to talk to my Jassie."

"Say hi for us," Daisha said.

After the girls left, Nattie sat at her desk, put her arms in front of her, and lay her head down. She blew her hair out of her face and tapped her fingernail on the desk while waiting for the phone to ring. She could smell the aroma of Daisha's perfume in the air.

Jase's heart ran wild with anticipation. He rode home from the bookstore as fast as he could and ran up to his room. He had to enter the number several times because he was so nervous and entered it wrong. "Hello?"

"Hi, Nattie!"

"Hi, Jassie! I have missed you so so much!"

"I'm going crazy without you. I love your letters though. I must have read each one like a thousand times."

Nattie laughed, "I did the same thing. This is so hard. I want to come home to be with you."

"Is the school that bad? You seemed to like it in your letters."

"No, I really like the school, my teachers, and my new friends but I just miss you all the time."

"I can't wait until we can video chat every night. I can't stand waiting so long to talk to you."

"I know. We have to wait another whole week."

"How hard are your classes?"

"So far, they aren't bad. I really like the things I'm learning. It would be perfect if you were here though. Tell me about the work program you wrote about."

"I only have to go to school for half a day, and then I work at the bookstore with Kimberly. I should have enough money for us to go to Voncara Cove by the time you come home."

"That's great. I can't wait."

They talked for several hours until Endnova and Daisha came home.

"Nattie, say hi for us."

"You hear, Jase?"

"Yeah, tell them I said hi."

"Jassie said hi!"

Jase and Nattie continued to talk very quietly until they noticed that the sun was coming up.

"Jassie, we talked all night. It's morning."

"Yeah, I didn't want to say anything." They were both so tired but neither wanted to say goodbye. "I guess we need to try to sleep some," Jase said.

"I don't want to go. It feels like you're here with me."

"I don't want to go either but I want to be able to talk to you later. Since it's the last time we can talk for another week."

"I hate this, Jassie. I am never leaving you again. I don't care what anyone says." They talked for another hour until Nattie's head started bobbing, she couldn't stay awake anymore.

"Jassie, I guess I need to go."

"I love you, Nattie."

"I love you too, my Jassie." They paused for a few moments. "Hang up, Jassie."

"No, you first."

"I don't want to."

"Let's hang up together."

"Okay"

"One, two, three."

"Jassie, wait!"

"What?"

"When do you want to talk again?"

"Well, I have to work a few hours later today but be ready in case Kimberly lets me go early. I will call you before I leave after lunch to make plans."

"Okay, bye."

"Bye, my Tristy." Nattie hung up, laid on her bed, and fell right to sleep. Jase set an alarm then fell asleep thinking about her.

Later on, Jase's alarm went off but he was so tired it didn't wake him. When he finally awoke, he was late for work. He rushed as fast as he could to get ready vond called Nattie. Endnova answered and said that Nattie was still sleeping and she didn't want to wake her. Jase agreed with Endnova and left a message with her to tell Nattie that he would call her as soon as he got off work.

Jase was so happy that afternoon. He was going about work

whistling and humming a tune.

"Boy, Jase. I really miss this," Kimberly said.

"What do you mean?"

"You are your old joyful self again. I guess you and Nattie were able to talk for a while?"

Jase laughed. "We talked till the sun came up."

Kimberly laughed, "That sounds like you two. I really miss the way things were. It's hard to think that things will never be same again."

"What do you mean?"

"Well, I will be gone when Nattie gets back."

"Won't you be coming home any?"

"Yes, I guess so but I don't know how long it will be."

Jase was able to leave the bookstore a little early and rushed home to talk to Nattie. He called but Endnova answered and said that Nattie was at the cafeteria eating. She made her go eat because she hadn't eaten anything all day.

"Don't worry, Jase. She will be back shortly and you two can talk all night again, at least until they shut off the connection."

"I wonder if they will shut off the GIN once we can start video chatting?"

"Yeah, they don't want us spending all night on the GIN making us too tired for our classes."

"Jase, here's Nattie. She just walked in. Nattie, it's Jase." Nattie threw her things on her bed and rushed to the phone.

"Hi, Jassie. I love you."

"I love you too, Nattie."

"I missed you so much this afternoon. I don't know how I'm going to make it another week to be able to talk to you." Jase and Nattie talked until the connection was turned off. Jase felt good, having the time to talk, but he also felt bad being cut off without telling her goodbye. He didn't like not having any control over when he was able to talk to her.

The next two days were kind of rough for both of them but the rest of the week went by quickly. Jase and Nattie were finally able to video chat. On days when Nattie was not in class, they would chat before Jase went to work and every evening. At first, they spent too much time talking and Nattie's schoolwork suffered a little. They had to limit their time, which wasn't too bad since they were able to talk twice a day.

Nattie wished that Jase would read to her but he simply replied, "Nattie, I really want to wait until you're with me. It's much better that way." She didn't push the issue thinking that Jase was being sentimental.

The days turned into weeks and before they knew it, two months had passed. Nattie was doing great in her classes and her final project for physics class was almost complete, even though she still had half a semester to finish. All she had left to do was some machine language programming, to set up the microprocessor, so that it would send out pulse-modulated signals into the electromagnetic device. Nattie became the favorite of all her teachers. Her rapport with the other students was fantastic and everyone was very nice to her. Other than missing Jase, she was on top of the world.

Jase was rather sharp with Kimberly in the bookstore and she could tell something was wrong. She walked up behind him and hugged him around the neck.

"What's wrong, Jase?"

"I don't know. It's like I'm mad all the time now. I can't explain it. I just am."

"You know it's because you miss Nattie."

"Her birthday is coming up and I'm going to miss it. I can't get past it. She will have a great time with her friends and I will miss all of it. It's like she has this whole other life without me."

Kimberly hugged him tighter, "Jase, why don't you go see her on her birthday?"

"How?"

"Just buy the tickets and go." Jase's whole body warmed, and he smiled at Kimberly.

He twisted his body back and looked at her, "I wonder how much it would cost. I am still saving for our Voncara Cove trip."

"You don't have to fly, you know. You can take the train."

"Oh! I never thought about that. You are so smart."

"Thanks, Jase."

They looked at the GIN on the computer in the bookstore. "Round trip tickets are only three hundred tutarian."

"See? That's pretty good." Jase bobbed his head back and forth, bouncing around a bit while he purchased the tickets.

"Woohoo!" He gave Kimberly a kiss on the cheek and called his mom to tell her he purchased the tickets. She was supportive, knowing how down Jase had been lately, and felt it was a good idea for him to spend time with Nattie on her birthday.

"Jase, you can go but you have to make up the schoolwork you miss and make sure you can have off those days at work."

"I love you, Mom!" Jase hopped around the bookstore whistling while he worked. Later that evening, he cleared everything with Mr. Alaxrandus, which was a good thing since the tickets were non-refundable.

Jase was all astir and could hardly wait. He sat down and wrote Endnova a letter telling her that he wanted to surprise Nattie on her birthday. He wrote, *Confidential,* as the return address. When Endnova received the letter, she cautiously opened it and found it was from Jase. She had been planning a surprise party for Nattie for a couple weeks, and had no problem finding students who wanted to attend in the back of Rashnaies Restaurant. Endnova wrote Jase back giving him details and told him that Daisha would meet him at the train station, only one sect from the school.

The next time they talked, Nattie wondered why Jase was in such a good mood. It was refreshing to see him so happy again so she didn't say anything. The next week took forever for Jase. He made lists of everything he wanted to take and thought about getting the perfect birthday gift. He decided on a golden bracelet, with an inscription inside. It said, *"To my beautiful Nattie, I will love you forever, Jase."*

Finally, the day Jase was waiting for had arrived. His mom drove him the hour to the train station and he arrived extra early. He walked along the tracks next to the immensely heavy passenger train, fascinated by the technology that allowed it to glide in the air, yet stay within the borders of the tracks. Powered by laviniun generators, the train could reach speeds of up to four hundred sects per hour.

When it was time, he boarded and found a comfy window seat. He sat tapping his foot on the floor watching out the window as the train sped increasingly down the tracks. The ride was quiet and smooth, even though he had hardly slept in anticipation of holding Nattie in his arms again. The train wasn't moving fast enough for him but he really enjoyed the ride, watching everything that passed by the window. *This is my greatest adventure ever.* After many hours, the train approached the city of Nightera. He stood up and stretched, gathered his things, and impatiently waited in line to exit.

Daisha stood waiting at the station. She knew exactly what Jase looked like from all the pictures Nattie had on her desk and seeing him on the video chat. She was a pretty girl with thick curly brown hair, blue eyes and was slightly heavy, yet rather petite. She was about five foot tall and had a very sweet sounding voice. She never had a boyfriend and was envious of Nattie's relationship with Jase. She imagined what it would be like to have him as a boyfriend.

Daisha walked up to Jase as he walked off of the train. "Hi, Jase!"

"Daisha?"

"Yep."

"How are you?"

"I'm good. How about you?"

"This is so great."

"Your first time in the city?"

"Yes."

"I hope you like it; it's quite big and noisy. You better put on a jacket. It's getting cold." They left the train station and walked down to the seawall to follow it all the way to the restaurant.

Daisha put her arm around Jase's and leaned on him as they walked. "Do you mind? I'm freezing."

"Not at all." They talked for a while as they walked, "Nattie is lucky to have a boyfriend like you."

"Awww, thank you. What is your boyfriend like?"

"I don't have a boyfriend."

"A beautiful lady like you? I figured you would have lots of guys interested."

"Awww, you're sweet, but interested is one thing. Wanting to be my boyfriend is another. How long have you and Nattie known each other?"

"Since we were about seven."

"Awww, young sweethearts."

"I imagine that you, Nattie, and Endnova have had some good times and shared some adventures?" Jase said.

Daisha laughed, "Not really. Nattie spends all of her time either doing schoolwork or talking about you. We can hardly get her to leave the room outside of school."

"Really?"

"Yeah, she really wants that scholarship bad."

"Wait. What scholarship?"

"You mean you don't know?"

"What am I missing?"

"If Nattie gets good enough grades, she will receive a scholarship. That's why she's here. Didn't she tell you?"

"No, why didn't she tell me?" Jase's smile diminished and he felt a tight coldness in his chest.

"She's doing it for you, ya know."

"What do you mean?"

"She was afraid that you would get into college and leave without her or something." Jase thought for a second. He understood but wondered why Nattie didn't just tell him. He realized it was wrong to doubt her.

"I just don't understand why she didn't tell me if everyone else knows."

"Jase, you are all she talks about. You are like a legend at school. They have the *About Teen Magazine* cover pinned up on the cafeteria wall with your picture on it. Plus Nattie talks about you all the time to everyone."

"Really?"

"Yeah, seriously. It's a bit much actually."

They arrived at the restaurant and walked back to the game room. Daisha told Jase to wait in the men's room until they were ready to surprise Nattie.

He went into bathroom and waited. There were benches along the wall in a carpeted area that led to a white decorative tile floor next to the bathroom stalls. There was a long mirror on the wall above the sinks. Jase straightened his hair and sat down on one of the benches. His heart rate was elevated and he couldn't sit still. He got back up and paced back and forth. He could hear some commotion going on outside the door as the students started to arrive and their voices carried.

Endnova planned everything. She couldn't wait to see the look on Nattie's face when she saw Jase. Nattie suspected that Endnova was up to something and figured she set up some outrageous surprise birthday party.

"Endnova, I'm not really feeling up to going out anywhere."

"I know, sweetie. You want to wait around on Jase so you two can chat."

"I miss him so much." Nattie started to cry.

Endnova was touched and felt hurt that Nattie was so upset on her birthday. She almost told her about Jase but held her tongue.

"Nattie, it's a few hours until Jase gets off work. Won't you come with me for a little celebration? You will feel better. Trust me."

"Okay, but only for like an hour, okay?"

"Okay."

"You promise?"

"I promise that you can come back any time you wish, you have my word. Dress up real nice though. I'm taking you somewhere special. Make yourself up like you would when you see Jase."

Nattie reluctantly put some effort into getting ready but her heart wasn't in it. Endnova tried to spray her with perfume but Nattie was expecting it and took off running. Endnova chased her down the hallway and into the common area where she cornered her. They were both laughing so hard they couldn't catch their breath. Endnova sprayed her with perfume on her neck and hands.

"It's not like there's anyone here I want to look good for, you know?"

"Ya never know."

"Shush," Nattie giggled.

Chapter 20

She followed Endnova to Rashnaies Restaurant.

"Hey, I thought you said somewhere special?"

"Trust me, girl. This will be special."

"What are you up to?"

"Come inside and see."

Nattie and Endnova walked to the back room and the lights were out. Endnova took her by the arm and pulled her into the room.

Everyone jumped out, "SURPRISE!"

Nattie jumped. She wasn't expecting the whole room to be packed full of students. More students showed up than expected because they caught wind of Nattie's big surprise and wanted to watch her reaction.

Everyone laughed at Nattie when she jumped in shock.

"Endnova! I said only an hour." Nattie lightly punched Endnova on the shoulder.

"Trust me, sweetie. You are gonna want to be here for this. I have a little surprise for you. Come over here."

Endnova held her hands over Nattie's eyes. Nattie smiled, "What are you up to?"

"Just relax." They brought Jase out and had him stand by the wall among the other students. His hands were shaking and he turned a bit red when everyone looked at him. He noticed that Nattie had grown a couple inches and gained a little weight. *I never could have imagined her being more beautiful than she was when she left.*

"Are you ready, Nattie?" Endnova asked.

"I don't know. Am I?"

"Do you trust me?"

"Come on, Endnova!"

"Everybody count to three."

"One, two, three…"

Endnova took away her hands from Nattie's eyes. She looked at all the students gazing at her, and wondered what the big deal was.

"Ya, so?" Endnova laughed and slapped her sides bending over holding her stomach. Everyone else started to laugh as well. Nattie smiled and started laughing, "What's so funny?" Then she glanced over at Daisha and did a double take with her eyes. She froze for a moment, and then put her hand over her mouth and chin. She began to shudder, her eyes watered up, and she started to sniffle.

"Awww, Nattie. Jase, come give this girl a hug." Jase barely took a step before Nattie ran and jumped on him, wrapping her legs around his waist, and kissing him all over his face. He held her and felt the back of her arms, forgetting how soft they were. Everyone clapped and rejoiced along with them.

Nattie put her legs down and gave Jase a real passionate kiss. "I'm so happy. I can't believe you're here. I love you so much. Why didn't you tell me?"

"I wanted it to be a surprise and besides, Endnova insisted."

Endnova walked over and hugged both of them.

"I love you, Endnova," Nattie said.

"Hi, Jase. We meet at last."

"Thank you, Endnova."

"Okay, enough of this mushy stuff. Let's party!" Endnova said.

Nattie and Jase were inseparable during the party. Everyone had a great time and Nattie's beautiful smile was so infectious. The students had never seen her quite like this before. She shined with joyful exuberance.

"How long are you here for, Jassie?"

"Three more days after today." Nattie looked up at Jase and smiled with the cutest dimple smile.

"Are you serious? I guess it's true what Endnova says."

"What's that?"

"A happy ending is determined by the controversy that precedes it. Today is a happy ending. I was so sad this morning and now I'm so happy." Jase put his arm around her waist and held her tight.

"I love you so much. I couldn't wait to get here. It seemed like it took forever."

"Did you fly?"

"No, I took the train because it was a lot cheaper since we are saving for our Voncara Cove trip."

"I still can't believe you are here. I love you, Jassie, so much." She kissed him tenderly on the lips.

Everyone had finished eating so Endnova carried out Nattie's birthday cake.

"Jase, why don't you say a few words," Endnova said. Jase was embarrassed. He didn't know hardly anyone there.

"Like what?"

"I don't know. Tell us what you love about Nattie."

"Oh, that's an easy one." Jase looked at Nattie and she waited to hear every word. "Where would I start? I love her beautiful smile, her loving heart, her playfulness, her unpredictability, and I love how tender hearted she is but at the same time, she is the toughest person I know. I would be lost without her." Nattie's eye's watered up and she hugged Jase.

"I couldn't live without you, my Jassie. I love you so much."

"Okay, let's cut the cake," Endnova said.

Everyone took a piece and there was plenty left for seconds. Jase sat next to Nattie at one of the tables and handed her the present that he bought her. She unwrapped the paper and opened the little box to reveal the pretty golden bracelet.

"Thank you, Jassie. It's so pretty."

"Just like you. Read the inscription." Nattie read the engraved inscription on the inside of the bracelet. She hugged him and kissed him on the neck. She let him put the bracelet on her little wrist.

"I'm never taking this off."

"You smell so good, Nattie." She giggled.

"What's funny?"

"Nothing." A few seconds later, she started giggling again.

"I miss that."

"Miss what?"

"When you start giggling for no reason." Nattie leaned forward and laughed loudly.

"Oh, there's always a reason." Now she couldn't stop giggling.

"What's so funny?" Endnova asked. That really got Nattie going. She tried to hold her lips to stop but that didn't help any. Then Endnova started to laugh. Nattie whispered in her ear about the great perfume chase and how Jase loved the way she smelled.

"I told you." Endnova said.

"Jase, is she always like this when she's around you?"

"Trust me; you haven't seen anything yet," Jase said.

"Nattie, I like you this way. You're finally out of your shell." Nattie stuck her tongue out at Endnova.

Jase and Nattie spent as much time together as they were allowed on a school night and then Jase went to his hotel room, within easy walking distance.

The next day, Jase was allowed to attend some of Nattie's classes with her under the primus that he was interested in the school. After their classes were completed for the week, Endnova insisted that

Nattie and Jase come and have fun with them.

"You don't have any excuse this time, Nattie, since you don't have to wait to talk to Jase."

"Okay, we'll go."

Endnova, Daisha, Nattie, and Jase had a great time visiting several of the many nightspots frequented by the school students. Nattie enjoyed every second with Jase to the fullest.

On their way back to the dorm for the night, Jase asked if they could see the city tomorrow.

"That's a great idea, Jase," Endnova said. "How about you, Daisha?"

"Count me in."

"Okay, we will meet you here tomorrow morning, Jase. Then we can get breakfast and go exploring the city."

"Sounds good to me."

The girls went upstairs, except for Nattie. She hugged Jase and said, "I don't want this day to end."

"I know. I wish you could come with me."

"At least I get to see you for two more days."

"I don't even want to think about you having to leave."

"Nattie, why didn't you tell me about the scholarship?"

"Who told you?"

"That doesn't matter. I never understood why you wanted to come here. Why didn't you tell me?"

Nattie started to get upset, "Jase, do I have to tell you?"

"What's wrong?"

"You will hate me."

"Awww, I could never hate you."

"I was so selfish, thinking about myself."

"What do you mean?"

"I was afraid that you would go to college without me and if I didn't get the scholarship, I didn't want to give you any ideas about going to college. I'm so sorry, Jase."

"Nattie, I could never be mad at you for something like that. I even asked you not to come here. Remember?"

"I'm so confused, Jase. I wish we were back home. This has been the hardest thing I have ever had to do. I mean, at least when you go to college, you are older and ready for it. I only had two weeks to get ready."

"Well, you are doing very well and it seems like everyone here just loves you."

"But, I miss you and my mom and Kimberly, and even Alrand sometimes." They both laughed.

"I'm sorry for being such a baby and crying all the time."

"Nattie, cry all you want. That's part of what makes you, you. I wouldn't change a single thing about you. I really love your tender heart." Nattie just hugged him for a long while.

"Hey, Nattie!" Endnova yelled. "You better get in here. They are dong the bed check."

"Okay! Bye, Jassie. I love you."

"I love you, baby. See you tomorrow morning."

"Oh! Jase, call me when you get there. I don't have your number over there."

"Okay, bye."

Jase called her from the hotel and they continued to talk for a few hours until Endnova told Nattie to go to bed, knowing they would be up talking all night.

Jase laid thinking about the wonderful day, how good Nattie smelled, and how soft she felt. A large deep sounding ship's horn echoed in the harbor reminding him of home. He took a deep breath and sank into a quiet sleep.

It was barely light when Jase awoke to get ready to meet the girls. It was a very chilly morning and a strange low-lying fog floated through the city from the warmer water of the docks. Jase watched it drifting as he waited for the girls to come down from the dorm. The air was cold and crisp and smelled slightly of burning diesel fuel from the ships and dockyard equipment from the other side of the inner harbor.

"Nattie, check out the fog," Jase said.

"Oh, that's neat." They all went to the cafeteria for breakfast and then headed out into the city to explore. Nattie held on close to Jase. Her little fingers were so cold. Jase warmed them as best as he could. They found a cute little souvenir shop that carried gloves so Jase purchased a pair for each of the girls.

"Thank you so much, Jase," Daisha said.

They visited many stores and shops and stopped to eat at a little sandwich market with excellent food for lunch. They sat down and warmed up while they ate. Jase asked the waitress about the best places to go in the city. She told them that they must visit the Charter Center Building, which allowed visitors access to an observation deck on the fiftieth floor.

When they finished eating, they made their way to the Charter building and rode the elevator up to the fiftieth floor. When they stepped out onto the observation deck, they could feel the very cold wind blowing and the girls were freezing. Jase opened his jacket and pulled the sides around Nattie to keep her warm. The sun was starting to set as the days were shorter that time of the year. The views of the city were spectacular and Jase took many pictures of the girls with the city in the background.

They all agreed to stay and freeze long enough to see the sun go down. They took turns walking inside to warm up so they didn't lose their great spot at the railing. Nattie kept her distance from the edge. She was not fond of the height. Just before the sun set, it started to snow. Jase and Nattie had not seen much snow in their lifetime so they were amazed at how pretty the falling snowflakes were in the spotlights on top of the building. Nattie ran around trying to catch them on her tongue.

"Nattie, you are so silly, girl," Endnova said. They all played in the snow for a little while until Nattie hit Jase with a snowball. Jase retaliated, chasing Nattie across the observation deck. A security guard then escorted the four of them to the elevator.

"There you go again, Jase, getting me into trouble," Nattie said.

"You started it this time," Jase said as he put his arm around her waist.

"I'm freezing, Jassie." Jase opened his jacket to let Nattie in and wrapped it around her on the elevator ride down.

Everyone was getting tired and worn out from so much walking. They decided to return to the dorm. Nattie made plans to meet up with Jase very early in the morning. She wanted Jase to herself until it was time for him to leave. Jase walked back to his hotel room and fell asleep. He was out for several hours when something woke him. Someone was calling.

"Hello?"

"Jassie."

"Hey, Nattie."

"I can't sleep."

"What's wrong?"

"I don't want you to leave."

"I wish I could stay."

"I know. Maybe we can get a ticket for me and I can come home with you?" Jase was still very sleepy. He thought for a minute.

"Are you serious, Nattie? I have enough saved that we can buy one." Jase was thrilled at the idea of Nattie riding on the train home with him.

"I really want to, Jase, but my mom would be so mad at me. What do you think?"

"I don't know what to say. My head is telling me that you have to stay but my heart wants you home with me."

"I know. I totally feel that way. Why is it that the things we have to do are so contrary to what is really in our hearts? Life isn't fair!"

"What's right, Nattie? Do we follow what's in our hearts or what our minds are telling us we have to do? What's the right thing to do?"

"I am so temped to come home with you. I hate this!"

"Maybe we need to think about it and get some sleep."

"I can't sleep, Jassie. I'm going to sneak out and come see you."

"Won't you get kicked out of the school if you do that?"

"I don't care; at least it would make the decision easier."

"Nattie, it's only a few hours until you are allowed to leave anyway. Why don't you get ready and meet me as soon as you can leave. We can take some time to think about it until then."

"Okay, I guess you're right. I will see you in a few hours."

"I love you, Nattie."

"I love you, Jassie." They hung up the phone and each lay on their beds contemplating their upcoming decision.

Nattie met up with Jase in the morning. He was already waiting with his suitcase at the dorm entranceway. Nattie ran to Jase and hugged him tight.

"Jassie, you want me to put your suitcase upstairs until it's time to leave?"

"Okay." Nattie took the suitcase upstairs and set it next to her bed.

"Nattie, you off to see Jase?" Endnova asked.

"Yes, I am thinking of going home with him."

"No, you're not! You are so close. You will definitely get the scholarship if you keep going the way you have been. If you leave now, you may regret it for the rest of your life."

"I don't care. I'm going home with Jase."

"How does he feel about this?"

"He wants me home with him."

"Wait up. I want to talk to you two." Endnova put something on quickly and followed Nattie outside. They met up with Jase and walked to the cafeteria to eat and talk.

"Jase, you know this is the wrong thing to do. You and Nattie have your whole lives ahead of you and this time will go by so fast. Trust me, I have been here three years. The time will fly by." Jase said nothing. He just held Nattie.

"My heart is hurting." Nattie said.

"You know the break is coming up in only six weeks, right? You get to go home for two weeks straight."

"I guess you're right. I can always make the decision not to come back after the break." Nattie felt a little better. She forgot about semester break just around the corner. She rubbed her chest with her hand. "Nattie, you okay?" Jase asked.

"My heart hurts."

"It will be okay, sweetie. I promise."

"Why does my chest hurt so?" Jase hugged her and kissed her neck.

Jase and Nattie spent the rest of the day alone together in the city. They walked along the seawall holding each other and talking. Nattie was so cold. They weren't used to the cold weather. Jase found a coat store and helped Nattie pick out a cute one. It was a bit pricy but Jase purchased it for her anyway because it was very heavy and warm.

"Thank you, Jassie. I love you."

"You're welcome, baby." They went to get Jase's suitcase, walked to the train station early, and found a little corner to sit and snuggle until it was time for Jase to leave. Endnova and Daisha snuck up on them and grabbed them from behind.

Chapter 21

Nattie jumped and smacked Endnova, "You brat!" Nattie said. "What are you doing here?"

"I'm not going to let you walk back to the dorm all by yourself."

"Yeah, right. You just want to make sure I don't get on the train."

"You know I love you two, right?"

"I know, Endnova."

The train heading for Summerset started to board. "I will miss you so much, Jassie."

"I love you, Nattie."

"I love you too. Thank you for coming for my birthday." They held each other until the last possible moment. Then Jase walked onboard. After the train left, Nattie started to tear up.

Endnova hugged her, "Nattie, it's only for a little while then you will be home."

"I know, but I will still miss him so much."

Jase found a seat. He was so sad and not looking forward to going back home without Nattie. He was relieved that Endnova showed up to take Nattie safely back to the dorm. *I'm so glad Nattie has a friend like Endnova watching over her.*

Jase arrived home a little before morning from his long train ride. He slept on the train so he could make it to school and work that day. He couldn't wait until the afternoon to talk with Nattie again. After school, he rushed home and connected to the GIN to video chat. Nattie was already connected and couldn't wait to talk with him.

"It's so strange, Jassie, to be so far away from you when I was able to hug you yesterday."

"I know. I was going crazy in school. It seemed like forever waiting to come home to talk to you." They talked until Jase had to head out for work.

When he arrived at work, he told Kimberly all about his amazing adventure in the city. It took a few days but Nattie and Jase adjusted back into their busy routines. Jase and Alrand worked out with his dad's weights in the basement. Jase always kept the GIN connected when they worked out in the event Nattie had a chance to connect early. Kimberly eventually decided to join them to get into shape for the Proelium Concordia.

They continued their workouts for several weeks leading up to the big pirate ship reenactment. Jase had no desire to go without Nattie. The night before the reenactment, he connected with her over video chat, "Jassie, why won't you go to the reenactment with Alrand and Kimberly?"

"I don't want to miss any time with you."

"I know but I have to go with Endnova to test my physics project. We have to rent a cruiser and drive outside the city to try it out in case something goes wrong. I won't be back here until the evening."

"I wish I could see your project in action. Can't you at least tell me what it does?"

"Okay, okay, but you can't laugh if it doesn't work."

"I won't. Tell me."

"Well, I modified a power receiver to work with different power transmitter frequencies based on the laviniun antigravity technology to try to boost power transmission."

"Wow, really?"

"Yes, it's like a power amplifier." Nattie smiled proudly; she could see Jase was impressed.

"That's amazing."

"I just hope it works."

"Will you still get the scholarship if it doesn't work?"

"My teacher said it's the research and processes that he cares about, not if the actual project works correctly. I just have to document everything."

"Sounds like a lot of hard work."

"It is but it would be so neat if it works. My instructor said he has never had a student try something this complicated or groundbreaking before so he is really interested in my results."

Nattie convinced Jase to watch the pirate ship reenactments while she and Endnova rode out of the city to test the small device. The girls were very excited to have permission to get away from the school for a while. As Endnova and Nattie got ready to leave, Endnova noticed Daisha was just sitting quietly on her bed.

"Daisha, what's wrong?"

"Nothing, I'm just bored."

"Why don't you come with us?" Nattie asked.

Daisha's face lit up and she scurried to get ready.

"Daisha, I'm sorry I didn't ask you sooner if you wanted to come, I just assumed you would be coming with us." Nattie said.

"I didn't know if you two wanted me to tag along. You seem to be so close now."

"Awww, Daisha, we love you. You know that, right?" Nattie gave her a hug and they walked downstairs to catch a shuttle.

The three girls picked up a rental and rode out of the city to a park with a huge empty field where Nattie could test her modified power receiver. They carried the test equipment about fifty feet away from the cruiser and Nattie set up everything to monitor the test. She ran wires all the way back to the area in front of the parking lot.

"You guys ready for this?"

"You're not going to blow us up or anything, are you?"

Nattie giggled, "You never know. Here we go." Once everything looked good, Nattie flipped the switch.

BANG! The girls jumped and Endnova screamed.

The cruiser behind them came crashing down to the pavement scaring the girls half to death.

"What in the world happened?!" Endnova shouted.

"I guess something went wrong with our rental," Nattie said.

"At the exact same time you turned on the device?" Daisha said.

"Wait." Nattie turned off her power receiver and the hovercraft lifted back to its normal position. "Wow! Well, that was unexpected," Nattie said.

"You think?" Endnova said. Nattie went to turn the switch back on but Endnova stopped her. "Are you crazy? Don't turn that thing back on."

"But I want to see if it is repeatable."

"Yeah, who's going to pay for the cruiser if it gets messed up?" They decided to maneuver the hovercraft over the soft grassy area and try the test once more. Nattie turned on the device and sure enough, the cruiser came crashing down to the ground. "Nattie, that's amazing!"

"Not really, it's not supposed to do that." They all laughed.

"Well you have to admit that's incredible, intentional or not." Nattie turned off the device and they collected up the equipment and packed it into the cruiser.

"Just make sure that thing is off on the way back to school."

"Don't worry. It's disconnected."

. . .

Jase met up with Alrand and they rode to pick up Kimberly. The three of them spent the day watching the pirate battles in the outer harbor area. Jase actually had a good time although he really missed Nattie and wished she were there with them. The roar of the cannons and the huge puffs of smoke floating across the water gave the battle a true sense of realism. The reenactments ran for several hours with four tall ships competing. After the battles were complete, the three of them went to Skaters to eat dinner.

"Hi, Jase. How's Nattie doing in school?" Jaftney asked.

"She's testing some project for her physics class today."

"I bet you really miss her?"

"I do."

"You two really do make a great couple, you know. Actually you both make great couples." Jaftney said speaking of Alrand and Kimberly.

"Thanks, Jaftney," Kimberly said as she hugged Alrand and give him a kiss.

"Jase, we have to tell you something," Alrand said.

"What?"

"I have decided to join the Proelium Concordia with Kimberly."

"Seriously?"

"Yes, we can join on the buddy system so that we will always be stationed at the same post and school."

"Sorry, Jase," Kimberly said. "We see how hard it is for you and Nattie and we don't want to go through that."

"We will be leaving the day after tomorrow. Sorry we won't be here when Nattie gets home." Jase felt all alone. Everyone was leaving and he was stuck there by himself. His head hung low and he stared down at the table thinking.

"Jase, say something," Alrand said. Kimberly moved over to Jase's side of the booth and hugged him.

"It will be okay. Nattie will be home for break in a few days. You have to be excited about that."

"I am but I will really miss you guys. I wish things could be the way they were."

"Jase, we will be back."

"Where will you be stationed?"

"At first, we will be training at the outer colonies."

"Really? Isn't that dangerous?"

"No, not really. The station has been operational for many years; it's pretty safe now."

The outer colonies were part of a military training and mining settlement on a huge moon of one of the neighboring planets in the solar system. The outpost was originally created as a space station for long-term, deep space, reconnaissance missions but was greatly expanded with the mining operations being so profitable.

That evening, Jase and Nattie talked all night again, sharing everything that happened in their eventful days.

"Jassie, I can't believe that Alrand and Kimberly will be gone when I get home." She told Jase about what happened when they tested her device.

"Nattie, that's so amazing. What do you think your teacher is going to say?"

"I don't know but if I do bad in the class, since the project is fifty percent of my grade, I won't be coming back next semester. I won't stay away from you if there is no chance of getting a scholarship."

"I can't wait. Only a few more days until you come home."

"I know. I'm so excited!"

The next day, Jase's mom invited Ms. Candella for dinner and asked Jase to set up his video chat downstairs where everyone could talk to Nattie. Jase arrived home and changed. He gathered his computer equipment to set up the video chat and proceeded downstairs. As Jase drew closer to the kitchen, he could hear his mom talking to Ms. Candella.

"Yes, that's true," Jase's mom said.

"When my husband died, Nattie stayed in her room most of the time crying. She was so sensitive to every little thing."

"Poor thing."

"One day, her best friend accidentally stepped on a little inchworm that they were playing with on the front porch. She was so heartbroken over that little green worm, she cried for hours. After that, she never wanted to talk to her little friend anymore. I just knew we had to get out of there and move back here around friends and family."

"That must have been so hard. My heart really goes out to the both of you."

"I'm so thankful for Jase. As soon as Nattie met up with him, everything changed. It has been so nice to see her happy and smiling again. I really hated to have to separate them but the academy is her only chance to get into college and she is so smart. Just like her dad."

"It's for the best, don't you think? They were moving really fast and needed a break anyway."

"I don't know. I hope you're right. Nattie hasn't been the same toward me since I talked her into going. I am so happy that she was able to see Jase on her birthday. I should have thought of that. She was so excited when she called me. I think that made a world of difference."

"I'm so glad. When Jase asked me to go, I was hesitant but I guess you have to let them go sometime. They grow up so fast. I'm glad everything is working out for the best."

"I hear she is doing well in all her classes and the semester will be over in a couple of days. I just hope it won't turn into a nightmare when she has to go back after being home for two weeks."

"Don't worry, I'll have a talk with Jase about that and see what we can do to help."

"That would be a huge relief. You know how much influence Jase has over Nattie. She would follow him to the outer colonies and back if he asked her to."

"Oh, speaking of which, I hear Kimberly will be going to the outer colonies for training when she goes off to school in the service."

"She's really brave. I don't know how her mom can handle it."

Jase felt bad for Nattie and really missed her. He thought and wished she were there so he could give her a hug. He quietly walked back up the stairs and then walked back down with heavy footsteps so they would think he just came downstairs. He set up the video chat and they all sat down for a late dinner. It was very exciting when Nattie connected and everyone was waiting to talk to her.

Nattie did most of the talking, telling everyone the latest news from school. Her final project turned out a complete success even though it had a completely different effect than was originally desired. Her teacher was very excited about it and said that she should keep the results under wrap because it wouldn't be good if her invention became public knowledge. Nattie expressed how excited she was about coming home for the semester break.

When they were finished, Jase took his computer back upstairs and connected with Nattie to talk alone for a while.

"Hey, sweetie."

"Hey, Jassie, I so can't wait to come home and be with you!"

"I know. I can hardly wait." That night, they were both so excited that neither wanted to disconnect. They talked as late as they could until the GIN was cut off at school.

The next day Jase's mom sat down with him to talk about encouraging Nattie to return to school for her final semester. Jase reluctantly agreed and said he would do his best.

The night before her flight, Nattie packed up all her possessions and books. "Nattie, you're packing like you're not coming back," Endnova said.

"Well, you never know."

"Girl, don't make me come and drag your butt back to school.

This place just wouldn't be the same without you."

"I'm going to miss you," Nattie said.

"Well, first you're coming with us tonight for a celebration. I'm not taking no for an answer. You don't have any schoolwork to do. Besides, you aced every one of your classes."

"Well, I have to talk..."

"To Jase, I know. Tell him I stole you away for a little while."

Nattie accompanied Endnova to the celebration. They all had a good time until Nattie noticed Daisha with a boyfriend from school. They were hugging and kissing. Nattie was happy for her but it made her miss Jase. She hurried back to the dorm.

She connected to the GIN. "Hi, Jassie."

"Hey, baby. How are you?"

"I'm doing great. Guess what?" Nattie started to giggle. "Daisha has a boyfriend."

"Why are you so tickled about that?"

"I guess I just want everyone to be in love like David and Tristy. Please read some for me, Jassie. I want to know what happened to Tristy."

"Not tonight, Nattie, I just want to talk to you."

Nattie made a frown at Jase on the video chat. "Why won't you read to me anymore?"

"Nattie, there's something I have to tell you but I want to wait until you get home on break first."

"Jassie, tell me now, please. What is it?"

"I will tell you tomorrow when you get home."

Nattie started to get upset and her feelings were a little bit hurt. "Jassie, I don't understand. What is it that you can't tell me?"

"Nattie, you know I love you and I just want you to be happy."

"Then tell me." Jase couldn't bear seeing Nattie get upset, which was what he was trying to avoid in the first place. He realized that he never should have told her anything.

"All right; wait a second." Jase picked up *Three Tall Ships*, which lay where he threw it a few months ago. Jase read to Nattie.

Finally, there was some news. Anderson was called to the makeshift hospital. When he arrived, Pamula walked out of Tristy's room, gave David a hug, and softly whispered.

"David, I'm afraid she's gone. There was nothing I could do to save her."

Anderson could hardly believe what he had heard. He went in next to Tristy's body and wept. He stroked her hair and kissed her forehead.

"This is not goodbye, my love, I will see you again on resurrection day, and we will be soulmates for all eternity."

"Oh no, Jassie, she died?"

Chapter 22

"**I**'m so sorry, Nattie." She wept aloud.

"That's so sad. I always imaged that we were them."

"I know. It's okay, Nattie." Now Jase felt bad because he knew how she would react.

"I guess I can't be your Tristy anymore."

"Nattie, you will always be my beautiful Tristy. Forever and ever."

"I love you, Jassie." They sat and looked at each other for a few minutes. "Can you read a little more for me Jassie, please?"

"Okay, sweetie." Jase continued to read where he left off.

Captain Wells arranged the funeral for Tristy Brody. He felt it was the very least he could do for her courageous actions that saved their ships and their town. He allowed Tristy's father to spread the word to all that desired to pay their respects. The day before the funeral proceedings, a tall ship made its way into the cove, captained by none other than Tristy's sister Angelica Brody.

"Jassie, that's her! Remember the girl that republished the book? She mentioned her on the back of the book!"

"Yes, it's right here,"

In fond memory of my great-grandmother Angelica Brody for whom I am named... You are so loved.

"Jassie, read some more, please."

"Okay, Nattie,"

Angelica was one of few woman captains but her reputation for being fierce and heartless infamously preceded her. Angelica walked into the town accompanied by her most loyal bodyguards. Anderson was summoned before the captain so he could be informed about Angelica. It was his job to guard against any treachery that may befall the town by Angelica's presence.

Angelica stood before David Anderson.

"So you're the one that my sister died for?"

"We were to be married."

"Is that so?" David could not believe the resemblance; it was as if he was looking at Tristy herself. He stood speechless.

"Why are you standing there like a statue?"

"You look like Tristy."

"She was my twin." I can hardly believe my eyes, thought David.

"She must have seen something special in you to die for you that way. She always said she would never marry or suffer my anguish." David wondered about the anguish Angelica spoke of but he stood silent.

The next day, Captain Wells presided over the funeral. Anderson spoke words of the heart about his love, forgiveness, and the goodness in all people.

"No matter how dark our hearts can be, there is light and hope in the Christ." After everyone left, Angelica stayed behind, alone. She stood over her sister and saw a note that David had lay on her chest. She was so touched by the note that she wept and fell to her knees. She thought of taking her own life rather than spend another day in sorrow.

She had lost her own love just a year before when they were attacked by the very pirates that took her sister's life. She took out her pistol and put it against her head. Just then, David rushed in and pulled the pistol away and it went off into the ceiling.

Angelica's bodyguards, not aware of the situation, ran into the room ready to kill David.

"Wait! Leave us," Angelica said.

"Angelica why would you want to kill yourself?" She just leaned forward, placing her head on the wooden plank floor

"Why did you stop me?"

"Because I don't want you to die."

"Why do you care?"

"Because you are Tristy's sister and I don't want to see you hurt."

"I can't go on. First, I lose my beloved Tierney, now Tristy. I can't take anymore. Will the killing ever stop?"

"You can go on vand I will help you. Together we can defeat them once and for all! We are developing a new weapon that will end their treachery." David reached out his hand and Angelica gave him hers. He pulled her to her feet. "Angelica, you don't have to go *through life alone." He sat her down on a bench and they talked until nightfall. David was infatuated by the stories she told. She was not a heartless killer but a hurting sole in need of rescue. She was quite taken with David and began to see what her sister saw in him.*

"Jassie, that's all so sad," Nattie said as she stuck out her lower lip.

"Can you believe Tristy had a twin?"

"I know. I wonder what's going to happen."

"I don't know but do you really think it's all true, that these things really happened?"

"Yes, I do. Remember what the author said. She was Angelica's great-granddaughter. That means that Angelica lived long enough to have children. So that proves it's all true and proves that the treasure is real, doesn't it?"

"I hope so, Nattie. We really need to go there this summer when school is out."

"I can't wait to see the rock where David carved his heart for Tristy. I can't believe she died and never got to see it. I don't want anyone else I know to die."

Nattie was silent for a little while and looked very sad over the video chat.

"Nattie, what is it?"

"Jassie, I want to tell you something. I've never told anyone this before."

"What is it?"

"Promise me that you won't tell anyone, ever."

"I won't. I promise."

Nattie hesitated, "Never mind."

"Nattie, why won't you tell me?"

"I can't."

"Why?"

"Sorry I said anything."

"Now it's going to drive me crazy. It must be something important. Please tell me."

"I will tell you when I get home, okay?"

"Is it something bad?"

"No, well, not really."

"Nattie, tell me, please."

"When I get home, okay?"

"You promise?"

"Yes."

"I wish you were here right now. I really want to give you a hug."

"I am counting the hours, Jassie. It's taking forever. They are going to shut off the GIN. Call me, okay?"

"Okay." Jase called Nattie and they talked well into the night since it was the weekend. They made plans for Jase to meet up with Nattie's mom so he could ride with her to the skyport to pick up Nattie. Jase said good night so she could have enough sleep to get up on time.

The next morning, Jase woke up earlier than expected. He was so excited but very tired. He could hardly function. He dropped his toothbrush on the floor and bumped his head on the counter when he tried to pick it up. Then he ran into the door trying to leave his room. *I guess it would help if I turned the doorknob*, he thought to himself and snickered. He quickly ate breakfast then hopped on his bike to ride to Ms. Candella's house.

Nattie's alarm sounded for quite a while before it woke her up. She jumped out of bed and rushed into the bathroom to get ready before the others. She wanted to look her best for Jase. When she finished and walked out of the bathroom, Endnova was waiting with perfume and caught Nattie off guard.

"Got ya, girly."

"Hey, now I'm going to stink up the whole ship!"

"You smell great and Jase is gonna love it," Endnova said.

Once all three of the girls were ready, they headed downstairs to catch a shuttle to the skytrans terminal. Nattie was so bubbly and chattered away. Many of the students waved and gave their goodbyes as the girls walked by, "Happy vacation, Nattie!"

Nattie was so anxious. The shuttle wasn't going fast enough for her. *Sheesh, I could get out and run faster than this*, she thought. Finally, they arrived at the skyport. Nattie was about to pull her hair out when she noticed that the ship's departure time was delayed. She found her departure gate and sat down on the end of a row of seats. She took off her cute coat that Jase bought her and laid it on the seat next to her. Her brilliant mind started to drift. She thought about Jase for a while, their struggles, their love, and their amazing adventures. A deep perplexing thought entered her head. *What makes us love? Is it our hearts or our minds? A physical heart can't love, so it must originate in the center of the mind. That must be our true heart. Will this stinking flight ever arrive so I can go see my Jassie?*

She laid her head back on the seat and closed her eyes taking a frustrating deep breath.

"Excuse me, miss?" a young man said.

"Yes?"

"Do you mind if I sit here?"

"But there's a whole row of empty seats?"

"Yes, but only one right next to a beautiful woman."

"Awww, thank you. You are sweet but I have a boyfriend."

"I figured as much. Would you mind if I sit over here so we can just talk a bit while waiting on our flights?"

"Sorry, but I have a lot on my mind. Not really in a talkative mood."

"That's okay. I'll sit quietly." A little while later, they announced the flight to Summerset was ready to board. Nattie struggled to get all of her bags situated.

"Here, let me help you with that," the young man said.

"Thanks."

"Sure, any time."

Nattie walked down the ramp and into the skyship. The flight was empty so she was relieved to have a row of seats to herself again. She figured she would be brave and try to sit next to the window and leave the shade up. She put her coat and a bag on the seat next to her so nobody would try to sit there.

Once everyone was boarded, the skyship lifted off into the air, accelerating at what seemed like an unbelievable rate. The ground disappeared in an instant. Nattie held on tight and pulled the shade down over the window. After she started to relax some, she decided to lift the shade just a little to take a peak outside, then she quickly pulled it shut.

"Are you afraid to look out of the window?" the stewardess asked.

"Yes, a little."

"It's all very safe, you know. There hasn't been a skyship crash in over fifty years."

"I know; it's just a little scary knowing we're up so high."

"Is this your first time flying?"

"No, my second. I'm returning home from school to see my boyfriend."

"How exciting."

"It is; it really is." Nattie took a chance and opened the shade. The sky was so beautiful. There were scattered puffy clouds, like fish in the sea, floating beneath the ship. The sky above the clouds was crystal clear and blue. Nattie had never before seen such a sight. She felt as if she could actually sit on top of a cloud, as if they were solid objects.

Jase and Ms. Candella drove to the skyport. When they arrived and stepped out of the cruiser, Jase's heart raced like crazy with anticipation. He felt like he was in a dream and waiting to wake up to see Nattie's beautiful face once again. He was shaking and nervous, as if he hadn't seen her in a hundred years.

"Jase, slow down. Where's the fire?"

"Sorry, Ms. Candella."

She laughed, "Why are you so nervous? You have all this nervous energy."

"I don't know. I didn't think this day would ever get here."

"Relax, you'll see Nattie soon enough."

"Let's see what gate we need to find."

"Awww, it looks like her flight is going to be late." That wasn't what Jase wanted to hear. They walked to the gate and waited for a good while.

Nattie gazed out the window, tapping her finger against the cabin wall as the ship began to descend. She liked the feeling of the ground getting ever closer. Everything beneath was so tiny, she felt like she could just pick up the homes with her fingers and move them around. From the air, she could see Summerset and the marina. Nattie smiled. *Oh, how I've missed everything.* Home was like paradise — so quiet, charming, and peaceful, and a million things to do, especially with Jase. There was never a dull moment.

Finally, the ship landed. Nattie took a deep breath and let it out. She shook like a shivering puppy. She felt both freezing cold and hot at the same time. She stood up to get her things ready to depart but her knees felt weak and she stumbled holding on to the seat in front of her. She struggled to pick up her things and took a last look around to make sure she didn't forget anything.

Jase waited, and waited, and waited. Everyone exited the gate except Nattie. He started to fear that she missed her flight. It appeared that everyone had already left the ship and no one else exited. He started to walk to the desk by the gate, when finally he could see her round the corner with all of her bags. He let out sigh of relief and walked toward her. Nattie looked around the crowded terminal and when her eyes gazed upon Jase, he was already looking at her and heading her way. She smiled and as soon as she cleared the gate, she dropped everything and ran to Jase. They hugged so tightly and neither wanted to let go. Jase put his hand on the back of Nattie's neck through her long black curly hair.

"Nattie, you smell so good."

"Thank you, my love." They rubbed noses and kissed. "I have missed you so much, Jassie."

"I have really missed you."

"I was thinking while sitting at the skyport waiting on my flight."

"About what?"

"Happy thoughts."

"Like?"

Nattie looked up at Jase and smiled with her beautiful dimple smile, "Jassie, today, let's forget our minds and only listen to our hearts. Our hearts are freedom and happiness; our minds enslave us. Today, let's listen to our hearts." Jase smiled and kissed her.

"Nattie, you're so sweet."

Chapter 23

"**I** love you, Jassie. I love it when you say sweet things about me. Am I dreaming?"

Jase laughed and loosened his grip around her waist. "No, you are really here with me. If it's a dream than I don't want to ever wake up."

"Me either."

"Nattie, it's been driving me crazy all night. Please tell me what you said you would tell me when you got home."

"Not here, later; here comes my mom."

Jase picked up all of Nattie's bags and her coat. She hugged her mom, "Hi, Mom, guess what?"

"What?"

"The school administrator said I could possibly be getting offered a scholarship when I return."

"Really? That's so wonderful. How do you like school now?"

"I like it because it's challenging. I just wish Jase could be there with me." They drove home from the skyport terminal. Nattie was so happy. She smiled and hugged Jase all the way home. Once they arrived, Nattie felt dirty and wanted to clean up and change. Jase sat on the swing on the front porch and waited.

Over time, the sky grew dark with storm clouds and the wind

started blowing. The air smelled of rain and dark black clouds swirled around as if they were dancing in harmony. Not yet being midday, it was as if it was night. Distant flashes of light illuminated the clouds and a deep crackling roiling thunder echoed along the waterway.

Nattie fixed herself up very nice for Jase and made sure to spray herself with perfume. She walked out of the front door and let out a little scream as a huge thunder burst let loose. At that moment, the flash of light reflecting off Nattie's beautiful, full, curly long black hair amazed Jase.

"Nattie, you look like an angel." Nattie smiled.

"I'm your Angelica." She put her hands on Jase's shoulder and leaned down to kiss him. She sat down on the swing next to him and they watched the approaching storm.

"Nattie, please tell me now."

"Okay, but don't think bad of me, okay?"

"I won't, just tell me."

"Remember how Angelica felt after Tristy died and how David saved her from killing herself?"

"Yes."

"That's how I felt after my dad died. I wanted to die but then you saved me." Nattie started to cry.

"How?" Jase said as he wiped her eyes.

"You came back into my life and gave me a reason to live." Jase started to tear up. He didn't know what to say.

He thought for a second, "Nattie, you mean more to me than anything in the world and I couldn't live without you." Nattie snuggled up close, as the rain grew heavy, to the point the gutters could not keep up. The water was like a streaming wall in front of the porch. Nattie put her arms around Jase and they kissed. The fierce wind blew Nattie's hair all around. Jase could feel it like feathers rubbing against his face. Nattie giggled and tried to gather her hair together.

"No, leave it; it feels nice."

"But I want to look good for you."

"Well, you look beautiful right now and a bit wild." Nattie giggled and kissed him. She snuggled up with her feet on the swing.

"I'm so happy, Jase. There is no place I would rather be. I could stay here with you forever." Nattie took a deep breath and let it out. After a few minutes, she fell asleep in Jase's arms to the sound of the rain.

Later, when the rain lessened and the clouds began to dissipate, extremely bright beams of light pierced through the cracks in glorious splendor. "Nattie, wake up." Nattie stretched her arms out, yawned, and wrapped them around Jase.

"Hey, honey," she said.

"Look, baby."

"Oh, Jase. That's so beautiful."

The rain had all but stopped so they walked off the porch to get a better view. Jase put his arm around Nattie as they walked toward the road. The wind blew high up in the sky, gradually taking the clouds away. A huge full rainbow appeared across the horizon all the way to the ground on both sides. The base was as wide as a house.

"Jassie, that's breathtaking!"

"That's the way I feel every time I look at you, Nattie. You are so amazing."

"Awww, Jassie. I love you." They stood and took in the magnificent sight before them. In time, the rainbow faded away and the air began to warm.

Jase and Nattie decided to ride into town. They walked all around to their favorite places and along the waterway, perusing through the shops. Nattie clung tightly to Jase everywhere they went. While walking toward the fairgrounds, Nattie had to use the bathroom. While Jase waited, he noticed something new. A small, three mast, sailing ship was docked at the boardwalk. He walked over to a little booth with some signs displaying the ship name. *The Nauti Sprinter. Daily and evening dinner cruises.*

Excitedly, he took a flyer and secretly tucked it away and met up with Nattie. They continued on, looking in the little shops along the waterway. Nattie picked up a cute hat and put it on her head.

"What do you think?"

"That's really you. Wow, you are so cute!" She put the hat back on the rack and Jase picked it up. "You have to have this, Nattie."

"Jase, it's too much. You're spending all your money on me."

"I can't help it. I've missed you so much." Nattie took the hat from Jase and put it back on the shelf.

"All I need is you." Jase grabbed the hat and ran to the teller counter with Nattie running close behind laughing.

"Come back here, you brat!"

"Nope." Jase dodged in and out of the racks of clothes, just barely keeping ahead of her. She finally grabbed his jacket and held on tight. Jase stopped and Nattie put her arms around his waist and they kissed. "You look to cute in this hat. I have to buy it for you."

"Okay, but this is it. You're not allowed to buy me anything else."

"Nothing else?"

"Well, at least not for the rest of the day," Nattie said with a huge smile on her face. They both laughed. Jase purchased the expensive red and black hat and put it on Nattie's head. She just started to giggle. "I love you so much, Jassie."

He kissed her on the cheek. "You own my heart, Nattie. It's all yours forever."

They rode home to Nattie's house and spent their last few hours together sitting on the porch until Nattie's mom told her to come in for the night.

The next week and a half, Jase and Nattie spent every possible second together. Their love for each other grew stronger every day. Every morning Jase could hardly wait to ride to Nattie's house to see her and every time she walked out onto the porch, she would take his breath away. She would always sit in the bookstore with Jase when he had to work; they would talk for hours. They spoke about Nattie's breakthrough invention.

"Just think, Nattie. It could cause not only cruiser crashes but skyship crashes also."

"I didn't think about that. I need to make sure when I travel that the power receiver is completely disconnected.

"Yeah, I think that would be a good idea." They both laughed.

"Jassie, it's slow in here today. Can you read some more to me, please?"

"How could I ever say no to you, cutie."

"I think that would be quite impossible," Nattie giggled. Nattie smiled and cuddled up to Jase.

He began to read from *Three Tall Ships* where they left off, with Nattie resting her head against his shoulder looking at the text:

Captain Wells was uneasy with Lieutenant Anderson growing so fond of the infamous Angelica Brody. He removed him from his assignment guarding the pirate crew and sent him on other missions, but every evening, he found the two of them spending time together. The captain summoned Angelica before him.

"I understand you have decided to extend your stay with us?"

"For now. It's been a long time since my crew has enjoyed safe harbor."

"What are your plans for the near future?"

"Is there an issue with our presence here?" Angelica said in a rather defensive manner.

"Not at all, provided your intentions are honorable,

not intending to be offensive but your reputation precedes you."

"Neither I or my crew has shown any aggression, nor do we have any cause. As far as my reputation, just ask your Lieutenant Anderson. He understands my plight."

"Speaking of which, I understand that the two of you have become quite close?"

"As manifested by your persistence to keep us apart by assigning him remedial tasks away from port."

Captain Wells thought for a second, understanding that Angelica was quite intelligent. He knew the harder he tried to separate the two of them, the more determined it would resolve them to be together.

Taking a leap of faith that Angelica would be honorable and hold true to her word, "Angelica, you, and your crew, are welcome here. Provided, I have your word that no harm will come to the citizens of Voncara Cove by your hand."

"Not only do you have my word but we will defend this port with our ship and our lives, if necessary."

Captain Wells stood, lifted his eyebrows, and felt warm. He shook Angelica's hand, "Then you have my liberty and hospitality. Stay as long as you please."

Angelica smiled at the captain, "Thank you."

David was happy that Angelica would be staying but he was confused in his heart because of his mourning of Tristy. He sensed that Angelica was in dire need of someone to care for her and noticed that her persona of ruthlessness faded in his presence. He found himself thinking about her throughout each day but he was concerned though, that another pirate attack was eminent.

Captain Wells formed an alliance with Angelica's father and asked Anderson if he would attempt to persuade Angelica to join as well. David thought it over and was very reluctant to ask her, not wanting to place her in any danger. David asked Angelica to walk with him along the shore so they could talk.

"Angelica, I was asked to make you a proposal to join our alliance but I want you to refuse."

"What do you mean?"

"I have grown fond of you and I don't want to take a chance of losing you too."

"David, I would be dead if it weren't for you. I know this is crazy but I think I love you. If you are going into battle, then so am I. If you die, then I will die right alongside you. Tell your commander that I will join the alliance but only if you captain my ship."

"Angelica, I care deeply about you and I don't want you there."

"Then I will tell Captain Wells myself. You are not going without me. I am keeping you close, no matter what happens. I have lost a love as well and I'm not going through that again."

"Listen, Angelica, I'm not supposed to tell anyone this, but Captain Wells has designed a new weapon. It will change the odds in our favor. You really don't need to be there."

"Tell me about this new weapon."

"I can't, please just trust me."

"David, if you don't trust me, then how am I supposed to trust you?"

"Okay, but you can't tell anyone I told you."

"David, you can trust me, I would die before I say anything."

"All right, it's called a Gatlin gun. It fires a large number of shot cartridges every minute."

"How many is a large number?"

"Three to four hundred per minute."

"How can this be?"

"We have superior technology available to us."

"What is technology?"

"It means that we can make things more powerful than the Blackrock pirates."

"Why didn't you use technology before?"

"We have; our long range cannons are based on advanced technology."

"How do you have this technology, David?"

"I could tell you, Angelica, but you wouldn't believe me or understand."

"Well, either way, I'm still coming with you, and that's final."

"I guess there's no getting around it then."

They talked to Captain Wells who agreed to let Lieutenant David Anderson captain the fifth ship of *the alliance. A plan was devised to attack the heart of the pirates by an assault on their town of Blackrock itself. No one had ever dared such a dangerous action but everyone agreed, once they witnessed a demonstration of the Gatlin gun's power.*

"Jassie, how is this possible...can they really be from the future?"

Chapter 24

"**I** don't see how but something's going on. I wish he told Angelica how they came by the advanced technology."

"I wonder why he thought that Angelica wouldn't understand or believe him."

"Well, if they were from the future, it would make sense," Nattie said with one eyebrow lifted in puzzlement. "I wonder what a Gatlin gun is."

"I don't know. I have never heard of anything like that. Nattie, if they were from the future, wouldn't we know about the Gatlin gun and even the RFI gun?"

"That's a great point, Jase. I don't know."

"We really need to go to Voncara Cove."

"I know but I spent so much money I will have to keep working during the summer to get enough to buy the tickets."

"I will get a job, Jassie, when I get home so we can get the money sooner."

"Where would you work?"

"Jaftney said they need help at Skaters so maybe I can work there. At least that way we will be close when we are working."

"That's a great idea. I can't wait until we can go on the trip. I feel like we are meant to figure out the books and find the treasure. I just wish we could find the last book."

"Read a little more, Jassie. I want to see what happens."

"Okay,"

The night before the planned assault, David stood at the bow of Angelica's ship, looking out over the water. He could remember standing with Tristy watching the moonlight shimmering with little dances of light on the water as it appeared to rise right up out of the ocean.

Angelica walked over and stood next to David. "I really miss her," David said.

"I miss her too." Angelica put her arm on David's shoulder. "Do you think that one day you could love me like you loved her?"

"Angelica, I do love you. Please don't go tomorrow."

"David, I will never leave your side. Ever!" David stopped trying to convince her. He put his arm around her and they leaned upon the railing watching the moonrise.

Just then, Jase had a wonderful idea but he kept it to himself. "Jassie, I'm glad David has Angelica but I miss Tristy."

"Sweetie, it's time to close up the bookstore for the night."

"Okay." Nattie helped Jase to lock up then he tickled her and chased her up to the second floor. They kissed for a few minutes then decided to head home before it got too late. Once they arrived at Nattie's house, they sat on the porch for a little while. "Jase, I can't believe the break is almost over."

"I know. I didn't want to think about it. It's so lonely here now when you are away with Alrand and Kimberly gone."

"I wish school was done now. I will miss you so much."

"You know you have to go back to school though. You've accomplished a lot."

"I know but it doesn't make it any easier."

"Nattie, make sure you're not doing anything the day before you leave for school, okay?"

"Why?"

"I have a little surprise."

"Ohhh, what is it?"

"It wouldn't be a surprise if I told you."

"Jassie! You know I can't stand when you do that to me."

"I know. Don't you just love it?" Nattie smacked Jase, laughed, and then they kissed for almost an hour. She felt so warm to Jase's touch and her face was bright red. He arranged her hair, pushing it back out of her face, so he could see her pretty, blue eyes. "I love you so much, Nattie."

"Jassie, I want to ask you something."

"What?"

The front door opened, "Nattie, it's time to come in now."

"Ugh! Okay, Mom."

"What were you going to ask me?"

"I have to go in now. I'll ask you later." They hugged and Nattie went inside. Jase waited until she waved to him from her bedroom window, on the second floor, before he set off for home. He wondered what Nattie was going to ask him.

Jase waited all night but when they met up the next day, Nattie turned all red and said she couldn't remember what she was going to ask.

"I was waiting forever. You sure you don't remember what you wanted to ask me?"

"Just never mind," Nattie said. They spent as much time together as they could over the next few days. Jase asked Nattie's mom if she could stay out late the night before she returned to school and let her in on his plans for Nattie's surprise date.

"Jase, that sounds wonderful," Ms. Candella said.

"Thanks, I took off work so we can spend the whole day together."

Jase arranged everything and told Nattie not to eat breakfast because he would be coming to pick her up early. Jase passed his driving test but wanted to surprise Nattie so he kept it a secret.

The dreaded day before the end of school break had arrived. Jase got up early in the morning and drove his mom's cruiser to Nattie's house and walked up to the porch. Nattie pranced out of the front door and hugged him around the neck.

"You brat! Why didn't you tell me you can drive?"

"It's a surprise."

"So that's the big surprise?" Nattie said as she smiled at Jase.

"Nope, that's not the surprise."

"Jassie! What is it?"

"Not telling." Jase tickled Nattie and she ran off the porch. He chased her around the house. She laughed so hard she couldn't keep running. Jase caught her and gave her a kiss. "I love you, Nattie."

"I love you, Jassie." They rubbed noses and put their foreheads together.

"Let's go!" Jase said. He helped her into the cruiser and they set out for the docks. Jase took Nattie to a little restaurant along the waterway. As they approached, they could smell the aroma of bacon and vanilla.

"Now I'm hungry, Jassie. It smells so yummy." It was chilly so they decided to sit inside but Jase arranged a table with a beautiful view of the harbor. They sat next to each other so they both could share the view. The sun was still low on the horizon and reflected off the rippling water. The sky was crystal blue without a single cloud. Slight little puffs of foggy mist slowly drifted past the boats in the marina and picked up yellow and orange tints from the rising sun. "This is so pretty." They held hands and looked at the menus.

After they ordered, they talked and kissed a little until their food was prepared.

After they finished eating, they walked arm in arm out to the end of the longest pier and sat down with their legs hanging over the edge. It was chilly so Nattie snuggled up close to Jase and he played with her long silky hair. "I love it when you play with my hair. It feels nice."

They watched the sun as it continued to climb higher into the sky cooking off the foggy mist floating across the water. Jase checked the time.

"Are you ready, baby?"

"For what?"

"Come on, I'll show you." They walked back to the cruiser.

"Where are we going, Jassie?"

"Just get in, beautiful. You will see." Jase put the top down so they could have a better view on their drive. He really loved seeing Nattie with wild, windblown, hair.

"Jassie, I'm going to freeze!" Jase laughed and lifted out a thick throw blanket from the back seat and covered Nattie. They drove about forty-five minutes north of town through the royal countryside. "We've never been here before."

"I know. Isn't it pretty?"

"It is. Maybe we should pull over somewhere," Nattie hinted and winked at Jase.

"We will, just a couple more sects."

"Jassie, where are we going?" Nattie said as she fidgeted in her seat.

"Just wait, you'll see."

"You really like driving me crazy, don't you?" Jase laughed.

"Evidently I do."

"How much longer?"

"Shush, just a couple minutes."

"You know I have been waiting forever for this surprise." Jase laughed loudly. "What's so funny?"

"I never said this was the surprise. That's not until tonight."

"Jassie!" Nattie bit Jase's arm.

"Hey!"

"That's what you get for driving me crazy," Nattie giggled. Jase tickled her and she squirmed in her seat.

"Now sit still. I'm trying to drive here!"

"Hey, you're the one tickling me! You brat!" Jase laughed.

He slowed and pulled into a parking area on the side of the road. A narrow trail led into the woods. Jase took Nattie by the hand. "Where are you taking me, you pirate?"

"To fight off scallywags and sea brigands."

"Am I your prisoner?"

"Totally," Jase laughed.

"What are you going to do with me? I hope something exciting," Nattie giggled.

"I'm taking you to see something I read about in a new book. And don't ask what it is because you'll just have to wait until we get there." Nattie took a deep breath and let out a little growl.

They walked through the woods and down a trail to the top of a gorge.

"Jassie, it's beautiful here and a little spooky. We can see so far."

"Especially since most of the trees are barren." They walked down a winding trail leading deep into the gorge. Nattie was really enjoying the hike, bouncing and skipping while she walked. "I love you, Nattie. You are so cute and silly."

"Long as I'm with you." She stopped Jase to fish for a hug and a kiss then they continued.

As they approached the bottom of the gorge, they could hear the sound of rushing water. The trail turned sharp to the left and followed along a high cliff above a river.

"Nattie, come look. We are so far up."

"That's okay. I'm just fine over here." Jase took Nattie's hand but she pulled away, "I'm not going over there."

"It's okay, just don't look down. We need to walk this way." He led Nattie up the trail following alongside the river. The further they walked the louder the sound of rushing water.

"Jassie, what is that? It's so loud."

"Just wait." The trail opened up to a rocky area and a spectacular seventy-foot high waterfall. The water crashing down into the gorge created a fog like mist in the air.

"Jassie, that's so incredible. The water is so powerful."

"Yeah, that's impressive." They walked as close as they could to the bottom of the waterfall. Other hikers had also gathered to take in the spectacular view. Jase had Nattie pose for a bunch of pictures in front of the crashing water. He positioned her on a huge rock and leaned her head back with her hair hanging down to take a few more shots.

"How's this, Jassie?"

"Beautiful, hold still."

The days were rather short this time of year and the sun started to disappear behind the cliffs of the gorge. They decide to start their long hike back up.

"Was it worth the hike, Nattie?"

"Of course, long as I'm with you." She put her arm around Jase as they reached the winding trail. "So, what's my surprise?" Jase had to laugh.

"It won't be long now, baby. Are you hungry?"

"I'm starving."

"Good."

"Why is that good?"

"You will see." Nattie punched Jase in the arm and stuck out her lower lip.

"Meany."

"You get to stay out late tonight."

"How so?"

"I asked your mom."

"Are we going somewhere to be alone?"

"Shush."

"Jassie, tell me!"

"Nope." Nattie tried to tickle Jase but he wasn't ticklish.

"That's just not fair. You should be ticklish so I can get you." Jase tried to tickle Nattie but she ran up the trail. He chased her but she was so fast. They quickly became winded, as the winding trail was quite steep. They paused to catch their breath. "Whew, it's so much harder going up," Nattie said.

"I know. I wish it was up hill getting to the waterfall so it would be downhill going back."

"It was such a pretty view though. Except for the cliffs above the river," Nattie said. Jase took Nattie's hand and they continued the rest of the way up the trail. When they reached the parking lot, Jase helped Nattie into the cruiser. He left the roof up because it was getting colder as the evening approached.

Nattie fell asleep while Jase drove back to the marina. He parked and woke her up. She stretched and said, "What are we doing now, Jassie?"

"Come with me, beautiful." Jase walked Nattie over to the *Nauti Sprinter*.

"Hello, can I help you?"

"Yes, we have two tickets for the sunset dinner cruise." Nattie could hardly contain herself. She started bouncing up and down on her toes in anticipation.

"Dinner will be served after sunset. Please step aboard." Jase and

Nattie walked up the ramp and onto the main deck.

"Jassie, this is so exciting. Is this my surprise?"

"Yes." Nattie hugged Jase tight and gave him a kiss. They walked around the ship and throughout the cabin looking at everything. The *Nauti Sprinter* was a square topsail schooner and was smaller than the tall ships present during the pirate battle reenactments but still impressive in size. The main cabin was specially designed to comfortably accommodate twenty-five guests for dinner.

The crew quickly rigged the sails on all three masts to set sail. Jase watched in fascination.

"Wouldn't it be neat to live on a boat like this, Nattie?"

"As long as it doesn't sink, I guess." Jase laughed.

The ship looked quite beautiful from the deck with all sails fully arrayed, pocketed by the wind with the sounds of the canvas cleaving forward. The sails were a light reddish yellow in color and fit perfectly with the beautiful sunset. As the sun set behind the horizon, the scattered clouds illuminated with shades of yellow, orange, and blue. The sky gradually dimmed beyond the rolling hills as the ship quietly sailed up the waterway. Jase and Nattie walked to the bow of the ship and leaned on the railings. Nattie put her arm around Jase.

"Just like Angelica and David," she said.

"I know; they gave me the idea for the surprise."

"It's a wonderful surprise, Jassie." They kissed and a crewman captured them with a camera. The picture was so perfect with the sails above their heads and the beautiful sunset as a background. After dark, the crew turned on strings of white lights around and above the deck, creating a beautiful romantic setting. "Jassie, this is the best surprise ever."

Everyone was invited into the cabin for a four-course dinner. Jase and Nattie were so hungry, since they hadn't eaten since breakfast. Each course was just as delicious as the previous.

"I love this, Jassie and I love you." She gave him a little kiss.

"I love you, Nattie. This is so excellent. I wish we could do this every day."

"That would be wonderful."

They picked out their desserts and started to eat them, "This is so yummy. I think you're going to have to roll me home after eating so much, Jassie." Jase laughed,

"You are so cute." They finished their dessert and stood to exit the cabin. Pictures of the guests were displayed at the main exit. Each couple received a free souvenir photo taken during the cruise. Everyone commented on Jase and Nattie's photo, which turned out superbly. The captain asked if he could have permission to use their image on postcards depicting the sunset cruse. Jase agreed. The captain thanked him by refunding his money. They exited the cabin and walked out to the deck.

"Look, Jase." Nattie took Jase's hand and pulled him to the bow of the ship.

"Nattie, isn't it funny how we always get free stuff? I think it's because you are so beautiful."

"I think it's because you're so dashing."

The ship made a wide turn to head back to port. Jase and Nattie watched as the moon rose up from behind the hills. The moonlight cast ghostly silhouettes of the barren trees across the hillsides.

"Nattie, that's so spooky."

"I love it. I want to go over there with you. We could..."

"Could what?" Nattie turned a little red and looked down at the deck.

"Nothing."

"What were you going to say, baby?"

"Nothing."

"Hey, you never told me what you were going to ask me the other night." Nattie turned bright red and wouldn't look at Jase. "What? Nattie?"

Chapter 25

"**I**t's nothing."

"Tell me."

"I can't."

"Why not?"

"Because." Jase laughed.

"Because why?"

"I just can't."

"You know you can tell me anything."

"I wish I didn't have to go back to school tomorrow." Nattie looked so sad. She took a deep breath in frustration and exhaled.

"What's wrong, Nattie?"

"I just want to be with you, Jassie." She put her head against Jase's chest.

"You're with me now, baby. At least for a little while." Nattie giggled. Jase held her until the ship reached the docks. Nattie took Jase's hand and hurried him off the ship. They briskly walked to the cruiser and climbed in.

Nattie put her arms around Jase and they kissed for a while. "I need to take you home, Nattie."

"Not yet. I'm not ready to go home."

"I promised your mom that I would have you home in time if she let us stay out late for the dinner cruise."

"But I have to leave tomorrow." Nattie sat back in her seat and crossed her arms.

"Sweetie, I'm sorry. You know I wish you didn't have to go. I can't wait until your school is done." Jase gave her a hug then drove her home. They walked up to the porch and kissed by the front door. Nattie's mom peered out and motioned them to come inside.

"How was your dinner on the ship, Nattie?" Nattie could only think about Jase and having to leave in the morning.

"It was good."

"Just good?"

"It was amazing, Ms. Candella." Nattie held Jase with her head against his chest and didn't say much. Jase rubbed her back as they stood there. "We also walked to a huge waterfall. I took lots of pictures of Nattie by the water."

"I'm glad you two had a good day. Nattie, are you all packed for tomorrow?"

"I'm ready. I just want to spend a little more time with Jase."

"Okay, but not too long. You have a long day ahead of you tomorrow." Jase and Nattie sat on the couch. She had a frown on her face and sat staring at Jase.

"Jassie, I don't want this day to end." She hugged him and they kissed a little until Jase's mom called.

"Nattie, time to say good night. Jase has to head home now." Nattie was nice and warm in Jase's arms. Neither of them wanted to say goodbye.

"I love you so much, Jassie. It's not any easier leaving you. I think it's actually harder."

"I love you, Nattie." They kissed for a few more minutes. "I better go, baby." Nattie walked Jase to the door. Her eyes welt up. "It will be okay, honey. I will be here early, okay?"

"You better be. I miss you already." Jase left to go home.

Nattie went up to her room and got ready for bed. She just laid there wide-awake. She felt like sneaking out to see Jase but instead she got up and wrote him a letter. She chose her words carefully and jotted them down in her own intelligible style using her signature twists and cute little fancy curls. She drew in a few scattered hearts around the words.

Jase set his alarm to get up extra early. He laid back on his bed and thought about their wonderful day. He glanced over at the pirate ship trophy Nattie won, sitting on his nightstand. *I'm going to miss her so much, her pretty, blue eyes and that cute dimple smile.* He drifted into a peaceful sleep.

Jase startled awake before his alarm even sounded. He sprung up from his bed and got ready to leave. He almost forgot to bring the little gift he purchased for Nattie a few days ago. He rushed to the Candella's house and knocked on the door. Nattie hardly slept and was already downstairs.

She ran to the door, "Hi, Jassie!"

"Hi, baby. Did you sleep well?"

"No, I didn't sleep at all."

"Awww, sweetie."

"All I could think about was you." They went into the kitchen and ate breakfast together.

"You all set, Nattie?"

"Yes, Mom," Nattie said in a negative tone.

"Someone got up on the wrong side of the bed. Did you sleep at all?"

"No." Jase packed Nattie's suitcases and her big coat into the cruiser while she and her mom had a little talk.

Ms. Candella drove them to the skyport. They found Nattie's gate and sat down to wait for the flight to board. Nattie snuggled up to Jase and laid her head against him. He put his arm around her and rubbed her arm and shoulder. They talked for a little while and made plans to talk on the GIN as soon as she arrived at school.

When the flight started to board, Jase handed Nattie the little gift he purchased for her. She removed the wrapper and opened the box to reveal a sapphire ring with the stones arranged in the shape of a small flower.

"Jassie! It's beautiful!"

"Just like you." Jase slid the ring onto her index finger.

"I love it, Jassie. I really do." Nattie was happy but sad at the same time. She was determined not to cry but she just couldn't help it. Her eyes teared up and her nose started running. "I'm sorry, Jassie. I didn't want to cry." Jase brought a tissue with him to wipe her eyes.

"It's okay, Nattie. You are so sweet and sensitive. Cry all you want."

"Awww, Jassie." Nattie hugged him tight, getting tears on his shirt. They announced the last boarding call for her flight so she kissed him and handed him the letter she wrote. "Jassie, wait until you are alone to read this, okay?"

"Okay, baby."

"At least I don't have to wait two weeks to talk to you this time." Nattie gave her mom a quick hug and ran for the gate. She paused to blow Jase a kiss, and then disappeared down the ramp.

After Ms. Candella dropped Jase off at home, he quickly walked up to his room. He could barely wait to open Nattie's nice-smelling note. He put it to his nose and took a whiff. *I miss you, Nattie,* he thought. He opened the note and looked at Nattie's pretty handwriting. *She writes so cute.*

"Dear Jassie, I had the most wonderful day with you yesterday. I really love our picture kissing on the boat. Sitting here, I miss you already. I can't stop thinking about you. I want to be able to kiss you goodnight every night before I fall asleep and see you smiling at me every morning when I wake up. I give myself to you completely, forever and ever. I want to spend the rest of my life with you. I could never love anyone else as I love you. I miss you, my Jassie, and I love you. I want to be with you so much.

With all my heart, Your Nattie."

Jase wiped his eyes and cleared his throat. *Ugh, over two months till I get to see my Nattie again.* Jase sat down and started to write her a letter but nothing seemed to be good enough. He put his chin in his hands and ran his fingers though his hair.

Nattie's flight landed and she went to pick up her luggage. She saw Endnova talking to someone in a corridor next to the flat escalators. *Hmmm, finally, a chance to get her back.*

She snuck around the corner and hid behind a tree in a planter. She ran over to the wall behind Endnova and walked in a normal inconspicuous manner. She walked right behind Endnova and grabbed her waist, shouting, "BOO!"

Endnova jumped in the air, startled half to death. It took her a second to realize it was Nattie.

"Girl! You trying to give me a heart attack?" Nattie laughed so hard that she couldn't stand and grabbed hold of Endnova to stop from falling.

"I so got you! Finally!"

"You just wait, girl."

"Hey, I'm just getting you back from all the times you got me." Endnova walked with Nattie to get her bags, and then they caught a ride on a shuttle to school.

"I'm so glad you came back, Nattie."

"I'm not," Nattie said as she tightened her lips and tapped her fingernails on the bus railing. "I'm so not ready for this."

"Relax, girl. We're gonna have a lot of fun!"

"Jase gave me the most excellent surprise yesterday."

"What surprise? Tell me."

"He took me on a romantic evening cruise on a sailing ship. We stood on the bow of the ship kissing in the moonlight."

"Oh my, that sounds wonderful! So what did you do after the cruse?"

"He took me home."

"No?"

"Yes. Look at my new ring he got me."

"Girl, that boy must really love you."

"He does and I miss him already." They grabbed their bags and stepped off the bus at their stop. Once they made it into their room, Nattie dropped her bags next to her bed and turned on the GIN as quickly as she could. She waited for the computer system to boot up, snapping her teeth together and tapping her foot on the floor. She sat straight up in the chair as the computer finally finished booting and opened the GIN. The computer displayed — GIN currently unavailable.

"Ugh!" Nattie's shoulders dropped and her head started to ache. She tensely got up, walked over to her bed, and plopped herself down staring up at the ceiling. "I'm so not ready for this again!"

Endnova walked over and knelt down next to her putting her elbows on the bed. "What ya doin'?"

"The stupid GIN is down." Nattie played with a lock of her hair. She wrapped it around her finger and pulled it tight.

"So tell me, have you two done it yet?" Nattie took in a deep heavy breath and let out.

"No."

"Really?"

"He can't take a hint for anything. All during the cruise, he was oblivious. I wanted to tell him but…"

"But what?"

"I couldn't."

"So what did you do?"

"I wrote him a note and gave it to him before I left."

"What did it say?"

"I'm not telling you that." Endnova tickled Nattie while holding her down. Nattie laughed and squirmed. "Stop, stop!" Nattie tried to catch her breath and grabbed Endnova's arms but they both were laughing so hard.

"You know, smarty pants, you can call him on the phone."

"Oh, yeah. Duh!" Nattie reached over and picked up the phone.

Jase sat waiting and waiting for Nattie to connect over the GIN. He read her letter over and over again until he memorized every word. The phone rang and Jase answered.

"Hi, Jassie!"

"Nattie! I thought you were going to turn on the GIN?"

"It's down so I had to call."

"Oh, I was going out of my mind waiting and missing you."

"What did you think about my letter?"

"I love you, Nattie. I want to be with you forever also."

"What did you think about the last part?"

"What do you mean?"

"Jase, the last part of the letter."

"It's wonderful." Nattie pulled on a lock of her hair so hard and took a deep breath. "What's wrong, Nattie?"

"Nothing."

"Something's bothering you."

"I want to be with you, Jase."

"I know, baby. I want to be with you too. I miss you."

"Ugh! Never mind."

"Nattie, what's wrong?" She took another deep breath and paused for a few seconds. "Nattie?"

"I love you, Jassie."

"I love you too." They talked for several hours until Endnova finally dragged Nattie away to eat.

Nattie stressed herself out over the next few days, desiring to be back home. She sat bored in her classes watching the clock and nodding off due to lack of sleep. It took her awhile, but with Endnova's help, she was able to finally get back into her normal routine and time passed more quickly. She and Jase talked as often as they could and counted the days until her return.

One day, as Jase was going through the mail at work, he gasped and stepped back a step. A shiver ran up his spine as he peered at a shocking flyer. The headline read, *Ancient book display presented by Jajaun Halfgrim in Barcastle, Fawneather. An open display of The Legend of the Blackrock Pirates, by U.S. Wells.*

The third book! Jase thought. He looked closely at the dates of the event but it had already started by the time the flyer arrived from overseas; it was to be over in only two days. *I have to see this book.* Jase's palms become clammy. He took off his vest to cool down a bit. He couldn't wait to tell Nattie and gave himself a headache trying to figure out a way to view the book, even if only the inside cover. Not knowing what to do, he fumbled around the bookstore until closing. He couldn't take his mind off the fact that the third book existed.

Jase rushed home as fast as he could after work. He turned on the GIN but Nattie wasn't on yet. He sat fidgeting in his chair until he couldn't stand the wait. He got up and paced back and forth in his room thinking. *Is she ever going to get on?* Being unable to think about anything else, he sat down at the computer and searched the location of Barcastle in Fawneather. *Hmm, that's not far from Voncara Cove*, he thought. Only a couple hundred sects.

Just then, the computer dinged as the video chat became active.

"Hi, my love."

"Hey, beautiful! Guess what?"

"What?"

"I found the third book!"

"Really, you have it?"

"No, but I know where it is."

"Tell me!"

"Some governor named Jajaun Halfgrim in Barcastle, Fawneather has it, and he put it on display for a few days in a book show."

"What's the title?"

"*The Legend of the Blackrock Pirates*."

"Oh, Jassie, that sounds great but how are we going to be able to see it?"

"I don't know. I haven't figured that part out yet. I was thinking maybe I could write Mr. Halfgrim a letter asking if he can send a copy of the first page and the cover so we can look at the markings."

"That's a good idea but I wonder if he would be willing to help us?"

"I don't know but it's worth a try. Anyway, he's not too far from Voncara Cove so maybe we can ask to see the book when we are over there visiting. I should have more than enough to pay for our trip by the time you get out of school, with all the hours I've been working."

"Jassie, I can't wait! Our trip will be so fun and I'm going out of my mind here. I'm so bored!"

"Why are you so bored?"

"I don't know. This semester is so easy. Oh! I found out today that I might be getting up to three scholarship offers!"

"That's great!"

"I know. I totally hid it from Endnova. She has been here for three years and hasn't been offered any. I wish I could give her one of mine."

"How do you know that you'll get them?"

"Well, it's not a done deal yet but all scholarships go through the Dean before they are approved. When he signs off on them, he lets us know. I had a slip in my mailbox this morning."

"What happens if you get all three?"

"I think I can accept up to two of them but there may be conditions, like a time limit. I want one without a time limit."

"You are doing so well there, Nattie. I am proud of you. You are so incredibly smart."

"Yeah right, not as smart as you."

"What do you mean? You're way smarter than I am."

"I'm only smart about technical stuff and science, things I can calculate or figure out. You are the one who knows all the real life stuff." Jase laughed. "I really love you. You are so cute and incredible."

"You think I'm incredible?"

"Of course." Nattie smiled with the biggest grin across her face. "I wish I was there right now. I want to kiss you."

"I can't wait till you get home on break. I miss you so much. It wouldn't be so bad if Alrand were still here. Oh, that reminds me. Alrand and Kimberly are almost finished with basic training. He said he loves it but Kimberly is struggling a little bit."

"Really? She was the one who wanted to join in the first place."

"Yeah, and I figured Alrand would have had a hard time but he said he has lost twenty bounds."

"Wow! Good for him."

"I wonder if they get to see each other much."

"Yeah, he said they have a little time together every day."

"So what do you have planned for us when I get home? And don't you dare tell me I have to wait and see or I'm going to bite you!"

Jase laughed. "Would I say that?"

"YES! Just to drive me crazy!"

"I have a few things planned."

"Tell me."

"Oh! I almost forgot. I found an old history book in the bookstore about a little church in Voncara Cove and guess what I found inside?"

"What?"

"Guess?"

"Jassie! Just tell me!"

"Okay, okay. There is a record of a Lieutenant Anderson marrying Angelica Brody."

"Are you serious?"

"Uh-huh," Jase shook his head yes.

"So the stories in Captain Wells' books must have at least some truth; this confirms it."

"And there's more. I think that Angelica and David had a daughter also named Angelica. There is another record, about eighteen years later, of an Angelica Anderson marrying a sea captain named Bruiser Simate."

"Oh, so she is the great grandmother of the girl who republished the second book."

"I think so." Nattie stuck out her lower lip and frowned. "What's wrong?"

"That means that Tristy really died." Nattie's eyes teared up a little. "It's so sad, Jassie."

"I know, baby, but that also means that there must really be a hidden treasure."

"I can't wait till we can go there."

"I wish we could go right now." Nattie flung her hair back and leaned her head on her hand. She let out a sigh.

"Nattie, it's only a week now. Then you will be home on break."

"Yeah, but then I have to come back again. I'm so tired of looking at you through this stupid computer screen. I want to hold you and be with you. After this, I never want us to be apart again, okay?"

"Okay."

"Promise me."

"I promise, Nattie." They talked until the GIN was disconnected.

The next day Jase wrote a letter to Jajaun Halfgrim using the address on the flyer. He asked for a copy of the cover and the first few pages in hopes that Mr. Halfgrim would grant his request. He smiled from ear to ear as he placed the latter in the mailbox at work. Just the thought of the trip to Voncara Cove with Nattie was exuberating.

With Nattie's school break just around the corner, Jase decided to go shopping for a welcome home gift. He browsed through a few shops but couldn't find anything special. He tried the jewelry store but everything nice was kind of expensive so he decided to wait and look again later. As he walked out, a pair of glimmering butterfly-shaped earrings caught his eye. *Hmm, the cost is a bit much but Nattie would love these and she would look so cute in them*, he thought. *I could definitely drive her crazy with these.*

He asked to look at the earrings but when he looked into the case, he saw a matching ring set that looked fascinating. He knew Nattie would really love the beautiful butterfly pattern.

"Sir, I can give you a great deal on that wedding ring if you're really interested. We have a great sale going on right now," the store clerk said. *What are you doing, Jase*, he whispered to himself. The ring was so intricate with many little colorful stones laid out in a compact, tasteful, arrangement that would look great on Nattie's skinny little finger. The more he thought about it, the more the idea grew on him. He thought, *I guess I can buy both gifts and then I can make up my mind later*. Jase made the purchase and asked that the earrings and the wedding ring be wrapped separately.

He walked back to work but couldn't sit still. He bounced around the bookstore whistling while he worked. He sat down on the steps and stared at the wrapped wedding ring in deep thought. After some time, he glanced at the clock. It was finally time to close. He locked up and headed home to get on the GIN. He sat tapping his pencil on the desk waiting for Nattie to sign on. Her normal connect time came and went but no Nattie. Jase put his elbow on the table to hold up his head because he started feeling sleepy.

"Where is she?" He got up and ran downstairs to get something to drink. When he came back up, the video chat was still silent. He sat back and tapped his foot while lightly stroking his eyebrows. He took a deep breath and leaned his head back in the chair starring at the ceiling. He started biting his lip when the computer finally dinged.

"Hi, Jassie. Sorry I took so long."

"I was getting worried, Nattie."

"I'm sorry, baby."

"What took so long?"

"Well, I was talking to my teachers. We have a big decision to make."

"About what?"

"Let's see if I can explain this right. If I stay during the break, I can meet with the scholarship people now and decide which ones I will accept. If I do this now rather than waiting until the end of the school year, I should be able to take my finals early and come home for good in about a month."

"So does this mean you're not coming next week?"

"That's what we have to decide. Should I come home next week or take the chance I can come home for good in only a month?"

"You don't know for sure if you can come home early though?"

"That's what I was talking to my teachers about. They all have to give me permission to take my finals early."

"What did they say?"

"I was able to talk to all but one and they all said that I could. I will have to wait until I talk with my last teacher to know for sure. What should I do, Jassie?"

Chapter 26

"**W**hat do you want to do?"

"I don't know. I miss you so much but I don't want to come home and have to leave you again. It's too hard."

"I was so looking forward to you coming home. I bought you a gift and everything."

"What did you get me?"

"I'm not telling. It's a surprise."

"Jase! You know I hate that. Why do you tell me if it's a surprise?"

"Because I know you love it." Nattie laughed,

"Not - ah. You just love to torment me."

"Just because I love you so much."

Nattie let out a long whimpering, "Jasssssie." Jase laughed. "So what should I do? You decide," Nattie said.

"I want to see you so badly but I want you home for good too. Just don't do it unless you know for sure you can come home early."

"Okay, so what did you get me?"

"I'm not telling. Guess you will have to wait a month until you get home."

"You brat!" Jase took a deep breath and let it out slowly.

"I can't stand this. I want you here with me. Four more weeks.

Ugh."

"I know, Jassie. I really want to come home. Did you get a response from your letter yet?"

"Not yet, but he probably just received it."

The following day, Nattie got approval from her last teacher to take her finals early, the week following the break. She selected two scholarships and then hit the books studying for finals. Jase made some extra money working longer hours at the bookstore during the break to pass time more quickly while missing Nattie. Since they were on break, they could talk all night long so neither of them got enough sleep. Nattie kept asking if Jase received a response to his letter about the book but he received nothing.

The last night of the break, Nattie opened the GIN right on time.

"Hi, my Jassie. Finals next week and then I can come home soon!"

"I so can't wait."

"And guess what?"

"What?"

"I have a surprise for you."

"You do? What is it?"

"Nope, not telling. You'll just have to wait and see." Jase stuck his tongue out at Nattie and laughed.

"Now who's the brat?"

"Don't like it, do you?" Jase laughed.

"Nattie, you are so cute. You know it doesn't bother me."

"Well, it should. You just wait. You will never guess in a million years what I got for you."

"Is it something I wear?"

"No hints. But you will love me so much when you find out what it is."

"Nattie, I already love very much. Don't think it's even possible for me to love you more than I do now."

"How much do you love me?"

"I would die for you. I couldn't live without you."

"Awww, Jassie, you are so sweet to me." Nattie sat and played with her sapphire ring that Jase gave her. They talked about everything they wanted to do when she got home and about their trip plans. Nattie's head started to bob as she kept jerking herself awake.

"Nattie, we need to sleep. When do you start your finals?"

"Not today; tomorrow." She let out a big yawn.

"Go to bed, sleepyhead."

"No, I'm okay." She pulled her hair back and laid her head on her hands on the desk. She closed her eyes for just a second and fell asleep.

Endnova and Daisha returned from break to find Nattie sitting at the computer sleeping and Jase asleep at his desk in front of the video camera. Endnova shut down the video chat and rubbed Nattie's back.

"Nattie? Wake up, sweetie."

"Hey, Endnova," she stretched and yawned.

"I see you've been talking to Jase all night again."

"I can't wait to go home."

"I'm gonna miss you, girl. I guess you're not coming back next year since you have a scholarship now."

"So do you."

"What?" Endnova got very serious.

"What are you talking about?"

"I'm giving you one of mine."

"That's not possible."

"Yes, it is. Since the scholarship guys were here, I asked one if I can give the scholarship to a friend since I can't use it."

"What did he say?"

"He said he would have to take a look at your coursework and if you qualify, it's yours."

"Wonder how long that will take?"

"Well, I looked in your mailbox and it's in there."

"Really! I love you, Nattie! I'm going to get my mail." Endnova took off running through the obstacle course of students to get to the mailboxes. She was in denial but hoping that there really was a scholarship waiting in her box. She took out a scholarship folder and screamed. She jumped up and down frantically shaking her paperwork in her hand. She ran back smiling and bouncing into the room, and gave Nattie a tight hug and a kiss on her cheek.

"I don't know how you pulled this off but thank you so much!"

"You're very welcome. If I waited until the end of the semester, he said he wouldn't have been able to do it."

"You are the sweetest person in the whole wide world, Nattellie Candella."

The whole next week Nattie spent studying and taking her final exams. She aced all but her composition final, which required a four-thousand-word literature paper on one of ten preselected subjects. Nattie decided to go with the nautical theme because she could get ideas from Jase. The next two days she concentrated on nothing else but finishing that paper. She and Jase spent as much time as allowed over the GIN exchanging ideas as she entered the storyline. Of course, Jase convinced her to write all about the pirates of Voncara Cove. Nattie could hardly keep up with Jase as he brilliantly rattled off colorful events about ancient battleships, dueling it out on rugged seas. Nattie added her own personal touch about a young sailor falling in love with a beautiful island girl who desired adventure and thirsted for knowledge of the lands beyond her shores. The character's features were based on her own personal attributes.

She turned in her final paper and began to pack up her things for the flight home. Daisha inconspicuously walked out of the dorm room while Endnova snuck up behind Nattie. She grabbed her waist, tickling her with a loud shout. Nattie jumped and fell forward onto her bed.

"GIRL!" Endnova laughed and took off running out of the room and down the hall with Nattie charging right behind.

"You are so going to get it!"

As soon as they ran into the dorm common area, a group of students shouted, "Surprise!"

About half the girls in the dorm showed up for a party in Nattie's honor. She turned all red with a big smile.

"I knew I would never get you away for a celebration, so I brought the party to you," Endnova said.

"You are so bad!"

"You didn't think I would let go without a proper goodbye, did ya?"

"I'm going to miss you, Endnova. You need to come visit me in Summerset some time. I don't think I could have made it without you."

"Who's got the present?" Endnova shouted. Daisha carried over a thin, wide, gift-wrapped box.

"Guys, you didn't have to do this."

"We wanted to. Everyone chipped in a little," Daisha said.

"You gonna open it, or what?" Endnova said. Nattie ripped off the wrapping and opened the box.

"NICE!" She held up a new stylish leather school jacket. "This is very nice. Thank you so much, everyone!"

"See my little upgrade?"

"Oh, that's cute, Endnova. Did you sew this on yourself?"

"Yep." The cute butterfly patch was sewed onto the right sleeve. "I know how much you love butterflies."

"You guys are too much. I am going to miss all of you." After the party, Nattie finished packing up her things and prepared for the flight home early the next morning. She couldn't sleep at all with her mind racing with so many thoughts.

. . .

Jase arrived at work early in the afternoon. "Hello, Mr. Alaxrandus."

"Hi, Jase, you're early."

"Well, I wanted to talk to you about tomorrow. Would it be possible for me to take off so I can meet Nattie at the skyport when her flight arrives?"

"Sure, Jase. I don't mind if you take off."

"Thanks, Mr. Alaxrandus."

"How's the search for the third book coming?"

"Oh, I forgot to tell you. I found it."

"What! You did?" Mr. Alaxrandus questioned with great interest.

"Yes, sir." Jase showed him the flyer for the book exhibit.

"This is amazing, Jase! I wish you had told me about this sooner. I would have liked to go see this."

"Sorry, I was so excited that I didn't even think about it."

"How do you plan on getting there?"

"I wrote a letter to Mr. Halfgrim but haven't received a reply."

"I have heard of him. He is a very wealthy and influential monarch in Barcastle. He supposedly owns a phenomenal book collection. I would love to get my hands on his library. I doubt you will ever receive a reply."

Jase didn't let this news dampen his spirits. He whistled while sweeping up the main entrance and reading areas. The bookstore had very little activity so Jase sat and leaned in a chair with his head tilted all the way back and closed his eyes. Time seemed to have completely stopped. Jase's stomach growled and grumbled loudly. He realized he hadn't eaten anything all day. He took a little break and walked to Skaters to grab a bite to eat.

After he finished eating, he slowly walked back to the bookstore. His shoulders hung low and he looked at the ground while he walked, thinking about Nattie. He took a deep breath to relieve his tension. *Doesn't seem like she will ever get here. So close yet so far away.* He opened the door to the bookstore and headed back toward the checkout counter.

He looked up and stopped dead in his tracks. He held his hand against his heart, and tried to catch his breath. He couldn't believe his eyes! There sat Nattie on the counter with a big smile on her face, swinging her feet back and forth. She wore a cute black and white horizontal stripped shirt. Her long curly hair bounced as her feet swung fore and aft.

Jase felt as if he had a knot in his throat and stood like a statue. Nattie squealed and jumped down off the counter and ran to Jase, bouncing on her tippy toes as she ran. She jumped up and Jase caught her midair. Nattie giggled and kissed him. Jase looked into her sparkling eyes.

"How? When?"

Nattie giggled, "What? What? What? I flew home early this morning. I wanted to surprise you."

"I can't believe how beautiful you look."

"You look yummy," Nattie giggled. Jase took a deep breath, taking in Nattie's perfume.

"Whew, you smell so good too."

"I love you, Jassie. We are never going to be apart again. Ever!"

"I still can't believe you're here. I missed you so bad."

"Awww, baby. You looked so sad when you walked into the store. I love the look on your face when you saw me."

"I think I almost had a heart attack." Nattie laughed and kissed him.

"Guess I got you good."

"I love you, brat!" Jase kissed her.

"Just wait until you get off work. I have a wonderful surprise for you."

"What is it?"

"Nope, have to wait and see."

"So where's my present, Jassie?"

"It's at home, silly." Jase kissed Nattie's cute cheeks and they walked over to the checkout counter. Jase leaned back and held Nattie close. She leaned her head against Jase's cheek and he gently rubbed her back. She felt so hot and her face turned a bit red.

"Jassie, when I'm with you, I don't care about anything else, as long as I can be with you. I love you so, so, much."

"I love you more than anything, Nattie. It was like my whole life was put on hold while you were away and I was waiting for you to get home so my life can begin again."

"Never again! I promise you." Jase motioned Nattie to sit down and pulled a chair up next to her.

"Jassie, do you have *Three Tall Ships* with you?"

"Yes, in my backpack."

"Since there are no customers in the store, can you read to me?"

"Okay, let me find where we left off." Nattie put her arm around Jase and her head against his shoulder so she could follow along.

"I love it so much when you read to me, especially when you get excited. Your voice is so calming, it relaxes me." Nattie played with the back of Jase's hair as he began to read.

David took a ship's boat and returned to his quarters ashore. It took him forever to fall asleep and he had not slept for long when something woke him. A bad dream about Tristy. He was unable to save her no matter how hard he tried. He got up all hot and sweaty, and walked down to the cove wall. The night sky was very clear with crisp cool air and the moon was high, reflecting off the waves as they crashed on the beach.

David was conflicted about his feelings for Angelica and mourning Tristy. He looked at the heart he carved for her on a stone in the wall. He looked up at the sky and thought about the future until he was finally at peace.

Maybe it's okay for me to love Angelica? Not knowing what to do, he climbed into a rowboat and headed out to Angelica's ship anchored in the cove. He quietly tied off the boat and climbed aboard. The guards were sleeping and didn't notice his presence. Quietly, he snuck into the captain's quarters. The rusty door hinges squeaked something awful but he continued anyway. He lit a candle and walked over to Angelica's bed. He tapped her on the shoulder and she awoke with a gasp. She sat up seeing David's face illuminated by the candlelight.

She whispered softly, "David, you scared me."

"I'm sorry. I had to come see you."

"It couldn't wait till morning?"

"No, I was afraid I wouldn't have the courage to say what I need to say in the morning."

"What's so important?"

"Not here. Will you come with me?"

"You know I will but don't try and convince me to stay behind during the battle."

"Okay, I won't."

"Wait, how did you get in here past the guards?"

"They are sleeping on duty."

"What? I'm gonna run um through, those scallywags!" Angelica put her frock coat on over her gown and slipped on her boots. She stomped out onto the deck and kicked the first of the two guards with all her might.

"Captain!" He cried with his arm up to protect

himself. Angelica drew her sword, ready to plunge it into his heart, but peered at the look on David's face. She belayed her sword and called for the quartermaster.

"Restrain these two and set a new watch. I will deal with these later."

Angelica followed David ashore and up the very steep incline to lookout point, the highest perch overlooking the cove. The steep climb took about thirty-five minutes to traverse.

"David, this is so beautiful. You can see the cove and the whole town from up here." The moon was so bright that it almost seemed as daylight. The ships anchored in the cove cast shadows like floating blankets on the water. David looked at Angelica; her face glowed in the moonlight. It was like staring into Tristy's eyes.

"Angelica, please sit with me." She sat down next to David on a large flat rock and leaned her head against his. "Angelica, I don't know what will happen tomorrow and I know I haven't been giving you the response that..."

Angelica held her finger to David's lips to silence him and leaned over to give him a long tender kiss.

"David, I know you have been holding back because of Tristy and it's okay."

"Angelica, I'm very much in love with you and there's something I wanted..."

"David! Look! Sails over the horizon!"

"Oh no! Hurry, we need to sound the alarm." They scurried down the huge hillside as quickly as possible.

"Angelica, I'm going to wake Captain Wells and rouse the men."

"I'm going to wake my father and return to my ship."

"Okay, good."

David ran into Captain Wells' chamber and shook him awake.

"Sir! Sail's on the horizon! Multiple ships approaching from the east."

"Can you identify them?"

"No, sir. They are still too far out."

"How could they know?"

"Sir?"

"I am afraid we may still have a spy among us."

"So, they may have learned of our attack plans which means they may know about the Gatlin gun."

"Quickly now, Lieutenant. Alert the ships and our ground forces. Prepare the long guns for battle."

"The ships are being alerted as we speak. Permission to take the Gatlin gun aboard Angelica's ship?"

"Granted. Make haste. Let's be ready for them. My guess is they will attack at dawn. Douse the lights on the ships and keep the men quiet and hidden. Let's not alert them just yet. Let them think we are unaware of their advance. Once they draw into the range of our long guns, make sail and attack. Try to get in close and use the Gatlin gun."

"Yes, sir!"

David roused the men to the long guns and set a watch on the overlook above the cove to signal when the ships drew close. He gathered four men to help load the Gatlin gun onto a longboat and rowed out to Angelica's ship.

"Angelica!"

"Yes?"

"Have the men quietly rig a tackle to hoist the Gatlin gun onto the ship. Give word to all crewmembers to stay out of sight as best as possible and douse all visible light."

"David, we make ready for sail."

"Not yet. We mean to surprise them. Wait until they sail into the range of the long guns, then we will attack." David climbed aboard the ship and directed the placement of the gun. The cannons were loaded and the crew hid waiting. Their heart rates elevated, anticipating the inevitable battle. Only the sound of the waves crashing upon the rocks of the cove could be heard as every man silently kneeled on the deck.

Chapter 27

The unidentified vessels halted their advance until the night sky was transformed by rays of the sun illuminating the clouds with shades of pink and red. A strong breeze cut across the cove from the northwest. Seagulls soared along the cliffs through the crisp morning air. The signal was given high up on the lookout. The ships were on the move.

"All crews, ready yourselves. Pass the word," said Lieutenant Anderson.

Angelica stood by his side as David gazed into the mist, awaiting what inevitably would follow. Anderson's hair stood up on the back of his neck as a strange feeling shivered down his body. He turned to Angelica and took her hands.

He looked into her eyes, "Angelica, will you marry me?" Angelica smiled at David,

"I thought you'd never ask. Will you feel this way once the battle is over?"

"I have felt this way for some time now."

"Then yes, I will be your wife."

BOOM! BOOM! BOOM!

Cannon fire rained forth from the long guns, signifying the approaching ships were hostile.

"Weigh anchor. Drop the sails. Hard to starboard," Anderson shouted.

As the ships drew near, their colors became plainly visible. Blockrock Pirates!

"Men, fire as she bears!"

"Six ships, they mean to wipe us out, sir."

"Four against six, not the best odds," Angelica said.

"Yes, but we have the shore batteries and the Gatlin gun."

"Signal all ships to draw the enemy as close to shore as possible." The battle became fierce.

"Down! Everyone down!" Angelica's ship received a full broadside from a thirty-two gun frigate. They passed at the mid-section, Anderson fired the Gatlin gun as fast as he could turn the handle, showering their deck with led balls and killing their captain.

"Throw the grappling hooks; board her, men!" Anderson's men fought their way onto the pirate vessel with little resistance.

Taking her for the captain, a pirate fired a shot striking Angelica hard in the chest, throwing her backwards. She let out a strange sounding scream as she fell.

"Angelica!" David rushed to her side and kneeled down next to her. "Oh no, don't you dare die on me!"

"David, help me, I can't breathe," Angelica gasped with all her strength. Anderson pulled a candy bar

from his coat pocket and ripped off the wrapper. He placed the wrapper over the gurgling wound in her chest and then applied a layer of cloth. He tied the dressing tight using hemp rope strands.

"Does that help any?"

"It hurts, David, but I can breathe better. I love you David."

"No, don't you say goodbye. You hang in there. I'm taking the ship ashore."

"David, you can't."

Jase closed the book and kissed Nattie on the forehead.

"Jassie, she can't die. You said they get married."

"That's what the church record book said."

"Where could he have possibly gotten a candy bar? They didn't have candy bars with wrappers back then."

"I know, just like the RFI gun and the Gatlin gun."

"Yeah, something strange is definitely going on but I don't want Angelica to die."

"Come on, baby. It's time to close up."

"Goodie! I can't wait to get to your house to give you your present."

"How big is it?" Nattie just giggled.

After closing up the bookstore, Jase drove Nattie back to his house. They walked into the kitchen.

"Hi, Mrs. Thunderbelt."

"Nattie? When did you get home?"

"Just a bit ago." She gave Nattie a hug. "I'm so glad you're home. It's nice to see Jase smiling again."

"My poor Jassie."

Nattie hugged him so tight he let out an, "Ugh." He put his arms around her little waist and leaned his head against hers.

"This feels so good. I have so missed you," Nattie said.

"Oh, come upstairs. I have your present."

"Wait, I want to give you yours first." Nattie handed Jase a large envelope.

"What's this?"

"Open it. It's an early birthday present." Nattie bounced and giggled with a huge smile on her face waiting for Jase's reaction. Jase opened the envelope and gasped. His eyes opened wide and his blood rushed to his head, turning his face red.

"No way! Nattie!" Jase bounced along with Nattie, "How did you do this?"

"Jase, what is it?"

"Mom, it's two tickets to Barcastle in Fawneather." Jase looked at Nattie with huge eyes opened wide, "How did you do this?"

"I wrote Mr. Halfgrim and told him we have the first book and would like to see his. Shortly after, I received an overnight package with an invitation for us to visit him at his castle and the envelope with the tickets. His only request was for us to bring your book along so he can take a look."

"Nattie, that's so clever," Jase's mom said. "When do you leave?"

Jase looked at the tickets, "This says, um, wow, in three days!"

"Jassie, since you don't have to pay for the trip, maybe we can get train tickets from Barcastle to Voncara Cove?"

"Definitely!" Jase jumped up and down and gave Nattie a kiss. "This is going to be so great."

"Jase, what about school and work?"

"Mom, I'm sure Mr. Alaxrandus will let me take off for this and I can make up what little schoolwork I will miss."

"I guess so. As long as your father has no objection, I guess you can go."

Jase took Nattie by the hand and they walked up to his room. "I still can't believe you're standing here."

"I know. I loved the look on your face when you walked into the bookstore. I felt like I could just explode waiting for you." Jase took

Nattie into his arms and they shared a long kiss. "Hey, where's my present?" Nattie stuck her lower lip out pretending to pout, so Jase kissed it.

"It's right here, baby." Jase handed Nattie the little gift box. It took her about two seconds to rip off the wrapping and open the box.

"Awww, Jassie, they're beautiful. I love my butterflies. Put them on me?"

Jase tenderly inserted her new earrings and kissed each ear. "You are so pretty, Nattie."

"Thank you, handsome."

"Jase, Nattie, come down for dinner," Jase's mom shouted from downstairs.

"Okay."

They headed downstairs to eat. Nattie chattered away all during dinner, talking about school, Daisha, and Endnova.

"You're not saying much, Jassie?"

"I'm just listening to you and thinking about our trip."

"Oh, I know. It's so exciting, isn't it?"

"I expect you both to behave yourselves and be careful," Jase's dad said.

"Don't worry; we will," Nattie said.

After dinner, Jase and Nattie worked out their travel plans and searched the GIN to find the locations of everything they wanted to see. Jase tickled Nattie. She jumped from the chair and ran to the bed, but Jase caught her and tickled her until she couldn't stand it.

"Let me breathe," She giggled. She climbed on Jase's back and pinned him against the bed. "Now what ya gonna do?"

"I'm gonna lay here with a monkey on my back." They both laughed.

"You're a silly boy and I love you so much."

"I love you, beautiful." They sat and talked for a while, and then Nattie pushed Jase back and leaned over him to kiss. Her long black silky hair surrounded his face. She giggled and pulled the hair away from his mouth.

Jase's mom yelled up the stairs, "Jase, time to take Nattie home."

"Jassie, I don't want to go home yet. It feels like I just got here."

"You did just get here. Funny how work drags on forever when I'm waiting to talk to you. Now that you're here, it feels like a blink of an eye."

"Jase, you hear me?" Jase got up and walked to the top of the staircase.

"Mom, she just got home. Can't she stay for a little while?"

"Jase, you have school tomorrow."

"Oh yeah. I totally forgot." Nattie laughed at Jase,

"Silly boy." Jase tried to help Nattie get up but she pulled him down to the bed and pinned his hands above his head.

"Am I squishing you?"

Jase laughed, "Not really. Feather weight." She kissed him until his mom called upstairs again. Jase took a deep breath, freed his hands, and tickled Nattie. She jumped off the bed to get away but Jase caught her. "We're coming, Mom!" After a long tender kiss, they headed downstairs.

"Goodbye, Mrs. Thunderbelt."

"Good night, Nattie. I'm glad you're finally back home."

Jase walked Nattie to the cruiser but she stopped,

"Jassie, let's just walk."

"You sure? It's a little cold out."

"Guess you'll just have to hold me to keep me warm." Jase smiled and took Nattie by the waist as he slowly walked her home, stopping occasionally for a kiss. A big full moon rose up from over the trees.

"Nattie, look at that moon. It's almost like daylight out here."

"Just like in the book."

"Can you believe we get to leave on our trip the day after

tomorrow? We can explore everything."

"I so can't wait. It will be so nice to be alone with you without anyone telling us it's time to go home." They arrived at Nattie's house and sat on the swing. Jase pulled her curly hair out of her face so they could kiss. "I so miss this."

Nattie put her arms around Jase's neck and passionately kissed him. The porch light came on and Nattie's mom walked outside, "Nattie, it's time to come in."

"Ugh! Geez, I am so ready for our trip! Okay, Mom. Can't we please have a second?"

"Just a second; then you need to come in." Her mom walked inside.

"I can't believe she makes me fly away to school all by myself for all that time. Then when I finally get home, I can't spend a few minutes with my boyfriend. Shesh!" Nattie flung her hair back and pulled Jase's head back by his hair to kiss him.

"Nattie, be careful. I don't want your mom to try to stop us from going on our trip." Nattie breathed in deeply and let out a shrugging long sigh.

She sat straight up. "Okay, you're right." She paused for a second. "Why don't we sneak out later?"

"I don't know, Nattie. If they catch us, there's no way they will let us go on our trip." Nattie got up and stomped into the house. Jase slowly walked from the swing toward the door with a puzzled look on his face. Nattie opened the screen door, leaned over, and kissed him.

"Turn on the GIN, okay?"

"Okay, Nattie."

"Good night, my love."

"Night, baby. Love you."

"I love you more."

"Doubtful." Nattie giggled and leaned over for one last kiss before closing the door.

When Jase returned home, he turned on the GIN. He and Nattie talked for hours. "Jassie, it seems silly to be stuck chatting again when you're so close."

"Yeah, all those nights anguishing because I couldn't hold you. Now you're home and we are still on the GIN. Maybe we should sneak out."

Nattie giggled, "Now you decide to sneak out. Now that I'm all sleepy and my hair is a mess."

"Ole, your hair is beautiful, like always."

"I'm getting really sleepy, Jase."

"I'm wide awake."

Nattie yawned, covering her mouth with her fingers. "You got up early, baby. You are probably really tired."

"I am. I can't say awake."

"Go to bed."

"No, you first." Nattie laid her head down on her desk and yawned again.

"Go to bed, Nattie. I'm disconnecting."

"Okay, love you."

"Night. Love you, baby."

In the morning when Jase's alarm went off, he was still very tired and dragging. His first class seemed so long. The classroom was warm and he kept bobbing his head as he fell asleep and jerked himself back awake. He kept looking at the clock and wished he had called Nattie before school but he decided to let her sleep. The bell rang and the students exited the classroom. Jase was the last one to get up to leave. He crept into the hallway and looked up to see Nattie running toward him.

"Jassie!" She jumped on him, knocking down his backpack and kissed him.

"What you doing here?"

"I missed you too much."

"I was going to call you but I wanted to make sure you had enough sleep."

"After we got off the GIN, I couldn't sleep at all."

"You didn't get any sleep again?"

"Not really. I couldn't stop thinking about you." Jase picked up his backpack and he walked arm in arm with Nattie to his next class.

"With your work study, how many more classes do you have today?"

"Three more. Are you staying here?"

"No, Mom is waiting for me. She wants me to go shopping with her. I will meet you at the bookstore later." Jase took Nattie by the waist and kissed her.

"I can't wait to get out of school today."

"Yeah, tonight we have to pack up for our trip." Nattie bounced and giggled.

"I can't wait! Bye, Jassie."

"Bye, beautiful." Jase briskly walked into his classroom and sat down. The next few hours were excruciating. He tapped his foot and shook his leg to stay awake. In his last class, he sat in the very back row and stood up so he wouldn't fall asleep again. He watched the second hand on the wall clock, oblivious to everything the teacher was saying. He got ready and darted out of the door the second the bell rang.

He swiftly maneuvered through the crowd of students to get outside. "Free at last!" He drove to the bookstore and opened the door. He walked toward the checkout counter but no Nattie. Another hour passed and still no Nattie. Jase frowned and felt a pain welling up deep inside. He tried to call her but there was no answer. He decided to go ahead and purchase the train tickets from Barcastle to Voncara Cove on the GIN. The weather report at the train station showed the temperature at twenty-two degrees.

Just as he finalized the purchase, Nattie skipped in the door with a big smile. Jase was so relieved. "Hi, Jassie!"

"I was worried about you. I figured you would be here waiting for me."

"Sorry, baby. Mom and I were shopping then I stopped off to get us something to eat. You hungry?"

"Starving." Jase gave Nattie a hug and they sat down to eat at one of the tables in the parlor. "Nattie, make sure you pack warm clothes and bring your heavy coat."

"Is it really that cold there?"

"Well, it's below freezing."

"Guess I'm going to freeze my butterflies off then," Nattie giggled.

"You are so silly, girl."

"I don't know why I said that." Nattie kept giggling. That got Jase laughing.

"What are you laughing about now?"

"I don't know. I'm just so happy." Nattie got up and massaged Jase's shoulders and kissed him on the neck. "I have something for you, Jase."

"Another present?"

"I think you will like this one better than the trip tickets."

"Really?" Nattie sat back down and winked at Jase,

"Really, and don't ask because you will find out soon enough."

"Find out about what?"

Nattie giggled louder. "I just said don't ask."

"I have ways of making you talk."

"Don't you dare!" Jase put his hands on the chair rails to stand up and Nattie took off running down the stairs. Jase caught her as they rounded one of the rows of bookshelves and tickled her. Nattie grabbed his hands and shoved him back into a bookcase, knocking off some books on the other side and kissed him. Mr. Alaxrandus entered the bookstore so they pretended to be dusting off the books. Nattie started whistling but couldn't stop giggling.

"What are you two up to today?"

"Hi, Mr. Alaxrandus. I have some great news."

"Yes?"

"Mr. Halfgrim purchased tickets for both Nattie and me to come visit his castle."

"Wow! That is amazing news. I wonder why he did that."

"Nattie told him we have the first book and that we would like to see his."

"Jase, be careful. I'm sure he wants to see your book for the same reason you want to see his, except he has a lot more resources available to him. I'm not sure that's the best move."

"What other choice do we have? We can't see his book unless we let him see ours. We are really looking forward to the trip."

"All I can say is be careful. I'm sure he has his own agenda."

Chapter 28

"We are supposed to leave tomorrow morning. Sorry for the short notice but I just found out last night."

"Trust me, I understand. I'll work something out."

"Thank you, Mr. Alaxrandus." Once Mr. Alaxrandus walked up to his office, Nattie bent over laughing, holding her stomach. "You hurt my head on that bookshelf."

"That's what you get for trying to tickle me. Let me kiss it better." Nattie kissed Jase on the lips. Jase smiled and she ended up kissing teeth.

"That's not where it hurts, silly."

"I know but I like this better." Nattie giggled and tried to tickle Jase.

"It's just not fair. You should be ticklish too."

Nattie followed Jase around the bookstore for the rest of the afternoon, helping him arrange books and straighten up.

"Jassie, should I eat something before we leave or do you want to eat at the skyport or something?"

"I want to eat with you. I don't care where."

"Okay, I'll wait to eat." Nattie hugged Jase tight. "I can't wait until tomorrow." She rubbed Jase's arm as he dusted off a row of books. "Jassie, can you scratch my back? It itches." Jase scratched her back as she wiggled around moving her shoulders to help him get the itch.

"Hold still."

"But it keeps moving," giggled Nattie. Her back felt so soft to Jase's touch. He put his arms around her, she leaned her head back so Jase could kiss the side of her cheek.

"It's almost time to close."

"What do you need me to do?"

"You can sweep up if you want while I count out the register."

"Okay. Jase, can you read to me tonight? I want to know what happens to Angelica. I hope she makes it."

"If we have time. We need to get ready for the trip." They finished up at the store and headed home to Jase's house.

Jase's mother already had dinner cooking. "Hi, Mrs. Thunderbelt, what smells so yummy?" Nattie giggled.

"Hi, Nattie. It's just a little stew." Nattie took a deep breath.

"Umm, it smells so good."

"Nattie, I talked to your mom. Since we're getting up so early, you're going to stay here tonight." Nattie smiled and bounced on her toes.

"Okay!"

"I figured that would make you two happy. Jase, Nattie will sleep in your room and you can sleep on the couch. Why don't you take Nattie home to get her things while I finish up dinner?"

"Okay, Mom."

Jase took Nattie by the waist and walked her to the cruiser. He opened the door and let her get in. "Thank you, handsome."

"You're welcome, hottie."

"I'm actually cold." Jase laughed as he got in. He drove to Nattie's house.

"Jase, I don't know what to pack. How long do you think we will be gone?"

"I was thinking about that. With the open-ended tickets, we could stay for a while. What do you think, maybe two weeks?"

"Hmm, let's see. Two weeks alone, traveling with my boyfriend. That would be fantastic."

"I do think we should try to travel light since our plans are kind of up in the air. I'm just going to take my backpack."

"But Jassie, I don't have a big enough backpack for all that."

"Want to go shopping for one in town?"

"Yes," Nattie said as she smiled and put her hand over her mouth to yawn.

"You getting sleepy too, baby?"

"A little." They let her mom know that they were going to the store to get a backpack.

Jase drove to a camping store. Nattie hugged him as they walked inside. She wrapped her arm around Jase's and they took their time wandering in and out of the various aisles of camping gear. Jase found a neat-looking survival knife with a built-in compass and a waterproof match compartment.

"Nattie, I really like this. Look at the design on the leather sheath and the blade."

"You should get it."

"It's a bit expensive."

"You always spend a lot on me but never yourself. I think you should get it."

"Okay, let's go find you a backpack." Nattie looked through the backpacks and strapped on a pink camouflage model with white clusters.

"Really?"

"What?"

"That's definitely not you."

"Why not? I like pink."

Jase laughed, "Go look in that mirror over there."

"You're right; doesn't look that good." Jase picked out a red and black quality backpack with lots of external pockets and international compartments.

"Nattie, what about this one?"

She strapped it on, "How do I look?"

"Very cute."

"Okay, then I want this one." Jase helped her off with the backpack. He looked at the price, rather expensive, but he said not a word and took Nattie's hand to go check out.

When they arrived back at Nattie's house, they headed straight up to Nattie's room to pack. Jase laid across the foot of the bed and propped up his head on a throw pillow. Nattie explored the pockets and compartments in her new backpack so she could figure out where everything should go.

"Jassie, I love this backpack."

"I knew you would. Lots of places in there to store your bricks."

Nattie jokingly gasped and smacked Jase. "I don't put bricks in there!"

"Please, I felt your little purse. I know you put bricks in there."

Nattie giggled, "I do not. Hush before I bite you."

Jase laid back and played with the lace fringe on Nattie's pillow while she laid out everything she planned on packing on the bed.

"Nattie, remember, we're packing light."

"Well, I can't pack too light if we are going to be away for two weeks." Jase opened up his new survival knife and fiddled with the compass.

"Hey, Nattie, look. It has a little flashlight built into the compass."

"Oh, that's neat."

"You can shine it on the compass or like a small flashlight."

"Okay, I think this is everything."

Jase laughed, "You're never going to get all that into your backpack." Nattie stuck her tongue out at Jase.

"Watch me." She tightly rolled all of her clothes and pajamas except for her shirts and a skirt, fitting them neatly into the compartments of her backpack. She saved one large compartment for her shirts and skirt, and put her bath and hair care items in the various external pockets. "Told you. Ha ha."

Nattie leaned over Jase and laid her head on his back. "I can't believe you got it all to fit."

"Oh, one last thing." Nattie put her little science project from school in the remaining external pocket.

"Why are you taking that?"

"Why not? I have room. I may want to play with it if I get bored."

"I don't think we will have a boring moment the whole trip."

"You promise?"

"Are you two about ready?" asked Ms. Candella.

"Yes, Mom."

"Good, Mrs. Thunderbelt has your dinner ready." Nattie gave her mom a hug goodbye. "You two be safe. Take care of my little girl, Jase. She's all I have."

"I will. I promise."

"Bye, Mom. I love you."

"Bye, Nattie. Have fun. Behave."

"No promises," Nattie said.

Jase laughed, "You're so ornery."

Nattie gasped and punched Jase lightly on the arm, "Am not!"

"You just wait till I put your pack of bricks down."

"Promises, promises," Nattie giggled.

They drove back to Jase's house and ate dinner with Jase's parents at the dining room table.

"This is really yummy."

"Thank you, Nattie. At least someone appreciates my cooking."

"Thanks, Mom, it is very good."

"You're welcome."

Mr. Thunderbelt spoke up as well. "Jase, you be careful on your trip. You and Nattie take care of each other and be safe. Let us know where you are before you travel."

"Okay, Dad." Nattie giggled. She tried to stop but couldn't. She tried holding her nose but then Jase looked at her silly and she couldn't help but to snort, sending her into laughter. Now she had everyone laughing.

"Nattie, what's so funny?" Jase's mother asked.

"Nothing," Nattie giggled, "I was just thinking."

"About what?" Jase asked.

"Mr. Thunderbelt, if Jase is bad should I tell on him?"

Everyone laughed, "Absolutely, you keep him in line."

Nattie turned bright red from laughing so hard. "Jase, you better do everything I say or I will tell on you!"

"Nattie, you're precious," Jase's mother said.

"Come on, Nattie, I need to finish packing up my things."

"Remember, you promised to read to me."

The two of them walked up to Jase's room and he finished packing. "Here, Jase, don't forget your new knife."

"Thanks, sweetie." They shared a kiss then gathered up their things into one spot by the front door so they could load up the cruiser in the morning. "I'm cold, Jase. Warm me up."

They walked back upstairs and Jase picked up the book to read to Nattie.

"Here, Jassie." She arranged some pillows at the head of the bed so they could sit up comfortably. Nattie snuggled up close to Jase and positioned herself so she could read along. She pulled up a throw blanket to warm up a bit.

"I love this, Jassie."

Jase gave her a little kiss. "I love you, baby." He found the place where they left off and read aloud in his dramatic voice.

"No, don't you say goodbye. You hang in there, I'm taking the ship ashore."

"David, you can't. The men need you. If we lose this battle, it won't matter if I live or die. You have to stay in command."

David's head hung low as he kneeled beside Angelica. He took her hand and kissed it; she felt so soft. His lips tightened. He jumped to his feet and kicked a wooden bucket across the deck. He banged his fist against the port railing.

BOOM! BOOM! BOOM! CRASH!

One of the pirate vessels got turned around in the cove and was hammered by the shore batteries until it was caught in the surf and thrown upon the rocks. The quartermaster ran up on deck, "Sir! We're sinking! The men cannot keep up with the inrush of water from the damaged hull."

"How long do we have?"

"Not long, sir. Maybe twenty minutes at most."

David could hear shouting in the distance. Captain Brody's ship was being attacked from both sides. Anderson took a step back and smiled with a big grin on his face. He took off his coat, stood up tall, and rolled up his sleeves.

"Sir, what are your orders?"

"Tell the men to abandon ship. Quickly move everything you can to the pirate vessel. Place the Gatlin gun on the quarterdeck."

David carried Angelica to the pirate ship captain's quarters and laid her on the bed.

"Hold on, Angelica, I will have you ashore momentarily."

"How, David?"

"This is going to be great!" He assigned men to care for her wound then walked out on deck,

"Quartermaster, take command of the ship."

"Sir, where are you going?"

"Give me two brave men. Have them set barrels of gunpowder on the bow of the ship with a short fuse. Cut away the grappling lines and set her loose."

Lieutenant Anderson jumped across to Angelica's sinking ship and set a course for Captain Brody's vessel. He maneuvered the ship against the wind until achieving the best angle to gain as much speed as possible. The ship started to list to one side. The ship still glided along nicely as the bow of the ship rode up the swells and crashed back down again with a thud.

Anderson held on to the helm tightly with the wind bucking against the sails. By the time the enemy noticed Anderson's advance, it was too late. There was no way for them to avoid the collision with the damaged ship. As he drew near, he motioned the men to light the fuse and jump off the ship. He waited until the very last second before abandoning the helm. He ran toward the railing jumping... Whoosh!

A brilliant fierce blanket of fire had burst forth with intense sound and pressure, completely splintering the enemy ship as if a thousand cannons fired at once. Anderson was caught in the blast and thrown violently from the ship into the sea. All the men on the nearby ships were startled and ducked *down out of instinct. They could feel the intense heat wave from the explosion and felt the pressure deep in their chests.*

Angelica cried out,

"David? Where is my David? What's happening?" Angelica tried to sit up.

"Captain, please rest. I will go find Lieutenant Anderson for you." The men gazed out at the sea but no sign of Anderson. The quartermaster guided the ship closer to the second vessel that was attacking Captain Brody's ship. He gave the order to open fire using the Gatlin gun but they quickly turned and fled.

Captain Wells' ship was heavily engaged in battle with the remaining two pirate vassals. He was able to avoid multiple attempts at boarding but his ship had taken quite a beating. Captain Brody ordered both ships to make sail to assist. When they drew near, the remaining pirate ships fled.

Captain Wells gave the order to stand down and launch boats to search for survivors. Captain Angelica's crew quickly made for the shore to get her medical care but her condition had already deteriorated.

Jase could hear Nattie sniffling and she tried to hide her face.

"You okay, Nattie?"

"No."

"What's wrong, sweetie?"

"I don't know."

Jase rubbed her arm, "They will be okay. Remember, they get married."

"I know." He reached for some tissues and handed a few to Nattie. She wiped her eyes and yawned. Jase set the book aside, laid back a bit, and let Nattie lay her head on his chest. She put her arm around him, took a deep breath, and closed her eyes. A few minutes later, she fell asleep. Jase, feeling very warm and content, soon followed.

About an hour passed before Jase's mother peeked through the door and saw the two of them on the bed.

Chapter 29

She walked over to Jase and lightly shook him.

"Jase?"

"Oh! Mom, I was reading the book and we fell asleep." Nattie startled awake and sat straight up with her hair covering her face. It took her a few seconds to realize where she was. She blew some of the hair out of her face and laid back down, putting her arm around Jase.

Jase's mom laughed. "Is she sleeping?"

Jase smiled and looked down at her. "I think so."

"Why don't you come downstairs and let her sleep." Jase wiggled out from under her arm and carefully rolled out of the bed.

"She is so tired," Jase said. He went downstairs and had a snack before lying down on the couch.

Nattie woke up in the morning and lay in bed nice and warm. She stared at her pirate competition trophy on the nightstand and drifted back to that wonderful day in her mind. She smiled and quickly jumped out of bed to go downstairs. She gently climbed on the couch and squeezed in between Jase and the back cushions. She put her arm around him and kissed the back of his neck.

Jase took a deep breath and stretched, "Raaah, morning, beautiful."

"Sorry, I was trying not to wake you."

"It's okay." Jase rubbed her soft arm with his hand. Nattie yawned with a deep inhale.

"You still tired, baby?"

"A little." They snuggled for a while until Nattie's stomach started growling.

"I'm getting hungry, Jassie."

"Yeah, I can hear." Nattie pinched Jase's side and he flinched. She kept pinching until Jase grabbed her hand.

"Oh, is someone ticklish!"

"Who, me?"

"Yes, you silly boy."

"Not ah."

"I felt you flinch."

"That's just your overactive imagination." Nattie climbed on Jase and held his wrists down.

"You are so bad." She sat up and moved her head back and forth, feathering her hair across his face. Jase freed his hands and grabbed Nattie's waist tickling her. She jumped up and tried to run but Jase caught her by the waist. "Don't you tickle me, mister!"

Jase looked into her pretty, blue eyes and rubbed his nose against hers. "I love you so much, Nattie." They put their arms around each other and their lips met for a long kiss.

"We are going to have so much fun, Jassie."

Jase's mom walked downstairs. Nattie ran over and hugged her.

"Good morning, Mom."

"Morning, Nattie. It's nice to see you're back to your spunky self."

"I finally got some sleep."

"Why don't you two get ready while I make you something to eat?"

After breakfast, Jase loaded their backpacks into the cruiser. They arrived at the skyport later than expected so Jase's mom dropped them off at the main entrance. "You two want me to come in with you?"

"That's okay, Mom. We have to rush."

"Have fun and be safe!"

"We will. Bye, Mom!"

Jase and Nattie hurried to their departure gate and made it with only a few minutes to spare. They stood nearby and waited to board.

"Does this bring back memories?"

"Well, this time you're coming with me." Nattie put her arms around Jase's waist and hugged him tight. "This is so exciting. I finally get to fly with you rather than all alone."

When they walked on board the skycraft, they had to wait in the aisle for the other passengers to stow their baggage. International flights were normally quite full and this one seemed to be packed to the gills.

"Nattie, is it normally like this?"

"No, this is crazy." A baby cried near the front of the ship and the passengers behind Nattie kept pushing forward. "Sheesh, I can't wait to sit down."

"Want to switch places with me, baby?"

"No, I'll wait." When they made it to the back of the skyship, Jase put their packs in the overhead compartments. "Jassie, do you want to sit by the window since you've never flown before?"

"I guess. Are you sure?"

"Yeah, we can always switch later if you don't like it."

"You're the one who's afraid of heights," Jase laughed.

Nattie smacked him, "Hey, you brat." Jase sat down and Nattie pulled up the armrest between them and snuggled up to Jase holding his arm and leaning her head against his shoulder. "This is so nice, flying with you." Jase opened the window cover and watched as the ship hovered into position for takeoff.

"Ladies and gentlemen, this is your captain for flight Five, Nine, Two, our flight time today will be approximately one hour and fifteen minutes and we will climb to an altitude of approximately 185 sects, entering a low orbit for about half an hour. We will cover a total distance of 4576 miles before arriving at the Barcastle Concordia Skyport. Please fasten your seat belts and prepare for takeoff."

The ship received clearance and began extreme astronomical ascension. Even with the damping effect of the laviniun generators, passengers still experienced some slight g-force effects. Jase tensely grabbed Nattie's knee and held the underside of the seat with his other hand. A few seconds later, he closed the window cover, looked at Nattie with big eyes, and lifted his eyebrows.

"Jassie, it's okay." Jase turned chalky white and sat straight up rigidly in his seat. Nattie rubbed his back and played with his hair. "Jassie, just sit back and relax." Jase eased back into the seat until the landing gear retracted and the wings swept back.

"What's that?" Jase asked as he tensed back up.

Nattie laughed, "Jassie, it's just the landing gear. Why don't you open the window cover and look out?"

"No, that's okay."

"Awww, honey. Look." Nattie reached over in front of Jase and slid up the window cover. "Look out, Jassie. You will love this." He peered out the window to see the ground disappearing. About ten minutes later, Jase watched as the brightness of the atmosphere faded into the blackness of space. Both Nattie and Jase stared out the window at the stars in amazement. Their bodies felt much lighter even though the laviniun generators produced artificial gravity.

"Nattie, this is remarkable."

"I know. It's so incredible."

"Why didn't you ever tell me about this?"

"My flights were too short. They never went into space."

"Oh."

Once the skyship settled into a stable orbit, the captain performed a slow barrel roll, allowing the passengers on both sides of the ship to see the planet.

"Nattie, it's phenomenal!"

"I know; that is impressive." They could see the various land masses and cloud formations on the planet's surface. The sun beamed rays of light that reflected off the atmosphere, forming a spectacular fanlike pattern around the circumference of the planet with amazing detail. "Look at all the colors," Nattie softly whispered.

"I can see now why Kimberly wanted to join the Proelium Concordia. This is just breathtaking."

"I know I could totally get into this. Nattie, I think I know what I want to do now."

"Jassie, you can't fly a pirate ship in space." They both laughed and Jase went to tickle Nattie but she grabbed his hand. "Don't you dare."

"Did I tell you that Alrand started fighter training?"

"No."

"Yeah, he just sent me a letter. He's loving it."

"I can see that. You both are so adventurous."

"He said he's a lieutenant now that basic training is complete."

"How's Kimberly doing?"

"She's doing a lot better now." Jase snapped a few pictures through the window.

"All passengers, please prepare for descent. We will be arriving shortly in Barcastle where it's a pleasant twenty-four degrees."

"Jassie, I'm going to freeze!"

"That's why we brought your heavy coat."

"I'm still going to freeze. You going to keep me warm?"

"Of course."

"You better or I'm telling your dad."

"You're so cute." Nattie smiled and kissed him.

"You two make a very sweet couple," a little lady said who was sitting on the other side across from Nattie.

"Well, thank you."

"Are you two going home?"

"No, ma'am. We are visiting the castle."

"Oh my, you are very blessed, young lady. No one ever gets to visit the castle. Are you related to the family?"

"No, ma'am. We were just invited."

"Well, I hope you have a good time."

"Awww, thank you so much," Nattie said.

The skyship started its descent down through the outer atmosphere. The ride started to get a little rough and the passengers could feel the fall in their stomachs. The ship rattled and made a few creaking sounds. Jase and Nattie held tight to each other and watched out the window. A red and yellow glow formed along the swept-back wingtips. As the ship accelerated downward, fire shot off the wings. As soon as the ship entered the lower atmosphere, the fire and bright red glow dissipated and thick long streams of mist formed off the wings as they slowly extended forward to catch the air.

"Nattie, what is that?"

"I think it's a vapor trail."

"That's really neat...oh, Nattie!"

"What?"

"I forgot to take pictures."

"Don't scare me like that." Nattie punched Jase on the arm. "You can get pictures on the way home."

"Whew, I didn't think about that. Good idea."

"What would you do without me?"

"Well, let me see. Since I just went crazy missing you while you were at school, I don't want to go through that ever again." She got serious and hugged Jase tight.

"Jassie, I'm with you now and forever. I'm not going anywhere else without you." They kissed until the ship landed at the skyport.

When they exited the ship, a well-dressed man in a black suit held a sign, standing by the gate. The sign said, "Candella – Party of Two."

"Hi, I'm Nattie Candella and this is my boyfriend, Jase Thunderbelt."

"Ah, please follow me, madam."

On the way out, Jase stopped off at a newsstand and purchased two maps, one of Barcastle and the second of Voncara Cove. They stopped at the main entranceway to put on their heavy coats. Nattie handed Jase her knitted hat so he could pull it over her head without messing up her hair too much. He folded it down to cover her ears then kissed her on the nose. Nattie smiled and stared at Jase the whole time.

"What?"

"Nothing," she said with a giggle. *She looked so cute*, Jase thought. They walked outside under the overhang in the loading zone and could see piles of snow on side of the road and huge snow-covered mountains in the distance to the north. The mountains were quite impressive in size and were actually in another country.

Nattie breathed in the cold dry crisp air and exhaled vanishing clouds of mist from her moist warm breath.

"Jassie, look." She arched her head back and puffed her breath like a smokestack on an old steam engine. Jase wrapped his arms around her and kissed her plump lips.

"You are so cute, you know that?"

"Yep," she answered. Jase couldn't help but to laugh.

The chauffeur walked them over to a very nice custom cruiser sitting right out in front of the main terminal and opened the back door for them. Nattie glanced at Jase for a second with a big dimple smile and climbed into the back seat.

"Oh, I love this," Nattie said as she played with all the buttons.

Jase smacked her hand jokingly, "Stop playing with stuff."

"Why don't you make me?"

Jase reached over to tickle her when the driver said, "Sir, we should arrive at our destination in about half an hour."

"Okay, thank you."

Meanwhile Nattie found the switch to raise a privacy divider so the driver couldn't see them.

"What are you up to, ornery?"

"Getting you." She took off her heavy coat and laid it on the seat in front of her. "Take off your coat, Jassie. It's in my way." Jase hardly got one arm out before Nattie pulled the coat from behind him. She climbed onto Jase's lap facing him and started kissing his neck. Jase put his arms around her waist. His heat rate quickened as he felt her smooth tender kisses. She became very warm to the touch. Nattie raised high up on her knees, grabbed the hair on the back of Jase's head, and pulled his head back.

"Tonight, you're all mine, Jassie," she said as she started kissing his lips.

A few minutes later, Jase said, "I love you, baby," with a soft voice as he started kissing down her neck, breathing heavily. She let out a squeal, lifted her shoulders, and tilted her head to cover her neck.

"That tickles!"

Jase laughed, "Is there any part of you that's not ticklish?"

"I guess you'll have to figure that out for yourself later tonight." Jase smiled and his face became flushed.

He looked into her intense glistening eyes, "Nattie, I want to be with you forever."

She smiled with a very ornery look on her face and giggled. "I could never love another like I love you, Jassie. Ever."

The cruiser slowed as they passed over a large hill by the side of the castle, providing an unobstructed view.

"Jassie, look!" His eyes widened and his jaw dropped.

"Oh my."

"You should see the look on your face," Nattie giggled.

"Do you see this place?"

"Yeah, it's impressive, but I'd rather be looking at you."

"Huh?"

The castle was nestled in the countryside far from any town or population. It was constructed out of charcoal-colored stone and was about a hundred and fifty meters long and one hundred meters wide. High cylindrical bastion towers guarded the four corners of the structure and shorter thick block-like, square towers attached the rest of the castle walls to the tall towers. Two heavy square towers stood on either side of the rustic majestic entranceway, constructed of dense ancient hardwoods. The main structure was ten stories high with a huge peaked roof.

A high stone curtain wall surrounded the grounds constructed from the same materials as the castle. A thick blanket of unblemished snow covered the courtyard and surrounding property.

They arrived at the huge towers of the main gate. The gate was of heavy woven cast iron construction hinged on huge pegs. The chauffeur lowered the window and pressed a button on a keypad. The gate slowly opened inward. The driver pulled forward and let them off at the front entranceway. They noticed a police cruiser sitting on the other side of the drive. Writing upon it displayed, *Chief of Police.*

Jase and Nattie walked up the stone steps to the large wooden doors. Several firewood lanterns were mounted on the sides and above the entranceway. Very large hinged doorknockers hung from iron lion-head castings. Jase tried to knock on the door but it was so thick and huge that it hardly made a sound and hurt his knuckles.

Nattie, being quite intrigued, pulled up on the heavy doorknocker and let it fall, producing a small little thud.

"Watch out, featherweight."

Nattie stepped back and pinched Jase a few times making him flinch, "Brat!"

Jase lifted up the knocker and slammed it down hard. A distinct boom echoed from inside. A little mouse dashed out from under the door and ran toward Nattie. She jumped back and held her hand to her chest with a little scream.

Jase laughed, "It's just a little mousey."

"That's not funny! It scared me half to death," Nattie giggled.

The large door creaked open. "Can I help you?"

"Yes, please. We are here to see Mr. Halfgrim."

"And who are you?"

"I'm Jase Thunderbelt and this is Nattie Candella."

"Yes, we have been expecting you. Please follow me."

Jase took Nattie's hand and they stepped through the doorway into an immense mezzanine. The ceiling was over two stories high and a large elegant chandelier hung down by a chain. The floors were tiled with large polished white and brown marble slabs. Exquisite wooden detailed moldings lined the windowsills, archways, and ceiling. Both Jase and Nattie walked with their heads tilted back looking at the amazing craftsmanship. They walked into the main hallway which opened up before them next to a grand winding staircase made of dark beautiful hardwood. Coats of armor were exhibited on both sides of the staircase and many more posed at intervals running down the long hallway to the left and right, each with a shield of varying patterns and colors.

They turned left and walked along the wide, tall, arched hallway and passed many chambers with beautiful wooden doors featuring decorative designs and patterns.

As they passed by a room labeled, *The Buttery*, Nattie giggled, "Jassie, you see that. It's my room."

Chapter 30

"**N**attie, that says buttery not butterfly."

"Oh," she giggled.

"What's a buttery?"

"It's where they keep the wine and ale."

"Well, I like it better as the butterfly room." Jase squeezed her and tickled her waist a little with his fingertips. Nattie squirmed, grabbed his fingers, and held them tight. She pinched her nose to try and stop from sneezing as she felt a tickle in her nostrils.

They caught wind of an alluring aroma of cuisine being prepared in the one of the kitchens.

"Umm, Jassie, I'm getting hungry."

"I know. Me too."

When they reached the end of the hall, they walked through an archway leading into a huge library. Jase counted eight chandeliers hanging down from the ceiling. Elegant brown wooden pillars extended from the marble floor all the way up to the high ceiling running down both sides of the rectangular chamber. The pillars were spaced about ten feet apart and sectional wooden bookcases sat back against the wall between them with one bookshelf turned facing out at each end, forming little recessed sectionals.

Each rustic bookshelf was enclosed behind window-paned doors.

The glass panels were displayed in a crisscross pattern with brown wooden muntins. Each door had a skeleton key lock at the center where the doors met. The sectional pattern was repeated along a high catwalk all around the room. Two spiral staircases on either side of the far wall led up to the catwalk.

Antique tables, chairs, and couches were arranged throughout the center of the library with an emphasis on a huge, beautiful, marble fireplace at the center of the far wall. An opening on the adjacent wall led into Mr. Halfgrim's study.

The butler had them sit on a couch next to the warm fireplace. As they sat down, they could hear talking coming from the study,

"... yes it will. Make sure they are fully prepared."

"Yes, sir, they will be ready."

"Sir, your guests have arrived," the butler said.

"Great!"

"I must go see to my guests."

The chief of police walked out of the study with his hat tucked under his arm and left the library.

Mr. Halfgrim walked out with the butler. He was a rather short and stocky man with brown and white hair and a graying beard and mustache. His face was slender but appeared to be pitted. He had baggy eyes hidden behind small round-wire-framed spectacles. His voice was moderately toned but a bit raspy.

He walked over to Jase and Nattie and they stood up to shake his hand. "I hope you had a nice trip."

"Yes, it was okay."

"Very good, very good. I have had a meal prepared for us before we get started. I suspect you would like to freshen up a bit before we eat."

"Yes, sir, that would be nice," Nattie said.

"I will have my man show you to your rooms."

"Thank you."

"Yes, thank you, and thank you for the tickets for our flight," Jase said.

"You're most welcome. I assume you have your book with you?"

"Yes, I have it right here."

"Would you mind if I have a quick look at it?"

Jase handed the book to Mr. Halfgrim, his eyes lit up when he touched the cover.

"Extraordinary!" He carefully opened the cover to look at the seal. "Well there's no doubt about it; it's genuine." He handed the book back to Jase. "I look forward to seeing more in a little while. Bernard..."

Mr. Halfgrim motioned for Jase and Nattie to follow the butler. They picked up their backpacks and headed down the hallway to the grand staircase. Nattie became a bit winded by the time they reached the second floor. Jase took her backpack on one shoulder and held his on the other. They climbed the remaining steps to the fourth floor and walked down a long hallway.

"Sir, your room is to the left, and madam, yours is on the right. Can you find your way back down to the main kitchen when you're ready?"

"Yes, sir, no problem," Jase said.

"The facilities are just down the hall to the left. Let me know if you require any assistance."

Jase carried Nattie's backpack into her room, which was very large, and laid it on her lacey white canopy bed. Nattie smiled but held her arms close to her body and her shoulders were up by her neck.

"You cold, baby?"

"I'm freezing."

"Want me to start a fire in the fireplace?"

"That would be great."

"Let me go put my bag in my room first."

"No! Jassie, stay in here with me."

"Are you sure?" Nattie just giggled and turned a little red.

Jase put his pack down and hugged her. They kissed for a moment.

"Jassie, I have to use the bathroom."

"Okay, go ahead. I'll start a fire."

Jase walked over to the window near the fireplace and looked outside at the breathtaking snow-covered view of the countryside behind the castle. He noticed strands of dried out vines growing outside, across the bottom of the window ledge from a trellis to the left. The inner windowsill was deep enough that someone could comfortably sit and read by the sunlight.

Next to the fireplace was a bin full of wood, kindling, and fire starter packets. Jase put half of the fire starters in the fireplace then piled on the kindling. He looked around but could not find anything to light the fire so he opened his backpack and grabbed his survival knife. He opened the waterproof handle and pulled out a match. By the time Nattie returned from the restroom, he had a blazing fire.

"I'm going to the bathroom now," Jase said.

"Okay." Nattie walked around the room admiring the artwork and tapestries on the walls. She tried out the antique sofa to the left of the fireplace. *It looks nice but feels a bit hard,* she thought.

Jase returned to find Nattie sitting in the window gazing outside. He walked over, "I figured you would be sitting up in here." Jase put his arms around her and gave her a kiss on the cheek.

"Why would you think that?"

"Because I know you; if there is ever anything you can do to look cute, guaranteed that's what you'll do."

"Not uh. I didn't do this to look cute. I just wanted to look outside."

"Well, doing cute things just comes naturally to you."

Nattie giggled, "You're so silly." Jase hugged her tight. "I'm starving, Jassie."

"Okay, baby. Let's go eat."

Jase grabbed a notepad and *Thundering Cannons* from his backpack. He took Nattie by the hand and they walked down the long hallway toward the staircase. Nattie be-bopped along, skipping, with her hair bouncing up and down. Jase walked fast to try and keep up.

"Come on, pokey."

"What's the hurry?"

"I'm hungry. If you don't hurry up I'm going to eat you," Nattie giggled. When they reached the kitchen, the butler showed them into an adjoining feasting hall where Mr. Halfgrim sat reading a newspaper.

"Ah, ready to eat?"

"Yes," Nattie said. Mr. Halfgrim motioned them to sit down. Jase walked around the large table and sat near the wall. Nattie followed and sat down next to him.

"Would you like me to set your book on the shelf here? We wouldn't want to take a chance that something could spill on it." Jase agreed and handed the book to Mr. Halfgrim. "I was quite confounded when I received your letter about finding this book. Can I ask how it came to be in your possession?" Mr. Halfgrim asked in a somewhat harsh tone with a very serious look on his face.

Jase lifted his eyebrows and thought for a second. "Um, I wasn't actually trying to find this book. I was just looking for a pirate book for some costume ideas in an old bookstore."

"Yeah, we found it by accident," Nattie said. The servants placed the main course on the table before them. The aroma was quite pleasant and Nattie started to dig in, being so hungry.

"Can I ask which bookstore you found it in?"

"Alaxrandus Rare Books."

"That old fool!" Both Jase and Nattie looked at Mr. Halfgrim with puzzled looks on their faces. "He told me the book was lost in a fire."

"Who? Mr. Alaxrandus?"

"Senior, yes."

"Well, he was very surprised when I found it because he did believe it was lost in a fire and we found it in the wrong section of the bookstore. He had no idea it was there. "So you know Mr. Alaxrandus then?" Jase asked.

"He and I go way back. I will make you the same offer I made him for the book. How does one million tutarian sound?" Jase looked at Nattie and she looked back at him with her eyes opened wide. She squinted her eyebrows and wrinkled her nose to show her disapproval. She could tell that Jase was overwhelmed by the offer.

"It's not for sale," Nattie said.

"Come now, a young couple like yourselves. You could make a pretty good life with that much money."

"It's not for sale," Nattie said very sharply.

"Don't get upset. I just wanted to make the offer. We can go up to the library after dinner and exchange books for a little while. I hope that's okay with you."

"Yes, sir, that's fine," Jase said.

"My offer still stands should you change your mind later."

There was silence during the rest of the meal. Nattie cleaned her plate and had dessert. "I can't believe you ate that much."

Nattie rubbed her tummy, "I was so hungry. Now I'm too stuffed to move."

Jase laughed, "Am I going to have to roll you over to the library?"

"I think so," Nattie giggled.

"Are we ready then?" Mr. Halfgrim asked.

"Yes, I think so."

"By the way, do you happen to know anything about the second book by U.S. Wells?"

Nattie, being suspicious, quickly questioned, "There's another book?"

"Yes, I'm surprised Mr. Alaxrandus didn't tell you about it. There are three books. You have the first and I have the third but the second book has not yet been revealed."

Jase removed his book from the shelf and they all walked to the library chamber. Jase and Nattie sat at one end of a table and placed his book at the center. Mr. Halfgrim walked up to the catwalk, unlocked one of the bookcase doors, and removed his book. He walked down, handed the book to Jase, and sat at the other end of the table.

The cover was made of a dark blue thick cloth that was kind of rough to the touch like denim. The title read, *The Legend of the Blackrock Pirates, by U.S. Wells*. A sketch on the front cover depicted a couple holding hands by a cliff along the sea with a large wooden gunship anchored nearby.

"Do you know who this couple is on the cover?" Nattie asked.

"I believe their names are David and Angelica." Nattie smiled at Jase and giggled a bit. He knew exactly what she was thinking.

He gently opened the front cover to find, as he expected, another crest with position information. However, this crest was a little different from the other two books. He looked over at Mr. Halfgrim who was also looking at the crest in his book and taking notes. Since Nattie had such good handwriting and was very good at drawing illustrations, Jase handed her the notepad so she could sketch the crest and markings.

The center pictograph was the same as the other two books but the position markings around the outer ring were different. There was a '3' to the left signifying book three and a 'NE' at the bottom, which obviously meant northeast.

The other markings were confusing. Centered on the right was a large 'X' in a box and about half an inch above and below were two X's.

Centered at the top was a '+50'. Jase looked at Nattie; she looked back and shrugged her shoulders.

Once she finished her sketch of the crest, Jase started paging through the book looking for any out of place text. Page after page, he searched but no change in font or structure.

Jase glanced over at Mr. Halfgrim to find him staring at a single page with his head resting in his hands, propped up by his elbows. He had turned a bit flush and rubbed his temples with his fingers.

Nattie whispered in Jase's ear, "What do you suppose he's looking at?"

"I don't know. Maybe the part about the RFI gun. This book hasn't revealed anything amazing other than the strange makings on the crest. He may be as confused as we were when we first saw the strange futuristic references," Jase whispered. He had finished scanning through all the pages but hadn't found anything that drew his attention.

Jase picked a page in the last quarter of the book that seemed interesting and started reading. Nattie sat fidgeting with her necklace. She slid back in her hard wooden chair and took a deep breath, held it in, and then let it out. She scratched her head, leaned back, and stared at the ceiling.

After waiting for what seemed like forever, Jase said, "Nattie, look at this. Read this." Nattie put her arm around Jase and started reading,

With the pirate's town defeated and the slaves freed, the remaining pirates scattered to the four winds with their battered ships. Without port of refuge, they became very dangerous, attacking merchant vessels for food and supplies. Captain Anderson was commissioned to hunt down the remaining pirates and to protect the local ports. Some of the most ruthless pirates formed a pact, which they named "The Blackrock Brotherhood." Anderson searched for months but was unable to find their secret base.

Angelica found it very difficult staying behind and was torn between her love for their newborn daughter

and the desire to sail at David's side. She longed for the sea but wished a better life for her daughter.

"Jassie!"

"I know."

"That's so wonderful."

"Shh." Jase looked over at Mr. Halfgrim who wiped his forehead with a handkerchief and stood up. He fanned himself with his notebook for a second. His face seemed distressed and red. He leaned with his palms against the table looking down at the book.

"Did you find something interesting?" Jase asked.

"Nothing unexpected or out of the usual," Mr. Halfgrim answered with a casual voice. Jase and Nattie both looked at each other for a moment then back at Mr. Halfgrim who seemed fixated on that same page. Nattie stood up, stretched with her hands above her head, and inconspicuously looked around the library while making her way behind Mr. Halfgrim.

When he noticed her coming near, he quickly closed the book and said, "I think that's enough for today. I will have the staff prepare a meal for you in a little while. I have to run into town on important business. We can pick up where we left off tomorrow." He and Jase exchanged books. "Feel free to explore the castle but try not to get lost. It's quite large."

"Okay, thank you."

"You can check in with the kitchen in a little while to eat." Mr. Halfgrim left the library taking his book with him.

"Jassie, do you really think it's possible that he is unaware of the second book?"

"I don't know. I get the feeling he's hiding something."

"Me too, something's going on."

"If he thought the book was of no help, then why was he just staring at some of the pages for so long?"

"Yeah, I was thinking the same thing and we know there are shocking statements in our book. You didn't find anything strange in his book?"

"Not so far but what do you think the markings on the crest mean?"

"I have to think about it. I'm not sure."

"Want to look around the castle?"

"Okay." Jase took Nattie by the hand and they walked up to her room so he could get his camera.

As they approached the door, the butler walked out of the room. "Can we help you with something?" Jase asked.

"No, sir. I was just lighting the fire but then I saw you had already started one. I did add a few more logs though."

"Could you tell us how to get to one of the tall towers? Mr. Halfgrim said we could explore some."

"I can draw you a little map." Nattie handed the butler Jase's notebook. "If you plan on roaming the castle at night, I suggest you take a coat. The outlying areas are not heated and are very cold. Also, you will find a housecoat in your rooms in the event you need to use the washroom during the night."

"Okay, thank you for the map."

After the butler walked away down the hall, Jase entered the room. Everything seemed in order. He quickly checked to make sure *Three Tall Ships* was still in his backpack. "Nattie, I think I will keep *Thundering Cannons* with me while we explore and hide *Three Tall Ships* at the bottom of my backpack."

"Good idea."

They walked across the hall to look in Jase's room and there was no fire started. "Very odd, don't you think?" Jase said.

"Yes, do you think he was looking in our stuff?"

"I don't know; maybe." Jase looked around a bit, "I like this room, Nattie. It's very rustic and pirate-looking."

Nattie laughed, "You want to stay in this room?"

"No, that's okay. You really like your room. Come on, let's get our coats and try to find the tower."

When they reached the end of the main hallway on the first floor, Nattie skipped up ahead and almost fell on the slick marble. Then she had a thought. "Jassie, watch this." She took off her shoes and sprinted down the hallway fast. She slid for a good distance in her socks.

"Hey, wait up!" Jase took off his shoes and ran towards her. He slid a long way but lost his balance and fell.

Nattie started laughing and helped him to his feet. "That wasn't really funny; it kinda hurt."

"I'm sorry, Jassie, but you should have seen your face when you lost your balance. Want me to kiss it better?"

"Oh, just kiss me, cutie."

A few moments later, they walked in their socks and followed the map until they ended up in a very long narrow corridor with an arched ceiling.

"Excellent!" Jase took off running as fast as he could with Nattie right behind. He slid really far but then Nattie couldn't stop in time and slid right into him.

She giggled, "Sorry, honey."

"No, you're not. You meant to do that."

"Yeah sure. I love to live dangerously." She pinched Jase and took off running and giggling while she flew down the long passageway with her hair flying back behind her. Jase ran as fast as he could without falling, to catch her.

Chapter 31

Nattie let out a little scream and ran faster. She slid up to the entrance of the tower where Jase finally caught her. She laughed so hard. She bent over holding her stomach, trying to stop Jase from tickling her. Jase put his arms around her waist and lifted her up then put her back down as they kissed. "Jassie, it's freezing. Let's hurry up the tower so you can get your pictures. I want to go somewhere warmer."

"You feel warm to me."

"Just wait until later," Nattie said as she winked at Jase and ran up the spiral staircase. About a third of the way up, she stopped to catch her breath. "Whew, there are so many steps and my feet are freezing."

"Put your shoes back on, silly."

"I can't now, look how black my socks are."

"Ew."

"Look at yours."

"That's nasty."

"Hurry, it's getting colder."

"Yeah, I think it's supposed to get really cold tonight.

When they reached the top of the tower, Jase walked to the wall and looked out over the grounds. "Nattie, come look."

"That's okay."

"It's perfectly safe." Jase took her by the waist and coaxed her over to the stone wall encompassing the top of the tower.

"It's such a very pretty view…look at that moon, Jassie." She looked down and started feeling dizzy. She backed away from the wall a bit.

Jase had her pose for a few pictures then she put her arms in his coat to hug him and try to warm up. Jase wrapped his open coat around her.

"I love you so much, Jassie."

"I love you, butterfly baby, and thank you."

"For what?"

"For getting us the invitation and tickets so we could come here."

"Awww, you're welcome."

"I'm getting a little hungry; how about you?"

"I could eat." They walked back down the tower and the long passageway. "Jassie, I want to know what happened with David and Angelica. Do you think you could read to me a little bit after we eat?"

"Yeah, we can read a little."

They found the feasting hall and the servants brought out their dinner. Nattie kept looking at Jase while he ate.

"What?"

Nattie smiled big, "Nothing."

"Why do you keep looking at me like that?"

"Like what?"

"Like you're going to eat me."

Nattie giggled and winked, "I might."

They finished eating vand returned up to Nattie's room. Jase bent down and hunted for *Three Tall Ships* in the bottom of his backpack.

"Jassie, turn around so I can change into my pajamas, and no peeking."

"No promises."

"You better not peek." Nattie took off her shirt as Jase turned his head. She quickly held her shirt over her chest and smacked him.

"You are so bad."

"I wasn't looking."

"I saw you!" She hurried and slipped on her pajamas. "Are you going to change, Jassie?"

"In a little bit."

Jase poked the fire and added a few logs. Nattie climbed up on the bed and plopped down, "Come read to me, Jassie." She patted her hand on the bed next to her, motioning Jase to come sit. He ran and jumped up on the high bed and leaned back against the pillows. Nattie snuggled up next to him and started kissing his neck. Jase turned his head to make it easier for her.

"You sure you want me to read?"

"Uh-huh, at least for a little while." Nattie said between her kisses. "We have all night and I'm going to make the best of it." Jase gave her a little tickle and she laughed with a deep voice. "Stop it." She bit Jase's shoulder and they both laughed. Jase found the area of the text where they left off and started reading,

Captain Wells walked into the makeshift field hospital to check in on the injured. Pamula had no time to provide an update with so many wounded to tend to.

"How can I help?" he asked.

"Help to apply direct pressure to their wounds until I can treat them."

"Any word on Anderson?"

"No, I have search parties out scouting the waters but no news thus far."

"It doesn't seem like there's much hope."

"I'm not giving up on Anderson just yet. How is Angelica?"

"She's stable for the moment but we brought limited medical equipment with us and we are almost out of penicillin. I'm worried about infections."

"Just do your best, I have great confidence in your abilities."

Later that evening, when the search parties returned for fresh lanterns, Captain Wells gathered the men together and called off the search.

"We have lost a great soldier today," His head hung low, "and a great friend. Thank you all for your efforts."

Angelica woke from a light coma, early the next morning. The room was full of men recovering from their injuries. She tried to sit up but felt excruciating pain in her chest.

"No, Angelica, lie still," Pamula said.

"Where's my David?"

"You need to rest now and heal."

"David!" She called out.

"Shh, Angelica, don't wake the men."

"Why won't you tell me?"

"Sweetie, I'm afraid he didn't make it."

"No! Please, no! Not again."

"Jassie, I don't understand. He can't be dead."

"Did you hear what Pamula said about the medical equipment?"

"Yes, I know it's not possible but they had to have traveled back from the future somehow."

"It seems that way; what other possibility could there be? Their advanced technology is way beyond anything of that time."

"Read some more, Jassie. I have to know."

Angelica turned away. Tears ran down her face. I have no reason left to live, she thought.

Later that morning, two men rushed into Captain Wells' quarters to wake him.

"What is it?"

"Sir! Lieutenant Anderson is alive!"

"He is? Where is he?"

"He's walking up from the cove."

Captain Wells ran out to meet him. David's clothing was partially burnt and some of his hair was melted and singed. His face had some patches of first and second-degree burns and his eyebrows were singed.

"You've looked better, David." David stood still, put his arm on his hip, and grinned.

"I've felt better too."

"What happened?"

"The explosion blew me a good distance from the ship and I was caught in an undertow. I was swept away, and when I finally broke free of the currents, I ended up alongside the cliffs far from the cove. I almost didn't make it but I was able to climb onto a ledge to escape the pounding surf. I had to wait until low tide so I could make it through to the beach."

"I'm very happy to see you alive. Let's get you looked at; those are some nasty burns."

"How's Angelica?"

"She's stable but not doing very well. I'm sure seeing you will make all the difference."

Captain Wells helped David to the hospital.

"Pamula, have you slept at all?" Captain Wells

asked.

Pamula turned around. She was so tired that it took her a second to focus. "David! You're alive!" She hugged him.

"Oh, I need to clean those burns, but first you need to follow me."

Pamula led David into the next room. Angelica had fallen back asleep. She looked so helpless. David sat down next to her bed and ran his hand gently through her long black hair. He took her hand and kissed it. Angelica cracked open her eyes to see David before her. She started to cry and held her arms up for a hug. David carefully leaned over her and put his cheek against hers. Angelica hugged him to tight and hurt herself.

"Ugh."

"You okay?"

"They told me you were dead, David."

"It's okay now. I'm here." Pamula walked over to David and turned his head with her hand under his chin. She cleaned and treated the burns on his face.

"I have to use the bathroom real quick," Nattie said.

"Go ahead."

"But I'm too warm to get up." She hugged Jase and he kissed her forehead. "I'm thirsty too. I'm going downstairs to get a drink. You want anything?"

"I'm good. You want me to come with you?"

"No, I want you to get ready for me when I get back." Nattie winked at Jase and kissed him. She giggled and got off the bed. She put on the warm fancy housecoat from the armoire.

"You look so sophisticated and beautiful."

"Thank you, honey. I'll be right back."

Nattie walked to the bathroom and Jase put away his book and cleaned up the room a bit.

Nattie walked down the four flights of steps and almost fell on the slippery marble in her dirty socks. She giggled and bounced along the hallway towards the kitchen. The castle was very dark but dimly lit lamps lined the walls about every ten feet, creating flickering shadows across the floor and walls. When she walked into the kitchen, she could hear voices from the next corridor.

It was dark and hard to see but she managed to pour herself a glass of fresh water. Being curious, she walked closer to the voices and hid outside the doorway in the shadows, to listen in on their conversation.

"...yes, I'm pretty sure."

"How sure?"

"Jajaun, I'm telling you. It must be inside the front cover."

"I want some assurance before we do this."

"The bottom line is, we won't know for sure until we slice it open."

A tall, bulky, ominous figure swaggered past Nattie, foreshadowing her attempt to conceal herself in the darkness. She held her breath, trying not to be discovered.

"Hello, Mr. Halfgrim."

"Ah, I see you received my note."

The large thug answered in a deep voice, "Yes sir, but I'm not totally clear..."

"Let me spell it out for you then. Kill the kids and bring me the two books. Try and make it look like an accident." Nattie gasped and quickly covered her mouth with her hand. She tried to stop breathing but couldn't hold her breath. The glass in her other hand shook and water spilled out onto the floor. The thug turned his head toward the door.

"What is it?"

"I think I heard something." He reached around the corner and turned on a light. "It's the girl!"

Nattie stood frozen as if she couldn't move. Her heart rate pulsed wildly, her body quivered.

"Get her, you idiot." Nattie let out a short scream as the thug reached out for her. The glass shattered across the floor as she ducked and ran into the hallway. She slid into the far wall and received a cut on her foot. She dashed toward the staircase with the thug lagging behind her. She tried to slow down to climb the stairs but fell and slid into the corner of the staircase, hurting her side. "Ugh." She tried to get up, being in pain, but the thug caught up to her. Nattie stood up quickly and drew a sword from the coat of armor next to the steps. She held the sword high in the air above her head.

"Ha ha, you gonna try to cut me, little girly?" Nattie backed up to the bottom of the steps.

"Stay away from me," she said in a frightened high-pitched voice.

"Be a good little girly and put down that sword. Nobody's gonna hurt you."

"Yeah right!"

The thug slowly reached down for his gun mounted in a holster on his belt.

Chapter 32

Nattie lunged forward, swinging down the sword with all her might, slicing his upper thigh through to the bone with the razor sharp blade.

The thug grabbed his wound with both hands and yelled with an ear-ringing cry. He fell to the ground hard, screaming at the top of his lungs. Nattie threw down the sword. It crashed down on the marble and bounced in the air. She ran up the first flight of steps as fast as she could, letting out a long moan of fright. She stopped momentarily to rip off the socks from her feet then continued up to the fourth floor. She sprinted down the long hallway towards her room like a burst of fire from a cannon, her hair streaming behind her. She left behind small splotches of blood from her bleeding foot.

Jase had just taken off his shirt when Nattie burst through the door and frantically locked it behind her.

"Nattie, what's wrong?" Her face was of fright and her eyes were so big, her eyebrows where stretched high on her forehead.

"Jassie, they're trying to kill us!"

"What?"

"I cut a man's leg off with a sword!"

"Nattie, what are you talking about?" She doubled over holding her stomach.

"This is not happening, this is not happening." She ran behind a large tapestry and a few seconds later, she moved behind another one.

"Nattie, what are you doing?"

"I'm looking for a secret passageway. Don't all castles have secret passageways? We have to escape!"

The doorknob turned and shook. Someone pounded on the door.

"Open up!"

"Jassie, we have to find a way out!"

"Hurry up with that key," a voice said from outside the bedroom door.

Jase pulled his shirt on and ran over to the window. "Here, Nattie, we can climb down the trellis."

"Oh, no, no, no, no, uh-uh,"

"Nattie, there's no other way out." They could hear someone trying to unlock the door with a key. Nattie panicked and ran to the window and looked down.

"Jassie, I can't do it," she cried with tears running down her face.

Jase hugged her tight, "I won't let you fall. If you're right, they will kill us if we stay."

"Try the next key! Hurry up!" someone shouted from outside the door.

"Okay, Jassie, I just can't believe this is happening." Jase threw their backpacks out the window and climbed out on the narrow ledge. Nattie followed.

"Don't look down, baby."

"Don't tell me that or that's what I'll do." Jase slowly shimmied along the edge and reached for the trellis. His foot slipped on some ice and he fell.

"JASSIE!"

His arm flung down into one of the crossbeams as he fell with a loud crack as the wood splintered. Jase grabbed on tight with his other arm and got his footing. "It's okay, baby. I'm fine." Voices could be heard inside the room. Nattie moved along the ledge, her bare feet melted into the ice as she maneuvered into position to grab the trellis. She reached out, grabbed hold with her left hand, and stretched out her right leg, placing it on a beam.

"That's it, baby. The hard part's over. Just take it one step at a time. Climb down to me."

"Where are they? They couldn't have just disappeared."

Jase and Nattie both froze in place when Mr. Halfgrim peered out of the window. "Did they climb out there?" he asked.

"They must have, where else could they be?"

"Hurry then. Everyone outside, we have to stop them."

"Jassie, I can't move. Help me." Jase climbed back up and helped her take the next step down.

"Just keep going, baby. One step at a time."

"But they are coming, Jase," she cried. Jase climbed down further to give Nattie more room. She took the next step and the board under her foot cracked in two. She screamed as she fell but Jase grabbed hold of her leg. Her upper body continued to fall back until she grabbed hold of a board with her hand. She let out a terrified frightening yell. Jase climbed down holding her leg until she was upright again. "I don't want to die, Jase," She cried. "I just wanted to be with you, that's all I wanted," she said as she held on with her arms entwined in the trellis.

"Nattie, look at me. We are going to make it. Don't you give up."

"Jassie, I can't move."

"Yes, you can. Remember the rope climbing competition? Just pretend you are only three feet off the ground, okay?"

"I'll try."

"Good girl." They continued to climb down one step at a time. "Look down, Nattie. Only a few more feet to go." Nattie let out a sigh of relief. Jase jumped down and waited for her. They could hear shouting in the distance.

Jase picked up both backpacks and they ran toward the stone

wall and the woods. The snow slowed them down considerably. As they ran through some trees, near the wall, they could hear shots and bullets whistling past their heads. Jase helped to push Nattie up high enough that she could grab hold of the wall and pull herself up. She lay flat on her tummy on the top of the wall, waiting and trying not to look down. Jase climbed a nearby tree and jumped for the wall. He slipped and fell as bullets ricocheted off the stones.

"Nattie, you okay?"

"Yes, hurry, Jase."

"Just jump down."

"No! Not without you." Jase climbed the tree again and jumped. He skinned his chin on the stones but managed to pull himself up. He jumped down the other side.

"Jump down, Nattie." He caught her as she fell.

"Jassie, my feet are so cold. I can't feel them."

Jase opened her backpack, removed a pair of socks, and placed them on her feet. He put her feet under his armpits to warm them for a few minutes. They could hear the men getting closer. Jase found Nattie's boots in her pack and put them on her feet. They ran into the woods and didn't stop for several sects until Nattie fell in the snow exhausted.

"Jassie, wait." Jase helped her up. She bent over and put her hands to her face. She started crying hysterically. Jase held her tight and tried to calm her down.

"Nattie, it will be okay."

"No it won't. They will find us and kill us."

"I won't let that happen, Nattie."

"I can't believe this…what are we going to do?"

"We get away and call the police."

"Jase, he owns the police. You saw the chief of police at his castle. He probably has them looking for us now. I'm sure he told them I cut that guy's leg off by now."

"How did that happen?"

She explained the whole story as they walked. "I can't believe you did that."

"Well, my instructor did say I was good with a sword…served him right!"

"My tough girl." Nattie smiled at Jase.

"I'm glad you're feeling a little better."

"I'm just happy we're alive and on the ground." They could hear the distant sound of dogs barking. "Ugh! That lasted for like what, ten seconds?" Nattie said in an aggravated tone.

"We better get going."

"Jassie, can the dogs track us in the snow?"

"I don't know but I'm sure they can follow our footprints. We need to find a way to lose them." Jase took out the map of Barcastle and oriented it with the compass on his knife. Using his little flashlight, he could see the map to guess their position.

"Nattie, we need to make it to here, the little town of Safrailium. It's the closest town outside of Barcastle."

"How far is it?"

"I'm guessing it's about twenty sects from here."

"Sheesh, it's so far to walk in this snow and I'm already freezing."

"Yeah, it's getting really cold."

"Jassie, the dogs are getting closer. What are we going to do?"

"There's a stream that runs all the way down here." Jase ran his finger across the map. "Maybe we can use it to lose them somehow. I'm sorry about all this, Nattie. Me and my stupid pirate stuff that got us into this mess."

"It's not your fault, Jassie. It's pit-faced Halfgrim's." Jase picked up both of their backpacks. "Jassie, let me carry mine. You shouldn't have to carry both of them."

"Well, how is your foot?"

"It still hurts but I can manage."

"Okay, we can switch back and forth. We have a long way to go."

They walked as fast as they could in the snow but the sounds of the dogs still grew closer. They reached a clearing and could see a road on their left.

"Nattie, that's it. If we walk on the road for a while, they will lose our footprints."

"What if someone comes? They will see us."

"If we see lights, we'll just run off the road. Give me your backpack for a little bit. Let's try to run and get ahead." They climbed over a small snow bank and onto the road. Jase helped Nattie to climb down and they ran.

The moon was high in the night sky, reflecting off the snow. It was almost like daylight. Nattie favored one leg as they ran.

"Are you doing okay, Nattie?"

"Let's just keep going."

"How's your leg?"

"Shhh. I'm trying not to think about the pain." She held her hand on her side as she ran.

It was so peaceful and quiet. The dogs had stopped barking and only the sounds of their footsteps and breathing could be heard. They rounded a curve in the road.

WOO, a siren sounded and lights strobed. Both their hearts skipped a few beats and they jumped. A police cruiser sat just off the road on the left, hidden by some bushes. Jase and Nattie jumped over the snow bank on the right hand side of the road and rolled down the embankment. Jase dropped the backpacks as he rolled, Nattie grabbed hold of hers and took off running. Jase picked up his backpack and ran after her as fast as he could in the snow. Nattie suddenly stopped and Jase almost tripped over her as she leaned over her backpack taking something out.

"Nattie, come on. What are you doing?"

"Just wait."

The police cruiser pulled up and over the embankment further down the road. It headed in their direction. Nattie quickly plugged in the auxiliary power connector on her school project and turned on the switch, causing the police cruiser to falter and barrel roll down the hill. It ended up landing upside down, wedged in the snow.

"Woohoo, that was phenomenal! Come on, Nattie; let's get out of here before they crawl out from under that thing."

They took off running back into the woods away from the road. Within a few minutes, they came upon the stream they were looking for.

"Wow, Nattie. It's frozen solid."

"There's not much snow on it though."

"Yeah, let's head down the stream for a while. Maybe we can get further ahead of them." Jase stepped down the bank onto the frozen stream and helped Nattie to climb down.

"Wait, Jassie, can you break off a branch of this evergreen tree?" Jase looked at her for a second.

"I love you, smarty. Great idea."

"How do you know what I was going to say?"

"Because I know how you think." Jase used his survival knife to cut a branch from the tree. They walked back and forth, leaving footprints all over the thin coating of snow leading in all directions.

"This is great," Nattie giggled. "They will be so confused."

They started walking down the stream, wiping their footprints from the snow with the evergreen branch as they walked.

"You really think this will fool them, Jassie?"

"Absolutely, the wind is causing the snow to smooth out more so after a while, they won't be able to see any footprints."

"Yeah but this wind is so cold. My ears and my nose are freezing."

"We need to find a safe place to start a fire. Come here, Nattie." Jase tied Nattie's hood a little tighter to try and keep the wind off her ears.

About half a sect down the stream, they stopped cleaning their tracks and hurried along at a faster pace. The stream grew wider as they walked and eventually led to a huge clearing. They walked for a while but Jase had a bad feeling.

"Nattie, let's head back into the woods. I don't like it out here in the open."

"I know, and the wind is stronger out here." As they walked, they could hear cracking sounds. "Oh no! Jassie, I think we're on a huge frozen lake."

"Quick, spread out some to lower our..." In an insane instance, Nattie fell through the ice and under the freezing water. Her head popped up out of the water and she let out a grueling scream, gasping for air. The water was up to her neck. She frantically tried to climb out but her hands just slipped on the ice and her backpack weighed her down. "NATTIE!" screamed Jase. He took off his backpack and lay on his stomach. He unfastened a shoulder strap and flung it to her. She just floated there as if staring into space.

"NATTIE! Grab hold, NATTIE!" She snapped to and held on as tight as she could, wrapping the strap around her wrist. Jase pulled her up on the ice. He stood up and dragged her across the lake to the embankment. He took off her soaking wet backpack and helped her to climb up. Her body went limp in his arms, her eyes rolled back in her head, and she fell backward. Jase tried to hold on to her but she rolled and fell face down into the snow.

"Oh no, Nattie?" Jase rolled her over and picked her up. She felt so heavy. "Nattie, hold on. Don't you die on me." He ran as fast as he could with her in his arms toward the woods so he could pull down some of the lower branches and make a fire. His heart pounded; he was totally in shock and panicked as he ran. The wind had picked up even more and it started to snow. The moon was very bright. He caught a reflection out of the corner of his eye and ran towards it. The snow was a little thinner in the woods, making it easier to run. He could see an outline of a structure through a little clearing up ahead. It was a little old cottage. Jase ran up to the small porch.

"Help us! Anyone please help us!" It appeared that the cottage was abandoned. Jase leaned back with Nattie in his arms and kicked the door several times until he smashed it open.

The wind filled the room blowing in snow that circled around inside. Jase laid her in front of the fireplace and propped the door shut with a wooden chair. He quickly searched around and found several blankets. He was rushing so much that he tripped over a chair and fell on the floor, hurting his wrists. He quickly got back up and ran to Nattie. He stripped the icy clothes from her lifeless body and wrapped her up in the blankets. He noticed a big black bruise on her side from where she slid into the staircase earlier. He stripped to his underwear and snuggled up next to her under the covers to warm her up. It was hard because her body felt like ice cubes.

Jase listened to her chest but couldn't hear a heartbeat. "No!" Jase cried; his tears dripped on Nattie's hair. He moved his ear closer to the center of her chest and listened. Finally, he heard a slight, thump, thump. Then nothing, then again a very slight thump, thump. He couldn't feel any breath from her mouth and her lips looked purple.

Chapter 33

Jase pinched her nose and breathed several easy warm breaths onto her lungs. He could see her chest rise each time. He desperately rubbed her arms and legs to try anything to warm her up. He listened to her chest again. He could hear a slight but more regular heartbeat. He could feel her breathing so he pulled the covers over their heads to trap as much heat as he could. After a few minutes, he could feel Nattie's body starting to twitch and shake.

Several more minutes passed and her whole body started uncontrollably shivering. "Jassie, help me," Nattie said very faintly.

Jase cried, "Nattie, are you okay?" There was no answer.

Some time passed and the shivering became more severe, "Jassie?"

"I'm here, Nattie."

"Where am I?"

"We're in a little cottage."

"I have to get back to school. I don't want to get into trouble."

"Nattie?" There was no answer. Jase lay there and cried. He kissed her shoulder. "Please be okay, Nattie. Please." Nattie's body started to calm a bit. He could see her lips were red again but she still felt cold. Another half hour passed before her shivering subsided, "Nattie?" Jase shook her a bit.

"Jassie, you're here."

"Are you okay?"

"I'm cold, so cold."

"I'm going to start a fire."

"But I have to finish my homework."

"Nattie, you're done with school."

"Does that mean I can come home with you?" She laid her head back down and fell asleep. Jase put his arm around her and lay his head against hers. His stomach felt like it was tied in knots. His chest hurt from the intense stress of the moment. He laid back and held his hands to his head. He had a pounding headache. His lips drew tight and his cheek muscles pulled at his chin. His hand clenched into a tight fist as he thought about Jajaun Halfgrim and all that had happened.

After he calmed a bit, he eased out from under the covers and got dressed. He had seen a small stack of wood on the porch so he moved the chair from the door and brought all the wood inside. He found some rope and cut a piece to hold the door shut. There were some old newspapers on the table so he placed them in the fireplace in small wads. He broke up several wooden chairs to use as kindling and used a match from his knife to start a fire. He strung up some rope for a clothesline near the fire and hung Nattie's icy clothes to dry.

He felt Nattie's forehead. She felt normal so he wrote her a note in case she woke up and went to find her backpack. The wind was really blowing and the snow seemed to be flying horizontally, making it hard to see. Jase used the compass and kicked up the snow as he walked to make sure he could find his way back. The lake was only a short distance from the cottage. He followed the edge of the lake until he tripped over the backpack and fell down. He had a rough time picking it up as it was partially frozen to the ground.

He quickly returned to the cottage and hung up as many things as he could to dry. He changed into dry pajamas and climbed into the blankets with Nattie. He kissed her and fell into an exhaustive sleep.

Morning had come and passed. A woodpecker, searching for a meal in the wood around the window, woke Jase. He felt Nattie. She was nice and toasty so he eased out from under the blankets and tucked her in nice and snug to keep her warm. He placed more wood on the embers in the fireplace and hung his coat over the window to keep the light out of her eyes. He wanted to let her get as much sleep as possible. He was so worried but didn't want to think about it. He looked for something to eat but there was nothing. He pulled out two candy bars from his backpack and placed them on the table for Nattie.

He stood over the table looking down at his map of Barcastle. Based on the position of the lake, he was able to determine both the distance and the direction they would need to take to reach Safrailium.

Nattie sat up and looked around. "Jase, where are we?" She looked down, realized she wasn't wearing any clothes, and quickly pulled the blankets up to cover her chest.

"Are you okay, Nattie?"

"What happened?"

"What's the last thing you remember?"

"I don't know. We were running from that jerky pit face idiot that wanted to kill us and the police cruiser rolled down the hill." Jase let out a sigh of relief and went to sit next to her. "Jassie what's wrong?" Jase frowned, wiped the tears from his eyes, and let out a little whimper. She hugged him, "Jassie, you okay?"

He started to cry. "I almost lost you, Nattie."

"How?"

"You fell into a frozen lake. If I hadn't found this place, you would be dead."

"So you saved my life."

"I had to. I couldn't live without you."

"You took my clothes off?" Jase laughed and wiped his nose.

"Yes, they were like ice. I had to warm you up. I hung them by the fire so they should be dry by now."

She looked at Jase in a funny way. "What?"

She smiled, "Never mind." She gave Jase a kiss. "Thank you for saving me, Jassie."

"You're welcome, baby." Jase got up and got the candy bars for her. "Here's breakfast."

"Aren't you going to eat one?"

"I already had mine. You eat those."

"I'm so hungry." It only took a few seconds for Nattie to devour both candy bars. She was so skinny that she got hungry every few hours. "Jassie, won't they find us here?"

"Well, our tracks were covered by the snow and wind last night, but the smoke from the fire could give us away if they get close enough. How are you feeling?"

"My chest hurts a little and I feel really tired."

"I wish we didn't have to move but they will eventually find us if we stay here."

"Do you think you're up to walking?"

"I guess it doesn't really matter. We can't stay here. How far do we have to go?"

"About fifteen sects."

"Sheesh, still that far."

"I'm betting that he has people in the town waiting for us."

"What are we going to do?"

"I'll figure that out when we get there. We need to take the train to Voncara Cove. I'm hoping they figure that we will try to fly out and not be looking at the train station."

"Maybe we should try to fly home?"

"I don't think that's a good idea. Even if we get home safely, he knows where we live. I don't want to have to worry about our parents."

"Jassie, my mom. I don't want anything to happen to her." Nattie started to get upset.

"Nattie, I'm sure your mom is fine. We can call her from Safrailium."

"We need to get going then." She got dressed and Jase helped her to pack her dry things back into her backpack.

They walked out into a beautiful fresh blanket of snow. The sky was clear and the warm sun was very bright reflecting off the white show. The air was cold and crisp but there was no wind so it didn't feel as bad. It was very quiet outside. They couldn't even hear their own footsteps in the fluffy snow, which made it difficult to walk. Jase held both backpacks and Nattie held his arm as they walked. He used his compass to guide their way but stayed away from the roadway.

After walking a couple sects, Jase could tell that Nattie wasn't feeling very well. She was normally such a chatterbox. "You okay? You're so quiet."

"I'm just thinking."

"Oh, I was wondering where that smoke was coming from." She smacked him.

"Ha ha, very funny. My brain doesn't smoke!"

"So what are you thinking about?"

"Lots of things — my mom, how much treasure there is, and how we can get back at that pit faced idiot."

"You really hate that guy."

"Don't you?"

"Of course; because of him I almost lost you three times. Maybe we should have sold him the book. We don't even know if the treasure is real."

"I don't care. He's never getting the book." Nattie's nostrils flared and her lips tightened. "I owe him a trip to the bottom of a frozen lake or a short trip out a fourth story window!"

"It all happened so fast, Nattie."

"Were you worried about me?"

"Are you kidding? I was terrified."

"I'm sorry, Jassie, but I'm glad it was me and not you."

"Wait. What's that coming?"

"It sounds like a cruiser."

"We must be closer to the road then I thought."

"Should we head back into the woods?"

"No, I have another idea. Can you get your invention back out?"

"I don't know if it will work, Jassie. It was all wet from the lake." She took out her science project and turned it on.

"Is it working?"

"I don't know. I think it's on but no way to know."

"Okay, keep it off but be ready to turn it on if someone comes. We can make much faster time on the road then in this deep snow."

They climbed over the snow bank and onto the road. They walked for about half an hour before they heard another cruiser in the distance. They hid behind a large boulder, in the tree line, on the hillside next to the road. Jase held Nattie and they waited. Sure enough, it was a police cruiser moving slowly. The men were glaring at the countryside as they passed by. Fortunately, they didn't spot their footprints.

"I guess old pit-face hasn't given up yet." They turned around and leaned back against the boulder for a while to rest. "Jassie, how are we going to make it before nightfall? We have such a long way to go. We will freeze if we stay out here all night."

"I guess we better pick up the pace a bit."

They continued down the road moving at an increased speed but Nattie had a hard time keeping up. After a few sects, she stopped and bent over a little.

"Nattie, what's wrong?"

"I don't know. My chest hurts." Jase threw the backpacks over the snow bank and picked her up. He carried her into the woods a short ways and sat her down by a tree.

"I think I need to lie down." Jase grabbed his backpack and helped her to lean back against it.

"How's that, baby?"

"Much better." She lay back and held her chest with her hand. Jase sat down next to her and held her close. "I don't think I'm going to make it, Jassie. It hurts too much," Nattie cried.

"Don't worry, I'll figure something out. Try to relax and rest." After a little while, Jase asked, "Does it still hurt?"

"It's better as long as I lay still."

Jase got up and pulled some thick dry branches from the trees. He tied together a makeshift rescue litter using the rope he took from the cottage so he could drag her behind him. Just before he was ready to try it out, they could hear a strange noise approaching on the road. Jase went to investigate and ran back a minute later.

"Nattie, it's an old-fashioned farm truck."

"You mean with wheels?"

"Yes, I have an idea. Come with me, quick." Jase helped her up and they climbed onto the roadway. "Nattie, wave them down as they get close."

"Me?"

"Yes, trust me on this." Nattie stood in the middle of the road and waved her arm while the truck was still a little ways off. She moved to the side as they slowed and opened the window.

"Sweetie, what are the two of you doing out here in the middle of nowhere in all this snow?" A cute little old lady asked from the passenger seat.

"It's a long, long, story."

"You must be freezing. Can we take you somewhere?" Nattie smiled with her big dimple smile,

"Yes, please. We are trying to get to Safrailium."

"That's where we're heading. You're welcome to come with us but it's going to be a little cramped."

"That's okay," Jase said quickly. He put their bags in the back and climbed in the truck. Nattie climbed in and sat on Jase's lap.

"I'm Millie and this is Daniel."

"Pleased to meet you. I'm Nattie, and this is Jase."

The truck bumped and pounded down the road, slipping here and there in the snow. "Boy, it's a bumpy ride."

"These old vehicles are like that. You feel every bump in the road."

"Well, it sure beats walking, and thank you for taking us."

"You're welcome, dear. How did you end up way out here?"

After a long pause, Nattie said, "It's really a long story. I wouldn't know where to start. We didn't mean to get caught out in the snow like this."

"Do you have a place to stay in town?"

"We aren't sure yet."

"It's so nice and warm in here." The truck went over a big hole in the road. The impact caused Nattie to grab her chest.

"You okay, sweetie?" Jase asked.

"I think so."

"Maybe we should just fly home when we get to town," Jase said.

"No, I like your plan better. We may never get another chance at this and we're already here," Nattie whispered.

She laid back and fell asleep on Jase. He held her tight with every bump of the truck during the hour and a half drive into town on the snowy roads.

"Where would you two like us to drop you?" Daniel asked.

"Where is the train station?"

"Would you like me to take you there?"

Jase thought for a second. He was worried that the police or some of Halfgrim's men could be watching the station.

"Can you drop us off nearby, maybe somewhere we can eat?"

"I know just the spot." Daniel stopped the truck a few blocks from the train station just outside of a little restaurant along a strip of shops. "The food here is the best in town, but it's not well known so you can normally get right in and eat without waiting."

"That's great, thank you. Nattie, wake up." Jase gave her a little shake. "We're here. You hungry, baby?"

"Starving." Jase took out their bags and shook Daniel's hand. "Thank you so much."

Jase cautiously looked around to make sure no one was looking for them. They slipped into an alley next to the restaurant. "Nattie, wait here. Let me make sure it's safe. If I take off running, stay hidden here and I'll come back for you, okay?"

"Okay, Jassie, but be careful." Jase walked into the restaurant, a cold shiver ran up his back.

"Can I help you?" a short young girl at the hostess counter asked.

"Can I see a menu please?"

"Sure, are you dining alone?" she said with a smile.

"No, I'm waiting on my girlfriend." She handed Jase a menu and walked into the kitchen for a second. Jase took a quick look around. It seemed okay and no one took an interest in him so he went to get Nattie.

Jase requested a table in the back of the restaurant where they could sit and watch the door as they ate.

There was a fireplace blazing on the back wall and the room was cozy and warm. They took off their coats and got comfortable. Jase noticed Nattie smiling as she looked at the menu. "You look like you're feeling better."

"I am."

The waitress walked over, "Hi, I'm Haddi, what can I get for you today?"

"I want one of everything on the menu," Nattie said with a giggle.

Jase and the waitress laughed. "You are so cute, Nattie."

"Well, I'm starving." They ordered their food and talked for a while.

"Jassie, do you think it will be safe at the train station?"

"Hopefully they think we are still in the woods and I would assume they would be watching the airport and not the train station. We need to be careful anyway."

"I wonder if it would be safe to go to the police here."

"I don't think we should take the chance. Would they even believe us anyway?"

"You're right. We better not say anything."

When they finished eating, they gathered up their things and headed towards the train station. They vigilantly watched for any suspicious individuals while they walked but there was very little traffic and hardly anyone on the sidewalks. It was a small station with a loading platform and a seating area made up of long wooden benches, outside the ticket office. The boarding area was wide open and almost appeared abandoned except for a small man at the ticket counter.

"Can I help you young folks?" Jase took out their tickets.

"Yes, sir. Could we possibly exchange these for tickets for today to Voncara Cove?"

Chapter 34

"Normally I would be happy to but there are no more trains today. The soonest is early tomorrow morning." Jase's shoulders dropped and he looked at Nattie.

"Can't we ever catch a break?" They looked so disappointed, the man at the ticket counter felt bad for them.

"I'll tell you what. I'm not supposed to do this but I will refund your tickets. There's a very special, old time scenic train leaving from here in just a little bit to Voncara Cove. It's an old-fashioned steam engine with luxurious passenger cars. It takes a little longer to get there but at least you won't have to wait until tomorrow. I think you will really enjoy it. I know my son did."

"That's perfect," Jase said.

"There's a little building a block down the road where you have to purchase the tickets. They are a private company not associated with the public railroad."

Nattie smiled, "Let's do it, Jassie. Sounds romantic."

"Okay." The teller refunded their tickets. "Thank you so much."

"You're welcome. Have a nice time."

They hurried to the building to purchase the new tickets. "This is exciting, Jassie." Nattie bounced along trying to pull Jase so he would pick up the pace.

"You know these backpacks aren't light."

"Hurry, pokey."

Jase laughed, "What's the hurry?"

"It sounds like fun, don't you think?"

"Yeah, I want to take pictures of the antique train."

They went in to purchase the tickets, there was a young girl working behind the counter. "Can I help you?"

"Yes, we would like to purchase..."

"Scenic train tickets?"

"Yes please."

"Would you like the dining car with a dinner meal or the first class car?" Jase looked at Nattie.

"We already ate dinner."

"Miss, we'll take the first class car."

"Are there any snacks on the train?" Nattie asked.

"Yes, ma'am. They sell drinks and snacks at the bar. Here are your tickets. The train arrives any minute and should board within the next hour." Jase paid for the tickets and they hurried back to the station to beat the train. Other passengers had already arrived and were sitting on the station benches.

No sooner did Jase and Nattie sit down that they heard a steam whistle blowing.

WOO, WOO. Jase got his camera ready to take pictures and positioned himself near the leading edge of the boarding ramp. The black locomotive with a yellow and red smokestack chugged along the tracks. Puffs of steam and smoke exhausted up into the air and blew backwards behind the train. Jase took lots of pictures as it approached and slowed into the station. He took pictures of the wheels, linkages, and the cab as the engine passed by. The huge spindle wheels were painted black with red spokes.

"Nattie, did you see the size of those wheels? I never knew they would be so big."

"Yeah, they were almost as tall as you." The passenger cars were brown with a maroon trim around the wooden windows and frame. Jase and Nattie walked along the eight cars until they reached the end.

With no caboose, Jase wanted to ride in the last car where they could see the tracks through the rear window. They waited there until it was time to board. A steward placed a set of steps by each doorway to make it easier for the passengers to step up onto the steel platforms.

Jase and Nattie were the first to board the luxurious car, which had been fully restored to its original luster. A fine red, black, and brown carpet lay on the floor with a fine tapestry pattern. There were individual, elegantly plush, antique chairs and love seats with end tables along both sides of the passenger car. Wooden sliding windows lined the walls providing a great view outside. Each car was equipped with a coal-burning stove and the interior was nice and warm.

Jase and Nattie sat in the loveseat nearest the back door. They took off their coats and put their things on the floor in front of them. Jase walked to the bar and purchased some snacks and drinks. The whistle blew one long and one short blast. The train jerked as the engine started to chug forward. Jase held onto the bar so he wouldn't fall. The train sped up on the tracks embarking on its three and a half hour journey to Voncara Cove. Jase wobbled as he walked back to their seat carrying their snacks. The train car swayed to the left and right making it hard to keep balance. He sat down quickly as the car swayed to the left and Nattie caught him holding on tight. She snuggled up and kissed him.

"I really love you, Jassie."

"I love you, baby."

"There's no place else in this world I would rather be than sitting here with you." Jase leaned over and they rubbed noses. He put his arm around her and they watched out the windows across from them, taking in the wonderful views of the countryside. The sky was so clear except for the occasional puff of smoke and little pieces of debris from the smokestack.

"It's so neat, the trail of smoke behind the train."

"Take a picture, Jassie." Jase took a few pictures then sat back down. It was so cozy that Nattie started yawning and feeling sleepy. Then Jase yawned.

"Nattie, stop that. You're making me yawn."

"Sorry, Jassie. I can't help it."

"How's your chest feeling?"

"It feels fine now." Nattie laid on Jase's lap using her coat as a pillow and fell asleep. Jase's head kept bobbing until he finally gave in and laid his head back to catch a nap. As the train approached Voncara Cove, a teen girl woke up Jase.

"Hi."

"Hey, are we there?"

"No, but I saw you had a camera. We are coming up on the canyon with the huge wooden bridge. I thought you might want to take a picture."

"Yes, thank you." Nattie sat up and stretched.

"Where are we?"

"Almost there." Jase got ready and when they approached the canyon, the views of the valley down below were breathtaking. The sun was just above the mountains to the west, providing the most perfect background lighting for taking pictures. Jase snapped picture after picture as the train passed over the bridge. Then he sat back down next to Nattie.

"Jassie, doesn't the past few days seem like a nightmare and we just woke up?"

"Yeah, a little, except they still want to kill us."

"Oh! That reminds me...something pit face said. Let me see the book." Nattie looked at the covering and felt around it with her fingertips.

"Jase hand me your knife."

"Nattie, what are you doing?"

"You trust me, right?"

"Of course." Nattie opened the book and used the knife to carefully cut the interior leather from the inside cover. It took a bit of effort but she was able to loosen the leather and fold it back. She reached inside the cover and pulled out a piece of very old yellowed paper, folded into a square. Jase's eyes opened wide with anticipation. "Open it."

"I'm working on it." Nattie unfolded the paper to reveal a hand-drawn map of Voncara Cove. "It's a treasure map!"

"Jase, shush!" Nattie giggled. "You're like a little kid looking at a lollipop."

"Look at those markings." Jase got out his notebook with Nattie's sketching of the crest in Halfgrim's book. "Look, if this drawing was to scale, I bet these X's would line up with the ones on the map."

"I think you're right."

"Look at the dotted line going up this trail on the side of the big hill."

"I think it's the starting point but how can we find it without the actual crest?"

"I guess we need to search for it."

"The path leads up the hill to this point and stops."

"Jassie, look. If the drawing was to scale, I think the outer crest circle's edge crosses over the treasure and the inner circle crosses through the starting point."

"So what about the +50? What do you think that stands for?" Nattie leaned forward and pulled her hair back so she could get a closer look.

"What does this mean, I wonder."

"What?"

"The small letters at the end of the trail? *Vace Tranecen.*"

CAVE
Lookout Point
vACE Traneen
N
E
S
W

"Sounds like another language."

"Yeah, it does, but what language?"

The train entered a very long tunnel through the mountain. The whistle blew echoing off the tunnel walls, intensifying the sound and causing some of the passengers to jump. Jase laughed and looked at Nattie.

She smiled and cleared her throat, "Ahem." She gave him a cute look with her head tilted and her shining hair hanging down to one side. A light shined down from the ceiling illuminating her hair and face. "You are so beautiful, Nattie." He put his arms around her waist and they shared a passionate kiss.

The train slowed as it exited the tunnel and made a sharp turn to the right. The tracks ran along the base of the mountains that isolated the cove from the outside world. They followed along the foothills until they reached the Voncara Cove station. Jase and Nattie intently watched outside the window as the train slowed to see if anyone suspicious stood nearby. Once they were satisfied that none of Halfgrim's men were around, they exited the train.

Voncara Cove was just a little town a lot like Summerset. They really felt right at home, walking down the narrow streets lined with shops and places to eat. Jase couldn't resist the antique shops, wanting to look for another rare pirate treasure for his costume.

Nattie kept pulling his arm, "Jase, we can look at all this stuff later. We need to find a safe place to stay. I don't want to freeze again tonight and I need a shower."

"How about just one if I'm quick?"

"Okay, if you promise not to take forever cuz it will be dark soon."

"Oh, this place is different. *The Cleric of Density.*"

They walked into the little shop of marvelous wonders. It was like stepping back in time with David and Tristy. Pirate artifacts covered the walls and shelves. There were several real carriage-mounted cannons in the center of the largest of three rooms.

"Figures."

"What?"

"You had to pick this one. Look at all this neat stuff."

"What's wrong with that?"

"Because you'll be in here forever."

"I'll just have a quick look around then we can go."

Jase asked the storeowner if he could take pictures of the artifacts. "Absolutely, feel free to tell all your friends about us. Are you two on vacation?"

"Yes, ma'am."

"If you like history, you will find many pieces here over six hundred years old."

"That's great; thank you."

Jase walked around taking lots of pictures.

"You have a very interesting name for your shop," Nattie said.

"Have you figured it out yet?"

"Figured out what?"

"Our name, it's an anagram."

"Oh, I love those." Nattie got into Jase's backpack laying by the counter and took out his notepad. She wrote down a few word arrangements. "I got it; it's *The Circle of Destiny*."

"Very good." Nattie thought, *how ironic*. She walked over to Jase who was admiring a historic sword in a display case.

"Jassie, can I see the little map?" she whispered softly.

"Nattie, look at the artwork on this sword." The detail was exquisite and quite unique. The entire blade was decorative with engraved designs. An inscription displayed, *Captain David Anderson, with love, Angelica.*

"Oh, Jase!"

"I know; it's actually David's sword."

"You so need to buy that."

"I wish I could, but it's four thousand tutarian."

"Really?"

"Yeah, it's way too much."

"But you have enough saved to buy it, don't you?"

"Yeah but that would take almost all of it."

"Jassie, you really need to buy it. You may never get another chance."

"No, it's just too much. We still have to get home."

"Nattie, what did you say before?"

"Oh yeah, let me see the little map." Jase handed Nattie the old map and she carefully unfolded it. She wrote in Jase's notebook for a few minutes.

"What are you doing, baby?"

"Shush." Jase smacked her butt and she wiggled.

"Hey, you brat." Nattie smiled with a big grin and looked at Jase.

"What?"

"I got it."

"Got what?"

"The words on the map silly...it's not another language, it's an anagram."

"What does it say?"

"*Vace Tranecen* is, *Cave Entrance*."

"Nattie, you are so amazing. How did you ever figure that out?"

"It's funny; you know the strange name of this shop?"

"Yeah."

"It's also an anagram. That's what got me thinking. This place is actually called *The Circle of Destiny*."

Jase laughed, "That's ironic."

"That's what I said," Nattie giggled. "Jassie, look at this." She pointed at the cave opening along the cliffs in the sea. "Remember the mesirage coordinates from the first two books pointed to this spot out in the water?"

"Yes."

"I bet that moving northeast of this position by fifty feet, based on the +50 and the NE from the seal in the third book, lines up with the cave entrance on the side of the large hill."

"If you're right, that will make it a lot easier to find."

They looked around the shop a little more and Nattie found what looked like a copper goblet but the top was as big as a cereal bowl. *This is strange*, she thought. She picked it up off the shelf and a funny-looking carved stick fell out of the top.

She bent down to pick it up and the shop owner walked over. "Do you know what that is?"

"I don't know. It's kind of heavy and too big to drink out of."

"Let me show you." The shop owner held the goblet by the base and ran the carved stick around the rim of the bowl. The brass hummed loudly with a beautiful tone. Nattie's eyes lit up and she smiled at the owner.

"Can I try?"

"Sure." Nattie ran the stick around the rim producing a wonderful tone. "I love this!"

"Nattie, you should get it," Jase said. She looked at the price tag, "No, it's too much."

"How much is it?"

"Forty-five tutarian."

Jase laughed, "You just told me I should buy a four thousand tutarian sword, and you think that's too much?"

"If you're truly interested in the sword, I will make you a special deal," the shop owner said. "I will sell you the sword for half off and you can have the Singing Bowl and Mallet for free." Nattie laughed and hiccupped at the same time.

"That's so neat, singing bowls. Jassie, you have to get the sword now. After all, it was David's."

"So you know the history of the Voncara Cove navy?" the shop owner asked.

"Um, a little," Nattie said.

"Captain Anderson led the navy's flagship hundreds of years ago. He's quite famous around here."

"What about Captain Wells?" Nattie asked.

"Who?"

"Okay, ma'am, we'll take you up on your offer. Can I see the sword?" She took David's sword from the case and handed it to Jase. He pulled it from the sheath and held it up.

"Wow, Jassie, look at all the nicks in the blade."

"Yeah, I think this sword has seen a lot of action but it still looks fantastic after all these years."

Jase paid for the sword and Nattie picked out the best singing bowl. She found a cute one with engraved purple butterflies at the base.

"Jassie, ask her about places to stay."

"Ma'am, would you happen to know of any places to stay that would be out of the way? Maybe something that most tourists wouldn't know about?"

"Yeah, sure, you want *Insurgent Point Tavern*. It was built upon the old site of Captain Anderson's headquarters. They have separate cabins with lots of privacy. They're quite fancy with fireplaces and nice decor."

"Oh that sounds nice, Jassie." Nattie winked at Jase and smiled.

"It's only a few blocks northeast of here and it's up on the hillside so you have a nice view looking down at the town and a nice view of the ocean."

"Thank you, that sounds great."

Jase and Nattie walked outside and headed for the tavern.

"Jassie, I want to see the ocean."

"Okay, let's get a hotel room, and then we can walk there." The tavern was a ways up on the hillside. Jase held both backpacks and Nattie held Jase's sword and her bag containing the singing bowl. They were out of breath by the time they reached the tavern office.

"Good evening. Can I help you?"

"Yes, we would like a room for the night please."

"Certainly."

"Are you very full tonight?"

"No, sir, quite empty actually. It's normally very slow during off-season but the rates are much better. Just fill out this form and I'll get you situated."

Jase filled out the paperwork and Nattie walked around the lobby looking at everything.

"All set?"

"Yes."

"Here's your key. I put you in one of our best cabins with a great view."

"Wonderful, thanks," Nattie said.

When they got to their cabin, they walked around the deck to the front where they could see way out over the ocean. The sun was setting beyond the mountains behind them and an amber glow reflected off the waves in the cove as they crashed on the beach. Jase took lots of pictures.

"Jassie, I need to sit down. My feet are killing me."

"Okay, sweetie." They walked into their cabin and put their things down.

"This is so nice. I love this."

"Yeah, this is really nice, and it was pretty cheap." Jase pulled off Nattie's boots as she stretched out on the bed.

"Ooh, this bed feels so good. Jassie, can you massage my feet? They hurt so bad. Actually my whole body aches."

Jase sat on the bottom of the bed.

"Give me your cute little foot." He started to massage her left foot but within just a few minutes, she had drifted off to sleep. Jase got up and found a blanket in the closet. He covered her up nice and snug, and gave her a kiss on the cheek. He made a fire in the fireplace and sat down to study the treasure map.

A bright light shined in through a crack in the curtains. He went to investigate. The moon was rising up as if out of the ocean and was quite brilliant. He could just imagine David and Angelica sitting up on the mountain looking at that same moon. He really wanted to wake Nattie but decided to let her sleep. He went out on the front deck and took pictures for her. He felt a little lonely out there all by himself so he went inside and got cleaned up. He then snuck in under the cover next to her. He put his arm around her, kissed her neck, and fell asleep.

Nattie woke up the next morning, well rested and full of energy. She eased out from under Jase's arm, trying not to wake him. She added a few logs to the fire and played with her singing bowl. Not wanting to wake up Jase, she took the bowl out to the front deck and closed the door behind her. She could smell the cool, salty sea air, blowing in from the ocean. With the tide coming in and the nice breeze, the waves in the cove were large and she could hear them roaring across the beach.

The sun was rising up above the ocean. She couldn't stand waiting anymore. She went in and stood above Jase, dragging her hair across his face. His nose twitched, then his cheek muscles. She tried not to laugh but couldn't help it. Her laughter shook the bed. Jase woke to see her standing over him laughing.

"Wake up, sleepyhead." Jase smiled up at her.

"You seem to be feeling well."

"Come on, Jassie. Get up; we have lots to see today." She grabbed his hand and pulled him sideways, halfway off the bed. "Come look." She led him outside to see the sun.

"Oh nice!"

"Told ya."

"I have to get my camera."

"Ahem, are you forgetting something?" She put her hand on her waist and tilted her head with a stern look. Jase laughed and put his arms around her.

Chapter 35

They shared a kiss in the orange glow of the rising sun.

"I love you, Nattie."

"I love you also. Now get ready. I want to see the ocean."

Jase laughed, "Okay, okay."

They got cleaned up and packed up their things. "Nattie, maybe we should just leave our packs here."

"What if Halfgrim shows up. If he finds out we're staying here, he could steal the books and your sword."

"Yeah, you're right."

They walked through the town toward the sea. "Jassie, look, a carriage ride."

"Nice."

"Can we go? Please? Pretty please."

"Sure, baby." Nattie jumped up and down. She grabbed Jase's arm and hurried him along to catch the carriage before anyone else could.

It was an open white carriage that could seat up to four people — two sitting forward, and two backwards. The carriage was pulled by a four-legged Sadrum Epod. They were a horse-like creature first discovered on the moons of Frailwar near the outer colonies. They were then bred by farmers because of their gentle demeanor, ease of taming, and their strong powerful legs that could pull heavy loads. They were smooth to the touch but had a scaly green skin.

Nattie pranced up to the carriage.

"Hi! Can you please take us to the ocean?" Nattie said with a big dimple smile on her face.

"We don't normally go that way. We have a set route we follow." Nattie stuck out her lower lip and clasped her hands together as if she was praying.

"Please..."

She looked so cute the driver laughed and said, "I guess I can make an exception just this once."

"Thank you, thank you, thank you." Jase picked up Nattie by the waist and put her on the first step of the carriage side rail. She hugged his neck and kissed him. "I can't wait to see the ocean, Jassie. Have you ever seen the ocean before?"

"Nope, well not up close, other than in pictures." A strange, rotten animal odor filled the air. Nattie fanned her face with her hand.

"What's that horrible smell?" Jase laughed and turned all red. "What's so funny?"

"It's the bag of poop behind the Epod." Nattie laughed loudly and held her nose.

"Ewwww, gross. Kinda takes the romance out of it, ha?"

"Don't worry; it won't smell bad once we get moving a little faster," the driver said. The Epod picked up the pace but silently marched with its elephant-like feet made up of fatty tissue.

"That's better," Nattie said. She grabbed Jase's hand and put his arm around her waist. Jase laughed and kissed her. "I'm getting hungry, Jassie."

"Me too."

"There's a great restaurant near the sea wall called *Every Morning* if you're interested," the driver said.

They passed by another street and Nattie suddenly pulled Jase down across the seat and kissed him. "Jase, stay down. I just saw one of Halfgrim's men."

"Are you sure?" Jase fearfully asked with his eyes wide open.

"Pretty sure, he looked like one of the men talking to him the night they chased me down the hallway. He's the one that thought the map was in the front of the book." Nattie continued to kiss Jase until they passed into the next street. She peeked up to make sure it was safe.

"Okay, he can't see us now." Jase sat up and looked around. He took a deep breath and let out a little growl.

"You know, I'm getting sick of this. Every time I'm having a good time with you, old pit-face has to ruin it."

"Nattie, maybe we should just give him the book. I'm so afraid he's going to hurt you."

"No way, he's not getting it. Even if we gave it to him, do you think he's just going to let us go?"

"I guess you're right." Jase hugged Nattie tight.

"I'm going to get that guy. You just wait and see. He's going to get what's coming to him and he's not ruining this for us. We have a sword and I'm not afraid to use it," Nattie said very boisterously.

Jase laughed and patted her back. "I'm not kidding. He messes with either one of us and he's gonna get it!"

They arrived at the sea wall. Jase paid the driver and Nattie thanked him. She stomped along in the sand as they walked toward an opening in the stone wall leading down to the beach. She stopped, standing perfectly still.

"What is it, Nattie?" She looked up at Jase with tears in her eyes. "Oh baby, what's wrong?" She pointed at the stone in the wall where David chiseled the words, *Tristy and David Forever*, inside a heart.

"I miss Tristy." She hugged Jase, "I don't want anyone else to die. I wish he would just leave us alone."

"Baby, it will be okay. I promise."

"I don't see how." Jase held her and rubbed her back. After a few minutes, she wiped her eyes, let out a few sniffles, and took a deep breath. "I'm okay now."

"You sure?"

"No." Her chin quivered a little and her lower lip protruded.

"Nattie, I will die before I let anything happen to you."

"That's what I'm afraid of."

"Come on, sweetie. Let's go see the ocean.

They walked down to the surf. Nattie closed her eyes and felt the sea wind in her hair. She took a deep breath and let it out, then took off her shoes and held her pants up as she walked out into the freezing surf.

"What are you doing, silly?"

"I want to feel it on my feet." The next wave flowed up the beach and tickled her feet with freezing seawater. It was deeper than she thought and got the bottom of her pants wet. She reached down, scoped up some water in her hand, and put it to her mouth for a little taste. "Yuck!" She spit it out.

"What's it taste like?"

"Like salt water. It's nasty."

"Well, I don't think you're supposed to drink it."

"I don't know how fish can like that stuff."

They held hands and walked down the beach with their backpacks on their backs. When they reached the foothills of Lookout Mountain, so named for its ideal position and height overlooking the town and the cove, they found an alternate path, leading up the side of the mountain not shown on the map. They decided to eat before starting their search for the cave. They found *Every Morning* restaurant and ate breakfast. The food was good but they excitedly rushed to finish.

Nattie gathered a bunch of pastries and cookies from the display at the counter. "Sweetie, what are you doing?"

"Getting snacks." Jase laughed. "It's not funny. I'm tired of being hungry all the time."

"I know, baby. You're just so cute grabbing up all these pastries." Jase gave her a kiss and they paid for their food and snacks.

"Jassie, I was thinking, and don't you dare say you see smoke." Jase laughed and gave her a hug.

"What are you thinking?"

"If the treasure is in a cave, maybe we should go get a bright flashlight or two."

"Good thinking, sweetie." They found a hardware store nearby and purchased Nattie a nice bright flashlight and Jase got a battery-operated spotlight with a built in electric lantern.

They set out on their journey, climbing the steep incline up the hillside. After a while, they passed through a little canyon with steep cliffs on both sides, which opened up to a large wooded area. They circled around up to the top of Lookout Mountain and sat on a flat boulder to rest. The view of the town and the sea was fantastic.

"Jassie, do you know where we are?" Nattie put her arm around him and leaned her head against him.

"Yes, this is where David brought Angelica the morning they saw the approaching enemy ships."

"I think this is the actual rock they sat on. Can you believe we're actually here?" Jase leaned Nattie's head back and kissed her tenderly, until a hawk flew by and screeched, startling them. Nattie jumped and giggled.

"Jassie, just think, we are the only ones in the whole world who know what really happened here with Tristy, David, and Angelica."

"Yeah, except for..."

Nattie put her finger against Jase's lips, "Don't even say it."

"Nattie, how far out do you think the book coordinates point to, out in the sea?"

"I'm not sure." Jase leaned over the edge of the cliff looking down at the surf pounding against the granite.

"Wow, Nattie, look."

"That's okay. I'm just fine over here."

"Just take a peek."

Nattie crawled on her tummy and peaked over the edge. "This is so high. I bet the cave at the sea is right under us."

"Do you think that's the cave entrance the map shows?"

"No, it couldn't be. It's not fifty feet northeast."

"But the only place there could have been a cave was in the canyon and there was nothing."

"What about the open area in the woods just past the canyon?"

"Hmm, let's go look around." They searched all along the cliffs and through the woods but found no cave. They heard voices so they hid behind some bushes next to the hillside. Nattie's heart raced and her face turned scarlet red. Jase shielded her and kept one hand on his sword, ready to strike. As the voices grew near, they could hear laughter.

Then a voice cried out, "ECHO," in the canyon.

"Shew, I think they're just tourists, Jassie."

"Nattie, look!" Jase pointed to a crest imprinted low in the stone cliff, behind the bushes.

"Jassie, that matches the images in the books."

"Yeah, except it's only the inner part with the hawk."

"The cave must be around here somewhere." They waited for the tourists, on their way to lookout point, to pass by, and then proceeded to examine the area around the engraved crest. They looked all over but no cave.

"Jase, what about this little hole in the rock?"

"It's just a hole."

"But what if there's something inside?"

"Why don't you stick your arm in and find out." Nattie laughed and punched Jase in the chest.

"I'm not sticking my hand in that! There could be bugs, spiders, or snakes in there."

"I'm just kidding, baby. Let's get a stick." Jase twirled a branch around in the hole then took it out. Nattie shined a flashlight inside and when she got close, a bird flew out skimming her head. She screamed, jumping backwards, tripping over Jase's shoes, and fell to the ground on the soft wet leaves.

She got up holding her chest with her heart racing and laughed, "Stupid bird, gave me a heart attack."

"You okay?"

"Yes, but now I'm all wet." She shook her hands to get off some of the moisture. Jase shined the flashlight and looked into the hole.

"Nattie, I think I see something."

"What is it?"

"Here, look."

"No, that's okay. I believe you."

Jase reached in with his hand and felt around. "I think it's a knob."

"Really?"

"Yeah but it's hard to get to. I need something to stand on. Can you get my backpack?" Nattie handed Jase his backpack and he stepped up to get a better grip. "I'm turning it but nothing's happening."

"Try pulling it."

"I don't want to break it."

"Wait...it's moving." He pulled it out until it stopped. They could hear a humming sound coming from behind the stone. The ground quaked for a second and they both stepped back a few steps. A rounded top door-sized crack appeared in the stone on the side of the cliff. With a deep sounding thud, a thick stone door slid inward, leaving an opening.

"Wow!"

"Incredible," Nattie said. Jase cautiously entered in first with Nattie right behind on her tippy toes, trying to look over his shoulder. A dark passageway led down a set of damp stone steps.

They turned on their lights and cautiously continued down. The further they walked the more humid the air became. The walls were damp and it stunk like wet rotten hemp rope.

"How far does this go?"

"I don't know. It seems to go forever." The passageway started to increase in size.

"Jassie, it's getting hard to breathe," Nattie said as she held onto the back of his coat. They walked a little further.

"Look, the cave opens up just ahead." They walked up to a drop-off that opened up into a huge cavern.

"Jassie, watch out." Jase just stood there and shined his spotlight.

Nattie walked up next to him and froze. Their hearts were beating frantically. They both were breathing very heavily, gasping in the humid air such that their whole bodies flexed with every breath. They could not believe what they were seeing. Nattie's knees felt weak. She held on to Jase. Their eyes were huge and their mouths hung open.

"This is unreal," Jase said as if he was mesmerized.

Nattie brushed her hair back to fully take in the incredible revelation. "I think I'm about to have a heart attack."

"Yeah, me too."

They gazed upon a huge, ancient alien gunship. It was so long they couldn't see the back end in the darkness. The ship was about a hundred and fifty feet long and about seventy feet wide including the wingtips. The fuselage was covered with a strange design of gray, charcoal, and black swirls all intermingling together. The nose of the ship faced them and had six small rectangular windows across the front upper cockpit area. Jase took a few pictures but the flash wasn't strong enough to capture a good image.

"We need to get closer."

They found steps leading down into the large cavern.

"Jassie, be careful; these stones are slippery."

"Wow, Nattie, look at all the damage." They could see serious battle scars all over the ship. The wings were scattered with blast holes and a long narrow diagonal charred impression ran across the length of the fuselage.

Jase started taking pictures all along the ship. He could hear the sound of waves crashing against the rocks near the back wall of the cave. Nattie climbed up on the large wing and walked over to look at an intricate technological device mounted against the fuselage. *Fascinating, I wonder what this is,* she thought. She felt the imprinted damage with her fingertips. It felt smooth to the touch as if the metal had been melted by extreme heat.

She walked over to what looked like a hatch. "Nattie, look at this. There's some writing on the tail."

"I can't; what's it look like?"

"It says, *USS Adversity, Mach 12.* Does that mean anything to you?"

"I never heard of anything like that before but how can we possibly read the writing on an ancient alien ship?"

"Good question."

Nattie pulled the release mechanism on the hatch and it started to fall loose.

"Jase, help me! Come quick." Jase ran up and helped her lift off the heavy panel before it fell. They stepped inside the alien ship. There were all kinds of gadgets mounted along the inner cockpit. Nattie sat down in the right-hand seat. She played with the various knobs, switches, and controls. Jase explored the rear of the ship using his spotlight. He walked into a huge bay and shined the light on the ceiling. It appeared as if the whole roof was made to open up via two huge panels. Nattie managed to toggle the main power switch, lighting up the gauges and dashboard. She quickly turned the power back off.

Chapter 36

Jase ran from the rear of the ship, "Nattie, the lights came on back there for a minute."

"Yeah, I know. I found the main power switch. I can't believe this thing still has power."

"What's that?" Jase noticed a leather-bound journal lying on the center console. Nattie picked it up and started reading. Jase sat in the left-hand seat and could imagine himself flying the ship through space. A cold chill ran up Nattie's spine when she looked at the title page in the journal. Her hair stood straight up on end from the shock of seeing the print:

Captain's Log

USS Adversity

National Aeronautics and Space Administration

United States of America

Captain Ulysses Stanton Wells

"Jassie, look at this! They weren't from the future. They were from another planet."

"What do you mean?"

"This ship belongs to David and Captain Wells."

"That explains it. This was the ship they sailed into the cave on the water. I knew it wasn't a tall sailing ship with only five crewmembers."

Nattie started reading through the logbook to learn as much as she could about the ship and its mission.

"Jassie, listen to this."

"We moved into position around the dark side of the moon to test the new RFI device. We aimed the weapon at the designated ground target. No sooner did we fire the weapon, than a terrible enemy appeared out of nowhere. They immediately fired on us. We took evasive action but their ships were more advanced and there was no way to outmaneuver them. We tried to destroy them with conventional weapons but they had no effect. There appeared to be some kind of shielding technology protecting their three ships. Lieutenant Anderson targeted one of their ships with the RFI and fired. The ship dissipated into oblivion. Their shielding technology had no effect against the RFI. We were struck by an enemy blast knocking out our targeting systems then three additional enemy ships appeared.

"Not wanting to give away Earth's position, we engaged the experimental, gravity shadow drive, and jettisoned through space beyond the speed of light for the first time. We knew the chances of ever finding our way back home were minimal but we had no other option. Just before the shadow drive was engaged, a communication was sent to Earth warning them not to use the RFI device or they could draw the enemy down upon them.

"We shut down the shadow drive and emerged in an unknown area of space. We flew to the nearest solar system and started scanning for inhabitable planets. To our surprise, we found one with human life but somehow the enemy was able to track us and appeared just as we were on final entry through the planet's atmosphere. We managed to hide our ship and escape their advance, but our shuttle sustained additional damage and I am afraid it will never fly again.

"We settled in Ushata Carry Contaviea, from the original language of the settlements, which is translated into Voncara Cove. The human population has been very helpful. We taught them our language and tried to advance their technology as they are able to bear it but I am afraid their technology will never reach a level to help us repair our ship in our lifetime. When we arrived, they were at a level of technology equal to our seventeenth century. We are over three hundred years more advanced than this society. They have been ravaged by rival nations through pirating warfare and enslavement. We are helping them to fight off their ruthless enemies through tactics and technology.

"Not knowing if we will ever be found, I created three books, stamped with the seal of the United States of America to be easily recognized, that provides the clues necessary to locate our ship. If you are reading this, then obviously you already made this discovery. My last journal entry is this: Never turn on the RFI because it could draw a horrible viscous enemy to your doorstep. Our neutron power source is capable of providing power for up to a thousand years but we have disconnected it from the device as a precaution."

"How amazing." Nattie took off her coat and fanned her face. Her heart rate was elevated and her face was flush. "Jassie, this is a major discovery. It proves there's life on other planets."

"I can hardly believe it," Jase said as he stood there thinking.

"What are we going to do now?" Nattie asked.

"I have an idea but I don't know if you're going to like it."

"What's that?"

"Well, Halfgrim is still looking for us and there's no actual treasure, we can't tell anyone about this..."

"Wait, why can't we tell anyone?"

"Nattie, think about it. First off, who would believe we found a hidden alien spaceship? Secondly, I don't want our lives to be endangered any more than they already are. Do you think our world can handle this revelation?"

"I see your point. What if they decide they want to cover it up? What happens to us?"

"Precisely, we need to be very careful."

"But what are we going to do about Halfgrim?" She paused a second. "Jassie, what if he already knows what's here? After all, they knew where to find the map in your book. They must have other sources of information about this."

"We join the Proelium Concordia."

"What? Are you serious?"

"Yeah, we join on the buddy system like Alrand and Kimberly. We get to be together out of Halfgrim's reach. We will be safe and I've actually been thinking about this since our flight to Barcastle. I want to fly in space."

Nattie sat thinking for a minute. "Are you sure about this, Jase?"

"Yeah, pretty sure."

"Well, as long as we get to be together, I don't care. Whatever you decide."

"You don't have to join up. It's up to you."

"You're not going anywhere without me. If you join, then I'm joining."

Jase laughed, "You can still go with me, silly."

"No, if you're joining then I'm joining."

"Okay, baby."

"We better get out of here and figure out how to close the entrance before Halfgrim shows up."

"I wonder if there is a recruiting office in Voncara Cove."

"I doubt it but we can check."

Nattie put the logbook into her backpack and they walked up the steps leading out. When they got to the entrance, Jase peeked out to make sure it was safe. He stepped on his backpack and reached into the hole in the cliff. He pushed the knob back into its original position but nothing happened.

"Oh great."

"What?"

"It didn't close." A few seconds later, they could hear a low-pitched hum and the stone slowly moved back into position.

"Jassie, you can see a crack outlining the door now."

"Let's find some mud to fill it in. When it dries, they won't be able to see it anymore."

They found some dirt matching the color of the stone by the canyon walls. They mixed it with water and sealed up the cracks.

"You want something to eat, Jassie?"

"Yes, I'm hungry." They walked down the trail while eating their snacks, heading for the town. Nattie went into one of the shops and inquired about a recruiting office.

"Jassie, there is an office here. They have naval personnel stationed here in the cove."

"Oh, I had no idea. Great." They headed toward the other side of town in search of the recruiting office.

"Jassie, are you sure this is what we should do?"

"Nattie, what else can we do?"

"I don't know," she frowned and looked down at the ground.

"What's wrong, baby?"

"Why would you think about joining without me?" Jase stopped and hugged her.

"I'm sorry, baby. I didn't mean it like that. You know I want you with me always, and forever." Nattie leaned her head against Jase's chest and held him tight.

"I was thinking that if we join up, we could eventually end up stationed with Alrand and Kimberly."

Nattie lifted her head up, "I didn't think about that. That could be fun."

They continued walking across town. "Jassie, what would I do? I don't really want to be a pilot. I'm not that crazy about flying."

"What about what Kimberly does?"

"That could work. I guess I can see what they have available."

"Yeah, we don't have to make a final decision until we are totally sure this is what we want." Nattie started feeling better about the idea.

They walked into the small recruiting office and a soldier sat behind a desk in uniform.

"What can I do for the two of you?"

"We would like to look into signing up on the buddy system," Jase said. "I want to fly."

"Let's not get ahead of ourselves. I need you two to fill out some forms and you need to take a placement test."

They filled out all the information and handed the forms back to the soldier. He placed Jase and Nattie on testing computers.

"Just follow the screens. They will guide you through the testing process." Jase wasn't so happy about having to muddle through so much testing but he hung in there and finished. The tests were different for each individual. The testing path was determined by the initial questions. When their testing was complete, he had them sit down and offered them some refreshments while their data was being computed. The soldier walked into an office for about half an hour then returned.

"Nattellie Candella."

"Yes?"

"You have had training at the Science Academy, is that right?"

"Yes, sir."

"I have been authorized to offer you an exceptional position with the Science Contingent in the Sky Brigade. There is a twenty thousand tutarian sign on bonus and you will be given the rank of

Captain on successful completion of basic training. You will have your choice of your first duty station. How does that sound?"

Nattie smiled and asked, "What about Jase?"

"Jase Thunderbelt, your scores are high enough for the Arial Combat Contingent, however, there is a very long waiting list. I can submit you to the program and sign you up for the infantry if you would like but there is no guarantee that you will be accepted."

"Never mind then. I have no desire to serve in the infantry."

"I wonder how Alrand got in."

"Sir, our friends joined up a while ago on the buddy system and got right into the flight program. There's no way Jase can be a pilot? I'm definitely not going to join up without him."

"Hmm, let me make a call. I will see what I can do."

"Thank you." The soldier walked into the office and shut the door.

"Nattie, that's fantastic. Your schooling is really paying off."

"Yeah, but I'm not going in without you."

"Well, if I can't fly, then it's not worth it."

"I hope he can do something for us. It sounds kind of exciting."

"Yeah, you get to be a captain."

Nattie laughed, "Then I get to boss you around and make you behave."

"Very funny." Nattie winked at Jase and grabbed his hand when he went to try and tickle her.

The office door opened and the soldier walked out smiling. "Well, Thunderbelt, fortune has smiled on you this day. Your girlfriend is going to get you the next spot in the flight training program."

"Really?" Nattie said.

"Evidently, they don't get many applicants with your skill level. They must want you badly." Jase smiled and looked at Nattie.

"I'm never going to live this one down, am I?"

Nattie giggled, "Nope."

"There's one problem though. The program is about to start so I have to get you there today. The next skyship leaves within the next two hours. You up for that?"

"Yeah, let's do it," Nattie said. "Jassie, I so can't believe we're doing this."

"I can't wait to fly my own ship."

"First, you both have to pass basic training. That will take a few months then off to your advanced training post."

"Is there a post in the outer colonies?"

"Yes, Cadet Candella, but you won't be sent there for the science contingent training."

"Jassie, that sounds so cute, Cadet Candella," Nattie said in a deep voice.

"You are cute, baby."

"Yes, sir, Cadet Thunderbelt," Nattie giggled.

"Okay, Cadets, your activation is complete. Just sign here and press your thumb into the reader." They both complied. "Congratulations, soldiers; you've just joined the elite of the elite. Let me be the first to salute you." He stood at attention and saluted Jase and Nattie who followed suit and saluted back. "Other hand, Cadet Candella."

Nattie giggled, "Oops. I'll have to remember that one."

"I will have a cruiser here in a few minutes to take you to the base so you can catch the next flight out."

"Sounds great."

"Cadet Thunderbelt, we did it."

"We sure did. Guess it was a good thing you finished school."

"Yeah, but I would have rather had that time with you." Nattie hugged Jase tight around the waist.

"I hope we get some time alone while we're in training."

"Me too, or I will miss you too much."

"We can always sneak out at night." Nattie winked at Jase.

The cruiser arrived and they were taken to the military base. As they passed through the gate, Nattie stuck her tongue out while looking out the window. Jase could see her reflection and laughed. "What was that for?"

"Oh, that was meant for Halfgrim. He can't touch us now." She smiled and put her arm around Jase.

The flight to their basic training post only took about an hour but the skyship had to ascend almost straight up to get over the mountains of the cove. Jase watched out the window, excited about flight school.

When they arrived at the skyport, they hurried onto a shuttle with several others, bound for the training compound. As they sped up past the gates, they could see tall guard towers with turret-mounted weapon systems. There were training areas with all kinds of obstacles constructed out of logs and ropes. There were towers with zip lines, knotted climbing ropes, and rope nets. *What have you gotten me into now, Jassie*, Nattie thought.

As soon as the shuttle set down, a soldier ran aboard screaming loudly commanding them to gather their things and get off as quickly as possible.

They joined a formation of eight women and twenty-four men. "Stand at attention with your mouths shut, shoulders back and stomach in. I am Major Lothen, your training instructor. You will address me as sir after every statement, is that clear?"

"Yes, sir," replied the young men and woman.

"What a bunch of Patters, I can't hear you!"

"YES, SIR!"

Patters were cute little furry animals that lived in the woods and often captured for use as pets.

The major inspected the new officer cadets and looked through their information on a small handheld computer as each announced their last name. When he reached Jase, he looked down at his sword laying on his civilian backpack.

"What's this, Cadet?"

"Cadet Thunderbelt, sir."

"There are no civilian weapons on my post, Thunderbelt. What are you doing with a sword?"

"Sir, we just signed up from Voncara Cove and were brought straight here. I just purchased this sword a few hours ago and it's a priceless artifact."

The Major looked at Jase's information. "Pilot…figures; you think you're some kind of general, fly boy?"

Nattie burst out laughing for a moment.

"You think that's funny, Cadet?"

"Yes, sir!"

"Get down and give me twenty."

"Sir?"

"Pushups, Cadet. Pushups."

"What's your name Cadet?"

"Cadet Candella, Sir."

"I can't hear you, Candella. Count em out!"

"One, two, three…" The Major looked at Nattie's information.

"A science officer…I see. Are you going to be a pain in my side, Cadet Smarty Pants?"

Jase laughed. "Now, you! Get down and give me thirty, fly boy."

Jase was still pretty buff from pumping iron in the basement the year Nattie was away at school. He got down and started knocking out pushups as if they were nothing. Nattie stopped and held herself up and looked at Jase next to her.

"Show off!" That got the whole platoon laughing, even the training instructor let out a little snicker.

"I can't hear you, Cadet Candella."

"One, two, three…"

"Smarty pants, did I tell you to start over? Shows how smart you are." Nattie burst out laughing and fell to her stomach, and then Jase started cracking up laughing.

"Okay you two, get up. It says here you two are in the buddy system?"

"Yes, sir!"

"Well I got my eye on you two."

"You have piqued my curiosity, Thunderbelt. Tell me about this priceless artifact."

"Sir, this sword actually belonged to Captain David Anderson of the Voncara Cove Navy."

"You are telling me this is his actual sword?"

"Yes, sir!"

"Would you mind if I take a look?"

"Absolutely, sir." He handed the major the sword. The major pulled the sword from the sheath and examined it.

"I must say, Cadet, I am impressed. This must have set you back quite a bit."

"It was worth it, sir."

Chapter 37

"**Y**ou make sure you put this in the safe when you turn in your civilian items."

"Yes, sir."

"Cadet Rails, front and center."

"Yes, sir!"

"Cadet, you are training for Tactics and Command, are you not?"

"Yes, sir."

"I am rating you platoon leader. You will take this sorry bunch of recruits to the supply depot to exchange their civilian clothing for their military issue. Then you will bring them back here to fall into the two barracks behind you. Girls on the left and men on the right. You follow me, Cadet?"

"Yes, sir!"

"If I catch any men in the woman's barracks, you will be out of here before you can say the word idiot. Do I make myself clear?"

"Yes, sir!" Nattie stood there with a big smile on her face.

"Wipe that smile off your face, Cadet Smarty Pants. I know what you're thinking."

"You do, sir?"

"I got my eye on you."

"Yes, sir."

"Move em out, Cadet Rails."

The cadets were taken to the supply depot where they were issued their military training clothing, boots, and bedding. A lieutenant guided them through the process and asked all those with valuables to come forward to be issued a personal lock box.

"Jassie, here, take the logbook also."

"Okay, be back in a few minutes." Jase put the two books by Captain Wells, the logbook from the spaceship, and Captain Anderson's sword into the lockbox. He was allowed to keep the key. Nattie stayed in line with the others.

"Cadets, move over here to the next line where you will be given regulation-length haircuts." Nattie stood with her mouth open then shook her head. *I didn't see this coming,* she thought as she let out a little whimper. A shy little farm girl who signed up to study botany on other planets stood in front of her in line. She turned around when she heard Nattie whine.

"Don't worry; I heard that you can ask them just to trim your hair a little. You have beautiful hair, by the way."

"Awww, thank you."

"No problem. I'm Kat." She shook Nattie's hand. "Kat Rudamin."

"Hi, I'm Nattie Candella."

"Is that Thunderbelt guy your brother or boyfriend?"

"He's my boyfriend."

"Oh, I was hoping he was just your brother." They both laughed. "He's a nice looking guy. How long have you two been together?"

"Since we were seven."

"Oh wow, so you two are childhood sweethearts."

"Yep, he's my Jassie."

"You're so lucky. It's so hard to find a good guy. Don't tell anyone but that's part of the reason I signed up. Plus I wanted to get out of my boring hometown."

Nattie was next to sit in the barber chair. "Can you just give me a little trim please?"

"As long as you can wear your hair up and have it all fit under your hat, but you have some thick hair. I suggest you let me take off at least five inches or you will never get it to fit."

"Okay, but please, only five inches."

After getting her hair trimmed, she sat down next to Kat with the other cadets. A few minutes later, Jase walked over, and his hair was shaved down to about a quarter of an inch.

"Jassie? Is that you?"

"Yes."

"Wow, you look so different. I almost didn't recognize you." He sat down next to Nattie. She couldn't resist feeling his head. "Oh my, I like that. It's so soft." Kat laughed. "Oh Jassie, this is Kat Rudamin."

"Hi, Jase, just call me Kat." They shook hands and the three of them talked until the cadets were taken to their barracks.

Nattie and Kat arranged to be bunkmates in the barracks. Nattie slept on the top bunk and Kat on the bottom.

An instructor showed them how to properly fold and put away their uniforms and how to make their beds regulation-style. They only had enough time to put their things away and change into their brightly colored uniforms before they were called out for an assembly for dinner.

When Jase ran outside, he could see Nattie standing in formation with the other ladies all wearing yellow uniforms. The ladies snickered a little bit at the guys when they saw them wearing their orange training uniforms. Jase ran over and formed up next to Nattie.

"Nice uniform, baby,"

Nattie giggled. "I knew you were going to say something. I knew it."

"Well, at least I won't lose sight of you." Nattie put her hand over her mouth as she snickered.

"I love you too, baby."

The training program wasn't very hard except for the fast pace. There was little time between classes and with the early start each day, they were exhausted by lights out. Nattie and Jase found a few set times each day where they could spend some time together. There was the morning run after physical training, the two hours they were given for lunch, and a little time just before lights out where they met behind the barracks for a hug and a kiss.

Occasionally, Nattie helped Kat with her studies and in the evenings, after lights out, Nattie would share stories about her and Jase's many adventures. Kat could scarcely believe some of the things that Nattie had been through. Some of the other young ladies in the nearby bunks also listened intently.

With the hectic daily schedule, time flew by and before they knew it, a couple months had passed. Both Jase and Nattie had very high scores and had earned the respect of their instructors until one day on the obstacle course. One of the obstacles was very high and consisted of logs stacked horizontally at vertical intervals of three to five feet. The cadets were expected to scale up one side, straddle the top, and then climb down the other side. Nattie climbed up to about the third log from the top and froze.

"Nattie, keep going," Kat said.

"I can't."

"You have to. Come on, you can do it." Nattie climbed back down to the disappointment of the training instructor.

"Candella, what's the problem here?"

"I can't do it, sir."

"Candella, you can and you will do it. Now get your butt up over that obstacle."

The girl's squad always trained apart from the men so Jase was not there to help. Nattie tried again but froze two logs from the top because there was larger spacing between the logs and she felt very vulnerable and was afraid she would fall. She climbed back down, "Sorry, sir. I can't do it," she said with watering eyes.

"Candella, if you don't scale this obstacle, you will not graduate."

"I will let you go today but you will have to complete this exercise for your final grading."

That night when Nattie met up with Jase, she started crying. "Jase, I'm going to fail. I can't do it. I'm too afraid."

Jase's throat felt tight and he frowned. He wiped her eyes. He hated to see Nattie so upset.

"Don't worry, baby. I will figure out something, okay?"

"I don't see how." Nattie wiped her nose on her shirt and her cheeks on her shoulder to wipe away the tears.

"Just take it easy. I will talk to our instructor."

"Okay, if you think it will help."

When she got back to the barracks, Kat gave her a hug. "You feeling better?"

"Yes, some."

"I know you can do it, Nattie. Just try not to think about it. Pretend you are only a foot off the ground."

Nattie let out a little laugh through her sorrow, "Now you sound like Jase."

"Well then, listen to him. I know you can do it. You still have some time before the physical finals."

The next day, Jase asked to speak with Major Lothen. He walked into his office and saluted.

"What can I do for you, Cadet Thunderbelt?"

"Sir, I wanted to talk to you about Cadet Candella."

"Go on."

"Sir, about the log climbing obstacle..."

"Thunderbelt, there are no exceptions. She has to complete every obstacle. I know you two are close and I was hoping I could count on you to help her find a way to manage her fear and complete the course."

"Yes, sir. If you can give us time to work on it, I know she can do it."

"The contingent needs recruits like her, so I am counting on you, Thunderbelt. I will give you both a pass just before dinner each night. Make it happen."

"Yes, sir."

Jase caught up with Nattie to give her the news.

"How did it go, Jassie?"

"Well, I have good news and bad news."

"Oh no, what's the bad news?"

"You have to climb over the obstacle, but he gave us both passes so we can work on it alone, each night, before dinner."

Nattie perked up a bit. "We get time alone, just me and you?"

"Yep, so I can help you."

Nattie smiled, "Okay."

The following evening Jase took Nattie out to the log climbing obstacle. She carefully climbed up to the log with the high separation.

"See, Jassie. I can't get past this one. It's too high and I can't hold onto the next log."

"Baby, it's just like the top log. You have to climb onto the log by itself then put your leg over it so you can straddle it."

"Kiss me first then I won't be thinking about it."

Jase moved closer and gave her a log kiss.

"I miss this," Nattie said.

"We are almost done, baby."

"I talked to Mom. She's flying out for graduation with your parents."

"Yeah but Alrand said they can't make it because they have training exercises. He said to do a video call after the ceremony."

"Wish they could come. I miss them."

"Now stop stalling, cutie, and climb."

"Jassie."

"I'm right here next to you. You can do this." Nattie put her arms over the high log and pulled herself up. Jase steadied her as she turned and put her leg over the log and sat up. Jase climbed up and sat in front of her. "Now stand up and hold the top log, then do the same thing again."

"Jassie, I'm scared; it's so high up."

"Baby, don't look down."

"I know. Pretend I'm only a few feet off the ground."

"It's a lot easier than climbing out of a forth story window."

"Yeah and I almost fell to my death, if you didn't catch me." Nattie stood up and put her arms around the top log. Her heart rate increased and her hands were sweaty. "Jassie, I'm going to fall. I can't hold on."

"I got you, baby. Let's do this." Nattie jumped up, swung her leg over the top log, and lay holding it tight. Jase climbed up with her. "Sit up, baby."

"I can't."

"Yes, you can." Jase leaned over and rubbed her back. He scooted closer and held her arms as she sat up. "Look at the great view from up here."

"It's such a pretty sunset." They sat on the top log for a while and kissed as the sun set behind the hills. Jase helped her to climb back down and they returned to the barracks. "Jassie, don't tell them I was able to do it yet, okay?"

"Of course not. You're going to climb it every day so you will be ready for the final grading. The faster you climb over, the more time we have alone together."

"Sounds good to me, except for the climbing part." Jase laughed and they kissed before heading to dinner.

Each evening, Jase coached Nattie over the obstacle until the week of final grading. They enjoyed their time together and Jase was very confident that Nattie would pass. She was so worried the night before the finals. She hardly slept and was very nervous but when it was her turn, she actually did very well and had no problem with the log climbing part of the course.

Only about two-thirds of the cadets passed their finals to move on to graduation, mostly due to the written examinations. Those who would graduate were taken to the supply depot to exchange their training uniforms for their active duty uniforms. Jase was given his lieutenant's insignias and Nattie was given her captain's insignias. Their uniforms were a light charcoal gray with gold trim for captain and silver trim for lieutenants. The uniforms were made with custom precision based on the individual cadet's measurements. Each was created as a single piece garment that zipped up in the front. Nattie's uniform had a science officer's patch on her left arm and the contingent's gold medal crest pinned on the right side, just right of her lapel. Her captain's insignia was complimented on the left side of her lapel. Jase didn't receive his wings as he would receive them during advanced training. He only had his contingent's silver medal on the right and his lieutenant's insignia on the left.

Jase also received his flight suit, flight gear, and fighter helmet. He walked out of the men's locker and saw Nattie standing next to Kat. He saluted, "Hi, Captain Candella."

She smiled when she saw him in his uniform and saluted him in return. "Jassie, you look so good. I could just eat you up." Kat smacked Nattie's butt and laughed.

"Kiss me, Jassie. That's an order."

"Guess I have to comply," Jase laughed. They held each other and kissed.

"Okay, you two. We better get back to the barracks and get ready for graduation tomorrow," Kat said.

"You look beautiful in your uniform by the way. So do you, Jassie."

"Guys don't look beautiful."

"To me, you do and thank you, Jassie."

"For what?"

"Helping me to get through this. I'm so happy we made it. I wasn't sure if I would."

"I never doubted. You are the most amazing person I know, Captain Candella."

Nattie smiled. "It's Nattie to you, mister. At least when no one else is around."

A new batch of recruits walked past and saluted them. "I could get used to this," Jase said.

Graduation day arrived and the new officers formed up with other training classes for the grand ceremony. Jase stood next to Nattie in formation and they could see their parents watching from the civilian stands. Nattie kept bending her knees a bit, as their commander was rather long-winded in his dedication speech. She was so excited and couldn't wait to see her mom. Finally, the moment came. Hats flew in the air in celebration. Nattie grabbed Jase's hand and pulled him along briskly to meet up with their parents. Her mom ran down from the stands and hugged her tight.

"Hi, Mom."

"Nattie, you look so cute in your uniform. What in the world made the two of you decide to join the Proelium Concordia?"

"Oh, that's a very long story, Mom."

Jase's dad congratulated him and told him how proud he was of him. "Dad, we need to make a video call to talk with Alrand and Kimberly then we can head into town for a while if you wish?"

"Sounds great, son."

They all went into the main building and found an available communications room and placed their call. Alrand and Kimberly were already waiting.

"Jase, Nat, congratulations!"

"Hi, guys, how are you two doing?"

"Fantastic," Kimberly said. "You want to tell them or should I?"

"You can tell them, I know your dying to tell someone."

"Tell someone what?" Nattie asked.

"We're getting married." Nattie clasped her arms and jumped up and down along with Kimberly on the other side. Kimberly held out her ring in front of the video camera so Nattie could see.

"That's so pretty, Kimberly." Nattie looked at Jase and stuck out her lower lip like she was pouting.

"Congratulations, guys. When is the big day?" Jase asked.

"Well, since you two are coming here after advanced training, we figured we would wait for you."

"That would be so great," Nattie said.

Jase's parents also congratulated them on their engagement.

The rest of the night, out with their parents, Nattie kept looking at Jase in a cute but strange way. She kept poking at him.

"What?"

"Nothing." Their parents dropped them off at the barracks as the next day they were to depart for their advanced training post.

Jase kissed Nattie goodnight. "Nattie, what's with you tonight?"

"Nothing, Jase."

"Yes something."

"It's not my place to say."

"Just say it, baby."

"No. If you don't know then I'm not saying," Nattie said in a harsh tone.

"Sweetie, what's wrong?"

Chapter 38

"**D**o you really love me, Jassie?"

"Of course I do."

"Well?"

"Well what?"

"Ugh! Why do I always have to think of everything and nudge you along? If you loved me, then you could make the first move for a change." Nattie ran into her barracks leaving Jase standing there. She walked to her bunk, sat down next to Kat, and put her head in her hands.

"Nattie, what's wrong?" She started crying. "Nattie, what is it?"

"He doesn't love me."

"Why would you say that?"

"Because our best friends are getting married, we have been together for a lot longer than them."

"Nattie, I see the way he looks at you. He loves you a lot."

"Can't he make the first move for a change to show he really loves me?"

Jase held his head low and walked into his barracks. His eyes watered and he sniffled. He lay in his bed, wide-awake, thinking about Nattie. Neither of them slept all night.

When Jase got up in the morning, he packed up his things as fast as he could and went outside to meet up with Nattie but she was still in her barracks. He waited for some time before she and Kat walked out with their bags. Jase picked up his things and walked toward Nattie but she just turned her head and walked toward the shuttle. Jase chased after her, "Nattie wait." She just kept walking and climbed onto the shuttle. Jase felt very alone, like part of him just died. He stepped up to the shuttle but didn't enter.

"Kat, what's he doing?"

"He's just standing by the door. Why don't you talk to him?" The shuttle left for the skyport but Jase waited behind for the next shuttle. "Nattie, Jase didn't get on the shuttle." She got scared and started crying.

"I need to get off."

"You can't." Her makeup ran with her tears. The whole ride to the skyport, Nattie sat and shook her leg nervously while biting her lip. She wanted to wait for the next shuttle to arrive but as soon as they exited, they ushered them to their respective flights.

Nattie sat in the embarkation area and waited by herself. Her tummy started hurting and she rocked back and forth holding her arms. She bit her fingernails and tried to hold back her tears. They announced the boarding of her flight but still no Jase. The flight officer asked for her orders and told her to board the ship. She walked on board and stowed her things. She stood at the seat assigned by the flight officer and watched the aisle. The final boarding call was made and shortly afterwards, Jase walked onto the ship. He was given a seat near the front of the craft. He could see Nattie standing about halfway down the aisle and her face look very red as if she had been crying. Jase sat down and shortly afterwards, the craft lifted off.

Nattie was relieved that Jase was safely on board the craft. When they reached cursing altitude, she boldly got up and walked to Jase's seat. He looked up at her and she handed him a note, and then she went back to her seat. Jase quickly opened the note and read, "Jassie, I'm so sorry and I love you so much!" Jase took a deep breath and let out a sigh of relief.

When the ship landed, Jase exited and waited with his things until Nattie walked out. She hurried over to him as fast as she could but didn't hug him as there were so many officers around them.

"Jassie, I'm so sorry."

"I'm sorry too. I know what you wanted and I want the same thing."

"Then why didn't you ask me?"

"Because I wanted it to be something special. I wanted to surprise you."

"I don't care about that. I just want you to want me."

"Nattie, I want you more than anything in this world. You scared me and it really hurt."

Nattie looked at Jase with a sad gaze. "Oh no, please, Jassie. I'm so sorry. I never meant to hurt you, ever. Will you please forgive me?"

"There's nothing to forgive, Nattie. I should have done this a long time ago." Jase rummaged around inside his flight bag, pulled out a little package, and handed it to Nattie. She paused, in a moment of fright.

"What's this?"

"Something I picked up for you while you were in school. I wanted to give it to you but so much has happened since you got home that I never had the chance." Jase got down on one knee. "I love you, Nattie. With all my heart, will you marry me?"

Nattie took one look at the cute butterfly patterned wedding ring, her chin quivered, her lips were sad, and she cried. "Yes, I will marry you." She hugged him, getting tears on his uniform. They were so caught up in the moment that they didn't realize they had an audience. Some of the soldiers and officers standing nearby started clapping. Nattie turned all red and smiled. Jase wiped the tears from her eyes and kissed her in front of everyone. Afterwards, some of the soldiers congratulated them and commented on the brave skyport proposal.

Jase slid the ring on her finger, a perfect fit. "You had this since I was in school?"

"Yes."

"So you planned on marrying me that long ago?"

"Of course, I was just waiting for the perfect time. I wanted to ask you at the castle but then all that stuff happened."

Nattie felt so relieved. She hugged Jase around his neck. "I'm sorry I ever doubted you, Jassie. I'm sorry I hurt you."

"It's okay, Nattie. Just don't ever do it again. I couldn't bear it."

"I promise." She kissed the tip of his nose.

They reported to the training facility not far from the skyport and were assigned their quarters. The training facility was a long, huge, three-story building that was quite impressive with its spacious interior. Everything they would need while in training was available within the walls of the facility, including post shopping, entertainment, officers club, and training division with classrooms and a large auditorium. The ceilings in the common areas opened up through all levels and had railings around each floor where the soldiers could stand and look down on the activities below.

Jase was given quarters closest to the airfield and flight training classes. His room was one of six connecting to a common area for his training squad. After he put away his gear and civilian items, he met the other officers in the squad. There were three guys and two ladies who would be in training with him.

Nattie was on the opposite side of the facility, located near the research labs. As a captain, she was assigned a decent-sized private room with a nice view outside. She rushed to put her things away, only stopping for a moment to admire her engagement ring. She hurried down the many corridors following a map of the building to find the officer's club where she and Jase planned to meet.

"Nattellie Candella! I thought that was you."

Nattie turned around. "Endnova, what are you doing here?" They both hugged.

"I'm an instructor cooperative for college."

"No way!"

"Yep, I didn't know you were joining the Concordia."

"I didn't ether."

"Let me guess, it was Jase's idea?"

Nattie giggled, "Yes."

"What contingent?"

"Science and Research."

"That's so funny. I may be your instructor for some of your classes."

"Really?"

"Yeah, tell me about it. You should probably be teaching me."

"No, I'm sure you will do great. I just can't believe you're here. Oh, I almost forgot, looky." Nattie held up her hand.

"No way, girl. He finally proposed?"

Nattie smiled, "Yep"

"When are you getting married?"

"We haven't set a date yet. I guess it will have to be some time after graduation. I can't wait to be Nattie Thunderbelt."

"How long have you been going over that one in your head?"

Nattie giggled, "All my life. I'm going to meet Jase now. You want to come?"

"I wish I could but I have to attend a teacher's orientation lecture."

"Sounds like fun."

"You're joking, right?"

Nattie laughed, "You know me."

"See you later, Misses Thunderbelt." Nattie smiled at the thought as she walked away.

She met up with Jase, just outside the officer's club. She hugged and kissed him. "I love you, Jassie, and I love my ring."

"I love you, beautiful."

"Guess what?"

"What?"

"Guess who's here."

"No idea."

"Endnova."

"That's a wild coincidence. So she joined up too?"

"No, she is an assistant teacher." Jase laughed.

"Didn't you have to help her with school?"

"Yeah, but she's smarter than she lets on."

Jase and Nattie entered the officer's club. Jase felt privileged being allowed in but Nattie felt as though they didn't belong. They met a few other young couples who had also just arrived and they all had a fun time, which put Nattie at ease. She was also the highest-ranking officer in the group. Jase met a seasoned pilot who didn't mind bragging about his experiences. Jase hung on every word and questioned the poor guy to death, desiring to learn anything he could. Nattie held his arm and leaned her head up against his shoulder. Being so tired, she eventually fell asleep.

"Lieutenant, I think your beautiful captain there is ready for bed."

"I think so. Thank you for the advice and information."

"Anytime," Jase could hardly wait to fly. Though not allowed inside, he escorted Nattie back to her room.

"You better get some sleep before classes start tomorrow."

"Not yet, I want to spend some more time with you alone." They walked outside where it was very dark and overcast. They stood at the edge of the building and kissed.

"Jassie, when should we get married?"

"Right now."

"I wish."

"I'm serious, Nattie. We should do it as soon as we can. Then we can share a larger room together."

"I want that. That would be so sweet to wake up in your arms every morning. You should have heard my mom when I told her."

"What did she say?"

"I'm not telling."

"That's mean."

"Okay, she said, it's about time," Nattie giggled.

"She said that?"

Nattie laughed, "No, I'm just kidding. She said she is very happy for us and glad we're going to be married. What did your dad say?"

"He said congratulations to the both of us and that this was totally expected."

Chapter 39

They started their first day of training the next morning. The initial lectures were so boring, at least until they took Jase and the other five trainees into the hangar to see a Sonic Fighter up close. Jase stood staring up at the ship with a bright glow about him. His eyes were wide open and he could hardly stand still. He could not believe the size of the thing. Any military clips he viewed made the ship look so small compared to real life. *How does this thing even fly?*

There were twelve sets of wings on each side, four in the midsection and eight in the back. Some of the wings were stubby and used for aerodynamic support of the advanced weapon systems. The remaining wings were wider for lift in the inner atmosphere but swept back to the rear for space flight and when parked in the hangar. The outer heat-resistant skin was porous to the touch but formed an air pocket that allowed the wings to slice through the air with little friction.

Each student was allowed to sit in both the pilot's seat and the navigator's seat behind. Jase held the flight stick and imagined flying through space.

Nattie was bored beyond belief in her classes and started to read through the class material until she found some interesting facts about weapons technology and targeting systems. She was rather excited to see schematics for laser radar used in the outer atmosphere and space. One of her teachers asked if she understood the information and was impressed with her perception and knowledge. She was happy to get the first boring day of classes out of the way.

Jase and Nattie were able to spend a lot of time together during training. They planned on having their wedding with Alrand and Kimberly once they graduated, in a double ceremony. Jase had to get through all of his written requirements and flight simulations before he could start to fly. He had trouble grasping some of the space navigation calculations so Nattie helped him through it. With her help, he quickly moved to the top of his class. His flight procedure and maneuvers in the simulator were excellent and the instructor said he was a real natural.

Nattie aced all her simple exams and was incredibly bored. She dreaded getting out of bed for classes every morning. Her primary instructor felt she was not being challenged and asked her to stop by her office after class.

Nattie reported as instructed, "Ma'am, Captain Candella reporting as requested."

"At ease, Captain. Have a seat."

"Yes, ma'am."

"I don't think you see this course as being very challenging, do you?" Nattie started thinking but didn't answer. "It's okay, you can answer truthfully."

"Well, I read though the manuals and some of the technology is very interesting but we don't really cover much in class."

"How would you like it if I had your course revised so that you can work in our weapons research program as an assistant to our developers?"

"Are you kidding?" Nattie sat up in her seat and smiled.

"That was the response I was looking for. You start tomorrow."

"Thank you so much." She handed Nattie the directions to the lab, a security pass, and the name of the director to whom she was to report.

After many days of studying, Jase passed his navigation final, which advanced him into the active flight portion of his training. He was so excited, he couldn't wait to tell Nattie. He found her outside of her quarters looking beautiful and smiling.

"Nattie."

"Jassie."

"Guess what?" They said at the same time.

They laughed. "You go first, Nattie."

"They are letting me work in the weapons development lab. No more boring classes."

"That's amazing. Great!"

"I know. I was so so bored. What's your news?"

"I passed. I'm in the flight program."

"Yay, Jassie! That's great. We need to celebrate."

"Yes, we do. Officer's club?"

"No, I have a better idea. Come with me."

They caught a shuttle and climbed aboard. "Where are we going, baby?"

"You'll see." Jase give her a little tickle and Nattie squirmed and grabbed his hand. "Stop it, you bad boy."

After a few minutes, Nattie took Jase by the hand and they got off at the far end of the skyport where the large military transports were tethered.

"Nattie, what are we doing?"

"Just come on."

"We can't get in there."

"Yes, we can." They walked up to the guard and he gave them a salute. He asked for identification and Nattie scanned her new access card. "He's with me, Sergeant."

"Yes, ma'am. Proceed."

They walked into the first hangar and stood before a huge battlecruiser.

"Wow, Nattie, how did you know this thing was here?"

"I didn't. I was just curious and I wanted to find the lab that I have to report to in the morning." They walked all the way around the enormous vessel. They must have walked several miles to get all the way around. The lift ramp was lowered to allow supply cruisers to enter. They asked a worker if they could board the ship to look around but he said they would have to get a service pass or he could get into trouble. They found the building where Nattie was to report in the morning, then returned to the training facility. They spent a few hours together then turned in for the night.

Jase sat holding the flight stick looking over the dashboard as the sun rose above the treeline and reflected off the runway. His flight instructor climbed into the navigation seat behind him.

"Lieutenant, your preflight checklist please."

Jase handed back the digital logbook, set to the preflight page.

"Prepare for departure." Jase clicked the switch to close and seal the canopy. He started the four turbine pulse engines that vibrated the ship as they spun up. The power of the engines felt very intimidating.

"Lieutenant, remember that the effects of the laviniun generators will be extremely responsive on the ground but will continually dissipate the further you are from the planet's surface."

"Tower this is flight five niner two, requesting clearance for takeoff."

"Five niner two, you are cleared for departure."

"Take her out, Lieutenant." Jase pulled back gently on the laviniun collective lever and nudged forward on the flight stick, just as he did in simulation hundreds of times. A slight crosswind blew the ship to the left but Jase gently corrected and sped down the runway. He climbed as he passed over buildings and banked left as he was instructed. It was so intriguing to look down at the tops of the buildings as he passed over.

"Excellent job, Lieutenant, you said this is your first time up?"

"Yes, sir."

"You handle the ship very well."

"Thank you, sir." Jase had a little difficulty trying to land the first time but by the end of the day, he had mastered all of the flight basics. He was the first one in his squad to fly and was considerably ahead of the others, still working on passing their navs.

Nattie reported to her new supervisor at the weapons research lab. He was swamped with priority work he had to complete and had little time for Nattie. He handed her a hand-drawn schematic and asked her to produce a prototype circuit. He didn't expect her to really understand the design but figured it would keep her busy for a few days while he got his work done. He was shocked when Nattie walked into his office a few hours later with a working circuit board, which she laid out and etched in a tank of ferric chloride solution. She soldered in the components by hand and tested the miniaturized motor control device with a few Salvo motors she found in the lab.

"Umm, did anyone help you with this?"

"No, sir. Everyone was very busy so I improvised."

"Where did you learn how to make your own circuit boards?"

"In electronics class at the Science Academy."

"I must say you did a great job."

Nattie smiled, "Thank you. It was fun."

"I'll tell you what. I'm going to pull up the latest targeting system project on a computer. Why don't you take a look so you can help me with testing when the prototype arrives?"

"Sounds good to me."

Jase and Nattie met up later that night and shared their experiences. Another month passed and Nattie became an integral part of the development and testing of the space-based targeting system. Jase was almost complete with the piloting portion of his program. He was only one parameter away from receiving his pilot's license. He was required to plot and fly a mission in space of a distance of no less than two hundred thousand sects, which was the approximate distance to the outer colonies. The only problem was, he had to have a navigator on board for the long flight. Since the rest of his class was too far behind to qualify to fly second seat. He had to find someone else to fill the seat but none of the current pilots had any desire to volunteer for a seventeen-hour mission.

Jase met Nattie in front of the supermarket so they could pick up a few things. Jase frowned and drooped as he walked.

"Poor baby," Nattie said. "Sill no success?"

"No, bunch of jerks. I would do it for them."

"How about your ace pilot friend?"

"I couldn't ask him." Jase took a deep breath and let it out. "I was looking forward to seeing Alrand again."

"Wish I could be your navigator. I want to see Kimberly."

"Wait, why not?"

"I'm not in the program."

"So, you can navigate just as good as any pilot here."

"But you said I couldn't fly with you until you get your license."

"If I get permission, will you come with me?"

"Hmm, let me see. Fly with my fiancé in a Sonic Fighter to a settlement on a moon where our best friends just happen to be stationed. Why in the world would I ever want to do that?" She squeezed Jase tight with her arms around his muscular waist. "Of course, I will. It sounds so exciting. I hope we can get permission."

Jase found his flight instructor and asked for a minute of his time. "Sir, would it be possible for a science officer to be my navigator for my space jump?"

"Is this officer also a navigator or pilot?"

"No, sir, but I guarantee she's the best navigator on this post."

The instructor laughed, "You think so?"

"Well, she helped me with my navigation studies and she understands space telemetry and communications. She also helps to design our targeting systems in the weapons research lab."

The instructor became a bit intrigued and curious. "Who is this officer?"

"Captain Candella."

"I think I've heard the Post Contingent Commander, Colonel Cantellous, mention her name. She's some kind of genius or something, right?"

"I think she's very smart...and she's willing to fly second seat...and I haven't been able to find anyone else willing."

"Do you think she would agree to take the navigation test?"

"I can ask her."

"You will still have to get permission from Colonel Cantellous but it would help you plead your case after she passes the test."

Jase found Nattie in the gym with Endnova. They liked to work out together in the evenings. He asked Nattie if she minded taking the test.

"Sure, Jassie, but I need to borrow your nav books tonight so I can study."

"Okay, I'm going to get cleaned up. Want to stop by when you're done here?" Nattie tilted her head and looked at Jase funny. He laughed and tickled her. "See you in a bit, baby."

Later on, Nattie showed up in the common area of Jase's squad. Several of pilots were sitting and studying their navs as she walked past. She and Jase hugged and kissed.

"Here are my nav books." They sat on a couch and Nattie started reading. She made some notes but started getting sleepy. She lay on Jase's lap looking up and reading until her arms got tired. "You need to go to bed, baby."

"You too."

"Yeah but I don't have anything to do tomorrow."

"I guess you're right." They started kissing again, which was a mistake. Nattie didn't want to leave.

She performed her normal work the following day and studied during breaks. When her work was complete, she met up with Jase and continued to study. After dinner, they met Jase's instructor in his office where Nattie was to take the test. They left her in the room for the two hours normally allowed for the test but she walked out after twenty minutes and handed the instructor the answers.

"My, how did you finish this so quickly?"

"I don't know. It was easy. It's just a lot of math."

The instructor laughed. "Just math...I think you finished it in record time." They walked into the office and sat down as the instructor graded the paper. "Well now, one hundred percent. Congratulations." He took a piece of paper, wrote a hand written note, and handed it to Jase. "This is for the commander. It's for his eyes only."

Jase set up an appointment to see the colonel. He and Nattie entered the commander's office. It was appropriate that the higher-ranking officer present a salute when appearing before a senior officer.

Nattie snapped a salute, "Captain Candella and Lieutenant Thunderbelt reporting, sir."

"At ease, Captain. Please have a seat."

"Sir, I have a note from my instructor for you." The colonel read the note then looked at Nattie.

"You are requesting second seat for Lieutenant Thunderbelt's space jump?"

"Yes, sir. I am."

"I see you have aced the navigation test and in record time. I have no problem granting your request but I would like to ask you why you volunteered?"

Nattie looked at Jase for a second then back at the commander. "Sir, Lieutenant Thunderbelt is ahead of his class and was unable to find a volunteer."

"Why you, Captain?" Nattie saw there was no way to skirt around the issue so she just told him.

"He's my fiancé, sir."

"Oh? You're a lucky guy, Thunderbelt. When's the big day?"

"As soon as we graduate and make it to our first duty station, sir," Jase said.

"Well, I wish the two of you the very best and have a safe flight." Nattie and Jase were all smiles and thanked the colonel. He gave Nattie orders that allowed her to draw flight gear and a helmet from the supply depot and a form for the flight instructor, allowing her to fly second seat on Jase's jump.

"Nattie, I will meet you at first light on the runway. Make sure you bring your snacks." Nattie punched Jase then kissed him.

"You're my snack, mister. Did you tell Alrand and Kimberly that we're coming?"

"Yep."

"What did they say?"

"They are very excited. They want to show us around and they said we are going to have a fantastic time."

"I can't wait, Jassie. This is the funnest thing we have ever done."

"Well, it's a very long flight though."

"It's only about eight hours. That won't be too bad. As long as your navs are right and you don't get us lost."

"Ooh, you're gonna get it." Jase chased Nattie through the hallway. She let out a little scream as she ran. Jase caught up with her and held her waist.

Nattie giggled and kissed him, "See you tomorrow, husband."

"See you tomorrow, Misses Thunderbelt to be." Nattie smiled and went into her room.

Jase was on the runway early to do his preflight. There was a nice cool breeze blowing in from the north. Nattie's hair blew around as she walked toward the aircraft with her flight bag in one hand and her helmet in the other.

"Wow."

"What?"

"You look so beautiful in that flight suit."

"Thank you, honey. You look nice yourself. Good enough to eat."

"Put your helmet on, silly." She put her helmet on and Jase started to laugh.

"What?"

"Your hair's not supposed to be hanging out of the helmet, baby." She went to pull it off. "Wait, leave it. You look so cute."

"What if someone sees me?"

"Who's going to see you?"

Jase took a few pictures of Nattie by the Sonic Fighter then she took a few of him. He got her situated in the navigator's seat and showed her a few things about working the flight controls.

"Nattie, the noise from the engines in the inner atmosphere will be too loud to talk so we have to use the intercom through our flight helmets. You press this button on the cord from your helmet to talk but be careful. It has two positions, one click for intercom and two clicks in for radio transmission."

"So if I press the button all the way down, I'm transmitting."

"Correct."

Chapter 40

"**O**kay, got it."

"Smarty." Jase gave her a kiss then climbed into the pilot's seat in front of her and closed the canopy.

The turbine engines wound up and commenced combustion, vibrating the ship. "Oh boy, what was I thinking," Nattie said.

"Don't worry, baby. I know it can be a little intimidating at first."

"A little intimidating? It feels like the engines are strapped to my back."

"I'll take it easy. It will be fine." Nattie put her muffin, still in the wrapper, on the side of the cockpit. She held on tight to her seat as Jase eased the ship into position. He received clearance and began a gentle assent.

"How you doing, Nattie?"

"Good." Jase throttled up the engines and pulled back on the collective lever to increase their rate of climb. Even with the anti-gravitational action of the laviniun generators, the pilots could still feel some gravity effects.

"This is kinda fun, Jassie." On an impulse, Jase jerked the flight stick left performing a barrel roll. Nattie screamed, "Jase! You trying to give me a heart attack?" She threw her muffin at Jase. It bounced off his helmet and landed on the dash. "Don't you do that again! That's an order." Jase laughed. "You are so going to get it, mister."

"Promises, promises."

"Yeah, you just wait. I'm not talking to you the whole trip." Jase laughed hysterically. "Okay, I'm not talking to you for the next thirty seconds."

"You're talking to me right now, sweetie."

"That doesn't count!" Then Nattie started laughing. "You are so bad. Give me back my muffin." Jase threw back her muffin over his head. "Dumb head," Nattie said.

A few seconds later, Nattie said, "You know, that was kinda fun."

"Want me to do another one? Nattie?"

"Wait a second, will ya? I'm trying to eat my muffin before you send it flying again…okay, now I'm ready. Warn me before you spin."

"Three, two, one…" Jase pushed forward on the stick and entered a steep dive. Nattie grabbed the bottom of her seat and screamed again. Jase did two and a half barrel rolls ending upside down.

"JASE!" Nattie said as she grabbed her chest. He rolled the ship back over and leveled out. "Ooh, you are so going to get it! I said spin!"

"I did."

"No, you scared me to death. You are such a brat."

"I love you, baby."

Nattie laughed, "You scared my tummy. Don't do that again."

"I'm going to make the jump into space."

"Okay." Jase pulled up hard on the collective lever and increased the turbine thrust, which pushed them back into their seats. The ship soared up through the outer atmosphere and into space. Nattie watched out the window as the vaporous white clouds dissipated into the dark night of space. The engines shut off and the ship flew quietly away from the planet. Jase set in the course and engaged the pulse engines. "It's all automatic from here."

"It's so amazing out here, Jassie. It feels so peaceful."

"You can take off your helmet now. The engines won't be nearly as loud." Jase and Nattie talked for several hours. Nattie was a total chatterbox but she noticed Jase wasn't saying anything after a while.

"Jase, you got really quiet."

"I was just thinking."

"About what?"

"Nothing really."

"Tell me."

"It's nothing, just thinking about how much fun we are going to have."

"Okay, so that's definitely not what you were thinking. Tell me, Jassie, please."

Jase took a deep breath, "You remember how Angelica felt at Tristy's funeral?"

"Yes." Jase was silent.

"Jase?"

"Never mind."

"Jassie, please tell me."

"I felt like that when you were mad at me and walked away from me after graduation in basic training."

"What made you think about that?"

"Your sweet voice."

"How?"

"It's just so nice to hear you talk, especially when you're silly or excited. You are such a part of me that I couldn't exist without you. That feeling was the same as the feeling I had at the lake when I thought I lost you."

"Jassie, you're going to make me cry."

"Sorry, baby."

"It's okay. I want to know how you feel, always."

"I am crazy about you. You are the only thing that I think of when I go to bed and you're my first thought when I wake up. By the time I get ready in the morning, I'm already missing you." Nattie was silent. "Nattie?"

She wiped her eyes. "I love you so much, Jassie."

After eight hours of flight time, the computer sounded a warning for the approaching destination. Jase woke Nattie from a little nap and reversed the thrust of the pulse engines to begin slowing. "Wow, Nattie; look out the window."

Nattie's jaw dropped as she viewed the huge planet, the blue and purple gas giant of Chasticka. The outer colonies were settled on one of her moons, which was similar in size and atmosphere to their home planet. Chasticka had two suns, allowing enough light for her moon to thrive with vegetation and animal life.

"Jassie, that is such an incredible sight. It makes me feel insignificant. I can't believe how huge it is."

"I know, and the laviniun input controls are very touchy."

"I bet. Be careful." Jase maneuvered the ship into a low orbit around the moon as the pulse engines continued to slow their momentum.

"Are you ready for descent through the atmosphere, baby?"

"I'm ready, honey." Jase set the angle of entry and started to descend. He didn't have to fully engage the laviniun generators with the gravitational effects of the nearby gas giant, so the transition through the atmosphere was quite smooth and constant. As they dropped in altitude, Jase flew around for a while to look at the surface of the moon.

"Jase, look at how pretty it is down there."

"I know. I didn't expect this. It's really tremendous. There are so many trees." Jase swerved and dropped down quickly to avoid a flying animal.

"Whew! Jase, what was that?"

"I don't know, some kind of funny-looking bird I guess."

Jase plotted a course for the settlement. "Nattie, want to take the stick?"

"Really?"

"Sure." Nattie held the flight stick with both hands.

"See the arrow on the gyrocompass?"

"Yes."

"Just try to keep that arrow lined up with the inner compass wheel and it will keep you on the course I entered." Nattie banked the ship left at the designated waypoint then back right a little while later, setting them on an approach vector to the skyport.

"You did great, Nattie."

"That was really easy."

Jase took back control of the ship so they could land. He climbed out onto the main wing and helped Nattie out of the cockpit. She stood on the wing and stretched.

They jumped down as Alrand and Kimberly ran out to meet them. Captain Alrand Dawlsome saluted Captain Nattie Candella. She returned the salute then jumped forward and gave Alrand a hug, then Kimberly. Jase hugged Kimberly and shook Alrand's hand. Nattie jumped up and down, holding Kimberly's hands.

"I have so missed you guys!" She said in a high pitch squealing voice. "You both look so good."

"Thank you, Nat."

"You two look great too."

"Thanks." Nattie showed Kimberly her ring.

"Oh, Nattie, it's so pretty."

"Jase, how ever did you find a butterfly wedding ring?"

"I'm not telling." Jase put his arm around Nattie and they all walked to Alrand's cruiser parked at the airfield.

"So Jase, you should start fighter training next, right?" Alrand asked.

"Yeah, I can't wait to dog fight." Nattie punched Jase in the arm hard.

"Hey!"

"I told you, you were going to get it. Kimberly, he was so bad."

"Let me guess, he scared the pants right off you?"

"He did! He was flying upside down." They all laughed.

"Alrand did the same thing to me."

"Boys! I'm telling you. What are we going to do with them?"

"Evidently we're marrying them." They all laughed and Nattie kissed Jase in the back seat.

Alrand and Kimberly crammed in as much excitement and sightseeing as they could for such a short stay. It didn't take long before things felt like old times. Jase and Nattie told them all about the events at the castle and about Halfgrim, but spoke not a word about the alien craft they found. Both Alrand and Kimberly were furious.

Nattie stayed overnight with Kimberly and Jase with Alrand. They all met up at first light for breakfast, before Jase and Nattie's departure. Alrand and Kimberly walked them out to their ship. It didn't take but a few seconds before Nattie and Kimberly welled up with tears as they said their goodbyes.

"I really love you guys," Nattie said. "I can't wait until we are stationed here with you. This place is so strange and wonderful."

"I know. I want to explore everything," Jase said.

"We will when you get here…love you both," Alrand said.

Nattie wiped her eyes and put on her helmet. Alrand laughed, "Nat, you're supposed to put your hair inside the helmet."

"No, Jase likes it this way. He says I'm cute."

"You guys are too much." Jase helped her into the ship. He waved goodbye to Alrand and Kimberly then fastened himself in for departure. They hovered out to the runway. Nattie could see Alrand and Kimberly standing there waving at them.

"I'm really going to miss them, Jassie. I didn't realize how much I missed them until we got here. It feels a little lonely without them."

"I know. Alrand has been my best friend since like, forever."

"At least we have each other and are together. That's the most important thing."

"Don't worry, baby. We'll be back in a few months after my training is completed."

They flew their long journey home. Nattie was exhausted and slept a good bit of the trip. Jase kept bobbing his head as he tried to stay awake. He wondered why Nattie always seemed to tire so exhaustively. He woke her up to help him stay alert. They talked about their wedding plans and Nattie encouraged him to do his best to complete the course so they could get married as soon as possible.

After arriving at the skyport, they reported to the flight commander to turn in the logbook. Jase received his pilot's license and advanced into the fighter-training program.

Jase jumped out of bed and ran to meet up with Nattie.

"Morning, baby." He gave her a kiss and a big hug.

"Hey, Jassie; today's the big day."

"Yep, I finally get to do some real combat maneuvers. I can't wait to get in the air."

"Go knock em out of the sky, handsome."

"Bye, baby." Jase ran off toward the skyport with his helmet under his arm. He accidentally ran into a female officer who was walking around a corner, knocking folders out from under her arm.

"Oh! I'm so sorry, Major." He picked up her papers.

"What's the big rush, Lieutenant?"

"First day of combat flight training, ma'am," Jase said quickly as he caught his breath.

"Well, chalk up your first kill, Lieutenant, direct hit."

"I'm so sorry about that."

"It's okay. I like your enthusiasm. As you were. Try not to score any more hits before you get into the air."

"Yes, ma'am," Jase laughed.

He joined a flight of three in formation. There were four flights engaged in the exercise. Jase held tight to his flight commander in the lead ship, forming the right side of a triangular flight pattern. They practiced a few aerobatics together before entering into the engagement zone.

"Nice flying, Thunderbelt. Keep it up. You will do well." Just then, "Watch it, fighters at three o'clock, high."

They executed evasive action as the opposing team had the jump on them. Jase was the first to be targeted and simulated being shot down. *Well, that lasted about two seconds*, he thought. The situation didn't improve much the remainder of the day. Jase was targeted at the offset of each engagement.

He pounded the dash with his fist multiple times and quickly spun down out of the sky to land. He opened the canopy, took off his helmet, and threw it out on the flight line. He sat staring at the sky watching his opponent's aerial tactics with his nostrils flaring.

Jase and the other pilots reported for their debriefing and the current tally of scores were posted. All of Jase's opponents had many kills. The tactics specialist stopped Jase and held him back after the debriefing was over.

"Thunderbelt, I can see you look a little frustrated. I think you're ready to go kick a cat."

"Yes, sir."

"It's just your first day. Cheer up; your opponents are a class ahead of you and have a lot more combat flight time. Hang in there. You will improve." Jase relaxed a bit. "Thunderbelt, worse case, your initial class will catch up with you, and then you will have the advantage."

"Yes, sir; it's just, I really expected to do much better. I was told I had a natural ability, but now I'm not so sure."

"It will come. Be patient."

Jase walked slowly with his head down, feeling exhausted from the stress. He caught up with Nattie and Endnova at the gym.

"Hi, Jassie," Nattie said with a bright smile.

"What's wrong, honey?"

"I don't want to talk about it."

"Okay." Nattie gave him a hug and kissed his neck. "I love you." She kissed his nose and pinched his tummy. Jase lifted his head and smiled.

"You always seem to have a way to make me feel better than I should. What am I going to do with you?"

"Marry me." She hugged him tight.

"Ugh, I so needed that. Massage right there."

"I'm guessing things didn't go so well today?" Nattie said as she massaged his back.

"I was just there for target practice, Nattie. I was the target."

Nattie giggled, "I bet you were the cutest target there though."

Jase grabbed her belly and tickled her. She tried to get away but she couldn't. Her face turned all red. She turned and pushed Jase's hands away.

"Stop it! You brat." She put her arms around his neck and they kissed. "I can't wait till we are married."

"Soon, baby. Soon. I just need to get a high enough score to graduate, and then we're out of here."

"Then you better get up there and kick some butt, buddy."

"I tried so hard, Nattie. I hardly lasted two seconds."

"You just need some practice, my love. It's only your first day."

Jase put his arm around Nattie and they started to walk to her quarters. "You said I can fly with you now, right?"

"Yes, but not during training."

"Let's go up now. You focus on practicing and I will keep track of our position." Jase laughed. "What's so funny? I'm serious."

"Yeah right, you go up with me flying maneuvers?"

"I can do it!"

"You sure about that?"

"If it helps get us out of here so we can get married, then yeah, I can do it."

"Okay, get your flight gear but no screaming."

"No promises there," Nattie giggled.

Every evening after the day's exercises, Jase and Nattie would go up training. Several weeks passed and Jase improved quite a bit. One day, he almost targeted an opponent but was reported shot down before he could get the kill. He was able to avoid being targeted for a greater duration but still had not accumulated any points. Nattie had finally reached a point where she stopped screaming every time Jase performed a precision maneuver. He gave Nattie flying lessons from time to time and taught her how to land. He continued to try so hard to score kills, but disappointingly fell short.

Nattie, being frustrated, waited until Jase started talking to his fellow pilots one evening at the officer's club. She walked over to the bar to talk with Jase's Ace fighter pilot friend, Major Slate.

Chapter 41

"**G**ood evening, Major."

"Ah, the beautiful Captain Candella." Nattie turned a little red and tilted her head a bit, brushing the hair out of her face. "Have a seat. Where's your Lieutenant?"

"He's over there talking," Nattie said as she sat down on the barstool.

"What can I get for you, Captain?"

"No no, that's okay. I just wanted to ask you a question."

"Shoot."

"Well," she took a deep breath and let it out. "Lieutenant Thunderbelt is ahead of his class, so he is training with more advanced pilots, with more experience."

"Let me guess, it's not going so well?"

"No, not at all," she said with a deep voice as she tilted her head down and rubbed the back of her neck. "Could you please help him? Please?"

"Are you sure he wants my help?"

"If he doesn't, I'm gonna punch his lights out."

The major laughed. "You are something, you know that?" Nattie giggled. He squeezed her arm then patted her on the back. "I'll see what I can do, Captain."

"Thank you very much."

The major walked over to Jase's table. The pilots stood at attention. "At ease, men. Thunderbelt, follow me." He took Jase out to his ship and ordered him into the pilot's seat. They climbed to altitude, "Show me what you got, Lieutenant. Simulate a fighter on your six. Go!" Jase spun and entered into a steep dive. He banked left and pulled in some collective shooting straight up. "Not bad. How many kills do you have?"

"None, sir."

"We will have to rectify that starting now. Tell me, how many evasive actions are there?" Jase started to describe many different techniques to avoid being shot down.

"Wrong! Forget everything you've learned. All that book smarts will just get you killed. Your mind is cluttered with too much information. There are only two types of evasion, controlled and sporadic. You have to have a feel for the ship and develop controlled responses. No more of this fly by impulse crap. You have real talent but you need to develop your responses and combine them end to end so that you are always in full control of the ship and are aware of your next maneuver. If you have to, turn down the power on the laviniun generators to get more of a feeling as you fly. You practice your responses like a guitar player practices cords. Once you know all the cords, you can combine them to create a magnificent sound. Are you following me, Lieutenant?"

"Absolutely, sir!"

"I will teach you your first thirty-six basic responses starting now."

Jase continued to learn new responses and practiced dog fighting against the major at night. Nattie would fly along with Jase and quietly sit holding on to her seat. She found the override for controlling the laviniun generators and wrote a little program to automatically adjust the output from her controls. She made sure to restore the setting each night when they returned to the skyport.

Within a week's time, he was able to avoid being targeted,

allowing him to score five kills. He climbed out of the cockpit as if he was still souring through the air. He jumped down off the primary wing and quickly ran to meet up with Nattie.

"Guess what?"

"What?" Nattie said excitedly.

"I got my fifth kill today."

"Really?" Nattie jumped up and down, and jumped up on Jase. He caught her and swung her around.

"You are so thin, Nattie. You feel like a feather."

"I love you so much, Jassie. What's the minimum score to be able to graduate this month?"

"Twenty-five."

"Jassie, I'm so proud…"

BERDOUN, BERDOUN, BERDOUN, the gut-pounding global alert siren began to sound throughout the complex and the whole military base.

Endnova ran quickly down the hallway, "Jase, Nattie, come quick!"

"What is it, Endnova?"

"We've been hit!"

"What do you mean?"

"The outer colonies have been wiped out!"

"What? NO!"

"By who?" Jase asked frantically.

"I don't know."

They ran to the central common area where students had gathered to watch the live video report. They saw images of unidentified ships, firing some type of powerful glowing streak of light that destroyed everything in its path.

"Were there any survivors?"

"No one knows."

"Come on, Nattie." Jase and Nattie ran to his quarters and tried to place a video call to the outer colonies. They tried multiple times but no response. Nattie was shaking all over as she stood next to Jase with her arm around him. Jase continued to try and contact Alrand but no success. They turned to leave but Alrand appeared on the monitor. His charred face was covered with black soot and dried blood. His eyes were red and teary.

Nattie ran close to the monitor, "Alrand, you're okay." He let his head fall to his chest, tears dropped from his face. "Alrand, what is it?"

He cried, "Kimberly's dead."

Nattie put her hand over her mouth. "Oh no!" Her whole body went numb as if someone just cut out half of her heart. She hugged Jase and cried, wiping her eyes and nose. "No, please no." Her tears dropped to the floor, splashing in big patters.

Jase was still, as if he couldn't breathe. "Alrand, what happened?" Alrand tried to clear his throat and wiped his charred face with his dirty sleeve.

"They just came out of nowhere. We couldn't get any ships up and the ones that did were blasted out of the sky just off the ground. They leveled everything." He started crying again, "I tried to save her but it all happened so fast. She got hit running from the skyport. I ran as fast as I could." He paused and gasped. "There was so much blood everywhere." He leaned his head down. "She told me she loved..."

The transmission was interrupted. Jase tried to place the call again but there was no receiver to accept the broadcast.

He sat down next to Nattie and held her tight.

"How, Jassie?"

"I don't know. We have no enemies."

"I can't believe she's gone." She hugged Jase and cried loudly on his shoulder.

BERDOUN, BERDOUN, BERDOUN, the alarm resounded.

"ATTENTION! All pilots report to the main contention area. Repeat, all pilots report to the main contention area."

Jase and Nattie ran to the assembly point and met up with the other pilots.

"Attention!"

Everyone stood as Colonel Cantellous entered the large room.

"At ease, please be seated. As you have undoubtedly heard, the outer colonies were attacked not long ago. I will make this short. We need as many pilots in the air as possible. Our enemy is powerful, very maneuverable, and has some type of shielding technology that greatly reduces the effectiveness of our weapons. However, they can be taken out with enough firepower. I want every able-bodied pilot and combat trainee suited up and ready to fly in fifteen minutes. We could very well be fighting for our very survival, people, and we have every reason to believe the enemy knows we're here. We are short of navigators so any volunteers would be greatly appreciated."

Nattie raised her hand in front of everyone. "Yes, Captain Candella?"

"I would like to volunteer to be Lieutenant Thunderbelt's navigator."

"Nattie, no!"

"You're not going up there without me, Jase."

"Nattie, it's too dangerous."

"No, Lieutenant, it's done. Let's get those ships in the air, people. Make it so."

Everyone hurried off to his or her required positions. "Nattie why did you do that?"

"I'm going with you, Jase. If you die, I die, remember? I'm not going to be the one left on the ground helpless to do anything, wondering if I will ever see you again." Nattie grabbed his flight suit by the collar and kissed him, "We do this together." Jase knew there was no changing her mind.

Jase and Nattie climbed into Jase's ship and sealed the canopy.

They flew to a position in space not far from the planet, powered down, and waited. Jase's heart rate was elevated and his breathing heavy.

"Jassie, relax. You can do this."

"I am relaxed. I'm just alert."

ZING

A bright light flashed across the squadron taking out multiple ships. They all scattered and engaged the enemy. Jase formed up with his flight group. In only moments, he was able to maneuver into position and fired on one of the enemy ships but he did little damage before the ship banked back hard and flew at his six. Jase tried to shake the alien ship but it stuck to him as if he was towing it with a tether.

"Nattie, I can't shake him," shouted Jase with a varying shaky tone of desperation.

"Jase, four more enemy ships just appeared." A shot was fired just as Jase banked left, ripping off one of the weapons pods which then struck the enemy ship and exploded.

"Whew, that was close." They could feel the heat from the blast inside the cockpit. "Nattie, did we destroy him?"

"No, he's coming back up behind us."

"Oh, great."

"Jassie, head closer to the planet.

"What? Why?"

"Just do it, trust me." Jase accelerated and headed back towards home. The enemy ship followed tightly, continually firing. Multiple strikes tore up parts of their ship. Jase performed one response after another but began to tire. Nattie enabled her laviniun generator program and quickly set in new parameters. "Jassie, on my mark, pull in full collective. Three, two, one, NOW!"

Using the gravitational forces of the planet, the new parameters burst the ship forward then effected a full reverse motion. The enemy ship flew right past. Jase set full throttle, targeted the enemy, and fired everything he had. The ship was destroyed in a great burst of fire, sending out a huge shock wave.

"Yes, Yes, Yes!" They flew back toward the squadron to try and draw another ship closer to their planet. Forty-five Concordia ships had already been destroyed and only two of the enemy. Jase targeted another enemy ship and fired the main cannon but the rounds seemed to spark into dust as they struck the shield. The enemy turned and chased Jase and Nattie toward the planet. They performed the same extreme maneuvers but Jase couldn't inflect enough damage.

"Jase, another ship directly behind us!" With a flash of light and a heat wave, the ship yawed sideways as if something struck it from the side cracking the fuselage and sending shrapnel flying.

Nattie screamed.

"Nattie? Are you okay, Nattie?" Jase looked back. Nattie was motionless with her head leaning forward against the console, swaying back and forth with the ship's motion. Blood was everywhere. "Nattie!"

The ship's atmosphere began to vent. Jase's flight suit automatically pressurized to one atmosphere but Nattie's, ripped apart from the shrapnel, could not inflate. In desperation, Jase darted down into the outer atmosphere of their planet. He forced a hard reentry, keeping the laviniun generators at a minimum while maintaining the steepest angle possible without burning up the ship. The bow turned bright red and yellow with flames flaring across the cockpit. He broke through the atmosphere and headed toward the base. The proximity alarm sounded, one of the alien ships followed him through reentry. Jase alerted the ground batteries and flew right past them. The enemy drew close to Jase so that they couldn't fire without further damaging his ship. Jase performed several of his learned responses, surprising the enemy, and fired armor piercing rounds with little effect. He veered off quickly and the ground batteries fired massive blasts, knocking the ship out of the sky.

Jase declared an emergency landing and requested medical personnel standby. On approach, one of the four engines flamed out and caught fire. He landed the ship and tried to unfasten Nattie's safety harness but it was jammed. He could feel the heat of the flames through his flight suit. The emergency crews tried to pull Jase away from the cockpit but he frantically fought them off and continued to try to free Nattie. He pulled his survival knife from his lower flight suit leg pocket and cut the restraining straps. He pulled her from the cockpit with all his might and handed Nattie off to rescue personnel. Just as Jase jumped from the wing, the whole rear end of the ship exploded, knocking everyone to the ground. The rescuers took Jase and Nattie to the post hospital.

En route, they cut off Nattie's flight suit and worked on stopping the bleeding from the serious shrapnel wounds. Jase was instructed to hold direct pressure over one of the punctures. Nattie regained partial consciousness and struggled to lift her head.

"Lay still, baby," Jase said in a subtle tone. He gently stroked her head.

"Jassie, it hurts." She closed her eyes and fell from consciousness. The short trip to the hospital felt like an eternity. They rushed Nattie into surgery to stabilize her enough to be placed into a medical pod. Jase was told to stay in the waiting room. He paced back and forth, going over the events in his head. He couldn't stand still and felt like he was going out of his mind.

Colonel Cantellous walked up to Jase. "How's she doing, son?"

Jase looked at the colonel with teary eyes, "All I know is that she is in surgery."

"I know how concerned you are and I have every confidence in our medical staff. I hate to ask this of you but I need you back up there. You are one of only a few pilots who have actually shot down one of these deathly terrors."

"I don't see how I can fly now. My mind will be focused on her."

"It was a mistake on my part allowing Candella to fly second seat. It's my fault."

"No, sir. If it wasn't for her, I would be dead."

"How is that?"

"She reprogrammed the laviniun generators to outmaneuver them and set up the primary fire button to expend all ordinance simultaneously, which is how I was able to shoot down the enemy."

"Impressive. I need that code. I hope we can extract it from the wreckage of your ship."

"If there's anything left after the explosion."

"This could be the key to winning this fight."

The colonel motioned over Captain Rails. "I need you to direct a science team to recover some custom code Captain Candella installed on Thunderbelt's ship. This is top priority."

"Yes, sir."

The doctor exited the surgical area and walked over to Jase.

"How is she?"

"She's stable for the moment. Do you know of any heart defects in her history?"

"No, sir; she has always been very healthy. Why?"

"One of her heart valves is damaged. I'm surprised she hasn't experienced a heart attack." Jase's heart was beating like crazy and his breathing was erratic.

"Is there anything you can do?"

"If we can get her stable enough to place her into a medical pod, we should be able to repair the damage."

"Why can't you put her in the pod now?"

"If she isn't stable enough and at least partially conscious, the pod could do more harm than good. It's unfortunate that this happened but it probably will save her life. Her heart would have eventually failed."

"Thunderbelt, she's in good hands. I need you on the airfield. We are regrouping for a second offensive." Jase wrote a sweet little note for Nattie and left it with a nurse.

Chapter 42

He walked to the airfield as if in a daze, thinking about Nattie in the surgery. His mind drifted and he had a frightening thought about that of Tristy and David. His heart skipped a beat and he desired to run back to Nattie.

"Thunderbelt." Jase continued walking. "Lieutenant Thunderbelt! Snap out of it," Colonel Cantellous said. "Men, Lieutenant Thunderbelt will explain a new tactic in fighting our enemy."

"Sir, were you successful in extracting the program?"

"That's correct. And we added a second fire button command. Additional weapon mounts have been added and the payload has been doubled. You get two shots to fire a full set of ordinance."

Jase explained how to use the laviniun-assisted maneuvers to outfly the enemy ships in low orbit based on Nattie's software modification. He also asserted that the main cannon was completely useless against their shields.

A loud rumbling could be heard in the distance as dark clouds drifted overhead. *The sky looks like I feel*, Jase thought. The flight of ten ships took to the sky with a vengeance, piercing through the rain and zero-visibility cloud cover. A few moments later, they emerged from the darkness into the bright blue sky. Jase's friend, Major Slate, led the attack.

"Men, prepare to target the enemy and make your jump into

space. Fire on them as soon as you can get them targeted. Don't hesitate."

Jase breathed very heavily and felt like he had a knot in his throat. He hesitated and looked back at the empty seat behind him. It felt cold and lonely without Nattie. He wanted to be angry with the enemy, but instead, he felt hurt and longed to know how Nattie was doing. He felt so bad not being there when, or if, she awoke. He prepared himself and reluctantly pulled in full collective while engaging the engines.

Jase's ship darted up through the atmosphere into space and slammed hard into a huge piece of wreckage, knocking out his laviniun generators and severely damaging the ship. He panicked as his ship twirled end over end out into space. Multiple alarms sounded in the speakers in his flight helmet. Only one ship remained, the Major's, and he desperately tried to evade the three remaining enemy vessels.

Jase cleared the alarms and used inertial actuators to regain control of his Sonic Fighter. He had a perfect opportunity to target the trailing enemy so he engaged the main engines and darted forward. The enemy was targeted and Jase fired the first full payload of rockets. The enemy craft performed some insane maneuvers and avoided the ordnance altogether, and then headed right toward him,

"Oh, great!"

Jase figured his best chance was to fly head-on toward the ship to give it little time to respond. He fully engaged all four engines, forcing him back tightly in his seat without the counter effects of the laviniun generators. He spun and swerved his ship back and forth trying to avoid the deadly beam repeatedly firing at him. His ship was struck multiple times, leaving holes in his wings. As the enemy drew dangerously close, he fired the second group of missiles but one of his engines was hit and blown clean off. It smashed into his rear vertical elevator, jamming his controls. He was on a collision course with the enemy with no way to maneuver. The missiles impacted the enemy's vessel, sending out a huge shockwave that changed Jase's trajectory, sending him down into the planet's atmosphere.

Without the laviniun generators and his vertical controls damaged, he couldn't correct his angle of entry and the ship started to heat drastically. Flames burst all around him as his ship soared through the atmosphere. Gnawing his teeth together and straining every muscle, he stretched out his legs pushing against the lower cockpit to pull back on the stick but the vertical elevator was totally jammed. Pieces of the gunship were stripped off by the fierce friction of the air as he plummeted downward. He broke through the outer atmosphere with the ship descending out of control. As the ground grew closer, he thought about Nattie and her disappointment. She was so looking forward to being married.

Jase tried one last time to free up the vertical elevator with all his might. Snap, the stick moved a few inches back but there wasn't enough time to level out. Then Jase remembered something that Captain Wells had said, "The ship kissed the water." He turned toward the sea, pulling back on the flight stick as hard as he could. He just missed hitting the top of a huge building in the city. He maneuvered the ship between the rows of buildings and almost hit cruisers on the roadway just before flying out over the beach. He smashed down hard on the water, ripping off the wings. The ship bounced several times hard on the water before breaking into pieces. Jase was ejected violently and landed in the water. His flight suit automatically inflated to keep him afloat and armed a distress beacon.

Nattie could see faint blurry lights passing by overhead. She could hear muffled voices and see blurry images of people around her as she was rushed down the hospital corridor. She felt tightness in her chest and couldn't move a muscle. They picked her up and lay her in a medical pod, the cover slid down and sealed above her.

"Doctor, is there any hope for her?" asked a nurse.

"It's not looking good. Her heart is failing and she has internal bleeding."

Rescue and recovery teams homed in on Jase's distress beacon. They transported him to the trauma center where skilled military surgeons worked frantically to preserve his life.

A few hours later, after being placed into the medical pod, Nattie awoke in the recovery room. She opened her eyes, grabbed her chest out of reflex, and instinctively felt about her body but everything felt wonderful. She sat up and looked around, not knowing where she was. When she realized she was in a hospital, she got up out of bed and started to walk, but felt dizzy and almost fell. A nurse ran into the room and grabbed hold of her.

"Sweetie, you need more time to recover before you can walk."

"Where's my Jassie?"

"Here, get right up..."

"Stop!" Nattie tried to pull free of her grip.

"Captain, you need to get back into bed."

"No, I have to find Jase."

"Marie, please come quickly and help me with her," yelled the nurse. The two nurses forced Nattie up on the bed.

"Please stop, please, I need to find Jase." Nattie pleaded with the nurse. "Please help me. I have to find my fiancé."

"Ma'am, I will see what I can do, but you need to stay here and rest."

"Can you tell me what happened? How did I get here?"

"Let me check your file. It says here you were treated for shrapnel wounds and heart trauma."

"Did we crash? Is Jase still alive?"

"Ma'am, I'm sorry but I don't know. Maybe if you give me a little more information. Who is Jase?"

"Lieutenant Thunderbelt, he was my pilot and he is my fiancé."

"I will check the log to see if he was admitted."

A few minutes later, the nurse walked back into the room with a shocking look on her face. She calmly stated,

"Captain, I am sorry to say. He was just admitted into the trauma center a little while ago. He's in critical condition."

"Oh no, how bad is it?"

"I don't know more than what I just told you."

"I need to go see how he is doing, please."

"Okay, let me get a wheelchair for you." The nurse pushed Nattie down to the emergency trauma unit. She went in to inquire about the severity of Jase's condition.

"Captain, they are doing the best they can."

"What does that mean? Tell me!"

"I'm so sorry." Nattie bent over holding her stomach and cried. "Sweetie, there's still a chance. They're doing everything they possibly can."

"What's wrong with him?"

"I better let the doctor explain when they're finished." Nattie wiped her mouth with the back of her hand. She was shaking so much and felt so cold. Her tears dripped on her lap and her nose kept running. "Why don't I take you back to your room? The doctor will come talk to you when there's news."

"No, please, I need to be here."

The nurse wrapped her up in a blanket. Nattie pulled her legs up in the wheelchair and leaned against the handle, curled up in a little ball. Being more alert, her mind raced, thinking about Jase and all the things they have done together. She felt numb all over and longed for Jase's embrace. She couldn't stand sitting, worrying, and doing nothing. She got up and walked around the waiting room. There was a huge explosion some distance away that shook the whole building, startling everyone. Nattie ran to the window to see the wreckage of an alien ship that was just shot down by the ground to air defenses. It was engulfed in flames and very heavy black smoke rose up into the air.

One of the doctors exited the surgery to talk with Nattie. She ran over to him crossing her arms and holding her elbows.

"Are you Captain Candella?"

"Yes, sir. Is he okay?" Nattie asked in a weak soft voice.

"He's alive at the moment. There's nothing more we can do now. The rest is up to him."

"How bad is it?"

"It's very serious. His backbone was broken in several locations. His arms and legs were broken along with a few ribs and a collarbone. He has severe burns over ninety percent of his body and several large lacerations. He needs to be placed into a medical pod but he has slipped into a coma."

"What if he comes out of the coma?"

"That would be great but I'm sorry to say, with his injuries, I don't think he will survive more than a few hours."

Nattie's shoulders clenched forward and her whole body tremored as she cried. She wiped her face and nose with her hospital gown and looked up at the doctor with her red puffy eyes.

"Can I please see him?"

"Just wait here a minute. I will let you know when he's ready for visitors." Nattie went and sat down. She put her head in her hands and cried until she felt like she had no tears left to cry. *I have to be strong for my Jassie,* she thought.

The doctor waved Nattie over. "Please take a second to prepare yourself."

Nattie took a deep breath and let it out. "Okay, I'm ready." They walked into the room. Jase was connected to several machines by tubes and wires. His body was almost entirely covered in bandages. He had a breathing tube coming out of his mouth connected to a respirator.

"Can he hear me if I talk to him?"

"It is possible, but doubtful." Nattie walked over to the bed and stood above Jase. She was afraid to touch him anywhere. She felt so hollow inside. She leaned down close to him and softly whispered, "Jassie, please don't die. I need you. I can't live without you. You are the love of my life. I could never love anyone else. Please, baby, come back to me."

Her warm tears dripped on the bandages around his forehead. She gently leaned forward and kissed his partially exposed ear. He felt warm to her lips. She squinted her eyes together. Everything was looking blurry. She searched for some tissues to wipe her face and blow her nose. She stood over Jase and began to prepare her heart. Colonel Cantellous walked into the room, Nattie tried to gain her composure but couldn't.

"How is he, Captain?" Nattie frowned and looked at the floor.

"He is a brave soldier," the colonel said. He patted Nattie on the back. "I put both of you in for medals of heroism." Nattie looked up at him with her sad watering eyes.

"I love him more than anything in this world."

"There have been many great losses in this fight. Unfortunately, it's not over yet. Thunderbelt saved the life of my flight commander, Major Slate, for which I am very grateful." He squeezed her shoulder, "He's a strong young man, Candella. Don't give up hope."

A nurse walked in as the colonel walked out to check on other wounded pilots. "Ma'am, there's a video call coming in for you from the outer colonies. You can take it here on the monitor. Oh, and a young man left me a note to give you yesterday but I couldn't find you until now. Sorry." She handed Nattie Jase's note and turned on the monitor.

"Alrand!"

"Hey, Nat. I heard about Jase. How is he?"

Nattie cried, "They say he only has hours to live and they can't put him in the medical pod." Alrand was silent. He bowed his head. After a few moments, he looked up at Nattie and wiped his eyes. In a teary, scratchy, voice, he said, "I'm so sorry, Nat. He was my best friend." He felt like crying but held it back, yet his voice was wavering.

"I know he was."

"Nat, I don't know how to tell you this but..."

"What is it?"

"You know I love you both, right?"

"I love you too, Alrand, but why are you saying this?"

"Nattie, they are forming an armada and heading your way. They have a huge battle cruiser and many ships. I believe it's an invasion force and they need to be stopped."

"Oh no!"

"I have been asked to fly special mission."

"What kind of mission?"

"I'm going to fly right into the middle of the armada and detonate a nuclear reflection device."

"Alrand, no! You will die. Everyone is dying. You can't do it," Nattie cried. "I can't lose you too. Tell them to pick someone else."

"Nat, I volunteered."

"But why?"

"I miss Kimberly too much and I don't want anyone else to have to die."

"Please, Alrand."

"Nat, the decision has been made. I just want you guys to know I love you."

Nattie stepped back and looked at Alrand. She stood straight up tall, her eyes opened wide, and her eyebrows lifted. Her lips drew tight as her nostrils flared. She put her hands on her waist and a vain pulsed in her neck as her heart rate soared.

"Nat?"

"You're not flying that mission, Alrand."

"Nat, I have to."

"No, you don't. I have a better idea."

"What are you talking about?"

"Trust me, Alrand, and promise me you won't fly that mission."

"I can't do that."

"Just give me a day, okay? Trust me, I mean it, do not fly that mission."

"Okay, but only a day. What do you have in mind?"

"I have to run. Just trust me."

Nattie ran out into the hallway to find Colonel Cantellous. She peaked into every room. A nurse caught up with her, "Ma'am, you should really be resting."

"Oh, shut up!" She spotted the Colonel exiting the wing and shouted, "Colonel Cantellous!" He stopped and waited while Nattie ran over to him. "Sir, I need to tell you something important."

"I'm listening, Captain."

"You are aware that I have been helping to design targeting systems for our fighters?"

"Yes, of course."

"Well, there's a device that can stop the armada that's heading our way."

"How do you know about that?"

"My best friend is the one who volunteered for the mission to stop them."

"What device are you referring to?"

"I know this will be hard to believe but..."

Nattie looked away for a second to think.

"Just spit it out, Captain."

"Okay, just before we joined up, Thunderbelt and I found an alien spaceship hidden in a cave in Voncara Cove. It's equipped with a weapon capable of obliterating the enemy."

"Wait, what?"

"I can show you the logbook from the ship if you don't believe me."

"Let me understand this. You found one of the alien ships and can understand their language enough to read their logbook?"

"No, sir; several hundred years ago a ship of humans, like us, was shot down, probably by the same enemy we now face. They hid their damaged ship in a cave. I have their logbook written in their language, which was taught to our ancestors. It's the same language we speak today."

"And you think this weapon can destroy our enemy?"

"Yes, sir."

"Why didn't you mention this before?"

"We didn't think anyone would believe us and I only thought about the weapon when Captain Dawlsome told me about his suicide mission."

"What do we have to do to make use of this weapon?"

"So you believe me?"

"I may have had a hard time believing this two days ago, but today most of our battalion has been destroyed by advanced hostile alien insurgents bent on wiping us out."

"Sir, if you can give me a few men to help carry the device and a shuttle, I can retrieve it and retrofit it onto one of our fighters."

"I'm sorry, Captain, but we don't have any pilots available."

"Then give me the men and I will fly the shuttle."

"Sir, I would like to volunteer to go along with Candella," Captain Rails said.

"I didn't know you were a pilot, Candella."

Chapter 43

"**S**ir, I'm not but Thunderbelt taught me how to fly."

"You two never cease to amaze me, Candella. It's a mission. Bring me that weapon. Captain Rails, find four strong soldiers to help carry that device and go with Candella. There is little time. Make haste."

Nattie read Jase's sweet and sincere letter that he left before flying his deadly mission. She took a quick moment to dry her eyes and prepare herself. She wrote Jase a short note:

"To my love, I will never forget you. My soul is empty without you. My heart may never beat again. I have ceased to exist, for without you, I am only an empty vessel. I love you far beyond this life into all eternity. If you should wake and I am not there, know that I go to Voncara Cove to retrieve the RFI to avenge you and to save Alrand. I love you now and always. Your Nattie."

Nattie remembered Captain Rails from basic training. He was strong and rather muscular like Jase. He gathered four pumped volunteers and met up with Nattie on the flight line. She plotted a course for Voncara Cove and received clearance from the tower. "You sure you know what you're doing?" Captain Rails asked.

"I have quite a few hours in the Sonic Fighters. I can't imagine this being much different."

She pulled up on the collective control and nosed forward, taking to the sky, smooth as silk.

"Nice job, Candella."

"Thanks."

They climbed to altitude and Nattie spared no fuel flying almost full throttle to get to Voncara Cove as quickly as possible. She tried to keep her mind on the task as not to dwell on Jase but partway through the flight, she teared up and wiped her cheeks. Her grief turned to anger and she pressed forward on the stick heading directly for the cove.

"Easy does it, Candella."

"I got it, we're fine." Nattie slowed and hovered over Point Lookout spotting for a place to land. She set the craft down in a tight clearing several hundred yards northwest of the cave entrance.

The men geared up and Sergeant Cascoya opened the rear hatch. The five of them followed Nattie through the woods.

"You sure you can find this cave again, Candella?"

"Blindfolded if I have to." They drew near the cliffs and walked into a clearing when thirteen men with pistols and rifles snuck up on them, catching them off guard.

"Freeze! Don't move a muscle."

"What's going on here?" Captain Rails asked. One of the men knocked him on the back of the head with the stock of his rifle, knocking him out.

"Anyone else have any questions?" Sergeant Cascoya assessed the situation, looking for an opportunity to throw a diversionary grenade, hoping to shock them to gain the upper hand. "Move it, this way." They made the other men drag Captain Rails and lead them toward the cave entrance. They held the soldiers arms behind their backs.

Nattie noticed that the cave was opened. There was a cargo cruiser sitting just inside the tree line. Wooden crates and pieces of equipment sat around the area and a campfire burned nearby. Nattie could hear a voice coming from inside the cave. She clenched her fist and her face drew cold. She turned red and tightened her lips. It was him. Halfgrim walked out of the cave with two of his large thugs with him, one walked with a serious limp.

"Well, well. Who do we have here?" Nattie held her tongue and looked away. Captain Rails regained consciousness and stood to his feet.

"Who is in charge here?"

"I am," Rails said as he rubbed the back of his bleeding head.

"What is your mission here?"

"What gives you the right to detain Concordia personnel?"

"I will ask the questions here." He looked at Nattie, "I don't believe my eyes." Halfgrim walked over to Nattie and grabbed her chin with his hand. She struggled and kicked him between the legs as hard as she could. Halfgrim fell to his knees, squealing in pain. He looked up at his limping thug and nodded his head. The thug limped over to Nattie and punched her upside the head with all his might. Her body went limp and fell to the ground.

"You idiot, I didn't tell you to kill her."

"She's not dead." Halfgrim got up. "See? She's still breathing."

"I need her conscious. Get their med kit and get her up." They got Nattie to her feet. She was dizzy and disoriented. Her face and eye had already started to darken with a bruise. Halfgrim drew close and backhanded her across the face. Rails and the other men tried to struggle free but the men put guns to their heads.

"Don't even think about it," one of the men said to Sergeant Cascoya. Halfgrim looked at Nattie's flight suit and her nametag.

"So this is why we couldn't find you, Captain Candella."

"Leave her alone or you're dead," Captain Rails said.

"Shut him up!" They punched Rails in the stomach multiple times, infuriating him.

"Tell me, Candella, how does this thing work?" Halfgrim walked to the transport cruiser and pulled the cover off the Resonate Frequency Injection gun.

Nattie's eyes opened wide, "You turned it on! Halfgrim, you half-witted, pit-faced, fool! We are at war because of you."

"You will answer my questions or die, Captain." Nattie spit the blood from her bleeding lips all over Halfgrim's face. He knocked Nattie to the ground and put his knee against her neck so that she couldn't breathe. The soldiers struggled to get free and Sergeant Cascoya tried to throw the diversionary grenade but couldn't pull the pin and was shot in the head.

Nattie's face started to turn blue as she struggled to breathe. "I have had it with you. Tell me how this thing works or you have taken your last breath." Halfgrim barely loosened the pressure against her neck.

"I will never help you, you stupid fool."

Halfgrim pulled back the hammer on his revolver and placed it to Nattie's head. She screamed and closed her eyes tight, squinting.

POW - POW - POW – POW

Four shots rang out, thumping into Halfgrim's chest, throwing him to the ground dead, five feet away from Nattie. Everyone instinctively ducked down as a Sonic Fighter blasted past overhead startling them. The soldiers pulled free and engaged Halfgrim's fleeing men. Those who were not killed escaped into the woods.

The Sonic Fighter circled overhead. Captain Rails got on the radio. "Away Team One to the fighter overhead, thank you for your assistance."

"My pleasure, is Nattie okay?" Nattie ran to the radio and grabbed it from Captain Rails' hand.

"JASSIE! Is that really you?"

"Hi, baby. Hope I'm not too late."

Nattie cried, "You were right on time, baby. I can't believe you're here." Nattie wiped her eyes and Rails looked at her neck, leaning her head to the side.

"I guess it was something about your note. A nurse read it to me and I woke up."

"Jase, we have to get the RFI back to the base as soon as possible."

"Okay, I'll fly cover. Be quick."

Nattie turned off the device. The men carried the RFI weapon system and Sergeant Cascoya's body to the shuttle. They flew back to the base as quickly as they could with their single fighter escort. Nattie hardly finished landing the shuttle when she burst out of the rear hatch and ran to Jase's fighter. He walked out on the wing and kneeled down, looking at Nattie standing there in the bright light of day, the wind blowing her long beautiful black hair. Nattie jumped up and down with her hands in the air, beckoning Jase to jump down. They held each other tightly.

"How do you feel, Jassie?"

"I feel wonderful. How about you? The whole side of your face and neck is bruised."

"I have never felt better, Jassie. I have you, and Halfgrim is dead."

"I could just imagine your face when you saw him."

"I have never been so mad in my entire life. If you were two seconds later, I would not be standing here."

"Whew, it was that close?"

"You have no idea."

Nattie worked with her boss and a science team to adapt the RFI gun to work with a new targeting system, that was recently developed. A brand new, advanced Sonic Fighter was fitted with the new weapon system.

"Candella, shouldn't we test the device at some point?"

"Not yet, it may draw the enemy down upon us. They are attracted to its energy emissions somehow. We will perform a test once the squadron is assembled and ready for this final battle."

. . .

Jase caught up with Colonel Cantellous and made a special request. "Thunderbelt, you know how crazy this is? This could be the end of our lives, if we lose this battle. That's why it makes so much sense."

"Very well, but we need to be quick."

Endnova walked up to Nattie in the hangar and took her by the hand. "Come with me."

"Wait, where are we going?"

"For once in your life, just shush and follow me."

Nattie laughed, "Endnova, I have to get ready."

"No, you have to follow me."

They walked into a large conference room with many soldiers standing inside. They all clapped their hands and cleared a path.

Endnova placed a white veil over Nattie's head.

Chapter 44

Jase stood at the far end of the room with Colonel Cantellous and Captain Rails. The men and women hummed a wedding march as Endnova walked Nattie down the center of the room. Her heart was beating so fast. She smiled and bounced a little on her toes.

Endnova walked her before the colonel and Jase, lifting her veil. The colonel spoke, "Men and Women, we are gathered together to bring these two special soldiers together in holy matrimony. Thunderbelt, you may pronounce your vows."

Jase held Nattie's hand, "Nattie, you are my one and only love. I promise to love you forever. I will protect you to my dying breath. You are the air that I breathe and without you, I would suffocate and die. You are part of me and I will never leave you or turn away from you, even throughout all eternity."

"Jassie, you're my best friend, my partner in life. I love you with all my heart and all my soul forever and ever. You are part of me so that nothing could ever change my desire to stand by your side. I will follow you anywhere and stand by you no matter what life brings our way. I promise to hold you and love you. I give my life to you fully."

"By the power vested in me as your colonel and confidante, I now pronounce you Husband and Wife."

Jase leaned Nattie backwards and held her in his arms kissing her. She put her arms around his neck. Knowing what becomes, everyone cheered and rejoiced, even for this short reprieve from the enemy's advance.

"May I present Mr. and Misses Thunderbelt," the colonel said. "I expect to see the two of you on the flight line in an hour." Jase looked at Nattie and her at him. They ran through the crowd and all the way back to Nattie's quarters. They burst in the door and locked it behind them. Jase was hesitant but Nattie wasted no time. She helped Jase off with his clothes and threw him back on the bed. They passionately made love for the very first time, but also, as if it was their last. They made use of every second they could before reporting to the flight line for battle.

Evening approached and the sun was set low in the sky. Bright orange and yellow puffy clouds floated calmly across the horizon. A warm gentle breeze blew out of the north. All of the remaining Concordia ships that were recalled for battle lined the runway, two hundred in all, plus Nattie's specially modified, Rioter Class, advanced Sonic Fighter. All of the pilots and their navigators stood by waiting for the Thunderbelts to make their way to a makeshift platform erected for Colonel Cantellous.

"Jassie, you seeing this?"

"Yeah, it's quite impressive. So many ships in one place." Jase and Nattie walked hand in hand and stood before the Colonel.

"Are the two of you ready for this?"

"Yes, sir," Nattie said confidently.

"I assume you will be flying second seat, Captain Thunderbelt?"

"Absolutely."

"Everything rests upon the two of you succeeding at your mission. Here are your objectives. First, you will need to destroy the enemy battleship's docking bay to prevent ships from entering and exiting. Your secondary objective is the battlecruiser itself. Take out as many fighters as you can but your primary objective has to be that docking bay."

"I understand, sir," Jase said.

The colonel stood at a microphone to address the pilots.

"Before we embark on this historic mission to save our planet, I have one piece of overdue business. Lieutenant Jase Thunderbelt, please step forward. Due to your outstanding courage in the face of grave danger and acts of heroism, I am ordering your immediate promotion to the rank and title of captain." The Colonel pinned the new rank insignia on Jase's lapel. Jase saluted and the colonel saluted in return.

"Men and Women, today we fight for the survival of our planet. We have a new weapon that will help to even the odds against them. This new fighter must make it though at all costs. You will defend it with your lives. Flight wing one will primarily attack the enemy fighters. Flight wing two, you will escort the special fighter to the battleship and defend it against all threats. Flight wing three, you will take up the rear position defending the planet. You must not allow the enemy to reach our home. Soldiers, today we truly live up to our name, Freedom Alliance! Fight to keep our freedom! Never back down! Never surrender!"

The pilots shouted and shook their fists in the air. "Mount up!" The skyport rumbled as the fighters spun up their turbines. The smell of burning JP-4 jet fuel filled the air.

Jase looked back at Nattie, "What are you smiling at?"

"Just thinking about you, no matter what happens, I'm happy because I finally got to have you."

"You're so silly, Misses Thunderbelt."

"Just like my husband," she giggled.

The flight wings lifted off in formation. Jase and Nattie took the lead position in the second flight group, which was the first to leave the atmosphere. They flew at full speed toward the alien battlecruiser, which had taken up position near the planet's largest moon. Before they could even get close, a contingent of alien fighters approached.

"Nattie, there are so many."

"I'm powering the weapon. I sure hope this works." The battle commenced as the second flight wing engaged the alien vessels. Ships exploded all around them. "Jassie, watch out; they're everywhere." Jase fired on the first target, blasting it instantly into oblivion.

"Nattie, how am I going to target them without hitting our own ships?"

"Jase, the system was designed to avoid our own fighters. Just fire at will and don't worry."

"Okay, here goes." Multiple enemy ships flew right though their flight wing causing everyone to scatter, performing evasive maneuvers. Jase fired repeatedly, taking out many of the enemy. He flew various responses to avoid enemy fire while approaching near to the battle cruiser. His flight wing kept the enemy off them as best as they could, but their numbers were diminishing quickly. Jase fired at the primary target causing massive damage to the battlecruiser's flight bay. The entire remaining enemy changed course, heading directly for Jase and Nattie. The battlecruiser fired globs of green plasma like bursts that instantly destroyed any Concordia ship but had no effect on the alien fighters.

Jase continually fired, destroying ship after ship but they kept coming. His ship was struck knocking off an unused weapons pod.

"Jase, that was too close."

"Okay, I'm heading away from the battlecruiser until these fighters are destroyed."

Jase sped up. The powerful engines vibrated such that they could feel it in their chests.

An enemy ship seemed to come out of nowhere and appeared right in front of them. Nattie screamed and Jase pushed down hard on the stick. His heart racing and his hands sweaty, they barely passed underneath as the engines shuttered from propulsion feedback against the hull of the enemy vessel. Jase banked hard left while Nattie targeted it,

"Jase, fire now!" Debris burst out in all directions as the ship violently exploded in a great ball of fire.

"Whew, that was so close," Jase said.

"Jase, can you smell that?"

He took a deep breath, "What is that?"

"I think it's some kind of electrical smell. It could be coming from the RFI power source I used to power the weapon systems."

"Is it safe?"

"I wish I knew."

The colonel hailed Jase on the radio, "Thunderbelt, make your run on the battlecruiser now before they repair that docking bay."

Several alliance ships formed up on Jase for the attack run. They flew toward the battlecruiser in a crazy shifting pattern to avoid the plasma blasts. One by one, the escort ships were destroyed from behind. The remaining ships had engaged the alien fighters but one got through and soared up behind Jase and Nattie. The final escort ship turned tail and ran.

"Jase! He left us!"

"Crap." Jase flew multiple responses end to end but could not shake the pursuing enemy. They were skimmed by a blast burning a grove into the outer hull of their ship.

"JASE, he has us!" Nattie closed her eyes and waited for the explosion.

KAWOSH.

The alien enemy's ship exploded in a huge fireball. The blast caused their ship to yaw sideways. They could feel the heat through the ship's hull.

"That one's for Kimberly!"

"Alrand, is that you?"

"It sure is."

"How did you get here?"

"I followed the armada, out of range. In the event you failed, I was going to blast them to infinity. Jase, you're clear. Let's take this thing down."

They flew at the battlecruiser, avoiding the plasma bursts. Jase fired shot after shot with the RFI and barely avoided one of the plasma bursts.

"Whew, that was close!"

"Jassie, take out their weapons." Jase flew along the length of the alien vessel, firing on their plasma cannons one after the other.

"Guys, we're not doing enough damage and we can't keep this up or we will end up getting hit."

"Alrand, you still have the reflective bomb on board, right?" Nattie asked.

"Yes, why?"

"I have an idea."

"What is it?"

"We fly as fast as we can toward home increasing our speed as much as possible. Then we slingshot around the planet. When we get close enough, you drop the bomb, armed for fifteen seconds. We should be able to maneuver behind the moon before it detonates."

"Nattie, we will be going too fast to slow down that quick."

"We won't have to. We just need to use the moon to block the blast."

"Let's do it," Alrand said. "Let's take these suckers out!"

Nattie set in the course and they sped ahead at full thrust. They performed a slingshot around their planet and adjusted course for the battlecruiser. They continually increased in speed as fast as they could.

"Alrand, you ready? We're only going to get one chance at this."

"Weapon armed and the target is locked."

Nattie called out the time, "Ready for deployment in...5...4...3...2...1...now, now, now."

Alrand released the weapon dead on as they continued toward the moon. "Start engine reverse in...3...2...1"

They maneuvered behind the moon, but still moving at a great velocity. "Quick, shut down all power," Nattie said. "Before the EMI shock wave is emitted."

The bomb detonated, melting every element of the alien battlecruiser with a fervent heat. The blast and heat wave pulsated out in all directions warming up the surface of the moon, turning it bright red. It could be seen by everyone on their planet. The burst of energy quickly dissipated but many could feel the ground quake under their feet as the blast penetrated their home atmosphere.

So many watched and waited for news as to the future of their planet. The actions of so few would determine their very existence. Once the news of victory reached the nations, there was a great celebration. Only a small handful of damaged Concordia ships made it back alive. The regiment waited but did not expect to hear from the heroes that saved their planet, figuring they were destroyed by the immense blast.

Chapter 45

"**H**ome base, this is Flight Team Two reporting in." The whole base cheered as the three heroes landed at the skyport. Jase, Alrand, and Nattie ran across the runway.

Major Slate limped out to meet them, "Let me be the first to salute you." He snapped to attention and saluted the three Captains. They returned the salute and received a hero's welcome by the men and women of the Concordia.

The military and the various governments of the planet decided to hold a formal presentation at the Proelium Concordia Events Stadium in Fawneather, to present the three heroes with an unprecedented alliance award before the whole world.

Nattie woke up early in the morning and played with Jase's hair, tickling his head. He smacked himself and Nattie shook the whole bed laughing at him.

"What are you up to, beautiful?"

"Playing with you. Today is the big day. How do my bruises look?"

Jase tried to focus, "I think they are about gone. You just need a little makeup and no one will notice." They got ready for their big presentation and met Alrand outside the hotel.

"Guys, we ready for this?" Alrand asked.

Nattie giggled, "Alrand, tuck your shirt in, in the back." Nattie put her arms around the two boys and they walked to the stadium.

Jase, Alrand, and Nattie stood before thousands. They felt honored that Colonel Cantellous along with the Concordia High Commander would be presenting them with medals of sacrificium virtus, a new metal of sacrificial heroism created specifically for them.

"Everyone, please observe a moment of silence for our fallen heroes who never returned from battle and those who were lost in the outer colony attack."

Jase, Alrand, and Nattie bowed their heads and felt sorrow for Kimberly and for those who were lost in battle. The three heroes wiped their eyes and felt choked up inside. Nattie tried not to think about Kimberly and keep it together.

After the moment passed, the colonel placed the medals around their necks, one by one, and the high commander shook their hands. They took a bow before the whole world while they received cheers and applause. Nattie was presented with a bouquet of flowers from the high commander. A band played a victory song and cameras flashed from all around the stadium.

A reporter was allowed on the platform and asked Alrand if he would like to say a few words. He bowed his head and refused, she moved on to Nattie. "Would you like to say anything, Captain?"

Nattie pulled the microphone close, "I love happy endings! And I love my husband." She put her arms around Jase and kissed him before the whole world.

THE END

"Jassie, I was just thinking."

"About what?"

"I would really like to get a good look at that Shadow Drive on that Earth vessel..."

Meet the Author

While sitting on a twentieth-floor terrace overlooking the ocean in Galveston TX, daydreaming about pirates on the high seas, George Babec decided to put his thoughts and imaginings onto paper. Having just visited an exhibit about real pirates, his active imagination was in overdrive. As he wrote, he thought back to when he was a boy and how he was always fascinated with old wooden battleships and love for the sea. He felt an allure of the technology of the past and freedom of the ocean. Even though he has embraced the information age as an Electronic Engineer, he has always had great respect for the adventurous inventors of past centuries, on whom our current technology stands. As a deep thinker, he pinned the plot and the adventurous theme of *Voncara*

Cove. The storyline connects the old and the new in a wondrous way. He found a new love of fiction writing, which was much more exhilarating than his passion for technical writing about his inventions and innovations.

George has always been adventurous and marvels at the feeling of discovery, like when he experienced a two-week wilderness canoe trip in Maine with the Boy Scouts. One day, as the scouts walked down a trail to meet their wilderness guide, they stumbled upon the neatest statue of a huge deer with giant antlers. It was so lifelike. They walked to the front and sides of the statue taking pictures. They were completely startled when the statue took off running, for it wasn't a statue at all! The deer just stood frozen, afraid to move a muscle.

George currently lives with his high school sweetheart and wife of thirty plus years in Knoxville, Tennessee. He has taken his wife and three daughters on many adventures and those experiences definitely have impacted his writing in a wonderful way. His military service in Army aviation provided some invaluable technology insights in the writing of *Voncara Cove.* He hopes the world will enjoy reading his novel as much as he has enjoyed writing it, and that it brings joy for others to share in his great literary adventure.

Visit George online at:
www.GeorgeBabec.com

ACKNOWLEDGMENTS

Special thanks to my wife for having patience during the writing of *Voncara Cove* and the countless hours spent on my many projects.

I would like to thank my mother, Linda Babec Jaffe, without her continuous support, encouragement, and expert help with my many publications; I never would have been able to achieve my aspirations.